Thank you for being so friendly

Gina

The Elusive Mr. Velucci

Tina Griffith

authorHOUSE

AuthorHouse™
1663 Liberty Drive
Bloomington, IN 47403
www.authorhouse.com
Phone: 1 (800) 839-8640

© 2018 Tina Griffith. All rights reserved.

No part of this book may be reproduced, stored in a retrieval system, or transmitted by any means without the written permission of the author.

Published by AuthorHouse 04/24/2018

ISBN: 978-1-5462-3707-5 (sc)
ISBN: 978-1-5462-3706-8 (e)

Print information available on the last page.

Any people depicted in stock imagery provided by Getty Images are models, and such images are being used for illustrative purposes only.
Certain stock imagery © Getty Images.

This book is printed on acid-free paper.

Because of the dynamic nature of the Internet, any web addresses or links contained in this book may have changed since publication and may no longer be valid. The views expressed in this work are solely those of the author and do not necessarily reflect the views of the publisher, and the publisher hereby disclaims any responsibility for them.

To Leo Mafrica; 'You found the song, and I created this story from it. Thank you so much for the beautiful inspiration. Your friend for life, TINA.

To Alberto Ruiz

Thank you for your patience, your encouragement, for always believing in me, and for loving me with all your heart. oxoxox

It was 10:32am on a bright but brisk Tuesday morning, and the newly-renovated, very popular coffee house in New York's east side, was already bubbling with reasonably loud and happy chatter. This was not a place for teenagers who were skipping class to be with their friends, but a throw-back space where you would envision hippies and dreamers to come to when they want to drink real coffee.

On this particular day, there were approximately twenty-five customers sipping their favorite drinks, while laughing at or replying to something that someone had just said. In the background, the coffee machines and latte spindles were whirling, a voice on the drive-through speaker was shouting an order, and two people were buying something at the counter. Almost every seat was being used in the cozy, brown room, and each person seemed to be deeply focused on the topics at hand.

And then, just when you thought this was as perfect as a famous painting, the ambience changed. It was abrupt and whimsical, as if somebody had sprinkled a handful of magic dust from the ceiling.

The sudden hush in the squared space was quite deafening, but the motionless position of every person in the room, was even more frightening. Their expressions and voices had stilled, anticipation had fused itself with every breath that was being taken, and every set of wide eyes had turned towards the front door.

Not a minute later, like an unexpected gush of wintry air, a perfectly proportioned woman stepped over the threshold and eased her shapely body inside. The statuesque beauty knew very well that she had a certain quality about her that made people stare with envy, and she loved it. Because of her conceit, she could have lingered in the entrance area for another minute or two, but she was on a mission. She removed her expensive sunglasses in order to allow her flawlessly made-up eyes to scan the room, while her painted lips parted ever-so-slightly. The short black dress which was hugging her body, enhanced the length of her long and shapely legs. Her feet were adorned by the cutest high heels, which cost what she made on a two-week paycheque, and she had now placed her Boho shawl over her arm. She was the center of everyone's attention, and she wouldn't want to have it any other way.

By the method in which she gazed into everyone's face, it was quite obvious that the 26-year old woman was looking for someone. While doing so, she ran a freshly manicured hand through the left side of her shiny hair, in a very slow and methodical motion. She heard soft sighs come from the mouths of some of the curious patrons, which caused her sensitive skin to tingle with extreme pleasure.

Halley James, an up-and-coming wedding planner, had arrived early to get a decent table. For the past few minutes, she had been getting things ready for when her friend and assistant, decided to breeze in.

Halley looked up when she heard the familiar ding of the bell over the hand-carved front door, and her heart

The Elusive Mr. Velucci

skipped a beat when she recognized who it was. Upon seeing her friend's classy attire, Halley rolled her eyes and then scoffed like a teenage girl; the not-too-low V-neck was cute and the cap shoulders made the dress seem quite refined, but she was quick to decide that the outfit was a little much for a working lunch.

"Terri! Over here!" Halley called in a thankful tone. She flashed her friend the fake smile which you give to a passing stranger on the street, while waving her hand to show Terri where she was sitting.

Terri's eyes followed the familiar voice. When she spotted Halley, she lifted her chin in the air and then strolled over to the table like a professional model. As she walked, she was very aware that her movements were being monitored by all the individuals in the room. She sucked her tummy in and was very cautious to look her best, just in case there was someone who might want to use her in a movie or on a magazine cover.

"Finally", Halley sighed under her breath. Even though she had been sitting in the booth at the coffee shop for almost fifteen minutes, she knew that she would have waited another ten or twenty for Terri to arrive; patience was a big part of Halley's personality.

Terri sat down, and then with extreme care, she laid her expensive fringed purse on the seat next to her. She folded her hands on the table in front of her, and was all set to begin the coffee date with her friend.

As if everyone else in the room had been in a dream-like trance, the potent spell was now broken. They all resumed their previous conversations, and went back to eating or drinking what was in front of them. The easy-listening overhead music began to play again, and life was how it was five minutes ago.

Terri was wearing a shrewd smile on her beautiful face, and was now able to focus on the semi-casually dressed woman sitting across the table from her. "Before you say anything, I got here as fast as I could", she confessed quickly; she knew that a lecture would be given if she didn't plead her innocence right away.

Halley, who was usually not flustered by much, shot her friend a stern glance of disappointment before she spoke. "Yah, I know", was what came out first. "You always do." It was followed by, "But this wedding is very important to me." She then shifted in her seat and rearranged the cutlery in front of her, while keeping her eyelashes lowered.

Terri suddenly felt like she'd been attacked. The guarded woman could feel her claws coming out and wanted to argue her case a little more, but then realized that she was the one in the wrong. The stylishly dressed woman was now embarrassed, and delivered a weak apology while lifting up a stiff menu. "Sorry", she offered quietly, but not very sincerely.

Halley heard the faint attempt of regret, and she could tell that her friend felt humbled. Because they really did need to finalize some decisions, she opted to forgive and forget. "Terri..." The soft, almost lyrical voice drifted towards Terri's side of the table. It was followed by a small tap of the tip of an index finger, which Halley had placed at the top of the menu.

Because what she was pretending to study was now being pulled away from her face, Terri let it drop to the table. "I am sorry", she repeated in a sincere tone.

The Elusive Mr. Velucci

Halley smiled with restrained amusement. "I know." She was secretly pleased that she had won that round. "And thank you." She reached across the solid flat surface and placed her hand on top of her friend's hand. "Are we ok, now?"

Terri smiled and nodded, and then placed her free hand on top of Halley's. "We're ok."

"Good! A wedding needs to be planned and we're running out of time."

"Just to be clear, there's no restriction of money, right?" Terri inquired. Her ideas and tastes were expensive, and she would hate to be told no when she suggested something that she thought would be perfect.

Halley smiled shyly and replied, "No, the groom is paying for the entire event."

A very kind barista came over and took their drink order, and once she was gone, the two friends continued with their discussion.

Minutes later, two pumpkin spice lattes were placed in front of them. "Enjoy", the waitress announced happily. She then gave her attention to another table.

"This one's mine!" Terri announced with total conviction, as she pulled the white mug without whipped cream towards her. Her glands were already salivating; she couldn't wait to enjoy her first sip of the seasonal hot drink.

Halley reached for her own cup and moved it closer to her spot on the table. "Oh, it smells so good", she stated in a voice that was smooth but insistent. She pursed her lips and blew across the top of her latte, and then took her first sip.

"This is amazing", Terri declared quite happily. "I don't know why they don't want to sell this all year round - it's really good." She was careful not to burn her upper lip while she took a second sip. "Mmm…", she moaned with extreme pleasure.

Halley fastened both of her hands around the very warm mug, as if to guard it against predators. "Give me another minute, and then we can talk about the wedding again."

Terri nodded and took another sip, and then she pushed her cup off to the side. She slid her pad of paper in front of her, and then looked for a pen in the bottom of her purse. "Ok, where did we leave off?"

Halley's mind tried to remember all that they had accomplished in their last meeting. "Let me see…" she began. "Did we check off that the flowers have already been ordered?"

Terri inspected her 28-point list. "Yes, there it is."

"Okay, good. Now we need to find a minister or a Justice of the Peace to perform the wedding."

Terri puckered her pillowy-soft lips, and took another sip of her hot beverage before she answered. "I could go through our books and records, and then call to see who's available."

"Great idea."

"Do we know yet, where the wedding will be held?" Terri asked with excitement in her voice. She was guaranteed to go, and had hopes that it would be somewhere exotic and far away.

"Not really", Halley replied, in a voice that didn't hold much confidence. "I'm not sure if they'll have the wedding in New York or in Italy, because both places hold such wonderful memories for them."

"Ok, but we'll need to know the location, soon. What

The Elusive Mr. Velucci

about the music?" Terri asked. She knew the theme for the wedding, but she was referring to which song will be played during the ceremony, and for the first dance as man and wife.

"If we don't already have that written down, I guess we'd better ask." Halley pulled her coffee cup towards her side of the table with one hand, while jotting down a note to herself with the other.

"And what about the invitations? Have they been approved?"

Halley checked her list and replied, "No, but I'll get on that today."

"That's a good idea, because we have to mail them out soon."

Both girls took a second to take another sip of their delicious drink.

It was then when something came into Terri's mind. "Did you know...?" she asked out loud. She had always been a romantic at heart, and loved hearing all the smallest of details of anyone who was getting married. "That I don't know the backstory to who these people are."

Halley's nicely-curved body stiffened up, and her eyes popped wide open with utter disbelief. "I've never told you that story?" Halley's voice had suddenly gone up an entire octave. She was baffled by how to answer, while an innocent look of sheer surprise covered her entire face.

"No", Terri replied softly, but there seemed to be a slight challenge lingering behind the simple word. Terri was quite interested in all of the couples who they worked for – how they met, what they did for a living, and where they go on their honeymoon. She loved hearing their stories, and felt that some of the information would be helpful to her, when and if she ever got married.

"Okay", Halley responded slowly, in an effort to buy some time. "But I can't believe you don't already know this." The senior wedding planner's skin began to glow pink, as a tumble of confused thoughts and feelings hurried towards her.

Terri suddenly got the feeling that this information would not only be juicy, but that it would take up a fair bit of time. "You know you have to tell me…" In one swift motion, Terri moved the pad of paper and pen off to the side with the back of her right hand. She blew across the top of her hot drink and placed it directly in front of her, and was now prepared to listen. "Ok, go!" she insisted eagerly. She had quickly turned into a bright-eyed little girl, who was on the verge of opening her first birthday present of the year.

"How do I begin?" Halley asked playfully. The pretty blonde grabbed hold of her cup and took a few sips, while a dozen thoughts ran through her head.

Terri loved how flustered her friend had become, and decided to play along. "How about from the day they met?" She took a sip from her own cup and urged Halley to begin. "Please…"

Terri had just embarked on a new relationship with a man named Tim, a successful record producer, and hoped that it would someday turn into a 'happily ever after'. They'd only gone out a few times, but she could already feel that she was falling in love with the 6' tall, bearded and handsome man. To Terri, romance was in the air, and she wanted to grab as much as life could throw at her. "You can trust me. Now talk!"

The Elusive Mr. Velucci

"Well…" she began timidly. "Did you know, that even though they are only getting married now, Enrico and Sadie met and fell in love 22 years ago?"

"What? Seriously?" Terri's mouth fell open and her eyes brightened; the disclosure had been totally unexpected. Her breath had got caught in her throat, her heart was now racing, and her impulsiveness was hard to hide. "Ok, wait a minute!" she urged, while holding her index finger up. Terri made a point to turn her cell phone off, because nothing was going to stop her from hearing everything that her friend was willing to share.

"It's the truth", she replied softly, and made a large 'x' on her chest. The charming performance was followed by a cute smirk that splashed across her lips, and a shiny spark of muted excitement which now radiated all over her face. And while an eyebrow had lifted in amusement, a glimmer of mischief glistened in her eyes.

Terri was on pins and needles waiting for the words to touch her heart, and hated that her friend was dragging it out.

"Ok." Halley crossed her ankles, held her warm cup firmly in her hands, and leaned her upper body forward before she proceeded to narrate the fascinating love story. "Allow me start from the beginning."

In amongst Italy's most picturesque attractions, lays a breathtaking coastline, enchanting getaways, and some spectacular ancient ruins. The sweet smell of garlic, basil, and oregano wafted freely through the cool air, assuring everyone that a lucky family was about to eat a hearty supper. It's been calculated that millions of people flock to Naples and Sorrento each year, to drink in all that the wonders of the land and its fine-looking people have to offer. And then there are those who have had the pleasure of actually living there, and calling that place home. Enrico Velucci was one of those lucky people.

The handsome man had been raised in Italy, with the authentic Italian culture and delicious foods. Whenever it touched his soul, he never failed to get up on his feet and dance to the seductive music. With his warm and captivating smile, and his sun-kissed, tanned skin, he had been persistently admired by the young and old of both sexes. His velvety voice and gentlemanly mannerisms had sent many a pulse racing, and he was only 19 years old.

After settling into his favorite spot, on the large beach in the Gulf of Sorrento, Enrico found a white piece of driftwood to sit upon. He had finished high school almost a year ago, and was taking these last few weeks to contemplate his future.

As he had done many times before today, Enrico slipped

The Elusive Mr. Velucci

his favorite sandals off of his feet, and dipped his toes into the cooler-than-body-temperature water. A twinkle of sunlight got caught in his dark eyes, as he looked out as far as he could see. His soul became lost in the beauty that was Italy, as he gazed over the vast body of gorgeous water. All around him were lights and music, boats and birds, and people of every nationality. But as rich and romantic as it was to foreigners, this was all part of his normal everyday life.

The tall man turned his attention upwards towards the mysterious and majestic mountains, and he could totally understand why people claimed that these rocks were reaching for the sky. And while Enrico loved the place where he was born, he felt like he needed to take a little break before beginning the next phase of his life. He had heard about the exciting adventures that one could find in America, from classmates and friends who had been there, and he decided that it might be nice to go to New York.

The very idea inspired him in ways that he had never felt before. As his mind explored this interesting notion, he realized that without a girlfriend or other ties to weigh him down, that he could travel right away.

Enrico suddenly felt uneasy when he thought about his parents; he would have to get them to agree before he could go. They were old and set in their ways, and he knew that they would love to have him there with them for every minute of every single day. He inhaled a deep and pained breath, and hoped that they would let him go – even for a short while.

His sensuous eyes took on a faraway look, and were then downcast as he entertained all the positive aspects about his future. Seconds later, a brilliant smile landed on his square face and his eyes began to glisten. At the same time, a fluttery feeling developed in his chest and his muscles began to tighten in readiness. He was focusing on what he had to do, and began to strategize the ways in which to argue his point - if that were to become necessary.

After placing his old and worn out sandals back onto his feet, Enrico hopped onto his bike and pedaled for almost an hour down the century-old streets. The space between the buildings was narrow, but throughout the years, he had become quite skilled on how to maneuver his overworked two-wheeler.

Minutes before arriving at his sandstone building, Enrico stopped at one of the countless shrines of The Virgin Mary, which adorn many of the walls in southern Italy. When he was done saying a prayer, Enrico turned his bike down a backstreet, and one block ahead, was a building with Juliette balconies hanging off of its side. This was where he had lived since he was born.

The young man jumped off his bike, and after tucking it precariously under his left arm, he carried it inside.

"Ciao!" he called to his parents, as he walked through the door. He spoke in a tone that was filled with immense love and respect. Enrico could already smell the delicious food which was gently making its way into his airways, and his taste buds instantly woke up.

"Come!" his mother shouted in Italian. She wiped her hands on her large and colorful apron, and then rushed over to hug and kiss her only son.

The Elusive Mr. Velucci

[1]"Ciao, Enrico." His father's voice was mellow and soft, and filled with great affection.

"Ciao, papa."

Enrico's mother dished the food onto her gorgeous son's plate, until it looked like there was enough to feed two grown men.

[2]"Grazie, mama", Enrico uttered lovingly. He then picked up his fork and began to devour all that laid before him.

Freshly baked and buttered bread was passed around, grated cheese was sprinkled very generously on top of everything they were eating, and it wasn't until five minutes later when any conversation began.

"How was your day?" Enrico's father asked in Italian - his first and only language.

"Good, papa", Enrico replied, also in Italian. "I gave a lot of thought to my future, just as you have taught me to do."

This pleased the older man, and it caused him to stop chewing. He immediately made eye contact with his wife of 22 years, and together they hoped that their son would deliver some good news.

"I have decided, that in order to better succeed in this world, that I need to explore more than this city has to offer." Enrico paused for dramatic effect, while looking first at his mother, and then at his father.

"What does that mean?" the older man asked. He was confused and no longer eating.

Enrico swallowed hard, and then provided his reply. "I

---

[1] Ciao = Hello

[2] Grazie = Thank you

would like to ask your permission to go abroad." He eyes glanced back and forth while he watched their reaction.

"To where?" Papa demanded. He was trying to keep his wrath in check, but a part of him was hoping that it wasn't true; their small family had never lived a day apart.

"New York, perhaps", he replied with quiet emphasis. He had tilted his head and changed his expression, in order to appear hopeful. "I want to study English", he began. "I want to learn about the culture of the American people - their foods, and their likes and dislikes."

"New York!?" mama cried. Her whole performance indicated panic and disbelief.

Enrico's eyes had grown wide and his throat was beginning to close up, from the insane possibility that he might not be able to leave Europe.

"How long were you thinking to go for?" Papa inquired.

After doing the math in his head, Enrico announced his timeline. "Six to eight months."

"Eight months?" mama cried with panic in her voice. This was both an observation as well as a question.

"That will bring me back here just in time to start school", Enrico explained.

Mama's reaction was written all over the delicate features on her matured face, but papa knew that Enrico was a grown man, and that he needed to spread his wings.

After a few minutes of profound soul-searching, the loving father knew what he had to do - he had to side with his son. But before he could give Enrico his blessing, he stood up to comfort his wife. As if he was shielding her from danger, the 5 foot 6 inch man held the refined woman gently against his own body.

The Elusive Mr.

"You have our permission to go, but only for months." Papa's words echoed through the room, as had just declared the 11th commandment. His ruling was firm, yet filled with love, for it was difficult for the older man to send his only son so far away from home.

"I have a brother in New York who will take care of you while you're there", he added, in a voice that was on the verge of breaking. "He and his wife own a store, so that will also give you something to do." Papa was trying to console the weeping woman who was nestled firmly in his arms, but now his own tears were welling in his eyes. He hoped that he could get through his speech before they fell down his cheeks. "I will call him tomorrow and tell him to expect you."

Enrico was extremely grateful of their decision. "Grazie, papa e mamma", he said in a loving tone. He rushed over to hug his parents and they quickly opened up their arms to hug him back.

[3]"Possa Dio vegliare su di te!" his mother stated through a hundred depressing tears.

"Grazie, mamma", he whispered against her neck. He then kissed the cheeks of each of his parents, and then held them very close to his body.

As soon as her son left the room, Enrico's mother pushed her face into the strong chest of her husband - the man she'd known and loved since she was 16 years old. As more tears began to fall from her eyes, she could feel her husband's tender arms tighten around her back and pull her even closer.

Salty water began to moisten his cheeks, as papa made

---

[3] Possa Dio vegliare su di te = May God watch over you

the sign of the cross on his body and sent a prayer to God. "Protect my son, oh Lord. See to it that he comes back to us, safe and sound. Amen."

"Amen", mama added. She was clutching a cotton handkerchief in her wrinkled fingers, while dabbing the many tears which were falling from her eyes.

Meanwhile, Enrico was in his bedroom, sifting through some pamphlets and schedules. Because he was nervous about flying, he had decided to embark on a large ship. He picked out his wardrobe and threw some books and pictures into a worn-out suitcase.

A large party was planned for the following week, which included friends as well as family. During those four hours, the music was playing all of his favorite songs, and the many dishes of food were decorative mounds of everything that he loved to eat. While the family members were wishing him well, they were crying at the heartbreak of his leaving.

On the morning of his departure, his mother and grandmother came to say good-bye. They had worked hours to make goodies for him to enjoy while he travelled, and they smothered him with dozens of kisses and hugs so that he wouldn't forget them. Minutes later, they all piled into the car and drove to the loading dock.

Just before the announcement came for all passengers to board the ship, Enrico's father held him by the shoulders. "Ti amo", the older man said, in a breath that reeked of whiskey. The tender words had slipped out of his old and quivering lips, and it broke both of their hearts.

Enrico choked back his own tears, and whispered the sentiment back to his father. "Ti amo, papa."

They all embraced, and then it was time for Enrico to

The Elusive Mr. Velucci

walk away. With mixed emotions, he picked up his suitcase and headed towards the ramp.

"Arrivederci!" they all called. [4]"Dio ti benedica!" they added. Tears were abundant, hearts were breaking, and hopes for a quick reunion were prevalent.

[5]"Ti amo, [6]entrambi!" he called to his parents.

"Ti amo, Enrico!" they called to him.

Sailing across the Atlantic was both physically and emotionally hard on the young man, as he had never been away from Italy before. He had no idea what being sea-sick entailed, so this often took his mind off of his loneliness for his home and family. At night there was nothing to see but miles and miles of cold and wavy water, so he lay in his bed and wished for the moment when he could step onto dry land again. In those last few days in the tiny cabin, that moment couldn't have come soon enough.

The large ship docked at the New York Passenger Ship Terminal, with Enrico being the 49th person to step foot onto American soil. He was quite elated and couldn't believe that he had finally made it.

"Enrico!"

His name had echoed throughout the entire brick building, and it had caught everyone's attention.

"Enrico!"

He looked around the room in order to see where the voice was coming from, and then he saw someone who looked very similar to his father. "Zio!" Enrico shouted, once he realized that it was Uncle Alberto - the oldest brother of

---

[4] Dio ti benedica = God bless you

[5] Ti amo = I love you

[6] entrambi = both

Tina Griffith

the five siblings, and the first one to come to the United States. Enrico's face glowed with pure relief, for he had just been assured that he was no longer alone.

"Enrico!" The short man was busting with pride and waving his right arm in a furious manner.

[7]"Zio!" Enrico called with great happiness, and quickly made his way over to where the older man was standing.

Aunt Gina was standing next to her husband, and she greeted Enrico with kisses to both of his cheeks. "Welcome to America!" the Italian woman stated loudly.

"Thank you", he replied shyly in his one and only language. "It is very nice to be here."

The formalities lasted several minutes, and then they all drove to the home of his American family. After getting the tour of the 2nd floor, 3-bedroom apartment, Enrico was subjected to a smaller celebration than the one which he had been given before he left Italy. It was then when he was able to get reacquainted with his cousins – Paulo and Franko.

The store in the East Village had been closed early, but the lingering smells coming from the family business below, were like gifts from heaven to Enrico's nose. If he closed his eyes, Enrico could tell that Sfogliatella, Cannoli, and Biscotti had been made fresh sometime that day. As well, he could tell that sandwiches with heaping amounts of salami, soppresata, prosciutto and/or pepperoni had been made and eaten on the premises. His mouth was watering just thinking about all the delicious foods that he would be eating while he was there.

"You will be staying in Franko's room", Aunt Gina stated.

---

[7] Zio = Uncle

The Elusive Mr. Velucci

"Anything you need or want, you ask us", Uncle Alberto added.

Enrico was beaming as he looked into the happy faces of his loving relatives, and he thanked them for letting him stay with them. "Grazie."

The next morning, they all went downstairs, and Enrico was shown around the store. By noon, the young man with an athletic physique, was sweeping floors, taking out the trash, and stocking shelves. He couldn't be of any assistance to the customers because he didn't speak a word of English, but plenty of women had gravitated towards him. They used their eyes and body language to entice him to help them, but he smiled and directed them towards the long counter.

The store closed at 7pm, and Enrico helped his uncle lock up. They were going upstairs for supper, when Zio had a brilliant idea.

"The boy must learn to speak English if he is to be of more help to us", the round man suggested sternly to his wife. He then turned to his oldest son and continued his thought. "Paulo, first thing tomorrow morning, you will find Enrico a tutor." It was a command, with no room for a rebuttal.

"Yes, papa", the 18-year old announced with obedience in his voice. Paulo's mind kicked into high gear, as he tried to recall everyone who he had gone to school with. "I will begin the task, tomorrow."

"Good!" papa shouted. He slammed his hand on the table and added, "And now, we will enjoy our meal."

A week later, a tutor was found. Her name was Sadie Lynn Adams.

Sadie had tutored plenty of students before today, but

because she was trying to get settled into a new apartment, she wasn't sure how much time she could devote to teaching someone English.

She was 21 years old, she was juggling two part time jobs, and while money was not filling up her bank account, she always managed to have enough to live on.

"Well?" the male voice asked. Paulo might have sounded impatient, but there was no threat of him hanging up before an answer was given.

Time was tight, but it suddenly occurred to her that having a little extra cash would be nice. "I'll do it", she sighed reluctantly into the phone.

"Good, we'll see you tomorrow." Before they ended the phone call, Paulo gave her the address, her student's name, his background, his age, and how much he wanted to learn.

Sadie hung up and then prepared all of the materials for their first visit.

They met at the quaint family restaurant, next door to Uncle Alberto's store, at 1pm the next day.

"Hi." Enrico let the single-syllable word slide slowly through his full lips, and was proud that he had used it exactly how he had been instructed to.

"Nice to meet you", she replied, as she tucked a lock of blonde hair behind her left ear. She was instantly mesmerized by his charming accent and his Mediterranean good looks, and immediately felt her breaths and heartbeat quicken.

'She was shy', was his first impression of her. Enrico couldn't help but smile as their eyes locked in an intimate embrace. His tutor was breathtaking, she dressed causal classic, and he loved that she wore her hair loose. Enrico could detect that she had sprayed a few drops of an exotic

The Elusive Mr. Velucci

perfume to certain parts of her body, which quickly seduced his senses and made every part of him come alive.

Sadie's cheeks were becoming warm, which embarrassed her, so she moved her eyes away from his. "Let's begin", she said in an unhurried fashion. She bent down and pulled the text book and binder of blank lined paper out from its carrying case. While she was arranging things on the table, Sadie felt strangely nervous. So he wouldn't pick up on that, she tried to command her expression to remain blank.

Enrico chuckled inwardly, as he had not expected to receive so much amusement from the stranger who had just come into his life. He leaned his taut body backwards in the chair, and began to study every movement that his teacher was making. As he watched Sadie get organized, he wondered if her wide-eyed innocence was merely a smoke screen to how she really was when no-one was looking. 'Perhaps she was the type who sings in the shower at the top of her lungs, or never hesitates to jump into a puddle when the mood strikes her', he assumed. After another minute of intense observation, Enrico could tell that Sadie was full of life, had experienced pain, and that she had unquenchable warmth in her soul. He also suspected that she was not yearning for a friendship from anyone, and yet, he felt an absolute eagerness for him, her new student, to stay close to her.

Sadie could feel him staring at her, and while it would be quite easy to throw herself into his arms, she was aware that she needed to stay strong; it was crucial that she remember that this was purely a business arrangement, and that's how it had to stay. Still, she was starting to become uncomfortable, and wished for him to let go of the strong hold which he had on her soul - even just a little.

Enrico was Italian, he oozed masculinity, and he was developing quite the interest in the beautiful woman sitting across from him. The way she moved, the way she spoke, and now in the way that she was trying to seem uninterested, it was all quite appealing to him.

Time passed and they were near the end of Lesson One. Sadie had been pronouncing each word on the page in English, and she had Enrico repeat it the best way he could. Pictures were explained in both English and Italian, but they were written in the English language.

Coincidently, when mistakes were made, faint sounds of chuckles and giggles could be heard from across the room. Sadie squinted her eyes and threw the young female strangers a wicked glare. Once she grasped that they had received the message which she was sending them, Sadie continued on with the lesson.

Enrico suddenly felt a slight air of protection around their table, while a part of him reveled in admiration of how powerful his tutor could be.

Before they knew it, their one hour class had turned into three hours. Enrico and Sadie were a lot more comfortable with each other by then, and it showed in their faces and body language. They were now laughing at their own mistakes, and not worrying about what anyone around them was saying or doing.

They stood up after Sadie had packed up all of her materials, and it was then when she noticed the slight difference in height – he was 2 inches taller than her.

"Good-bye, and thank you for allowing me to have so

The Elusive Mr. Velucci

much of your time today", he whispered in a low, soft voice. "I had fun, but I also learned a lot." He gazed deep into her eyes as he spoke in the language which he knew by heart, and it only prolonged her departure.

Sadie could tell that she was blushing, but she mirrored what he was doing and agreed with his sentiments. "I also had a lot of fun", she professed whole heartedly. She couldn't help but feel an uncanny sadness that their time together was ending. "Should we make plans to have another lesson?" she added. Her mastery of the Italian language was flawless.

The approval on his face, echoed in his voice. "Most definitely. Are you free the day after tomorrow?" He studied her eyes while he waited for her to answer.

Sadie agreed, and then they said good-bye. With each meeting that they had after that, they dressed up and looked better than the last one. With each hour that they had spent together, Sadie's attraction for Enrico had grown stronger, and vice versa.

A month after their first lesson, Enrico was no longer just a student to Sadie; whether he was in her company or not, he had become the shimmering full moon in her dark sky at Christmas.

It was not until their fourth month together, when Enrico did something that surprised Sadie. They were talking nonchalantly, in a language which was comprised of both English and Italian, and then he looked into her face for a full minute. As she tried to figure out why he wasn't saying anything, she noticed that his eyes were sparkling, his lips had formed into an irresistible grin, and then he exhaled a rather long sigh of satisfaction. All the while, he continued his persistent gaze into her flawless face.

Sadie breathed out and felt a warm glow flow right through her. It was delightfully distracting, and while she tried to interpret what it meant, she lowered her eyelashes and chin. Seconds later, it occurred to her that he was now seeing a woman instead of a teacher, and her mouth curved into an unconscious smile.

Enrico's grin went from ear-to-ear, for Sadie had no idea how captivating she looked. Just then, he realized that he preferred being with her over anyone else. He loved that her eyes twinkled when she giggled and that her entire attention was always on him. He could even feel himself getting lost in the way she tilted her head, every time she smiled.

Sadie raised her chin and saw an open invitation in the smoldering power of his olive-black eyes, which seemed to entice her to stay within his reach. It was intoxicating, but there was no threat that she would walk away from him.

Enrico was undeniably looking at her as if he were photographing her with his eyes. It was seductive and bold, and he made sure to study everything from the creamy expanse of her neck, to the full breasts which lay snug beneath her silky, short-sleeved blouse.

Suddenly, someone walked a little too close to their table, which put a stop to Enrico's absent-minded staring. Without missing a beat, he leaned his body forward and began to go over his notes.

In those quiet moments when her student was reading, Sadie found herself stealing a few glances at his profile or his hands, and sometimes she had gotten caught.

Enrico could always feel when she was sneaking a peek, and passion promptly took hold of him. Amusement

The Elusive Mr. Velucci

flickered on Enrico's face when his eyes met hers, and it made her turn her head away.

Those awkward seconds had caused her heart to pump harder and her cheeks to grow pink from embarrassment, but it didn't stop her from checking out all that he had to offer.

Enrico felt strongly towards Sadie, and he was suddenly very aware of what was happening between them. He would only be in America for a short while, and because he had not had the good fortune to fall in love before, he wasn't sure that it should be with a woman from another country. However, as much as he wanted to prove to himself that he was immune to her, he was not. They hadn't known each other for very long, but it was becoming clear that he was now under her spell.

Sadie had a lot going on in her life, and she couldn't afford to be confused by silly romantic notions. With Enrico going back to Italy, she would be left in New York without him. She didn't want the heartache that that would bring to her soul, but it was becoming quite evident that she was falling for him.

"I go to the market to get my food", he recited slowly. The words were laden with a heavy Italian accent, but were spoken with perfect English.

Sadie raised her eyes and watched as her student explained what he had just learned. As she listened, she found herself unintentionally staring at his magnificent mouth; how moist and soft it must be, how it changed positions for each syllable which he tried to sound out, and how it would feel to have those lips pressed against her own.

A soft sigh of desire escaped from her throat, from the very idea of the two of them kissing.

Enrico had gotten to the end of the page, and he was now waiting for his tutor to speak.

Sadie was shocked and wondered if he had heard her sigh. She hoped not, and cleared her throat. But when she tried to talk, her voice had trembled. This troubled her, and she almost lost her train of thought.

Enrico felt somewhat sorry for her, as he watched her struggle to maintain her self-control.

Her sweaty hands, which were hidden from sight, were now twisting nervously in her lap. "Good job!" she insisted loudly. Sadie then reached one hand up and turned the page. "Read the next paragraph", she instructed quietly. She kept her eyelashes lowered, as she scolded herself for behaving in an unprofessional manner.

It was in that very moment when Enrico realized that he was fighting his own battle of self-control. Every fiber in his body had warned him against getting too close to her, but he was having trouble denying the spark of excitement that had begun to build within his body. In fact, the mere prospect of them evolving into more than just friends, was now spinning into reality. And because of how she was acting today, it had become clear to him that she felt the same way as he did.

For weeks they had spent at least three hours or more per lesson, speaking in Italian but learning English. They had grown closer, but always kept the line of student and teacher in full view. In that same time period, they had skipped the classroom setting several times, so that Sadie could show her handsome protégé all the wonderful sights that New York and its regions had to offer.

There had certainly been a few awkward moments between them, like when their hands or fingers had touched and neither one was willing to move theirs away first. Or when they locked eyes for a little longer than what was necessary, and neither felt the need to utter a single word to fill the interlude of awkward silence. They even found themselves becoming giddy when they finished the other person's sentences, and when they've had the same thoughts at the same time. After any of these things had happened, their hearts immediately raced with desire. There was definitely love growing between the student and the teacher, but neither one was willing to speak about it.

The changing weather conditions, which had marched through three of the four seasons, was a great teaching tool, and it had given them so much more to talk about. Ice skating while being totally bundled up, had turned into afternoon walks with sunglasses and a light sweater. Where they were once too shy to accidentally touch, they now felt freer to pat or hold onto a shoulder or an arm, while laughing intimately when the other person said or did something funny. When they said hello or good-night, they embraced with undeniable affection. And these days, they stared into each other's eyes, because they were connected on a level that was different from any they had ever known before.

It wasn't being said out loud, but the more time that passed, the more the fear and reality of being without the other, was creeping in. Before they knew it, they had two weeks left before it was time for Enrico to go back to Italy.

Tina Griffith

In those 14 days, their one-hour lessons had stretched to five or more hours, and everything they did when they were together, was a reflection of what was sitting deep in their hearts.

Two nights before Enrico was to leave America, his aunt and uncle invited him and Sadie to enjoy a fancy dinner at their home. The music was loud, the drinks were flowing, and there was more food than everyone could eat at one sitting. Paulo and Franko were there with a few of their friends, and Alberto and Gina had also asked a few of their friends and customers to stop by. On the whole, it was both a happy and sad time for all of them, for nobody wanted to see Enrico go.

The next night, which was his last night in New York, Enrico and Sadie decided to go out on the town. It wasn't classified as a date, but it felt like they were going to the prom.

Enrico borrowed shoes from his cousin, he wore a rented tux, he had his hair slicked back, and he held a colorful corsage in his hand.

Sadie had her hair and nails done, she applied an adequate amount of make-up to her face, she wore a white layered dress that cost more than she made in a month, and she walked in shoes that hurt her toes.

Uncle Alberto drove his nephew to Sadie's home in his 1967, yellow Chevrolet - his pride and joy. With Aunt Gina sitting in the front seat beside him, they watched as Enrico walked up to the front door of Sadie's apartment building. He buzzed, and she came down.

Enrico's face lit up when he saw her. "You look quite

The Elusive Mr. Velu...

beautiful", he gushed in perfect English. His voice was deep and sensual, and filled with a ton of admiration.

While Enrico inspected her from head to toe, he was unaware that those four words had sent a ripple of excitement straight to Sadie's soul. "Thank you. And you also look very handsome", she answered in a weak and shy whisper. She was swooning and scarcely aware that she was even talking.

He placed the corsage onto Sadie's wrist, while his aunt and uncle watched from twenty feet away. After they all said Hi to one another, Uncle Alberto drove to a place called, 'Caruso's Hideaway'.

"Have a good time!" Aunt Gina called, after Sadie and Enrico got out of the car.

"We will!" they declared as one voice.

The young couple held hands while they went inside the loud and lively establishment. They were shown to a small table, and each ordered a rum and coke. They took their time to look at everything that was around them, and watched with intense interest as the dozen or so strangers danced across the parquet floor. On more than a few occasions, they found themselves laughing while trying to talk over the music, and they were making silly excuses to toast everything; their friendship, the amount of English which Enrico had learned, and to Enrico's last night in America. Neither Enrico nor Sadie were thinking about tomorrow or the day after that; they both wanted to enjoy tonight, and this magnificent moment.

Thirty-two minutes after they had arrived, the first few notes of a particular song began to play, and something in the back of Enrico's mind popped. He stood up in a robotic manner, stretched out his hand, and then asked Sadie to dance.

Sadie's heart automatically leaped into her throat. She smiled and nodded before she verbally agreed, and then reached for his hand.

The instant their skin touched, all forms of sensibility went out the window. Their business arrangement had suddenly ended, for tonight there would be no shadows of regret across her heart - only the memories of their last night together.

The lights dimmed as the handsome couple made their way into the middle of the dance floor. He took her hand in his, and all their fingers intertwined and shot out to the side. His other hand was placed at her waist, and the instant it touched, both of their bodies trembled with delight.

On the down beat they took their first step, and began to glide around the wooden surface. Enrico steered his partner with a firm hand, while Sadie tip toed gracefully around the floor in her heels. They kept their bodies a proper distance apart and sent invisible messages to anyone who might ask, that they did not want to dance with any person other than who they were with.

The music swelled and stayed heightened for several beats, and it caused all of the dancers to keep perfect time with the rhythm.

Everyone was watching Enrico and Sadie, and they were all spellbound by what they were witnessing. It was beyond dancing now - more like a ballet or an opera - and it looked as if those two had been together since the beginning of time; they each knew what the other was about to do. The whole thing was hypnotic and the crowd didn't dare look way, for fear of missing out on how it would end.

Outwardly, Sadie appeared to be calm and composed.

The Elusive Mr. Velucci

Secretly, she was scared and she couldn't breathe; his nearness was quite overwhelming. Her pulse was increasing with excitement, at the mere thought that he was now standing closer to her than he ever had before. So close, that she could feel the heat emanating from his body.

At first they were dancing as friends, and by the time the first song had ended, something had changed between them.

Sadie was now aware of the hard muscles which lay under his clothing, and the shallow way in which he was breathing.

Enrico had clearly noticed that her nipples were now protruding beneath the thin fabric of her dress, and that her skin had become sweaty by the mere touch of his hand.

The music suddenly went from a fast-paced melody, with dozens of colored lights all blinking at the same time, to a slow-paced ballad with steady, soft white lighting. Violins and cellos began to call out the notes to the new song, while the voices of a dozen angels sang the words in each bar. During the chorus, a dry ice machine produced a thick, white fog that hung no more than a foot off the floor.

It was all so intense, and Sadie was sure that it was designed to make everyone feel like they were floating on a cloud.

Without confirming it out loud, the young couple had agreed to stay on the floor for another song. Their breathing was in sync, their eyes were locked, and they spoke volumes without saying a word.

The air around them was roaring with vibration and mingling sounds of music and voices, and the melody was more than compelling. While they moved around the floor like professionals, both Enrico and Sadie were surprised to find that her soft curves were unconsciously trying to mold themselves into the contours of his firm body. Even more surprising, was that he wasn't doing anything to stop it from happening. And when the music to their third song stopped, they did not. Everyone else in the room stood up and clapped at the marvelous performance, but the two people whose eyes were still locked together, didn't hear or see anyone else in the room.

Sometime in the last ten minutes, Enrico had recognized how truly lovely Sadie was. He then took notice of her luscious mouth, her gorgeous eyes, her picture-perfect face, and the fact that she smelled like lilacs in full bloom.

It felt odd that Enrico was studying her as if he was analyzing her - like a Monet painting that was worth a million dollars. His eyes were drinking in all that he saw, and it sent a shiver up her spine. Sadie was strangely flattered by his interest, and now hoped that he would kiss her before the night was over.

Enrico was completely caught off guard; this was his English teacher and he was having inappropriate thoughts about her. But she was also a regular person and this was his last night in America. 'Would it be proper to tell her how he felt?' he wondered. As Enrico looked deep into her eyes, he thought he could feel an eager affection radiating from Sadie's body.

When his gaze met hers, her heart turned over in response. Sadie hoped that she was sending all the right signals, but she wasn't sure. 'Kiss me, already!' she screamed inside of her head.

Enrico looked into her eyes, which glowed with a savage inner fire, and the desire to kiss her became even stronger.

He couldn't deny the thrill he got at the prospect of what he was thinking, and it was making him weak in the knees.

Sadie was by no means blind to his attraction towards her, and her curiosity, as well as her vanity, was more than aroused. She was shocked by her own eagerness, and raised her chin in hopes of meeting his lips.

For the past eight months, they had been fighting off any and all feelings that they might have for the other person, but in that very moment, they could no longer hide the fact that they both felt an ache of obsession between them.

As he held her close to his body, Enrico detected a stronger meaning to what was going on between them. They were no longer just dancing, for this was more like a game of chess – he moved, which guided her to make the next move. His heavy lashes suddenly flew up. He then chuckled when he thought about the delight he would get, when he took away one of her defenses.

Sadie saw something playful and evil twinkle in his eyes, and it sent waves of eagerness throughout her body. Her dance partner was not hard to read, and she quickly felt her pulse increase with hunger for him.

The music thundered loudly in its last chorus of life, while Enrico's heartbeat had skyrocketed. Enrico could feel tiny ripples of pleasure exploding under the hand which was touching her skin, and this made him want to jump for joy. He could actually feel his hot blood coursing through his veins like a freshly awakened river, and he inhaled quite sharply.

His hand on her hip grabbed her a little tighter, and seemed to pull her a little closer to his body. Not surprisingly, they were now standing so close that only a whisper could pass between them.

Sadie was captivated by his warm touch, and she was secretly drawn to a height of passion that she had never known before. And because the dormant sexuality of her body had now been woken up, she wasn't sure how she would ever be able to walk away from him.

Enrico's heart was now pounding in his ears, while his breath had been caught in his throat. He wasn't about to let her go, and he gathered up all the force in his body to prove it.

Before the current song had played its very last note, Enrico stopped moving his feet.

Sadie gasped and became a little teary-eyed, for while he might be thinking that he was fulfilling a moment of physical desire, she was about to allow him to tear her soul apart.

His hands came up and cupped her beautiful face, and then he pulled her head gently towards his. Without asking, he pushed his lips onto hers, which summoned an incredible yearning that touched every cell in his body.

A passionate fluttering arose at the back of her neck, as she felt her lips pucker up to meet his. She let out a short gasp of delight, a split second before their mouths touched, and was now moaning with pleasure from the actual contact.

Enrico also moaned as he drank in the sweetness of how her lips had felt against his own. It was like drinking the finest wine that had ever been made, while listening to the most beautiful orchestral arrangement that had ever been written. In short, it was more pleasurable than he could have ever imagined, and now his body was shouting for more.

The Elusive Mr. Velucci

As his lips were merging with hers, Enrico felt an immediate and total attraction to her. A brief shiver rippled up his spine, bringing with it an awareness that he'd never experienced before. And as he roused his own passion, he could sense that hers was also growing stronger.

Enrico ended the kiss and stepped back, and then stared lovingly into Sadie's stunning face. He could see surprise in her eyes, but he could also see that she wanted more.

Sadie was completely lost; the kiss was as challenging as it was rewarding, and she did indeed want more. She knew very well that they shouldn't get involved, but they were beginning to, and now she hoped that they wouldn't stop.

Without being too obvious, he shifted how he was standing and then took a step closer. He closed his eyes and recaptured her mouth - more demanding this time - and when he felt her lips begging to open, it was enough to send him over the moon.

There was a dreamy essence to their second kiss, one where the very fabric of reality was all but gone. They seemed to be the only two people on the earth, and nothing else mattered except the two of them being together.

Sadie's body was bursting with hunger. She couldn't believe what was happening, but she gave herself freely to the passion of the moment. She had been able to part her lips, and the feel of his tongue against hers, sent the pit of her stomach into a wild swirl of sensations.

Enrico had waited for months to kiss her, and the prolonged anticipation had been almost unbearable. Now that they were engaged in the foreplay of lovemaking, his body was as erratic as a tornado; he was overcome by his craving for her and wanted nothing more than to rip her clothes off.

Sadie felt him move even closer, and then he wrapped his hands behind her back. The entire front of his body was pressed tightly against the entire front of hers, and she could now feel something solid against her groin. Enrico was crushing his lips against hers for the third time, weakening her knees, and silencing all of her thoughts. His actions were demanding and non-stop, and she wasn't doing anything to slow him down.

Enrico was drowning in the heat of the moment, and he wanted nothing more than to take this to the next level. He was undeniably hard, and his lower body was burning with the anticipation of sex. He no longer wanted to be standing, and his mind was adrift in everything that could be happening in the next hour.

And then everything changed.

Enrico felt a hard tap against his left shoulder. That simple gesture completely shattered the spell that he was in, and quickly brought him back into the large dance room. The gorgeous Italian was surprised to find that the whole area was in total quiet, which made things that much more awkward for everyone concerned.

"Sir?" came from a well-dressed man who was trying to get the dancer's attention.

Enrico was too stunned to speak, and was becoming more embarrassed by the second.

"Sir?" the man repeated.

Enrico's wide eyes began to scan the room, and he could see that everyone was looking at him with a surprised look on their face. It wasn't tough to figure out that they had probably been watching him making out with Sadie, and he wished that he was anywhere but there.

"Sir!" the man called loudly.

Enrico wiped his mouth with the back of his hand and replied, "Yes?"

"We're going to have to ask you to stop what you're doing; everyone is complaining."

It was now Sadie's turn to look around, which she did in slow motion. "We're so sorry", she responded shyly. She was also terribly embarrassed, and wished that she had the power to disappear.

Enrico looked at Sadie and then back at the man in front of him. "Thank you for telling us." He bowed his head, which he hoped showed his remorse at the situation, and then placed his left hand against Sadie's back. "Come on", he whispered with force. He led her back to their table, helped her grab her things, and then they left the building.

"Taxi!" he called loudly, once they were outside. He stuck his hand out to flag down a cab, and then turned to observe Sadie's reaction. "Don't be afraid." His mellow voice was edged with control. "Everything's going to be ok."

"I'm not", she said matter-of-factly, and lowered her chin. In truth, a million thoughts were rushing through her brain. Sadie had a desperate need to be close to the man who now held her heart in his hands, but she couldn't tell him. She honestly thought that he was taking her home, but she didn't want the night to end. She knew that she was not guaranteed of any more time other than these last eight months, but she prayed for another hour.

The cab arrived, they both got in, and several minutes later, the cab stopped.

Tina Griffith

When Sadie read the words on the flashing neon sign, a smile appeared, for she now understood what was about to happen. Without an ounce of hesitation, she took a deep breath and followed Enrico's lead.

After checking into the 24-room motel, Enrico walked with Sadie to #21. He unlocked the door and allowed her to go in first. Once inside, he kicked the door shut with his foot.

They were standing approximately three feet apart, frozen to their spots on the floor, and every time he refreshed his smile, her heart beat faster.

Enrico exhaled a long sigh of contentment, for he was finally alone with Sadie Adams – his tutor, his friend, and after tonight, his lover.

A soft whimper escaped from Sadie's throat, for she knew what he wanted to do.

He was amazed by how beautiful she looked in the soft lighting in the room, and he couldn't wait to hold her in his arms again.

Sadie felt completely powerless - like a breathless teenager who was standing in front of a rich and famous singing idol.

He did it slowly and seductively, and Sadie watched with utter curiosity, as his gaze slid down the entire length of her body.

Enrico made no attempt to hide the fact that he was looking at her as if he wanted to have his way with her. He truly wanted to devour every part of her body; kiss, lick, and touch everything that she had to offer, until she screamed for mercy.

Her fingers ached to reach out and touch him, but she

The Elusive Mr. Velucci

knew that he would have to make the first move; she wasn't brave enough to begin what they were about to do.

And as if he had been reading her mind, he took two large steps towards her and clutched her body tightly against his own. He looked into her eyes as if he was seeking permission, and then lowered his mouth and kissed her with a wild intensity. His tongue was going everywhere, and he knew that it was driving her crazy.

A small cry of relief broke from her throat, as she locked herself into his forceful embrace. She had no intentions of backing away from him; she had wanted this for quite a while now. Because the urgency in his kiss had upset her balance and made her weak in the knees, she now longed for the protectiveness of his strong arms.

Enrico pulled his head back so that he could see the expression on her face. He was wearing a serious look, and he wanted her to know that his body was full of lust and that he meant to get everything that she was offering.

Sadie could now smell the sweet and powerful musk of his sweat, and she wanted to faint. She was quite mindful of where parts of his warm body was touching her own, because that's where her skin felt unrestrained.

Enrico moved his soft, wet lips close to her ear, and he said her name like no one on earth had ever said it before. "Sadie Lynn." He whispered that he wanted her, and suddenly the air around them was hot and thick with desire.

Without thinking, she released a soft moan of approval. Butterflies were fluttering in her tummy while her bones seemed to be melting away, but she wasn't about to move from the spot where she was nestled tightly in his arms.

With the tip of his index finger, he raised her chin, and

kissed her eager mouth for a second time. It wasn't long before he was wrapped in an invisible heat so strong, that he never wanted to break free from it.

Sadie had succumbed to the forceful domination of his lips, yet again. She even surprised herself when she began kissing him with a need that was as strong as he was delivering. Just then, a shudder passed through her as her body urged him to do more.

Enrico could feel the bindings of the tangible bond that had been built up between them these past few months, and he now felt that he was ready to give them a night to remember.

"Take me", her heart whispered, but the words never left her mouth. Her head was swimming and her body was aching for his touch, and even though they weren't supposed to get this close, she wanted to be together with him for however long they had.

Their closeness was like a drug to him, lulling him to euphoria, and he could tell that she felt the same exact way as he did. He boldly slid the zipper down on the back of her dress, and then he helped it fall to the floor. To his surprise, all she was wearing was a bra and underwear. Out of curiosity, his hand seared a path from her breast bone to the top of her panties. Enrico had never touched a naked woman's body before, and because it brought him great pleasure, he now knew that he would do it as often as possible.

As his fingers lightly brushed against her exposed skin, she wanted to scream with joy; the very idea of what they were about to do, sent currents of desire to her loins.

The Elusive Mr. Velucci

Instinctively, her body automatically arched towards him, while a soft sigh left her accessible lips.

His hands touched her breasts over the fabric of her bra, which made her toss her head back from unbelievable gratification. He eased the lacy cup aside in order to release the mound of flesh which was being held captive. He moved his head closer and used his tongue to tantalize the firm, pink buds, which had swollen to their fullest capacity.

While he was introducing himself to her smooth breasts, she felt him reach for her hands. He then encouraged her to touch his body.

She was cautious at first, but became an expert quite quickly. After unbuttoning his shirt, she traced the muscles from his neck down to his navel – just as he had done to her. The sparse black hair on his chest was wiry, but it did not cause her to withdraw her attention. Instead, she stood silent, kept her eyes locked with his, and then she felt her body shiver. Sadie was beginning to get the hang of what she was doing, and slid her hand across the smooth skin on his slightly-hairy belly. She watched his stomach muscles quiver, as her fingers grazed every single inch from the right side of his waist to the left, and it brought a satisfied grin to her bruised lips.

His exposed nipples were licking the cool air, while Sadie was propelling the nerves on his skin to shatter into an orgasm. She saw something in his eyes that caused her to hold her breath, which in turn sent their foreplay into another level.

With one swoop, Enrico lifted her up and laid her down in the middle of the bed. He was pleased when she didn't object to him removing the rest of her clothing, and then he proceeded to take off his own.

Once they were both naked, he climbed on top of her, and swooped in to steal another kiss. He then traced kisses down her slender throat, all the way to her flat belly. Before he went lower, he gave her body a bold sweeping glance and then searched her eyes.

Her pupils were dilated and dark with desire. She ached for the fulfillment of all he had to offer, and couldn't wait to be crushed in his powerful embrace.

Enrico lowered his mouth and descended on her lips, while his hand was discovering other parts of her body.

She was soon teetering on the brink and then fell into unmanageable pleasure, with Enrico only seconds behind her.

They lay there giggling and panting in the afterglow, while wrapped in each other's arms. They had now been joined together by more than just flesh; it was by love in their souls and a biological need to be as one.

They used the next several hours to explore their bodies and awaken their senses. Hands and mouths were going everywhere, and Enrico and Sadie were learning of private places that only married people should know or talk about. Muscles were quivering, pulses were racing, and sweat was making everything wet. Eyes began to water, noses began to run, positions kept changing, and blankets had been thrown to the floor. Because passion and adrenaline was pushed to the limit, neither Sadie nor Enrico could stop what they were doing.

More than a few times that night, their worlds had spun out of control and had careened on its axis, because

The Elusive Mr. Velucci

the gratification was so pure and unpredictable. They had both gasped in sweet agony of the pleasure which they were experiencing, and they had both shattered into a million lustrous stars after each orgasm.

It was all so magical and there was so much to learn, and both partners were very willing to gain as much experience as possible. They had fallen asleep a few times during the course of the last few hours, but neither one wanted to waste too much time sleeping when they could be doing other things.

Time after time, he saw her brilliant smile beam brightly across her sweaty face, after he calmed his burning arousal by sliding his moist body on top of hers.

Sadie immediately responded to the seduction of his passion, by raising her hips to meet his. And with each thrust, she couldn't control the volume of her delight.

Enrico moaned aloud with erotic pleasure himself, and they both knew when another searing moment was about to happen.

Together, their bodies began to vibrate from an uncontrollable flow of energy, which soon flooded their souls with a bursting of unbelievable sensations.

Around 4am, the exhausted man gathered his partner's naked body into his sweaty arms, and he was holding her as if he would never let her go. Smiles of contentment shone on both their faces, while songs of love sang in their hearts. It was evident that their friendship had turned into devotion, which had just been heightened with extreme satisfaction, and now neither wanted their time together, to end.

"Are you okay?" he asked lovingly. Enrico felt he might

have been a little too rough that last time. He searched her eyes for an answer even before she could speak.

Sadie smiled with a love that one has for a newborn baby. "I'm okay", she sighed happily. She reached up and kissed his mouth as tenderly as she could, to convince him that she truly was fine.

Her mouth on his, relaxed whatever thoughts were dancing in his head. He then wrapped himself around her body, and they surrendered themselves to the numbed sleep of satisfied lovers.

The dark of evening soon turned into the light of a new day, which told them that their time together was about to end.

As they lay there under the white and flimsy, wrinkled sheets, Enrico stroked Sadie's matted hair. As they stared into each other's eyes, they hated that he was about to leave. The words, 'stay here', hovered in the air all around them, even though they were never spoken out loud. Prayers had been quietly delivered to the Lord up above, while wishes that things could be different, filled their souls.

Genuine love floated from his heart to hers, but the actual words were never spoken. Because of where each of them lived, they couldn't bring themselves to talk about how their relationship could possibly work. They each felt that there was no sense lingering on the possibly that he was going to remain here, because they both knew that he couldn't.

With absolute reluctance, Enrico called for a cab, and then he called his aunt and uncle. He asked them to bring his suitcase when they came to say good-bye, and they were only too happy to oblige.

The Elusive Mr. Velucci

After he hung up, it was clear that the ambience in the room had turned somber, but it didn't change what had happened or what was about to happen. Enrico and Sadie got up and dressed, and then they gathered their belongings. Fifteen minutes later, when they opened the door to the motel room, both of them had to stop and take in what they were seeing. The beauty of the gorgeous sunrise in the east, was completely shattered by the fact that Enrico and Sadie needed to walk away from the shabby room where they had just shared something special.

Sadie wasn't sure that she could leave the motel, and began to cry with incredible sadness; along with the tears and pain of sheer heartbreak, was the feeling that they had started something which both of them wanted to keep going.

Enrico also didn't want to leave the room where they had just consummated their love, but there was a time limit, and that threshold had now passed.

As Enrico and Sadie got into the cab, it was very clear that they were in love. No sounds were made, but their body language professed an unending amount of words which spoke volumes about how they felt. They were quite comfortable in each other's company, and they both moved with an elegance, as if it had all been choreographed months ago.

From the outside looking in, it was as if they could read or anticipate the other person's thoughts and feelings. From within their own selves, they had just confirmed and strengthened what had been growing since they first met.

Sadly, their time was now up, and there was nothing that either of them could do to change things; they had to say good-bye.

Enrico looked out of the side window while a million thoughts raced around his head. He considered the consequences of what would happen if he were to stay in America for another little while, and could already envision some problems. He contemplated another avenue, but his mind suddenly became inundated with the promise that he had made to his parents; he had to go home to them, and to start school in September. These and other obligations needed to be filled and he knew it, but it was making him miserable. He reached for Sadie's hand and held in lovingly within his own. He squeezed it several times, in hopes that she could read his last few thoughts.

Sadie was looking out of her own window and trying not to burst into tears; she was already missing him, and he hadn't even left yet. She could feel his hand wrap around hers, and she squeezed him back with her own messages.

While her heart was breaking, her mind kept going over the pictures of them making love. How he touched her, how he kissed her, and how he made her feel were all she could think about. As tears ran down her face, she wondered if she had the right to ask him to stay. Even though her voice couldn't say the words out loud, she turned her head and looked in his direction, and pushed the sentiments towards his heart. "Please don't go", her soul begged, as it ripped the frayed essence of her very being in half.

Enrico turned and looked into her eyes. Her flushed skin and tear-stained appearance was easy to read, and he knew what she wanted - for him to stay. His own tears welled up behind his eyes, and he wished with all his might that he could, but sadly, it was not possible. Because of that, he turned his head away and cursed under his breath. He

The Elusive Mr. Velucci

then hoped that she had not seen the single tear which had escaped from his right eye, and was now sliding down the black bristles of his cheek.

Sadie inhaled quite quickly when he turned away, and even though she hated that he had to leave, she understood the situation. She looked out of her window again, and sobbed without hiding the sound of her own crying.

Unbeknownst to the woman who sat beside him, Enrico had hoped for a miracle that would allow him to remain in America – even for a little while longer. Because he could feel the anguish in every breath that was leaving her body, he lowered his head and wept for her, and for himself.

The cab arrived at the front entrance of the terminal and came to a halt. Sadie got out of her side while Enrico paid the driver. They walked into the building holding hands, unaware that Enrico's relatives were standing nearby.

As soon as they saw him, Uncle Alberto and Aunt Gina raced over to their nephew. As they approached, they could see that something life-changing had happened between Enrico and Sadie, and out of respect, the older couple said nothing to embarrass them.

They both said HI to Sadie and gave her a hug, and then Aunt Gina shoved a large bag of food into her nephew's hands. "Enjoy", she said, even though she had intended to say so much more.

Being a woman, Gina could see beyond the emotions which Enrico and Sadie were displaying, for she had detected that they had fallen in love and were now having a hard time saying good-bye.

"Say Hi to your parents for us", Zio stated sincerely. He

kissed Enrico's cheeks and then moved aside so that his wife could also say good-bye.

"Have a good trip", Aunt Gina whispered lovingly. She kissed both of his cheeks, and then hugged him as if she would never see him again.

"Ciao!" they called, as they walked away.

"Ciao!" Enrico cried. He waved and suddenly felt ill at ease; he was leaving a place and people who he had grown to love, and going back to his parents and his country of birth. He was nervous, and suddenly felt much younger than the age on his passport.

Enrico and Sadie were now standing alone, and it was their turn to say good-bye. They faced each other, he took her hands in his, and he spoke in an extremely compassionate tone.

"I didn't realize how much you would mean to me when we first met", he whispered with total sincerity. His eyes had filled up and he could hardly see, and with everything in his soul, he very much wanted to stay right where he was. He was miserable because he knew he couldn't, so he promised to come back as soon as possible.

"Enrico", she whimpered, as she looked lovingly into his eyes. Her voice had a gentle softness to it, with undertones of abandonment. She wanted to say a thousand more words, but they got stuck in her throat.

"I know", he revealed, in a voice that was fragile and shaking. It was quite evident to everyone around them, that he wasn't prepared to say good-bye to the beautiful girl standing in front of him. He brought his forehead forward until it was touching hers, and they cried with immense fear that they would never see each other again.

The Elusive Mr. Velucci

An announcement came over the P.A., which stated that all passengers must get checked in. It was in that moment when Enrico knew in his heart, that no miracle was coming and that he would have to leave. He pulled his head back from hers and looked deep into Sadie's unhappy eyes. He had not expected to fall in love, and now he could feel his own heart breaking.

Enrico placed both of his hands against the sides of her face, and slowly closed his eyes. With all the love he had inside of him, he kissed her forehead, her cheeks, her nose, and then her mouth. It baffled him that this woman had provided him with the absolute need to love another living soul, for he would not have guessed that to be possible. He wanted to hold her, take care of her, know her whereabouts, and love her for the rest of his life, but he could not; he had waited too long to change the course of his immediate future.

Enrico was becoming frustrated that he had taken eight months to get to know her, but he had only had six hours to really love her. He pulled her body closer to his, and then held on tight. 'If only I had known or acted sooner...' he whispered.

Enrico needed to go, so he ended their embrace as hurriedly as it had begun.

A flash of wild grief suddenly ripped through her soul, as Sadie realized the true reality of what was happening. "Enrico!" she cried from every pore in her body. Her eyes were begging him to stay, while her heart was breaking into a million pieces. The whole thing suddenly felt very real, and severe panic began to fill every fiber of her being.

Enrico examined her face and he knew what she wanted.

"I'll be back", he assured her, in a voice that was both soft and trying to stay strong. He picked up his suitcase with one hand, and he placed something in her hand with the other.

Without looking to see what it was, she swaddled the object safely in the palm of her hand, while keeping her eyes locked with his.

Enrico twisted his upper body to face his family and shouted, "Good-bye everyone!" He turned around to take one more look into the face of his beloved Sadie, and then he began to walk away.

"No!" she shouted loudly. The simple word dissolved into the air like a crispy leaf in the fall.

Enrico hadn't gotten very far, and now it was him who was falling apart. He took one more look in her direction, put his hand to his mouth, and blew her a kiss. "Bye for now!" he said quietly. As he faced forward again, he began to cry. Not full-out crying like a small child who had gotten hurt on the playground, but a grown man's frustration and enormous displeasure of things that he couldn't fix or change.

Nothing in her mind or body was able to let him go, and now Sadie felt like she couldn't breathe. Her muscles were paralyzed and she was experiencing numbness all over. Her eyebrows were raised, her eyes were wide open, and a look of extreme anxiety shot across her face.

While Enrico was moving his feet, he was trying to hide his appearance from the other travelers. He was utterly depressed and having a hard time forcing his emotions to stay down. He tried to make it look like he was holding back a sneeze rather than a flood of tears, but when one or two drops of salty water leaked out from their moist

The Elusive Mr. Velucci

environment, Enrico wiped them off of his face with the sleeve of his right arm and kept going.

Sadie had been watching the man she loves walk away, and with an incredible amount of courage, she boldly took a few steps towards him. "En-ri-co!" She shouted his name as she extended her left hand far in front of her body, but he didn't turn around. With sheer desperation gushing from the very core of her soul, she wanted to run after him, to hold him one last time, but she knew she couldn't; their time was up.

Enrico heard her calling him, but he couldn't bear to turn around again; he knew that if he saw her, he would run back into her arms and he would never let go. Instead, he made himself a promise to return to New York as soon as he could.

Sadie stood frozen in her tracks, while anxiety guided her every thought. She watched Enrico, as he continued to walk in a hurried pace, and she wanted him to come back. "Enrico", she sighed, with little air passing through her trembling lips. "I love you." Her head was bent in sorrow while the world was crashing down around her.

After Enrico boarded the large vessel, he made sure to stand on the very end of the large deck. He was facing her, but they were so far apart. His hand leaped high into the air and swayed back and forth, as he watched her wave back to him. He could tell that she was beckoning him to come back, and it was killing him that he couldn't.

Sadie's heart leaped in her chest when she saw him. "Enrico!" she called loudly. She saw him waving, and she waved back with as much energy as she could muster. She couldn't take her eyes off of the handsome man, who only ours ago, had made passionate love to her. "I'm here!" she cried. Her voice had cracked and was full of raw emotion.

Enrico's face was wearing the biggest smile of his life, and he waved with all of his might. "Sadie!" he called, as if she could hear him.

"Enrico!" she shouted. She knew in that instance that he was the man who she would love for the rest of her life.

The ship blew its horn a few times, and then it slowly pulled away from the dock.

"No!" she screamed, as her body went into an even bigger panic mode. Tears were trickling down her moist and flushed cheeks, as her soul was being smashed into a thousand different pieces. "Please don't leave!" she pleaded at the top of her lungs. She was yelling with as much force as she had in her body, and was stunned that no-one was looking in her direction. 'Why were they not helping me get him back?' she wondered wildly.

"Sadie!" Enrico called, but the sound of his words were not as clear anymore. "I love you!" he added happily. "Can you hear me?"

With all the noise that was around her, Sadie's ears didn't get to receive his tender words. "How will I go on without you?" she cried, while choking on her own tears. Her heart was in her throat, her will to live had been taken away, and now there was a horrible, empty ache in her soul.

"Enrico!" Sadie shouted at full volume. She continued to step closer and closer to the edge of the platform, as the ship appeared to go further and further away from the shore. "No-o-o-o-o!" she screamed, as if that would somehow stop what was happening.

With each moment that passed, their hearts were

The Elusive Mr. Velucci

growing heavier with the sadness that was now weighing them down. Minute-by-minute, their emotional pain was getting worse, and almost an hour later, the ship was nothing more than a mere dot on the large body of water.

Sadie had fallen to her knees before the ship had totally disappeared, and it was then when she discovered what Enrico had placed in her closed fist - a beautiful silver locket. On the left side of the elaborately engraved heart, was a picture of Enrico. On the right, was a picture of her.

Sadie was quite overwhelmed and couldn't get any words to come out of her mouth, but her spirit was filled with a thousand sentiments. Surprise and confusion went through her entire body, and then she began to cry again, but from the love of a gift that she would hold onto for the rest of her life.

As the ship began to sail across the Atlantic Ocean, Sadie slowly made her way back to her apartment. She looked side-to-side as she walked, and was astounded that everything in her world seemed different, even though the backdrops of New York were still the same. 'Does anyone know that the love of my life has been ripped away from me?' she wanted to scream, but didn't. Instead, she planted one foot in front of the other, and tried to appear as if nothing was going on.

Enrico was looking forward to seeing his parents and friends again, but he couldn't stop thinking about Sadie. His attractive smile broadened as he remembered how it felt to be in her arms; her scent, her soft hair, her smooth skin, and how her curves molded so well with his. The thought of her mouth on his, sent a new surge of warmth throughout his entire body. Enrico bent his head and immediately placed his index and middle finger upon his lips. Suddenly, memories of how he had caressed her mouth and the whole outline of her naked body, rushed to the forefront of his mind. The memory of all that they had shared, brought perfect harmony to all of his senses. Sadie brought him to life and to manhood, and he was glad that he had not shared that with anyone else.

As Enrico repositioned himself against the railing of the ship, her beautiful face appeared before him. Her hair was flowing freely in the wind, and she was smiling as if she was also agreeing that their time together had been more than amazing. It sent shivers down his spine and goose bumps to his skin, and it was then when he decided to go and find his cabin.

During the next several days, there were many nights where Sadie couldn't sleep, and too many moments where she couldn't stop crying. All of her thoughts were on Enrico and the things which they had done together. More than a thousand pictures flashed through her mind at great speed, and even though she would have liked to grab one out of the air and reflect on what they had done in that particular moment, she couldn't; there were too many of them. It was as if they were attached to a movie reel and the action could not be stopped until the film got to the end. The experience was both terrifying and satisfying, for while she truly enjoyed that time period, she hated that it was now over.

Once again, she began to cry, but it was because they didn't surrender to their unspoken passion until it was too late. They fought it, and ultimately let all the wasted moments drift away. It was so heartbreaking for her to think about, because now he was gone, and she wasn't sure if she would ever see him again.

The Elusive Mr. Velucci

Sadie's upper body bent forward and she sobbed for a love that had been unfairly pulled away from her. She was not ready to say good-bye to Enrico, but at least she was left with the memories.

From the first moment when Sadie was back at work, or in the company of her friends, she tried to appear to be ok. She spent the rest of her time studying and working, and hoping to hear from Enrico.

When the ship docked in Italy, Enrico was greeted by a large group of friends and family members. They all cheered when they saw him, and welcomed him with tears and open arms.

"Enrico!" his parents shouted loudly, with a happiness that only a parent can explain and understand. It was also out of relief for a child who they had not seen in a very long time. Their appreciation that he had come back, was sincere and overwhelming, and their hearts pounded when he hugged them.

"I came home, just as I promised", he whispered through his own tears.

"And for that, we are so happy", they rejoiced.

For the next twenty-four hours, his childhood home was filled with food, music, people, and a lot of questions.

"How was the weather?" asked his cousin.

"What about the food? Did you like it?" asked his mother's sister.

"What about the women?" asked his friend from school.

Enrico was tired and answered each topic with a 3-5 word reply.

As he looked around his childhood home, he became terribly nostalgic; it was wonderful to be there, in familiar

Tina Griffith

surroundings with people who he loved and knew, but something was different.

Another question shot across the room, and it was clear that everyone was anxious to learn all that he had done while he was away.

Enrico tried to answer everyone as best he could, and then his mother came to his rescue and eventually sent everyone home.

When Enrico was able to lay his head down on his pillow, he stared up at the ceiling and wished that Sadie was there with him. A large tear leaked from his left eye, as he wondered what and how she was doing. In his imagination, he tried to envision her. He could see her wearing a long, flowing sheer gown with long billowy sleeves and a scoop neck. There was a slight breeze blowing all around her, which disturbed her hair but not her beauty. She was looking directly at him, gesturing for him to be with her, to kiss her and to hold her, and it was all done without words.

Enrico rolled onto his side, and pulled at the blankets until they were high enough to cover his ear. Another tear pushed through the barrier of his left eye, and fell without shame, onto his pillow. He had clearly fallen in love with Sadie, and because they were now so far apart, he vowed to keep her in his heart for the rest of his life. Sadly, the idea that he might never see her again, burst his soul into a million pieces.

Enrico shifted his body until he was laying with his chest against the mattress, and then he pushed his face deep into his pillow to forbid the sound of his heartbreak to leave his room. He cried like a small boy, until he was exhausted and finally able to sleep.

The Elusive Mr. Velucci

The next morning, he awoke with a new sense of self. He was still Enrico Velucci, but he was no longer the child who had left Italy all those months ago. Today he lifted his nose into the air as a man, and looked forward to the responsibilities which lay before him.

A week later, Enrico attended his first day of University. He had always loved music, and his dream was to become an orchestra conductor.

School was tough, and there was a lot more to learn than he had originally understood. Unfortunately, between the heavy load of attending University, completing his homework, and working at his part time job, that didn't leave him much time for anything else. Eating the evening meal with his parents was the only luxury which he allowed himself to have. Otherwise, his life was kept to such a strict schedule, that he only thought about Sadie when he was dreaming.

Sadie hadn't been feeling well for the last couple of weeks, and she thought she might have the flu. Five weeks after Enrico's first day at school, she found out that she was pregnant. Her first thought was to tell Enrico, but since they had not exchanged any contact information, she made her way to Uncle Alberto's deli. The lights were off and the business was locked up, which was strange for a Thursday morning. She then read the hand-written note that was stuck on the front door and gasped.

'Closed Due to a Family Emergency'

As her hands rushed up to grip the sides of her head, her eyes widened and her heart began to pound in panic.

"What?" she called, but to no-one in particular. After a split second where her breathing had become suspended, she felt a flush of adrenaline start sprinting through her body. She was staring at the note and seemed frozen to the spot, and she wanted to faint. She looked up to see if she had the right address, and quickly became embarrassed and disoriented at the same time. 'What do I do now?' screamed through her mind, but there were no answers.

It took a few minutes before she turned around and made her way back to her own apartment, but she did so in a daze of disbelief and confusion.

Sadie had no way of knowing that Enrico's father had taken ill and had been put into the hospital. Family members from far and wide had been asked to come and see him and his family - to bring them food, and to extend their condolences. The bed-ridden man thought they were there to wish him well, but little did he know that everyone had actually come to say their good-byes.

Sadie went back to the deli a few weeks later, and again, the door was locked and a note was hanging off the front door.

'Closed - Death in the Family'

Enrico's father had passed away, but Sadie would not know this until many years later.

Sadie was pregnant and not feeling well. She was terribly frightened and had no family to fall back on. She didn't know how to get hold of Enrico, and when she went back to the deli two weeks later, she broke out in tears because it was still closed.

The Elusive Mr. Velucci

With desperation swimming through her veins, Sadie reached out to friends and co-workers, who encouraged her to go to the public welfare offices. The lady assigned to her was very nice, and gave her baby clothes and bottles, a large laundry basket for the newborn to sleep in, and a few vouchers for food and rent. It was all sincerely appreciated, but it wasn't enough; the mom-to-be wanted to be with the father of her child.

Enrico had taken a little time off from work and school when his father's health had taken a turn for the worse. When the older man died, everyone was devastated. They gathered around his widow and son, and took care of them for as long as they could. When the appropriate amount of time had passed, one-by-one they left, and let Enrico and his mother fend for themselves.

Enrico was now the man of the house. Because of his new responsibilities, he pushed his own activities to the side and directed all of his energy towards his mother and her well-being. He was grieving the loss of his father, along with the grey-haired woman who had given him life, but there was no time to pause; there was food to shop for and prepare, housework to do, and taking his mother back and forth to the church on a daily basis. There were phone calls to answer and the front door to open, from people who were wondering how Enrico and his mother were doing.

At night, after he had tucked his mother into bed, he sometimes wished that he had a minute to breathe, but everything and everyone was demanding such a large amount of his attention, that he couldn't get any time alone. He couldn't do anything that he wanted, and that also meant that Sadie was slowly turning into a lovely memory.

To the outside world, Sadie maintained that she was fine. However, inside she was a complete mess; her hormones were all over the place and she cried at the silliest things. When she saw couples holding hands or kissing, she lowered her head and cried, because she wanted to do those things with Enrico. When she listened to song lyrics on the radio, she became emotional. And she wouldn't dare watch a romantic movie, for fear that the man and woman would end up together. She desperately wanted that to happen to her, but as the weeks rolled by, she was slowly losing hope that it would.

Three months later, around 6pm on Christmas Eve, Sadie made her way to Rockefeller Center. After she parked her car and walked the last few blocks in Midtown Manhattan, she took in all that was around her; the buildings which were lit up in cheery holiday colors, the decorations which had been carefully draped over doorways and trees, the enormous element of excitement for all that that time of year was about, and the very idea of strangers rushing around while trying to buy their last minute gifts. It felt quite magical to have the holiday season drape itself around her.

The air was crisp and filled with the smell of roasted chestnuts, which were being sold by vendors on several street corners. Christmas music was more than just a faint sound in the background, and the mix of rich people with the ones who lived from paycheck-to-paycheck, was quite amusing; they were all laughing and interacting as if they had known each other since birth.

Sadie soon found herself standing in front of the unbelievably beautiful, and very famous Christmas tree, which had been lit up and decorated to perfection. It seemed

The Elusive Mr. Velucci

taller than it looked on TV, and she couldn't begin to count how many large red bows had been strategically placed on every bough. Sadie was mesmerized by the magnificent spectacle, and admired it as if she was a kid seeing it for the first time.

As she gazed at every ribbon and ornament, her vision slid downward, as the reflection of the colored lights glistened in her eyes. Her smile had widened with a multitude of appreciation by the time she got to the bottom of the tree, for there stood the triumphant collection of metal wire, herald angels. They were standing guard in the Channel Gardens, while seeming to blow their horns. Sadie became immediately overwhelmed, for it was all so utterly magnificent.

Sadie stood admiring all that she could see, for a good 15 minutes or so, and then she was ready to do what she had come to do. She closed her eyes, laced her fingers together, and allowed the tender words to flow gracefully from her heart. "I know that it was foolish for me to fall in love with Enrico, because it had been clearly told to me that he would have to go home when his time in New York was over. But fall in love I did, and now I want to be with him every second of every day."

Her swollen belly was moving, which caused her to become even more emotional. A tear fell from her right eye and her lips began to quiver, but she continued. "I miss him with everything I have, and now I am going to have his child. If I can receive any wish tonight, I wish that I could see Enrico again. I would very much like to talk with him, hold him, and let him know that I will always love him."

A cold chill raced up the length of her spine, which

startled her and triggered her to suspend her speech for a brief second. She looked around, but because she was on a mission, she didn't care that she was fenced in by an unsurmountable number of people. Sadie closed her eyes and positioned her hands in front of her face. With everything in her soul, she prayed towards the gigantic tree and the heavens above it. "Please", she begged loudly, and then broke out crying. "Please let me see him again, and let it be soon; I love him and miss him very much, and I want him to know that he is about to become a father."

The very minute the last few words left her mouth, Sadie felt big, fluffy, flakes of powdered snow drift down from the sky and land on her face. She immediately opened her eyes, and the joy in her heart repeated in her laughter and shone on her skin; the wet flakes were kissing everything that they were touching. 'Was this a sign that my wish had been heard?' she asked aloud. Sadie looked straight up and tried to catch a snowflake on her tongue. When one landed, she instantly felt a sense of complete satisfaction.

Minutes later, Sadie tucked the ends of her warm coat tightly across her chest. As she stared at the very top of the beautiful tree, she hoped with all her might that the universe had heard her wish.

Suddenly, and without being able to explain it, she could feel Enrico all around her and it caused her to inhale sharply. The experience was dreamlike, even though she was awake. It took over all of her senses and it made her doubt her own sanity, but she could smell him. She was sure that he was near, and yet he was so far away.

Once she understood that there was no logic to the

The Elusive Mr. Velucci

intuition that she was having, she chalked it up to wishful thinking.

Another tear fell down her reddened face, and Sadie decided that it was time to leave. She looked down and lovingly caressed her bulging tummy. "You want to go home now, precious?" She was speaking to her baby, who had just jumped at the sound of her voice. This made her smile, and because there was a definite chill in the air, she made her way back to her car.

Many minutes later, Sadie arrived at her home, but before she went into her apartment, she looked up at the sky and whispered softly, "Have a good Christmas, my love. Perhaps in the new year, we will see each other again."

Little did Sadie know that Enrico was also praying that night. He had made his way to his favorite spot by the water, in the gulf of Sorrento. As he walked, in the distance he could hear a Christmas Concert by the Sorrento Symphony Chamber Orchestra. They were playing classical music by Corelli, Bach, and Mozart, while the Blue Gospel Choir was singing Christmas songs in both English and Italian.

Enrico was suddenly transported back to his childhood, and how his family had gone to the ice rink at the Piazza A. Lauro on Corso Italia, near the train station. He remembered how his father had taught him how to stand on the blades and then glide across the bumpy ice, while his mother cheered him on from the ridge between the slippery surface and the grass. There was plenty of hot chocolate afterwards, along with several sweet treats for his efforts.

Enrico lowered his face and smiled, for that seemed like such a long time ago. He then envisioned all the children and adults who were spending a happy hour or two, skating and laughing while soaking up the carnival atmosphere on this festive night. "Ah, what wonderful memories they are making", he sighed in Italian.

Sadie popped into his head and he wondered what she was doing. He couldn't believe how much he was missing her, but his life had changed since he left New York, and there was still a lot to do before he could make his way back to her arms. Enrico looked up to the heavens, and searched until he spotted the brightest star that he had ever seen. It was glorious and he wished that he could share the experience with her, but it wasn't meant to be.

His mother had died two weeks ago, from what some people were calling, a broken heart. He was now all alone and extremely sad, and as a form of comfort, he said a prayer. In Italian, he wished for his parents to have a very Happy Christmas, and he hoped that they were together. He then paused before he spoke the next part in English.

"My darling, Sadie", he began quietly. His tear-smothered voice had cracked and he knew it, but he had to continue. "I know you can't hear me, but I hope you are well. I miss you more than you could ever know, and I wish that I was there with you, in your arms, looking up at the same sky, on this blessed night."

Tears were now streaming down his cheeks, but he refused to wipe them away; he wanted to feel the pain of loneliness with every breath that he took. "I hope you have a good Christmas, Sadie", he whispered. "Please know that I am always thinking of you."

There was no way that he could ignore the immense love that he had for the girl he had given his heart to, but he needed to push onward as best he could. He felt that in doing

The Elusive Mr. Velucci

so, that it would enable him to have a better future. He was quite sure that that would also include Sadie, and therefore, this was the concept that kept him moving forward.

Suddenly, everything about her and their time together, appeared in stunning detail in the forefront of his mind. Especially the memory of how Sadie had spoken his name during their last night together; her voice had such a compassionate tone to it, that it seemed to linger for several seconds longer than it needed to.

His eyelashes and chin lowered towards his chest, for the mere memory brought tears and goose bumps to his soul. He truly believed that no other person on this earth had ever been able to make him feel like that, and he doubted that anyone ever could again.

Enrico released a loud sigh in total wonder of his tutor's power and beauty. He loved her and he knew it, and he wished that they could have had a few more days to be together. And even though their distance was tearing him apart, he needed to resign himself to the fact that they would have to be separated for a little while longer.

Enrico's body bent forward with utter despair, as many tears slid down his cheeks; being apart was not what he wanted, but it was what had to happen.

Hours later, when the clock stuck midnight in New York and 6am in Naples, Enrico was just getting up while Sadie had only been in bed for two hours. It was Christmas Day, all around the world, and everyone was celebrating.

Even though Enrico and Sadie were on different continents, they moved their blankets aside and got themselves into a sitting position on the bed. They closed their eyes and wished like they had never wished before, that they could be together again – even for one last time. A loud rush of wind and snow brushed against their bedroom windows, and it caused them to open their eyes. They weren't sure if it was a sign or not, but their mouths slid into an encouraging smile. With hope cheering them on, they looked towards the ceiling, as their hearts sent a prayer of thanks to the heavens.

A moment later, they crawled back into the warmth of their beds. They felt especially close in that moment, which made them believe that all was not lost.

The images of them during her sleep were delightful, but the reality was that Sadie could feel Enrico slipping away. His essence, his kisses, and how it felt to be in his arms, were all things that she did not want to lose. And yet, she was worried that that's all she would be left with… lovely memories.

Enrico's life was very full, and he still had so much to do before he could reunite with Sadie. It was a goal that he was working towards, even though there were days when it seemed beyond difficult. He tried to be strong though, and only surrendered his power when he slept. The dark of the night was the best time of his day, for that's when he got to be with Sadie.

Sadie loved closing her eyes and seeing Enrico. She had recently developed a fear of having already lost him, and decided that if she could only be with him in her dreams, then she wanted to be comatose all the time.

The weeks turned into months, which eventually spun into years of no contact. Enrico and Sadie continued to keep their unspoiled memories safe in their hearts, and never lost sight of the possibility that they would one day be together.

The Elusive Mr. Velucci

Throughout the last few years, Enrico had gone through school, and was now perfecting his new occupation as a conductor of the finest orchestras in the world. He was living in his parent's home and keeping himself quite busy, while acquiring the respect and acknowledgement that came from his line of work.

Meanwhile, Sadie had given birth to a beautiful little girl, and because she now worked mostly from home, the new mom had been able to watch her darling daughter grow up.

Sadie had very little experience with taking care of babies or children, and would have loved to have had her own mother be there with her - to guide her and to help her - but it was not mean to be.

When Sadie was thirteen years old, she began to babysit for the neighbors in the next block. Both couples had been friends for ten years or more, and when Sadie became of age, Mr. and Mrs. Whitmore asked if she could look after their two little girls.

It was a life-changing moment for Sadie's parents, for they still looked upon her as their infant daughter. After talking with Sadie and realizing that she was quite competent, they agreed.

The little girls were two and four, and were sleeping when Sadie arrived. Before the couple left the house, the TV was turned on and the snacks had been placed on the coffee table. Because the evening had gone so very well, Sadie was asked to watch over the children, several more times, over the next year.

Mr. Whitmore had often had improper thoughts about Sadie, and continually hugged her longer and closer than he should have. He also made a few crude comments and gestures when he was alone with her. "Come here and sit by me", he'd say casually. He would then string his lengthy arm across her adolescent shoulders, and pull her entire body closer to his own. He proceeded to compliment her on her attire or good looks, much like a man does on a first date.

Sadie hated every minute of it.

"Mmm…, you smell really good", he'd whisper, while his nose was pressed up against her hair. Then he would inhale a long breath with his eyes closed, as if he was making a memory for later.

His wife had been spying and saw everything from the sidelines. It was despicable how her husband had acted in the young lady's company, and she couldn't help but cringe at a few of his lewd comments. On more than a few occasions, Mrs. Whitmore had come out of hiding to speak with her husband. She bravely pointed out how indecent he was being towards Sadie, but because Mr. Whitmore would feel embarrassed at what his wife had accused him of, he rushed towards her and slapped her across the face with all his might. The astonished woman pressed a flat hand against the hot, burning flesh, and without uttering another word, she ran from the room in tears.

Sadly, this was not the only time that he had hit her, and it wouldn't be the last. It would, however, not stop the brave woman from continuing to battle her husband, whenever she thought he was being inappropriate; she had been assaulted when she was a child, and she vowed to protect as many children as she needed to, and she would suffer whatever consequences were thrown at her.

With his wife out of the room, Mr. Whitmore sat down next to Sadie and tried to pick up where he had left off. He

The Elusive Mr. Velucci

leaned towards her and tried to look down her blouse, even though her breasts were still blooming. He placed his hand on her thigh when he pretended to chuckle, hoping to slide it higher up her leg.

All of this made Sadie feel quite uncomfortable, and when she gathered enough courage, she forced her body to react. With a surprising amount of power, she removed Mr. Whitmore's hand and stood up. "I have to go", she stated loudly, and made her way to the front door.

Mrs. Whitmore, who could see everything from behind the corner of the wall, was proud of the young girl for knowing when to run away.

Sadie ran to her house as quickly as she could, and told her parents the majority of what went on in the neighbor's home. Her mother held her tightly while her father suggested that she not go back again, but Sadie was headstrong and disagreed with his advice.

The next morning, on her way to school, Sadie saw Mrs. Whitmore and her two little girls looking out of the front window. They were smiling and waving while saying HI, and Sadie came to the conclusion that the situation might not be as bad as she had thought. And when they asked for her services again, Sadie agreed, with only a moment's hesitation.

Sadie was young, but she knew the fundamentals of sex. She certainly didn't want to have it at thirteen, but being a stubborn teenager, she was positive that she could fight off anyone, if she needed to.

Mr. Whitmore's advances had become more frequent and more aggressive in the last two months, but nothing was ever done inside of his own home. They did, however, happen on the short walk to Sadie's house.

Sadie was starting to become intimated, and asked her father if he could walk her home. She was delighted when he said yes. Sadly, Mr. Whitmore protested against her phoning her parents at the end of her shift. When she asked why, he came up with a number of wild and unbelievable excuses; "It was too late to call", "The phone wasn't working", "It would be faster to just walk there", etc...

Sadie was surprised by his constant arguments, and asked Mrs. Whitmore if she could walk her home. Not surprisingly, Mr. Whitmore always said no, insisting sharply that it was his job.

Sadie was soon at the point where she had to choose between her safety and looking after the kids. Because she was half-certain that her neighbor was all talk and no action, she agreed to babysit again and again.

Then came that very last night – the one which changed all of their lives... forever.

It was around midnight and Mr. Whitmore had come home very drunk. He was more aggressive than usual, and insisted on walking Sadie home.

Mrs. Whitmore had had enough of her husband's attitude for the night, and her only concern was to check on her two children. She looked frazzled as she rushed up the stairs, but made sure to say good-night to Sadie. Because she felt her husband needed to get some cold air slapped against his warm skin, she didn't stop him from stepping outside and breathing it into his inebriated lungs. As the front door opened, she silently wished that the walk would be quick, and that Sadie would get home safe and sound.

Sadie could sense the scary situation before her, and she vowed to run fast so that she could to get home unscathed.

"Hey!" he called, which was enough to slow her down.

Sadie pulled her shoulders in, crossed her arms across her chest, tucked her fingers into her elbows, and tried to keep a bit of distance between the two of them as they walked.

"What's the matter with you tonight?" he asked, in words that slurred and smelled of stale beer.

"Nothing", she replied. "It's just a little cool outside and I want to get home." She lowered her head while she spoke, and hoped that he would walk quicker.

Mr. Whitmore hated that she was rushing ahead of him, so he extended his arm and grabbed the back of her clothing. "Walk with me, damn it!" he ordered loudly. He had forced his words out through clenched teeth, and then stumbled for a quick second because he had stretched out further than his normal reach had allowed.

Sadie was more than surprised by how strong his grip was, and it made her stop in her tracks with fear of what he would do next.

"Caught ya!" he gloated. His smile was lopsided, his eyes could not focus in the dark, and he was getting turned on by the thrill of finally having his victim in his clutches.

Sadie's eyes were cast ahead, while her brain quickly calculated how many more steps it would take for her to get to her front door.

"Now, come here", he demanded. He placed his hands on her shoulders and shifted their bodies until she was facing him.

"What for?" she asked, while panic rushed through every one of her veins.

As his body got closer to hers, his mind began to conjure up an experience that was totally unsuitable for a young teenager to be part of.

He looked hideous and smelled of alcohol and cigarettes, and she hated that he wanted her to stand so close to him. She kept a firm hand on his chest in order to keep a little distance between them, but his arms were around her, pushing her chest towards his.

"I want to kiss you", he stated matter-of-factly. A second later, he was puckering his lips like a cartoon character, so that they stretched out further than the edge of his face. He even made awkward kissy noises towards her, in an attempt to get her to kiss him back.

Sadie's mind was exploding with a million thoughts of how to get away. And before she could act out even one single plan, Mr. Whitmore forced their lips together. The kiss was repulsive, very wet and sloppy, and the whole experience brought fear and disgust to the very core of her soul. "Stop it!" she insisted loudly, once their lips had parted. She squirmed as if her life depended on it, and hated that he was so strong. "I have to get home!" she screamed.

"Not yet", he insisted. He was now focused and angry, but he felt like he wouldn't be able to hold her still for much longer. He hadn't counted on her struggling so hard, so he used his right leg to sweep her legs out from under her, and then they were both on the ground.

Sadie's head hit the grass a little too hard, and the pain from the fall and the fact that he was on top of her - pawing at her and trying to rip her clothes off - caused her to cry. Adrenaline kept her aware of her surroundings, and enabled her to want to fight back. She used her hands to pull his hair out, and punched him in the throat as hard as she could. She used her legs to push him off of her, and also slammed her heels into his back and hip area. She even used her last bit of strength to poke him in the eyes with her thumbs. She was losing the battle and she knew it, but she was adamant and did not want to give up.

"Stop wrestling me, kid!" he ordered harshly. He was unsympathetic about how she was feeling, and totally determined to get what he was after.

Sadie found her voice and screamed for help, but he quickly covered her mouth and nose with his hand. She was not able to breathe now. She thrashed her head from side-to-side to get free of him, while her muffled screams were barely heard. The only sounds that anyone could hear were perceived as grunts, slaps, inaudible cries for help, and a lot of rustling around.

An elderly woman from across the two-lane road, was letting her feisty dog outside for a quick pee. The two-year old schnauzer had been barking non-stop for the past ten minutes, and was obviously aware that something was going on. The second the door opened, he raced across the street with an abundant amount of energy. He rushed straight towards the couple on the ground, and made himself quite known.

'Bark, Bark, Bark!' His rear-end was high in the air and his tail was as stiff as a broom handle. 'Bark, Bark, Bark!' He was filled with curiosity as to what they were doing.

"Shit!" the older man shouted aggressively. "Go away!" He was quite angry at the dog for possibly attracting unwanted interested in what was going on. For a brief second, he removed his center of attention off of Sadie and onto the bothersome pooch. "Shut up!" he screamed with all his might. In his drunken stupor, he hadn't noticed that his hand had been moved from Sadie's mouth.

Sadie was now free to scream, and she did so with all the force she had in her young body. "He-e-e-e-e-lp!"

Oddly enough, it took a minute before Mr. Whitmore figured out where the sound was coming from; he had alcohol trickling through his veins, a young girl pleading for her life underneath him, and a dog barking in his face. He was confused and drunk, and felt as if he was having an out of body experience.

"Who's out there?" the Schnauzer's owner called. The old woman placed an unsteady hand upon her forehead, as if to block out the bright light of the nearest street lamp. Because no-one called back, she assumed that it was a few stray dogs playing, and didn't give it another thought.

Once Mr. Whitmore heard the neighbor's question, he was suddenly more aware of his surroundings. He looked down and into Sadie's tear-stained face, and he immediately presented her with dozens of apologies. "I'm so sorry", he declared with complete sincerity.

"Let me up!" Sadie cried loudly, as she fought to get out from under his overweight body.

"I'm sorry!" he professed, as he tried to roll off to the side. He was still swimming in the haze of his liquor binge, and wasn't entirely sure of what had happened.

She was caught under one of his legs and using both hands to get free. "Get off of me!" she cried.

Mr. Whitmore kept apologizing and hoped that by being nice, that she would forgive him. He felt ashamed as he watched his babysitter stand up and run away, but he could not stand up quick enough to comfort her. Instead, he lay there, his face now pressed into the slightly-damp grass, and he cursed himself for being so stupid.

Sadie ran as fast as she could, and was sobbing wildly by the time she reached her front door.

The Elusive Mr. Velucci

The old man with the white wispy hair, struck his tight fist into the ground a few more times, before a horrible thought occurred to him. 'What if, when Sadie's father finds out what I have done, he runs down the street to kill me?' The very idea of a gruesome death by an angry father was not one that he liked, so Mr. Whitmore shifted his body into an upright position and marched himself home.

Sadie's parents had been waiting in their bed, and breathed a sigh of relief when they heard her come in.

Sadie ran straight to her bedroom and flung herself onto her bed. She pushed her face into her pillow, and hid her tears and child-like bawling as best she could.

"Night, baby girl!" they called. They turned out their light and were now able to go to sleep.

After entering his home, Mr. Whitmore bolted his front door, and then walked around the house to make sure that every port of entry was tightly shut and locked. Only then did he make his way up the stairs to his bedroom.

Sadie's parents had not heard Sadie cries of shock and disbelief, nor had they seen her saddened face. They were just satisfied that their daughter was home, safe and sound.

Sadie, on the other hand, was not content; she kept playing those same horrifying minutes, over-and-over again in her mind. And no matter how hard she tried, she couldn't quiet the sounds or the terror of what had happened. 'How could he do that to me?' she questioned, while trying to search for a plausible answer.

After climbing into bed, Mr. Whitmore lay on his back with the blankets pulled up to his chin. It was not usual for the house to be settling when the weather got colder, but tonight, every creak made his ears perk up and his eyes widen.

Tina Griffith

Outside, the night air began to blow with a cool and gentle simplicity. Mr. Whitmore tried to relax his overwrought muscles, by concentrating on the whistling and humming sounds which the wind was making, while it danced through the crispy leaves of the willow tree out back. This had worked for a few minutes, and then a tree branch had knocked loudly against the master bedroom window, and it made his heart race a little too wildly.

The older man's eyes were wider than before, and his breathing had now become labored. He was fully awake and extremely anxious, and more than petrified of being murdered in his sleep.

Mrs. Whitmore snored loudly, which brought her to a semi-conscious state. She rolled over onto her left side, and accidently slammed her forearm across her husband's throat.

That was the very moment when Mr. Whitmore died from sheer fright.

Meanwhile, Sadie was still struggling with what had happened in the dark, a block away from her home. She had now become terrified of being outside at night, and vowed to never babysit anywhere, ever again.

She felt somewhat better and stronger after making that decision, and pulled herself into a sitting position. She dried her tears with the palms of her hands, turned her pillow over, and got herself ready for bed.

Sadie went to the bathroom and cleaned the blood of her skin, and yelped quietly from the pain between her legs. She tucked her dress and panties into the laundry hamper, and tried to hide them under whatever else was in there.

She was becoming angry and ashamed at what had happened, and wondered if she had done something to cause

The Elusive Mr. Velucci

it. As she changed into her pajamas and got into bed, her jaw had tensed up and exposed her deep frustrations. She closed her eyes and doubted that sleep would come, but it did, and almost immediately.

Morning came quickly, but there was a strange vibe in the air. As she got out of bed, Sadie realized that she had been able to sleep fairly well, despite what had happened a few hours before. Her new strength brought a shy smile to her face, and she hoped that her problems were now behind her.

That same afternoon, after she had come home from school, her mother informed her that Mr. Whitmore had died in his sleep.

"He did?" she stated, and her eyes opened wide with shock. She wanted to say more, but her first thought was that she had done something to cause his death.

"He did", her mother confirmed. "The funeral will be announced sometime in the next few days." And as if she was changing the subject on purpose, she asked, "Do you have any homework?"

Sadie nodded, while a blank stare masked the look of surprise on her face.

Up until that very moment, Sadie had planned on telling her parents what Mr. Whitmore had done, but not until they were finished eating their supper. Because of the news that he had died, she was now reluctant to speak about those few moments to anyone. 'What if he had died because of me?' raced through her mind. 'If she had been with him only hours before his death, there would be thousands of questions fired at her, from people who were urging her to tell them all that she knew.'

Supper had been served and she was called to the table.

Sadie's heart was pounding and her chest was now

tightening, as she forced the food to go into her mouth and down her throat. She wasn't even sure what she was eating, but she didn't know what else to do but sit there with her parents safely around her.

"Are we done?" her mother asked politely. She stood up to grab the plates and bring them into the kitchen.

"Good meal, mother", Sadie's father stated happily.

Sadie pushed the last forkful of food into her mouth and then stood up. "Can I be excused?" She shifted her focus between her mom and dad, as she waited for one of them to give their permission.

"Are you ok, honey?" her mother asked. "You don't look well." She came forward to feel her daughter's forehead, but Sadie's father interrupted.

"She's fine, mother. Stop fussing." He wiped his mouth with the back of his hand and pushed himself away from the table. "I'm going to watch TV."

"You're probably right", she replied softly. Sadie's mother felt embarrassed by her husband's order, so she lowered her eyes and continued to bring the dirty dishes into the kitchen.

Sadie was sorry for what had just happened, but instead of going to comfort her mother, she rushed to her bedroom and shut the door.

Sadie hated that she couldn't tell her parents what Mr. Whitmore had done, and then wondered if she would ever be able to tell anyone.

Sadie stayed in her room for the rest of the night, and then went to school the next day. The pain in her body had subsided a bit, and there was no longer any spots of blood between her legs. She knew that she would never be the same again, but would act as if nothing had ever happened.

The Elusive Mr. Velucci

Sadie kept to herself from that night on, and was often reminded to be aware of anyone who could ever try to hurt her.

Mrs. Whitmore moved away from the neighborhood, a month after her husband's funeral. Sadie liked Mrs. Whitmore and the two kids, but she hated that they reminded her of the reason that she would be emotionally scarred for the rest of her life.

It took a few weeks, but Sadie's frame of mind eventually recovered to a slightly, less-than-perfect, mirror image of who she used to be. She very happily let school work dominate the next few years of her life, while music and television took her soul to somewhere more psychologically manageable.

She didn't date when the other girls did, and if she went out, it was always with other people around her. Her danger radar was always up, and constantly cautioning her that 'things like that' could happen at any time. It was a hard way to live and very exhausting to always be on the lookout for trouble, but it was necessary to do, in order for her to survive.

Sadie's parents died in a horrific car accident, while coming home drunk on New Year's Eve – she was barely nineteen years old. Instead of having to navigate in that large and empty house all alone, Sadie and Nicole, her best friend since Grade 5, moved into a 2-bedroom apartment. It wasn't too long after that when Nicole met Hunter – a.k.a. her 'soul-mate'. After a few months of dating, they decided to move in together, and started a family a year later.

Sadie stayed in the apartment, and took on a few part-time jobs in order to pay the bills. When it wasn't enough, she downsized to a smaller place. She was twenty-one years old now, and still lived with a sense of emotional and physical danger all around her. Little did she know then, that all the cautious feelings would fly out the window, once she met Enrico Velucci.

As they got to know each other, her soul had coupled with his, and she eventually welcomed him into her heart. Before their time together was over, Sadie had learned how to experience life as if she had never been broken. She had fallen in love with him and never wanted the glorious feeling to end. But, as quickly as Enrico had come into her life, he had disappeared. In his place, he had unknowingly left a precious gift – a daughter, who looked exactly like him. This exquisite souvenir was the only connection she had, from the man who she loved with all her heart and soul.

Because of the many unforeseen obstacles which had jumped in the way of them reconnecting, they had been apart for many years. During that time, both Enrico and Sadie's lives had gotten quite demanding and chaotic, but they never lost hope of seeing each other again.

It was almost six years ago since he left New York, when Enrico received an invitation to go to America. Because of the destination, his mind automatically drifted to Sadie. It didn't take long before he decided to pay her a visit; seeing her was something that had weighed heavily on his mind for the past few years. He now hoped that she still lived in the same place.

Thirteen days later, and an hour after his plane had landed, Enrico was at Sadie's apartment. He knocked, but unfortunately, she wasn't home. He couldn't leave a note because he didn't have a pen or any paper with him, so he opted to come back the next day.

The Elusive Mr. Velucci

It was a Wednesday afternoon and Sadie had gone to pick Sophie up from Kindergarten. They drove to an indoor play area, where they waited until five of Sophie's friends from school could join them. For the next hour, the kids scaled walls and raced around, while the parents sat and watched. Cake was served, presents were opened, and then the kids spent another hour having fun. When the party was over, it was mother/daughter time at a local theatre.

That same afternoon, Enrico met with the musicians and directors of the New York Philharmonic Orchestra, at the Lincoln Centre. He couldn't begin to describe the honor that he felt, to be standing in the illustrious building, and conducting one of the oldest musical institutions in the United States; it had been a dream of his since he was seventeen years old.

Enrico looked around and his mind suddenly became inundated with very interesting information, about the many festivals which had been held there in the past, the glorious history of the orchestra, and of the landmark which stood close to the Juilliard School and the Metropolitan Opera House. He couldn't help but envision all of the famous people who had travelled across the world just to listen to what was being played there. And then he scanned all the chairs which were crowding around him, and noted that the heavenly music had been heard by all walks of life.

Enrico developed goose bumps all over his body, but there was no more time to dwell; the group needed to practice all of the pieces which they would be playing on Friday and Saturday night. Enrico took his coat off and he rolled up his sleeves, and after everyone was sitting down, he guided his musicians with a baton and a vast number of familiar hand gestures.

Sophie had had a very long and wonderful day, and was already quite sleepy by the time they got home. As she was being tucked into bed, the little girl watched her mother yawn. "You look tired, mommy."

"I am tired", Sadie chuckled lightly. "But I had a lot of fun today."

"Me, too", Sophie giggled.

"And tomorrow after school, it will be just the two of us celebrating your birthday." She touched her daughter's nose with her index finger and wiggled the round tip from side-to-side.

Sophie stuck both of her thumbs into the air and repeated, "Just me and you!" She loved having birthday parties with her friends, but she also loved having the yearly, quiet celebration with her mom.

Sadie kissed Sophie's cheeks and then walked towards the bedroom door. "Night, sweetheart", she said quietly, as she took one last look at her beautiful little girl.

"Night, mommy", Sophie called, and then she rolled over and closed her eyes.

Minutes later, Sadie was putting herself to bed.

Little did she know that Enrico was in a hotel, not too far from where she lived. He had just come back from the bathroom, and was lifting the covers of the blanket so that he could climb into bed.

Both adults were exhausted, but very happy about how their day had gone. Now they were laying there, in the dark, staring up at the ceiling, and they wondered what the other person was doing.

The Elusive Mr. Velucci

Sadie wished that Enrico knew about Sophie, and the fact that tomorrow she would be turning five years old. She wasn't sure that he even wanted to be a dad, but she had no doubt that he would love his little girl.

Enrico was a little sad that Sadie wasn't at home when he was there, but he vowed to keep trying. And he hoped that if and when he did get hold of Sadie, that he could persuade her to come to the Lincoln Centre to watch him perform.

They were both smiling as they closed their eyes for the night, and then they drifted off to sleep.

Thursday was the last day for rehearsals, which meant that Enrico had a full day ahead of him. Even so, he made sure to be at Sadie's home at 9am, and then again at 5pm. He knocked and then listened at the door to see if anyone was home, and was disappointed when she didn't answer.

Sadie had rushed around all morning, and up to the moment when Sophie was finished with her afternoon class at school. Together they did a bit of grocery shopping, ate a take-out supper at 5:30, and gobbled down cake and ice cream while watching a cartoon movie at home. At bedtime, Sophie professed that it was the best birthday she ever had. Little did she know that her mother had another surprise up her sleeve.

Enrico was still getting used to the time difference, and was exhausted by the time he was able to get into his bed. When the room went dark, his eyes suddenly lit up, because the bright moon was now shining in from the window and onto his face. He wished that Sadie was there to enjoy it with him, but because he still had time, he hoped that he could share it with her before he went back home.

Friday was even more hectic for Enrico, for that night was

going to be his first performance in America. Nonetheless, he found the time to make his way to her apartment. He knocked on her door in the morning and then again in the afternoon, and while he felt miserable that she wasn't there, he was hopeful because he still had tomorrow.

Because Sophie had the day off from Kindergarten on Friday, Sadie wanted to make the most of it and took her daughter on a week-end trip to Bronx, New York. They checked into their hotel room around 11, and played in the pool within minutes after they arrived. After enjoying the afternoon and eating a late supper, they climbed into bed and watched TV until they fell asleep.

Meanwhile, Enrico turned in an amazing performance, and didn't get to bed until closer to midnight.

After breakfast on Saturday morning, mother and daughter made their way to the Bronx Zoo.

Enrico arrived at Sadie's apartment before noon, and once again, he knocked on her door and got no response. Hoping that she would return shortly, he bought a coffee and something to eat from a nearby street vendor. He then sat down on one of the eight steps which led up to the front door of her building, and waited.

After lunch, Sadie and her daughter took the subway to the Staten Island Ferry terminal.

It had been three hours since he arrived at Sadie's building, but now Enrico needed to get himself ready for that night's concert. He went up to her apartment and knocked on her door one more time, just in case she had come in the back way. She didn't answer, but this time he was disappointed but not surprised. He left her building with his head down and made his way back to his hotel.

The Elusive Mr. Velucci

Enrico actually cried while he was having a shower, and it wasn't because the water was scalding his skin. Despair was twisting and turning inside of his body, and with a defeated heart, he raised his tormented expression towards the shower head, in hopes that the many drops would eventually wash his tears of emotional pain away.

By suppertime, Sadie and Sophie were exhausted. They enjoyed a light meal on their tiny balcony, and fell into bed soon after.

The curtain came down on another spectacular performance, and Enrico lowered his head in a deep bow. He did so with gratitude for the clapping and cheering, but also to hide his sorrow that Sadie was not sitting in the audience.

Hours later, as he entered his hotel room for the last time, his heart ached from the loss of his efforts in reuniting with Sadie. He had tossed and turned that night in bed, but he always ended up on his right side in the fetal position. When sleep did come, the dreams had him chasing something that was inches away from his reach.

He was a shattered mess when he woke up the next morning, and all he could think of was getting hold of Sadie.

On Sunday morning, two hours before he needed to board the plane back to Italy, Enrico was standing in front of Sadie's door. He knocked and was devastated that she didn't answer, but today he had been prepared; Enrico had written Sadie a long letter, making sure to add his phone number and address on the bottom. He apologized to her for the length of time that it took for him to write, and professed that he still loved her and thought about her every single day.

Tina Griffith

Enrico kissed the sealed white envelope, and then placed it in the cluster of mailboxes in the front entrance of her apartment building. He tapped the slot twice for good luck, and then walked to his rental car.

Unbeknownst to Enrico, while he was driving towards the airport, Sadie was coming from the other direction. She had arrived at her home five minutes after he had left, but she would never know that he had even been there; Enrico had unknowingly dropped the envelope into the wrong mail slot.

Enrico was filled with unbelievable anticipation as he flew back to Italy, for two reasons; he had received a standing ovation for his performance on Friday night, and then again on Saturday night. And he had been praised backstage by both his peers, and by several members of the orchestra for his outstanding good work.

Enrico was also terribly nervous about leaving a letter for Sadie, and hoped that she would jump for joy when she read it.

Enrico leaned his head backwards against the headrest, and envisioned every detail of how his reunion with Sadie was going to play out. He was very sure that she would be ecstatic to hear from him, and trusted that they would get to talk and/or see each other, sometime in the near future.

Many hours later, after he had arrived in the safety of his home, Enrico began the anxious task of waiting for Sadie's reply. He checked his mailbox twice a day, but when weeks went by and Sadie still hadn't responded, he understood it to mean that she was no longer interested in having a relationship with him.

This hit Enrico very hard, and he ended up in bed for

The Elusive Mr. Velucci

a week. When he felt better, he carried on with his life as best he could, for he realized that he had at least tried to reach out to her.

Two years later, Enrico landed on American soil again. This time he had been asked to conduct The New York Pop Orchestra for an award's benefit – a very significant honor for him.

Going to New York made him think about Sadie. He had never given up hope of ever seeing her again, and had thought about her every single day for the past two years. After renting a car at the airport, he drove straight to her home.

Sadie was busy volunteering at her daughter's school, so she wasn't there when Enrico thumped his knuckles loudly against the hard surface of her door.

He was terribly disappointed when she didn't answer, but because he only had two hours to get checked into his hotel and arrive at the venue before rehearsals began, Enrico decided to go back to her apartment the next day. For now, he had no choice but to walk away.

Rehearsals went very well, and that night he ended up in bed, totally exhausted. The next morning he had breakfast and then raced to Sadie's home. She was out buying groceries with Sophie, so she wasn't there to answer her door.

The night of the award's benefit show went better than anyone could have predicted; every note was hit with perfection, and every speaker had read their lines without a flaw.

After lingering around backstage to take pictures and say HI to all those people who he knew and didn't know, Enrico made a beeline to Sadie's home. He was catching a midnight flight back to Italy and had less than three hours before he needed to board the plane. Because this was his last chance, he didn't want to miss it.

He knocked lightly, and then leaned his ear against the door in order to hear if anyone was there.

Sadie had been mindlessly flipping through a magazine and fell asleep with the TV playing softly in the background, so she didn't hear anyone tapping at her door.

Enrico felt dejected, but because of the time, it occurred to him that Sadie might have been sleeping. He reached into his pocket as he walked down the stairs, and pulled an envelope out. He had attached his business card to a 2-paged, warm and sincere letter, and placed it into what he thought was her mailbox.

This letter was basically the same as the last one, but with more apologies and more of an explanation of why he didn't contact her until two years ago. He hoped that it sounded mushy and romantic, as well as terribly unhappy that they were apart; he really wanted her to call him this time.

As he drove away from Sadie's building, Enrico couldn't help but wonder if he was wasting his time by chasing after her. In the next second he scolded himself for having those thoughts, and concentrated on having a positive outlook on the situation.

But when the weeks went by and there was still no word from Sadie, it gave him further proof that she just didn't want to have anything to do with him. This sent him into an eating frenzy, where he consumed everything in sight and stayed indoors as much as possible.

Soon the cupboards were bare and he had no other choice but to venture out to the markets. He hated that he

The Elusive Mr. Velucci

had to shower and get dressed, but he felt better by being outside and around people again. When he got back home, he answered a call from a friend of his, who asked him if he'd like to go back to work. Enrico thought about it for a minute, and then agreed. In the next few weeks, he went on to conduct the Sarajevo Philharmonic Orchestra in Bosnia, the Dubrovnik Symphony Orchestra in Croatia, and the National Symphony Orchestra in Estonia. Granted, these were smaller venues than what he was used to, but it was what brought him out of his bout of melancholy.

Three years after his last trip to New York, Enrico was told that he would be receiving a Grammy for Best Orchestra Performance. The invitation said that he needed to be in New York on the 5th of September, which was two weeks away, and Enrico shouted for joy.

As much as he wanted to kid himself, he was still very much in love with Sadie. He also knew that he would wait for as long as it took and would go as far as he needed to, just for the pleasure of seeing her again.

Enrico arrived a day earlier than he had to, and the first thing he did after getting off the plane, was to go to Sadie's home.

He was filled with uncertainty as he knocked on her door, but he didn't back down. This time when she didn't answer, he went to the neighbor's apartment across the hall.

Mrs. Lilly Thomas looked through her peep hole, and was surprised to find a well-dressed man standing in her hallway. "Hello?" she called sharply. "Who's there?"

She was 83-years old and stood all of 4'11", and because she didn't recognize him, she kept her door bolted. After the stranger explained that he was looking for Sadie Adams,

Tina Griffith

Mrs. Thomas relented. She kept the chain on, but now had an opening to speak through.

"She lives across the hall." She pointed her crooked index finger in the direction that he needed to go. "Why are you bothering me?"

Enrico hung his head with disappointment. "I've knocked on that door several times, but she's never home", he confessed sadly. "Perhaps you can tell her that I've stopped by?"

Mrs. Thomas suddenly felt sorry for the young man; she could tell that he was unhappy, so she nodded and agreed. "Yes, I can do that for you." Her voice was frail, and she seemed enthusiastic to help.

Enrico wanted to jump out of his skin for joy. "Thank you so much." He shoved a business card into her hand, and kindly asked her to give it to Sadie. "I really appreciate this", he said firmly, and thanked her again for helping him.

After saying good-bye, Enrico skipped down the stairs. Before reaching the front door, he stuck his business card into what he thought was Sadie's mailbox. As he drove to the hotel, his heart was soaring with hope that Sadie would call and that they would meet up. Hours later, when that didn't happen, he wondered what had gone wrong.

The next day, Enrico went to the apartment building where Sadie and Mrs. Thomas lived. He knocked on Sadie's door and she didn't answer. He jiggled the door knob and found that it was locked, and after shamefully listening at the door, he got down on his knees to see if there were any lights on. Surprisingly, there was no space at the bottom of her door to stick a straw through.

His eyebrows pulled into a disappointed frown, as Enrico

The Elusive Mr. Velucci

stood up and made his way across the hall. He knocked on Mrs. Thomas's door, but she appeared not to know him.

"I was here yesterday", he stated with total confidence. "I gave you my business card and asked you to give it to your neighbor." He tried to remain calm as he pointed towards Sadie's door, but his frustration was getting the better of him. "Do you remember that?" he asked, as he took a step closer to her entrance. His eyes were quite wide and his voice was a little too loud.

The little, old, wrinkled woman stared at him with a shocked expression. She was frightened by how anxious he was, and silenced by the dark and angry look on his face.

Enrico obviously didn't realize how he must look or sound to an elderly lady who lived alone. "Look…", he said, after quieting his tone.

Mrs. Thomas had moderate dementia, so she had good days and bad ones. Today her brain was not functioning well at all, and she couldn't even recall what she had for breakfast. There was no way that she would remember him or his request from yesterday.

"No!" she screamed, as she cowered behind her door. "Go away! I don't know you!" She was adamant and scared, and used the door as a shield to protect herself from the man who might harm her.

Because he felt like he was losing out on his last and only chance to get hold of Sadie, Enrico got down on his knees. "Please!" he begged at full volume. His hands were in front of his face and shaking, and all of his fingers were intertwined. His eyes were glistening with tears that hadn't fallen yet, but they were very close to being released. "Please!" he cried.

Mrs. Thomas had watched the last two minutes with

Tina Griffith

horror written all over her face, and because she was now completely terrified, she slammed the door closed.

"No!" he screamed in desperation, and placed his right hand flat against the wooden barrier. Enrico could now hear and feel all the locks clicking together on the inside of her home.

"Go away!" she demanded in a shrill voice. "Or I will call the police!" Mrs. Thomas began to cry, and walked quickly towards the safety of her bedroom.

Enrico's eyebrows shot up with great surprise, and he became stunned beyond all reason. All of his hopes had now vanished, and he hated that he was back to square one.

After taking a second to analyze the situation, Enrico stood up and dusted the clothing by his knees. He felt terribly lost and didn't know what to do, and now contemplated the fact that maybe he just wasn't meant to be with Sadie.

And suddenly, as if a lightning bolt had tickled the top of his head, his mind snapped to attention; with all that had happened with Mrs. Thomas, Enrico almost forgot that he was being given an award that night. He looked at his watch and quickly calculated how much time he had to get ready. He muttered something inaudible under his breath, and then began to move his feet.

As Enrico raced down the stairs, he was certain that if he didn't have to board the plane an hour after the presentation, he would be back at Sadie's door that evening.

In the meantime, Sadie was dining out and having quite the talk with her 10-year old child. She had always told Sophie that her father had been killed overseas, and it had released her from extending the conversation… until today. At school that very morning, they had learned about war

The Elusive Mr. Velucci

and other places where soldiers were being dispatched to keep the peace. Because of that topic, Sophie had been bombarded with questions about where her father had been stationed, and how he had died.

"Gosh, I'm so sorry", Sadie whispered, as she held her daughter tightly against her own body. "What can I do to make things better?"

"You've told me about him, but do you have any pictures of him?" Sophie asked, with the wide-eyed innocence of a sweet child.

Sadie had one, but it was tiny, and it had been placed in the silver locket which Enrico had given her. She hadn't shown it to anyone, because she didn't want it to get damaged or lost. Her fingers unconsciously reached up and caressed the jeweled trinket, as her thoughts drifted back to the day when Enrico left to go back to Italy.

"Mommy?" Her soft voice broke the dreamlike trance which Sadie was in.

Sadie blushed and exhaled before she said no. "All of our pictures were destroyed in a fire." It was a lie and she knew it, but she thought it might buy her a little more time before this discussion came up again.

"Oh." Sophie lowered her chin to her chest and looked like she was about to cry.

Sadie could see that she needed to take the focus off of the topic at hand, so she came up with an idea. "How about we check out that brand new ice cream parlor? I know you want to." Sadie had purposely put a bit of bounce in her voice, in hopes that her daughter would accept the offer.

Sophie looked up and smiled as if that had been her plan all along. "Ok!"

Tina Griffith

Sadie smiled too, for she was glad that she had been able to sidestep that problem. She knew that Sophie watched other children with their fathers, and it made her sad that Enrico was not in their life. Regardless, Sadie had always been both mother and father to Sophie, and would continue to do whatever was needed in order to keep her daughter safe and happy.

Sadie made a silly face and mocked her daughter. "Ok", she said in a weird voice. It was enough to make Sophie laugh, and that's all that counted.

In the same moment as Sadie was driving to the ice cream place, Enrico was on stage, accepting his award. Three hours later, he was flying back to Italy while she was putting their daughter to bed.

Enrico's head was leaning against the padded headrest, while he stared at the clouds through the small, round window. Because the gorgeous Italian man had been left terribly heartbroken by this last visit to America, he decided not to accept any more offers to go back; Enrico firmly believed that Sadie was no longer interested in him, or she would have tried to get hold of him long before now.

A stewardess asked him if wanted to have a drink, and he said yes. "I'll have a large glass of red wine, please."

The stewardess could see that he was depressed about something, and filled the see-through, plastic cup all the way to the rim. "Here you go, and call me when you want some more." She spoke in a soft and sensual voice, added a wink and a wicked smile to the offer, and hoped that he would ask her to come back.

Enrico reached for the glass and did nothing more than nod in her direction. He fell asleep after he finished the

The Elusive Mr. Velucci

second glass of wine, and by the time the plane had landed in Italy, he resigned himself to the fact that Sadie would not be part of his future.

Enrico was not one to give up, but he had no more tears to cry and felt that all he could do now was surrender an awkward smile. It was unsettling to think how ridiculous he had been to chase after her for so long, but he knew it was because he truly loved her.

Two years had rushed by since Enrico had been in New York, and while Sophie was turning twelve, Sadie had received another promotion. She still hadn't replied to any of Enrico's letters, which left a huge hole in his heart. He continued to think about her at least once every hour, but he was getting tired of waiting for something that might not ever happen. Because of this, he was now going to place most of his focus on having a life without, Sadie Adams.

In those quiet moments, when he wasn't travelling or conducting an orchestra, Enrico enjoyed being in the home which he had once shared with his parents. There were mornings where he loved life and couldn't wait to get out of bed, and then there were the times when he felt gloomy and quite bored, and he wondered if he'd ever find happiness again.

And then one day, without warning, a miracle happened which changed his life forever.

Maria Angelina Fuentes, the only child of a Spanish Math teacher and an Italian nurse, had gone through eight years of school with Enrico Velucci. Even though they had been ultimate best friends when they were little, they sometimes acted like they were mortal enemies during their teen years. They were each other's sounding board and even gave advice on clothing and potential dates, but they were never more than friends.

Mario became engaged to a boy named Luciano, on May 24, the day that they graduated from High School. Enrico had attended the wedding on August 29, three months later, but lost touch with Maria before she found out that she was pregnant. Angelo Romeo Moretti was born the following October, weighing 7 lbs and 2 ozs. He was the spitting image of his father, which had Luciano busting with pride.

Maria's marriage was wonderful in every way possible, and she honestly believed that it would last forever. Sadly, her husband died in a horrific motorcycle accident a few years later, and it left her completely devastated.

The families of Maria and Antonio rushed to the young widow's side, in order to give her as much love and comfort as she needed. Maria's mom, Sylvia Fuentes, and Luciano's mom, Anna Moretti, lived full-time with Maria and Angelo, for four and a half months following Luciano's funeral.

The Elusive Mr. Velucci

After that, the moms moved out and only crowded Maria's home during the daytime hours. They divided the cooking and cleaning, and other day-to-day chores, while dozens of relatives came and went at all hours of the day.

Maria loved the attention, but after a year of being babysat, she asked them all to leave her alone. It was a tough decision because she knew that their hearts were in the right place, but Luciano was gone and she had to get on with her life.

Being alone was quite hard, and the financial part was even harder. Maria lived off their savings, and any money that came in from the insurance company, or family and friends. When she noticed that the money was running out, Maria decided to go to work. She had no experience of any kind, but soon found employment in a bakery, not far from their modest home.

It was there where Maria became reunited with Enrico.

He was out walking, enjoying a day off, when he smelled the warm and sweet fragrance of the freshly baked goodies. He pulled the decorated glass door open and stepped inside, and was instantly greeted by a friendly clerk.

"What can I get you?" Maria asked, in a voice that was as lovely and down-to-earth as she was. As the handsome man got closer, her eyes widened and she felt her breath hitch in her throat; there was something very familiar about him. The more she studied his face, the more she questioned who he might be.

Enrico felt her staring, but he pretended not to notice.

"Oh my goodness!" she gasped quietly, when it hit her. Her entire face lit up, for she now knew who he was. She had seen him on magazine covers and talk shows on TV, and while she had foolishly turned into a swooning fan in the last few seconds, she forced herself not to act so silly.

A blurred light of desire and familiarity passed through him when he glanced in Maria's direction, but Enrico tried to keep his feelings hidden. He looked up at the menu board while he contemplated what to buy, but he couldn't help sneaking a peek or two at the stunningly beautiful woman who was serving him.

'Could I ask him for an autograph?' she wondered. 'No!' her mind shouted. 'He's a celebrity and therefore deserves his privacy.' Maria tried to remain calm as she waited for him to place his order.

Enrico found something to buy, and took a few steps towards the counter. "I'd like two bagels and a loaf of bread, please." And it was when he was handing her the money that he recognized her face. He checked her name tag and then read it out loud. "Maria?"

The sudden impact of him saying her name, brought all of their memories to the forefront of her brain. "Enrico?" she asked, even though it wasn't a question. He was no longer the famous orchestra conductor, but the child who she had gone to school with.

"It's me!" they blurted out in the same breath. Within seconds, it felt like time had stood still, while their childhood connection pulled their souls together.

Lots of tears, a warm hug, and a short break from work to get reacquainted, was followed by supper at her house, with her son. They talked about everything that had happened since high school had ended, and before the night was over, the three of them had become friends.

Weeks went by, and when it became known that Angelo

The Elusive Mr. Velucci

was by himself for two hours before Maria came home from work, Enrico offered to look after him.

"I have to go out of town because of my occupation, but on my days off, I'd love to help you out."

Maria jumped at the offer, as did Angelo.

From that day on, Enrico picked Angelo up from school, and he soon found that he liked having someone little to take care of.

Angelo loved spending time with his mother's friend, and he began to look forward to the 3:00 bell, more than before. The boy no longer had a father and Enrico no longer had parents, therefore, their friendship seemed like a perfect match.

Angelo and his mother had been able to fill the empty void which Enrico had in his life, while gifting him with many joyous reasons to celebrate the future. Meanwhile, Sadie, who would always hold a piece of Enrico's heart, was slowing becoming a treasured part of his past.

Within a year, Maria and Enrico had become engaged. They both lived in small apartments and wanted something bigger, so that Maria could have a garden and Angelo had somewhere to play. They found their dream home very quickly, and they all moved in shortly after.

Enrico kept his parent's home and used it as an office; it was nice for him to go back there from time-to-time.

On their wedding day, all three of them wore white, and stood at the homemade altar in their backyard. A minister presided over the ten minute ceremony, and made sure to include Angelo in all of the questions. "I do", they proclaimed in perfect harmony. Maria and Enrico were now husband and wife, and Angelo was legally adopted as

Enrico's son. His last name was changed to Velucci, and he called Enrico 'dad', from that day forward.

During their first few years of married life, the couple were sad that they had not been able to give Angelo a sibling. But it wasn't for a lack of trying, for they went to clinics, got tested, changed their diets, and took medications, but they could not produce a biological child.

On Angelo's thirteenth birthday, they decided to take a break from the frustrating demands of making a baby. Enrico and his beautiful wife resolved to be satisfied with all the joy which Angelo brought into their lives, and were no longer going to do anything but focus on him, from then on.

Five years after receiving the Grammy Award for the Best Orchestra Performance, Enrico was asked to be part of the New York Philharmonic, Young People's Concert. He would only be gone for three days, and with Maria working and Angelo in school, they decided that he should go to New York by himself.

The lavish event was being held on Saturday, June 4 at 2:00 pm, and it would only take up three hours of his time. Enrico took almost thirty minutes to leaf through the captivating brochure, in order to review all that he could expect to see and do during that afternoon. He quickly noted that the lavish event would be exploring the classical elegance through the music of Mozart and Haydn, and how it influenced the romantic composer, Tchaikovsky.

Further down on the second page, Enrico's name was listed as the conductor to 'Mozart's Overture to The Marriage of Figaro'. His eyes filled with an inner glow and began to tear up, as this was his favorite piece of music of all time.

The Elusive Mr. Velucci

And when Enrico turned to the last page of the program, he spotted his name listed in yet another capacity - teaching kids how composers inspire a child's mind and life.

Since teaching inspires him in the same way as conducting does, a sincere smile appeared on his perfectly symmetrical, thirty-two year old face. And because the whole thing will be televised, Enrico knew that his family would be glued to the television set, from start to finish.

Just the thought of Maria and Angelo watching him, made Enrico blush with pride; he had no doubt that they would be proud of him.

On the bottom of the last page, Enrico noted that during the finale, all the composers would be paying tribute to one another. He couldn't help but exhale a long sigh of contentment, for some of those people were his friends, some he had never met but had always looked up to, and others he had worked with once or twice.

Enrico placed the colorful presentation face down on his lap, and covered it with both of his hands. He then turned his head and stared out of the nearby window. He took a few minutes to study the hauntingly beautiful horizon, which showcased where the denim blue water touched the impeccably clear sky, and then his mind drifted back to the Young People's Concert. He teared up thinking about how truly significant this experience in New York was going to be, and now he couldn't wait to get there.

During the flight to America, Enrico's tummy had sent him to the bathroom at least a dozen times. He was quite anxious about being in the same city as Sadie, and twirled his gold wedding band around and around rather roughly, as a form of punishment. He didn't know why he felt so guilty about being married, but he did, and he tried to brush it off, but he couldn't.

To make matters worse, a woman in the row in front of him, had been watching a movie and now it was over. As the credits rolled, a song came on, and he could hear it as she took her head phones off and laid them on the seat beside her.

> ♫ I need one moment in time
> When all my dreams are a heartbeat away
> And all the answers are before me ♪

She turned the TV off, and even though the song had disappeared, Enrico's mind continued to sing the words. "One moment in time", he repeated, in a voice that was as quiet as a hint of a whisper. He moved his face to the left, and as he gazed out the window at the fluffy clouds below the plane, the catchphrase 'what if' flew from his soul.

There were a hundred meanings to those two simple words, and throughout the last three hours of the flight, Enrico contemplated each and every one of them.

What if he saw her? What if they hugged and talked for a while? What if the sparks were still there? What if it came to a point where he had to choose between Maria and Sadie?

Enrico's skin went pale and he began to panic. He went back and forth, weighing the pros and cons about a hundred times, but he felt that there was nothing he could do; Enrico was committed to Maria, but he had a strong craving to be in Sadie's company. It was an overpowering attraction that had no imperfections. It was more than just a basic need, and it crossed over an ocean and many glorious mountains.

The Elusive Mr. Velucci

Enrico was now staring down at his hands, and touching the ring as if it would give him the strength and answers which he needed.

By the time the plane landed, he had pretty much decided that it was probably not a good idea to see her. But when he started the motor on his rented vehicle, it was with the intention that he would be at her door within the hour.

The building looked exactly the same, but her mailbox had a new name on it. He shrugged his shoulders and shook his head in surprise, and with a look of determination in his eyes, he went up the stairs. He knocked on Sadie's door, and was dazed and speechless when a stranger answered.

Enrico's eyes were the widest they could be, as he let a loud gasp escape from his throat. He looked intently at the number on the door, and then back at the person who had opened it.

"Can I help you?" the man asked. His grey eyes were hooded like those of a hawk, and now they were suddenly narrowing. "You're not selling anything, are you?" he asked with suspicion seeping through his veins.

"No, no!" Enrico said a little too loudly. The stature of the large man and his obvious discontent from being disturbed, brought fear into Enrico's heart. "Is Sadie home?" He realized that his voice had quivered, but he was progressively turning into a giant bundle of nerves.

"Oh, you mean the previous tenant. She moved out of here a year ago, and no, there is no forwarding address", shot the man in a sleeveless, black t-shirt. He was unshaven, unkempt, had a beer in his hand, and it was quite obvious that he did not want to have any company.

Enrico was speechless and couldn't breathe, so he just

stood there with his bottom lip hanging open. A thousand sentences flew through his mind, but none would come out. He wondered where Sadie had gone to, and then doubted if he should continue his search for her.

The stranger was obviously busy and had no patience, and since the man at his door looked lost, he decided to end their visit. "Ok, we're done."

When the door to Sadie's apartment slammed shut, Enrico stood frozen for another full minute. He slowly made his way across the hall, hoping to speak with Mrs. Thomas.

'Knock, Knock, Knock'

"She's not going to answer!" the disheveled man yelled from the inside of Sadie's old apartment. "She died a few months ago."

Enrico wasn't sure how to define what he was feeling, other than ill-fated. And once again, his posture appeared lifeless as he made his way to the front door of the building. He felt bad for the old woman and had no way to get hold of Sadie, and with the big event happening tomorrow, there was no time to begin a search for his former tutor.

Enrico was in shock as he sat down in the driver's seat of the off-white, compact car. He had a vague glaze on his face and one hand on the steering wheel, while the fingers on the other hand were fanned out and carving uneven paths through his thick, dark hair. He tried to ignore the tightening feeling in his stomach, and eventually made his way to the hotel.

Minutes after checking in, he dialed his home number. As soon as he heard his wife's familiar voice, he felt a lot better; she had a soft and soothing motherly tone, a very kind demeanor, and because they spoke in Italian, it brought him

The Elusive Mr. Velucci

back to the comfort of home. All of this helped immensely, with calming down his troubled soul.

Maria only knew that he had left Italy feeling queasy. She had no idea that anything else had made him upset. She offered him some medical advice, for which he was quite grateful. She ended their phone call with, "You have a good sleep and please call me when you wake up."

"Thank you, sweetheart. I will. Say hello to Angelo, and know that I love you both, very much."

"We love you, too."

Enrico had a difficult sleep, but felt a little better when he woke up on Saturday morning. While having his shower, he decided to push Sadie aside and put all of his energies into his family, and the magnificent event which lay ahead of him.

The moment he stepped his foot inside of the large venue, he was tossed into a totally different frame of mind. The spacious room was infused with laughter and talking, and it completely surrounded him on all sides. The music, the orchestra, the kids, the other conductors, and the impressive setting, triggered an appreciative and well-deserved sigh of awe from his lips.

Both adults and children recognized him and asked for autographs and pictures, and then he was led backstage. Enrico got to meet some of the young people, and was reintroduced to the musicians in the orchestra, as well as with the current director of the venue.

He couldn't believe how inspiring it was to be there, and with every minute that passed, Enrico's enthusiasm continued to swell to great heights.

Three hours and four-five minutes later, Enrico was

exhausted but very happy. He had had an amazing time, he taught and performed with perfection, and he even received a standing ovation.

As he eased his toned body into the rental car, it was then when he realized what was really important – his music, and being with his family in Italy.

Enrico flew back home, and ran into the arms of the people who he loved the most in the world. He had no idea what had happened to Sadie, but he regarded this trip as a final acknowledgement that their time together had truly ended. All he had left was their memories, which he kept sacred and deep in the soft nook of his heart.

Years later, Maria and Enrico were excited to attend Angelo's High School graduation ceremony. They all had a really good time, pictures were taken, and then they parted ways. Maria left in her own car because she had to go back to work. Since Angelo was going to a party with his friends, Enrico headed straight home.

Ten minutes later, Maria suffered a serious stroke while she was driving, which blinded her and caused her car to swerve all over the road.

According to the police report, witnesses said that the car had flipped 360° before striking the steel support of an overhead highway sign. The impact folded the vehicle in half, which killed her instantly.

Because of the indescribable grief which he had sustained after his wife died, Enrico had cancelled all work for the next six months. During that same time period, he thanked God every single day that he still had Angelo in his life.

Near the end of summer, Enrico saw his son come into the house with a brand new suitcase. It confused him at first,

The Elusive Mr. Velucci

and then he was reminded that Angelo was going away to college.

"When are you scheduled to leave?" Enrico asked, in a voice that dripped of tears and exhaustion.

Angelo was placing the suitcase in his bedroom while he answered. "I won't be leaving for another week, why?" When he walked back into the living room, he looked into his father's weary face and could see that he was troubled. As he guided the older man towards the couch, Angelo took hold of his arm and asked, "Will you be ok while I'm gone?"

Enrico was a proud man, but welcomed the physical support which Angelo was offering. "I'll be ok", he replied, but the words had been dotted with emotional pain. "I have friends and neighbors around me, and I will be going back to work before the year is up. I'll be ok", he promised, in a voice which was thick with grief.

It had been months since his mother died, and Angelo could read the blank expression on his father's face. He then noticed the wrinkles which had not been there before, and the slight greying in his dad's thick head of hair. All of this made Enrico look prematurely old, and it scared the younger man. "New York is not that far away", Angelo claimed with conviction. "And I could come back within a day, if you asked me to." He kept the details simple, hoping to put a smile on his father's face.

"Thank you", Enrico stated sadly. He knew what Angelo was trying to do, but it wasn't working.

Suddenly, the words, 'New York', echoed in his ears, and it brought a boat load of emotions and memories into the forefront of Enrico's mind. Tears were forming in his eyes, as he realized that he was about the same age as Angelo is now, when he had travelled away from home for the very first time.

Thinking about that whole time period was bringing a shy smile to the older man's face; he was now recalling all the wonderful memories which he had had when he was in America. Seeing Uncle Alberto's family again, exploring all that New York had to offer, learning what he could in English, and then spending that last night with Sadie Lynn Adams - it was something that Enrico would remember fondly for the rest of his life.

Enrico lowered his head and wished that Maria was in the room with them; she always knew just what to say in times like this, and she would have been a sturdy rock for him to lean on. But she wasn't, and he hated that he had to endure this next phase of his life alone.

Enrico didn't know what delightful adventures lie ahead of Angelo, but he did know that he could not deny his son this wonderful experience.

"Dad? Are you ok?" Angelo became concerned as he watched his father seem to go into a trance.

Enrico lifted his head and looked lovingly into his son's dark brown eyes. He reached out and patted Angelo's hand for further reassurance. "I am just fine."

And he truly was; he was happy for Angelo, he felt blessed for having had a wonderful life with Maria, and now he was going to enjoy sifting through the memories of being in New York with Sadie.

Angelo sighed with great relief, but felt he needed to continue to keep an eye on his father.

Over the next few days, Enrico watched his son pack. They spent that time talking about the flight, how to get

The Elusive Mr. Velucci

out of the New York airport, and things pertaining to college. While Enrico tried to give Angelo the benefits of his wisdom, he plastered a fake smile on his weathered face, and proceeded to suggest places where Angelo could go and things that he could do. After a minute of talking, he soon found that he was describing all the same things which he had done with Sadie.

'Knock, Knock, Knock'

Angelo went to answer the front door and returned in a heightened mood. "My friends are here", he stated happily. Angelo changed his clothes while he explained that they had come to take him out for the evening. "I won't be too late", he promised, as he rushed out the door.

Enrico wished him well, and then made himself comfortable in front of the TV. He leaned his head backwards and rested it against the back of the couch. He then wondered what his life would have been like, had he gone back to New York a year or two after he said good-bye to Sadie. A second later, he had closed his eyes, and was visualizing a complete scenario about seeing the blonde beauty on one of his trips to New York.

He had no idea how long the daydream had lasted, but he woke up brooding. Enrico did not regret marrying Maria or having Angelo in his life, and he was very happy that he had met Sadie and that they had experienced so much together. However, it did bring him a great deal of sadness that he had never able to get hold of her. Especially after all the tears and the promises which they had shared while saying good-bye.

Enrico remained in a pensive mood for the next two hours, and then he turned the TV off and went to bed.

When his room was dark, he reminisced about being with Sadie – from saying hello at their first meeting, to all that they had done on their last night together.

When he got to the part where they were having sex, the whole thing seemed so true-to-life, that he actually thought he had been transported back in time.

* * * * * * * *

Enrico was suddenly out of breath and he could feel how hard his heart was pounding. He felt Sadie squirm when he touched any part of her delicious body, and he could hear the guttural animal sounds which she made when she liked something that he was doing. He could smell the passion and the salty sweat in the room, which was building between them while they were making love. And when they were done, he gazed lovingly into her face, and then he scanned the perfect body which lay limp beneath him. He smiled as he marveled that it was fit and toned with a light dusting of freckles, and he knew that he would never tire of admiring it.

"Enrico", she sighed slowly, with desire in her voice. Her hair was flat and wet, and her skin was moist as she wrapped her hands around the back of his neck. She pursed her lips and brought him close so that she could kiss him. He was very quick to learn that kissing was not the only thing that she had on her mind.

* * * * * * * *

Everything had played out exactly as it had been on their last night together. Not a single detail had been left

The Elusive Mr. Velucci

out, and everything that he had just relived, felt as real as the wrinkled lines on his hands and face.

Enrico woke up the next morning on moist sheets, while his mind danced between happiness and being sad. His body was covered in sweat from the sex dream he had just experienced, while tears of sorrow soaked his pillow from the realization that he might never see Sadie again.

Enrico sat up on the side of his bed, and he could feel how heavy his chest had become from all that he had lost in his life – his parents, Sadie, and of course, Maria. He was now an adult with a nineteen year old son, but he knew that life needed to go on.

He brushed the emotional remnants of the last few hours off his shoulders, and got himself ready to start his day. As he stood up, Enrico pushed his shoulders back and placed Sadie where she belonged - in a special corner of his heart. When he was ready to face the world, he made his way downstairs.

While he was eating breakfast, Enrico realized that Angelo would be leaving to go to America in less than twenty-four hours. Because of that, Enrico decided that he had no time to feel sorry for himself. He plastered a fake smile on his face and gave his son his entire attention.

They had a father and son day, driving here and there, and enjoyed all the Italian food that Angelo would miss while he was in New York. They talked about what each of them would be doing for the next week or so, and promised to stay in touch as often as possible.

They said good-bye at the airport early the next morning, and hugged like they would never see each other again. Before parting ways, schedules for phone calls were confirmed, as well as flights back and forth at least once every six months.

"I'll see you soon", Enrico demanded lightly.

"Of course, papa", Angelo cried. He felt quite sad that his dad would now be alone. "Ti amo!" he called, as he walked away.

"Ti amo, Angelo!" Enrico waited until his son was out of sight, and then he walked out of the terminal, sat in his car, and released all of his emotions.

Over the next twelve months, Enrico regained his will to live. He had conducted seven different orchestras in countries around the world, and travelled to his favorite spot in the gulf of Sorrento, on his days off.

Angelo was in school during the week and worked part-time on Wednesday, Thursday, and Friday nights. They spent three hours on the phone every Sunday afternoon, and Angelo flew home once every six months, as promised.

Eighteen months after Angelo began taking classes in New York, he was visiting his father in Italy, on Easter break. It was a regular 6-month visit, but this time it felt special.

"I'll need you to sit down for this", Angelo began. It had been a firm statement, and now he was a ball of nerves.

Enrico could tell that there was something going on; Angelo had a look of yearning on his youthful face, and he had adopted a silly, love-struck tone of voice when speaking. His eyes were wide and glistening with happiness, but he looked nervous and excited at the same time.

Angelo felt a fluttering in the pit of his stomach, as he was standing in front of his father. He was energized and almost couldn't contain himself, and it was because he was about to make a huge announcement.

The Elusive Mr. Velucci

"What is it, Angelo?" Enrico asked with trepidation in his voice.

"Papa, I'm getting married", Angelo blurted out. The news was delivered in one breath, as he spread his fingers wide open and began to shake his hands in the air.

In that same twenty year time period, Sadie had been busy raising a beautiful little girl. Enrico eventually turned into a fond memory, but one that Sadie saw every time she looked into her daughter's exquisite face.

Sophie was a cheeky child at times, but she was also very loving, kind, and well-disciplined. She was of average height, had dark eyes and dark thick hair, and the same magnificent pouting lips that her father wore on his handsome face. She basically resembled her dad in every way possible, except that she was a girl, and her mannerisms mirrored her mother's.

Sadie very happily devoted her whole life to her daughter, and her work and friends. She had been set up on many blind dates, but none had worked out. Mostly because she wasn't actively searching for a husband or a boyfriend.

Sadie was still in love with Enrico and hoped that they would one day be together again, but she wasn't holding her breath over it. She thought about him every single day, but kept herself busy so that he wouldn't consume too much of her time.

Sadie received a huge promotion before Sophie turned 13, and the extra money allowed them to move to a bigger place. Thankfully, it was in the same district as where they already lived, so that Sophie could continue going to the same school as her friends. For Sadie, it meant working more in an office rather than from home. That part wasn't a deal breaker, because life with a teenage girl was better when they had a bit of space between them.

Elementary School turned into High School, and other than the 'when was she old enough to begin dating', and 'when could she start to wear make-up' discussions, there weren't too many problems between mother and daughter.

Graduation from High School came and went, and then the week before Sophie began college, arrived.

Everything was packed, and both Sadie and Sophie were suffering with their own anxieties.

Sophie was eighteen years old, and had become an attractive young lady. She had her own sense of fashion, was well-read, enjoyed Opera and classical music, but she also rocked out to groups like 'Poison', which Sadie did not enjoy.

"I'm going to miss you so much", Sadie stated softly, as she looked around her child's half-empty room. She wanted to cry, because she hated that Sophie had grown up to the age where she was going off to college, but she knew that it had to happen one day. That day had just come too fast for Sadie's mind to process.

"Will you be ok?" Sophie called out, as she rushed into her mother's arms. She had never been away from her mother before, except for the odd sleep over at a friend's home during her days in elementary school.

"I will be, but it won't be easy; I'm going to miss you like crazy!" As she spoke, Sadie hugged her daughter hard and close to her chest. She was worried that once she let go, Sophie would be gone and everything between them would change. It was quite unsettling that this might be the last moment that mother and daughter would be living in the

The Elusive Mr. Velucci

same home together, so Sadie closed her eyes and tried to make this moment a memory.

Sophie could hear her mother's heart beating wildly inside of her chest. While it scared her, she knew that it was racing out of love and sadness. "It's going to be ok, and we'll see each other at least four times a month", she promised.

Sadie pushed her daughter off of her body and studied her face. "I better see you more than just four times a month!" It was a firm statement, but one that was delivered with a lot of love.

Sophie couldn't help but laugh. "You will, because I know if I don't come home, you will drive down to see me." The long-haired beauty rolled her eyes, but it was meant as a joke.

Sadie leaned her face close to her daughter's, and kissed her cheeks a few dozen times. "You know me so well."

"That I do", she agreed.

As they resumed their hug, Sadie recognized that her daughter needed to live life as an adult. She was not willing to allow their lives to transform into anything but what they had always deemed to be normal, even though she knew it probably would. She also knew that everything special started with the first step.

Sadie broke their embrace rather abruptly. "Let's get all of this into the car", she ordered. She had suddenly realized that she had to distance herself from the sentiments in order to save herself more grief, and that also meant that she had to be strong.

Sophie's face showed both surprise and confusion to her mother pulling away, but she willingly complied to her mother's request.

A few hours later, Sadie was driving her daughter to the school. It took four trips to get everything from the car up to her dorm room, and after unpacking and making sure that Sophie was ok, they said good-bye.

"I'm going to miss you, mom." Her eyes had welled up and her bottom lip was trying not to quiver.

"I'm going to miss you, too. Call me whenever you want, and I'll always answer."

"I love you."

"Love you, too."

Leaving her child at the large college was heartbreaking, and Sadie drove home while crying buckets of tears. She already missed her darling daughter, and knew that the next week or so would be quite intimidating for both of them; Sadie hadn't been alone since the night when Sophie was born, and now Sophie had just walked into a whole new world. They were going to live miles and miles apart from each other, with only the phone and a computer to connect them.

Sophie began school a week later, formed a few friendships, and always kept her mother in the forefront of her mind.

Sadie wasn't sure that she liked the new routine; she had coffee alone in the morning, she watched TV alone at night, and she went to sleep without saying good-night to her favorite person on the planet. Sadie knew that there would be a lot of adjustments to make, but she didn't expect to feel so lonely.

'R-i-i-i-i-ng'

After Sadie heard her daughter's voice, her nerves became a lot more settled. They laughed and talked about

The Elusive Mr. Velucci

everything; school, food, clothing, and work. They also spoke about the possibility of talking for a few minutes every night, instead of having a long conversation once every other day.

Sophie could tell that this separation was very hard on her mother, and that's why she agreed to them talking more often. Secretly, Sophie was much too busy and excited to feel as sad as her mother was, but she certainly had her moments when she felt lonely and homesick.

Sadie loved the new routine, and waited for each nightly phone call with baited breath. On the days when Sophie came to the house, their conversations filled the air with gossip, work, shopping, and all that was happening at school.

While Sophie spoke, she watched her mother hold onto every single word, as if it were dusted with gold and dotted with diamonds.

Sadie relished those days when Sophie drove home for the week-end, and she smothered her daughter with as much love and attention as the young girl could stand. She would like to say that it was just like old times when Sophie came home, but there were definite differences now. These days, they were two adult women instead of a mother caring for her toddler. This made Sadie take stock of how much she no longer needed to do for Sophie, for her daughter could certainly take care of herself.

As she watched Sophie move around their home, tidying things up or making them something to eat, Sadie's eyes got misty; she missed the old days when she did everything for her daughter. As she watched how much Sophie was babying her, she realized that it would take time to get used to this new relationship.

One day, near the end of the first year of school, Sophie came home in a ball of energy. It was quite evident that she had something to say, and she did so when Sadie was sitting comfortably.

"I would like to move out of the dorm and share an apartment with my friend, Gisela", Sophie stated firmly. She held her gaze steady, but her stomach was in knots. "We want a 2-bedroom apartment, slightly off campus, and we'll both get jobs!" The words burst through her lips with total rapture, in hopes that her mother would give her, her blessing. "What do you think? Is it ok?" She was totally eager for the answer and was having trouble controlling her enthusiasm.

Sadie loved that her daughter would be out of the dorm, for there were far too many parties and other distractions there. But living away from the school would also bring its own concerns; travelling back and forth, boys staying overnight, and work might interfere with school. These were all valid points, but after looking into her daughter's pleading expression, Sadie had to agree.

Because her mom hadn't responded, Sophie brought new elements to the discussion, in order to gain her mother's approval. "She's a great cook, she's very clean, and I know she'll keep me on my toes."

Sadie laughed while she threw her hands into the air in a surrendering pose. "Listen", she stated slowly. "As your mother, I think it'll be ok, but I need to enforce the short phone calls every night, for obvious reasons."

Sophie squealed without really hearing anything more than her mother saying, 'it'll be ok', and then she jumped

The Elusive Mr. Velucci

for joy. "Yeeah! Thank you!" She rushed over and gave her mother a huge hug.

All the details of their agreement had been written down in long-hand, and then the paper had been tacked up onto the wall, by the phone in the kitchen. "And I'll need to meet Gisela", she added sternly.

Sophie gave her mother a thumbs-up. "You got it, mom."

Not long after Sophie had driven away from her mother's house, Sadie's mind went into overdrive from phrases like 'living on her own' and 'off campus'.

Because her parents had died when she was 19 years old, Sadie had no choice but to live on her own. She couldn't help but remember how difficult it was to find work and a place to live, and she barely managed to make ends meet. That was not the life that she wanted for Sophie, but she wasn't sure how to convey this to her determined daughter.

All of a sudden, another thought entered her brain; Enrico was a year older than Sophie was now, when he met Sadie. It brought to mind how enamored she had been, by his good looks, his charming accent, and his tales of travelling across the ocean in a large ship. And, he had done it without knowing a word of English!

Sadie had been quite impressed by Enrico's fortitude, and suddenly realized that she saw that same trait in her daughter.

"Enrico", she sighed softly. She missed him so much, and the mere mention of his name brought shivers up her spine.

Sadie lowered her eyes and allowed her subconscious thoughts to float to the surface. She hadn't thought so strongly about Enrico in years, and now she didn't know if she wanted to stop. With increasing speed, every detail about him came forward and made her smile; his scent, his slightly curly hair, his soft hands, and his arresting good looks, that had captured her attention from the first moment they met.

If she was being truthful, she would suppose that she had been drawn to him right away, as if they'd known each other since birth. The knowledge behind that thought, made her aware of the dull ache in her chest from the memory of those forgotten feelings.

Because she didn't want to dwell on him and their time together, she forced herself to stand up and walk around her home. Normally that had worked, but today she was alone, and with Sophie entering into a new chapter in her life, Sadie felt herself being suffocated by Enrico's image.

As she carried on with her day, everything reminded her of something they had done together; a song which they had danced to was playing on the radio. A commercial which advertised travel and touring, jogged her memory of all the places which she had gone to with Enrico. And when she was doing laundry and spotted a romance book in one of the boxes in her basement, she was immediately transported back into Enrico's arms.

A couple of hours later, when Sophie called to say goodnight, it conjured up even more memories for Sadie to linger in. All of them were dreamlike, and all of them made her happy and sad at the same time.

After they hung up the phone, Sadie got herself ready for bed. After sliding under the covers, she suddenly remembered every single detail of their last night together. How he had swept her up, seemingly weightless, into his

The Elusive Mr. Velucci

sturdy arms. And how she had locked herself into his warm embrace, and never wanted to let go. Once he had placed her on the bed, he caressed her lips with his mouth, and then he continued to kiss all the contours of her body.

Sadie understood that she was day-dreaming, but it all felt so real. And as if he was right there and they were reenacting the whole night again, her body was playing along with it.

A moan of desire slid through her lips, when she remembered the way she had responded when he was thrusting away on top of her. Her back arched involuntarily and sweat began to bead on her forehead, from the heat which was now surging throughout her entire body.

'It was all so vivid, but why was it happening?' she wondered. 'Why had he suddenly popped into my head with such vigor?'

Sadie was now beyond the point where 'shutting things down' was literally impossible, so she brought herself to a shuddering orgasm. A rush of pink now stained her cheeks, and she had to bite her bottom lip to stifle the outcry of uninhibited delight. A brief shiver rippled through her body, while her heart thumped uncontrollably. Once it had quieted down, she was fully awake, and she watched as her breasts rose and fell under her now-steady breathing.

Sadie used the bathroom, and studied her reflection in the mirror as she washed her hands. She was no longer twenty-one, but she could still see a few remnants of the young lady that she had once been.

After Sadie climbed back into bed, she turned off the light and tried to go to sleep, but her dreams were all about Enrico. She woke up the next morning drenched in her own sweat, exactly as she had done after their decadent night of great passion. She ripped the blankets off her moist body and jumped into a warm shower. As she washed her hair, she tried to scrub the images of Enrico and their time together, out of her mind. Within minutes, she was in tears from missing him, and she wondered if this was healthy. After weighing the pros and cons of having these unnecessary thoughts, she was mentally and emotionally exhausted. After all the soap had been removed from her body, she turned the water a little warmer, with hopes of making herself invisible in the white fog.

Sadie came out of the shower feeling a bit better, but it was because she had decided not to think about Enrico for the rest of the day.

While she was getting dressed, she involuntarily continued to argue her point. 'Since he left, he has not come back or even tried to contact me.' Her mind was debating the issue without her consent. 'I even wonder if the time that we spent together, means more to me than it does to him.' She was reflecting on a few things at the same time, and her emotions were starting to get the better of her. 'At least I went to the deli to see if his aunt or uncle could pass a message onto him. It wasn't my fault that the store was closed.' She was trying to calm down, but everything seemed to hit her at the same time. 'He obviously doesn't want me, or he would have reached out to me long before now.'

By the time she had entered the kitchen to make some breakfast, she was in a stronger frame of mind; she was no longer upset, and had pretty much decided to keep Enrico as a wonderful memory, and not as a vital element of her life.

The first year of Sophie living away from home was

The Elusive Mr. Velucci

emotionally crazy, but Sadie did her best to push through the loneliness and sadness. She kept busy with newer and bigger projects at work, and rushed home to receive Sophie's phone calls, every single night. In those hours when it was dark outside and there was nothing on TV, Sadie's mind drifted back to Enrico, and she wondered what he was doing. She made sure not to dwell on him for longer than a minute, but it was clear that she still carried his heart in the palm of her hand.

Half-way through her second year in college, Sophie rushed home with a huge announcement. She had it all planned out - how it would go and what she would say - and couldn't wait to act it out.

Sophie walked into the house with her face beaming with sheer happiness. "Guess what?!" she shouted with a great deal of force. She was literally bouncing inside and out, as she waited for her mother to return a similar question.

"What?" she answered calmly. Sadie's first thought was that her daughter had won an award or been asked to speak during an assembly of some sort. Because Sophie looked like she was going to bust, she finished straightening the table cloth and then gave her daughter her full attention. "Tell me."

Sadie could see that Sophie was more excited today than any other day; she was more touchy-feely, more anxious, and she held an extremely strong eye contact with her mother. Her eyes sparkled and blinked very little, and she was taking large, deep, savoring breaths at least once every minute.

"Mom", she giggled, when she was ready. Her smile was wide and bright, and she was lightly jogging in place from having too much happiness in her body. "I need you to sit down."

Sadie could tell that what her daughter wanted to share was quite big, and now it was her who was becoming anxious. "Sophie, you're scaring me."

"It's ok; you're going to like this", Sophie squealed, as she stood directly in front of her mother. She had had both of her hands hidden behind her back, and suddenly whipped the left one forward. All the fingers on that delicate hand were dangling and moving rapidly, as if to draw attention to the most obvious reason for any girl to be that excited. "Look!" she shrieked with pure joy. "I'm engaged!"

Almost two hours had passed since Halley had begun to tell the story, and now that she'd taken a dramatic moment to pause, she had become fully aware of all that was going on around her. And while she didn't know when it had happened, the entire room had gone completely quiet and all eyes and ears were on her.

Loud gasps, huge inhales of air, and long sighs could be heard from every table. Some people were wiping tears from their eyes, while others were fanning themselves in order to stop them from full-out crying. Everyone had deserted their own conversations, and had turned their entire attention onto the story which Halley was narrating. Coffee orders were done in whispers, no-one had gone out for a cigarette, and anyone who dared to make any kind of noise, were quickly reprimanded by the strangers around them.

"Don't start again until I come back", someone pleaded loud enough for Halley to hear. The lady had to use the restroom, but did so on tippy toe. It seemed that everyone wanted to continue to hear every single word of the delightful story, regardless of the time, because they were all deeply caught up in the web of romance.

Both Halley and Terri were fascinated by the fact that they could hold an audience's interest for so long, and on such an unfathomable scale.

As Halley looked into the many faces that were staring

back at her, she sighed in wonder. "Perhaps I've already said too much", she confessed. Halley lowered her eyelashes and was now feeling quite shy.

Fear filled every pore in Terri's body, that Halley had become spooked and might not want to continue. She reached her hand across the table and tried to convince her friend not to worry. "It's all ok."

And then, from somewhere in the far side of the coffee shop, a crisp question shocked everyone in the room. "And then what happened?" the stranger asked. Suddenly, a little life had been bought back into the quiet, artsy environment.

"Not yet, not yet!" the lady from the bathroom called from within the tiny room. "I'm almost done. Wait for me!" The toilet flushed, the soap dispenser was banged, the water turned on, and seconds later, the door opened. The lady rushed to her seat and sat down, and then motioned without speaking, that Halley could continue.

Terri's heart was racing and her eyes were bugging out, from the sheer surprise of Sophie's news. She was shaking with an abundance of curiosity as she looked directly into Halley's eyes. "Please, continue", she pleaded.

Halley had been mildly disturbed that she had caught the attention of so many people at the same time, but she noted that this could be free advertising for her Wedding Planner business. She pushed her shoulders back, and pretended that her and Terri were the only two people in the room.

"Wait a minute!" Terri asked in a moment of clarity. "They're both engaged?" She suddenly caught on to what was happening, and with complete naivety, she was beside herself with utter confusion. "Oh my gosh!" she stated,

The Elusive Mr. Velucci

while she tried her best to figure out all the ways in which this could end.

All of a sudden, gasps were leaving the mouths of several people in the room. Disagreeing hushes that they couldn't possibly be engaged to each other were also abundant, as were the swoons from the few people who loved the idea of love in the air.

It took another minute or two before Terri connected the dots, and then her entire world shifted on its axis. "Shut the front door!" she shouted. Terri slammed her hands onto the table, and was partially standing because she was totally blinded by the weirdness of the situation. "Are you sure? "I mean…"

"Yes, I'm sure", Halley replied happily, as she continued to laugh softly. She loved how everyone was reacting, because of course, she was the only person in the room who knew the full story.

Meanwhile, Terri was dumbfounded and lowered her face towards the table. "Wow!" was all she could say. She reached for her cup, which was now cold, as she tried to fit the pieces of the puzzle together. When she saw that her mug was empty, she became flustered. "I totally need some wine."

All around them, people at every table in the room had their own opinions about the four people in the story, and whispered their ideas softly to each other. No-one had been spared the shock of how the story was unfolding, and not one single person was physically or mentally able to leave the coffee shop, until they knew how it all ended.

Halley watched as her friend's sophisticated mind worked its magic through the bizarre set of circumstances, and then she shot back a whole new bucket of questions.

Tina Griffith

"If they are brother and sister, they can't get married, right? Love or not, it wouldn't work."

Several patrons fired their questions and/or thoughts across the room at full volume, which had Terri replying to people who she didn't even know – not her favorite sport.

It only took five more minutes before Halley called a halt to the impromptu interrogation. "Okay!" she called loudly. "Enough!" She extended one flat hand toward her friend and the other towards the crowd, while her eyes were closed and her expression was serious. "Let me fill in the blanks for you." And as if she was conducting a huge block party, Halley spoke to the entire room at the same time, "You're all going to like this next part, because this is where Enrico and Sadie meet for the first time in over 20 years." She added that last sentence while wearing a wide, manic, unsettling grin on her face. It was almost sinister, and she suddenly felt like she had great power.

"Ok, everyone. Sh-h-h-h-h! I wanna hear how this plays out!" the manager instructed loudly. She was walking around the room trying to quiet everyone down, because she had become as invested in this story as the rest of the crowd was.

Halley thanked her by nodding in her direction.

As soon as the crowd was settled, Terri looked across the table. "Ok, go!" she ordered. She sat on the very edge of the bench across from Halley, folded her hands on the table in front of her, and she took a few deep breaths. She really wanted to pay attention to every word that was about to drift towards her, but not surprisingly, so did every single person in the entire room; chairs had been turned to face the conversation, and all eyes and ears were focused on hearing the rest of the story.

To ensure that there would be no more interruptions, the manager of the coffee shop placed a 'closed sign' on the front door, and then sat down not far from the table where Terri and Halley were sitting.

The ambience in the room was now filled with total anxiety, while the hushed crowd was on pins and needles, silently pleading for Halley to continue.

"If you're all set, let me pick up in the same moment where I left off…"

"What?" Sadie's face went from scared to amazement after she heard her daughter's announcement. She involuntarily sucked in a quick breath, and she was laughing but terribly confused. She wanted to scream for joy and dance around, but her body couldn't move, and she was both elated that her daughter was going to get married, and sad that her daughter was going to get married. "Oh my gosh!" she gushed loudly. Sadie hadn't noticed that her voice was now an octave higher than normal, but she was in shock.

"Ye-e-e-ah!" Sophie shouted. She was over the moon with happiness, and could hardly believe her good fortune.

"Let me see it!" she urged wildly. With both hands, Sadie held onto her daughter's ring finger and drank in the beauty of the magnificent looking diamond.

"Isn't it just the most gorgeous thing you've ever seen in your whole entire life?" Sophie asked in an infatuated tone of voice. "I'm so happy, mom. I just can't believe it."

"Congratulations, honey." Sadie was stunned. "I'm so happy for you." She let go of her daughter's hand, and gathered her child as close as possible to her own body. They embraced with a strong hug, and didn't let go for several minutes.

This had developed into a big bonding moment for Sadie and Sophie - a moment when no words were necessary to convey what they were thinking or feeling. A moment used

The Elusive Mr. Velucci

to reflect the fact, that once Sophie was married, nothing would ever be the same again, for their lives would play out very differently from then on.

When Sophie was hugging her mom, she became very aware of the fact that she was going to have to move out of her mother's home. It was a little scary, but when she realized that it was no different than the arrangement which they have right now, it eased her mind.

Of course Sadie had always understood that the time would come when her daughter would leave the nest, but now that it was here, it was terrifying. To Sadie it implied, that she would live out the rest of her life all alone. A tentative smile spread across her mouth as the chilly, two-syllable word sunk into her brain.

Alone. The word literally means separated, isolated, or apart from others. It felt so disheartening and lonely to think about, and Sadie wasn't sure how she was going to cope. Before the power of the word took control over her senses, she remembered that Sophie would only be a phone call away. This relaxed her and gave her hope that everything will be ok.

When the embrace ended, and they had both dried their tears, Sadie spoke first. "We have so much to do, so after breakfast tomorrow, how about if we go shopping?" She watched her daughter nod in slow motion.

"I'd love that, thank you." Sophie's teary-eyed face looked down at the diamond ring on her left hand, and the concept of a wedding became her entire focus for the next few seconds.

Sadie broke the silence by speaking up. "When will I get to meet the man who is going to join our little family?" She brought her right hand up and stroked her daughter's silky hair, as she waited for the answer.

Sadie had heard about the boy who Sophie was dating, but they had never met. Apparently he was busy with school, work, and travelling overseas once every few months, to make an appearance in Sadie's home.

Sophie spoke without taking her eyes off of the shiny ring. "I've invited both him and his father here for supper, on the Friday after next."

"Father and son?"

She stopped speaking and looked directly into her mother's eyes. "Should I have come to you first?" she asked with sincerity. "I guess I hoped that it would be ok."

"Um... no, it'll be fine", Sadie assured her daughter, but inside she was frightened beyond belief.

"Are you sure? I mean, I could reschedule?"

"No. It's ok." As Sadie gazed into her daughter's beautiful, chocolate-colored eyes, she could see that Sophie had become a grown woman. Enrico's DNA had embedded itself into everything that Sophie was today, but because Sadie had raised her, she was going to take the majority part of the glory for how this young lady had turned out.

"Mom", she said in a softer tone. "I haven't met the father, but if he's anything like Angelo, I'm sure that we will love him." She wrapped her arms around her mother's neck and added, "I hope you love them both!"

With her face pushed into the spot between her daughter's neck and shoulder, Sadie whispered to herself, 'I hope so, too.'

She was secretly thankful that the father didn't live in North America, because then they wouldn't have to see each

The Elusive Mr. Velucci

other very often. She then realized that there really wasn't much to stress over, because it didn't matter if any of them got along or not; her only wish was for Sophie to be happy.

For the next two weeks, menus were planned, food was bought, the house was cleaned from top to bottom, hair and nails got done, and all was accomplished before the morning of the big meeting.

Both Sadie and Sophie were nervous wrecks, and neither one was sure of how the visit would go.

Ten minutes before Angelo predicted that they would arrive, muffled male voices could be heard speaking on the other side of the solid door.

'Ding Dong'

"Mom!" she shouted, with both surprise and utter delight in her voice. "They're here!" Sophie's heart quickened as she touched her hair and her clothing, one last time. When she ran to open the door, her eyes glistened with ultimate bliss. When she saw his face, her smile widened and her face radiated with love.

"Sophie", he breathed, in the most seductive manner possible. Angelo released an appreciative sigh through his full lips, while laying a tanned, rugged hand over his heart. "Let me look at you." His eyes made a complete inventory of her body, and then he reached for both of her hands and spread them out to the sides. And as if they hadn't seen each other in years, his eyes scanned every inch of her face. "Very beautiful", he confirmed.

Sophie giggled as all girls do when they're happy but embarrassed, and then she quickly composed herself. "Come!" she ordered playfully. She grabbed one of his hands and gently dragged him further into the house, forgetting for

Tina Griffith

a brief second that her fiancé's father was behind him. [8]"Mi scusi, signore!" she stated firmly to the older gentleman; she hadn't meant to be rude. [9]"Per favore, avanti!"

"Grazie", he stated softly. The older man smiled knowingly and nodded his head, for he remembered what it felt like to be young and in love. He bent over and lifted his suitcase off the cement porch, and with appreciation shining across his face, he stepped over the threshold. As he moved himself into the small but quaint living room, he made a point to look around.

The area was very lovely; well-maintained, with small, almost dainty furniture. A few plants were scattered here and there, but nothing was larger than a man's head. He ventured to guess that the pictures on the walls were probably hand-painted or bought at thrift stores, and then he took notice of the charming ambience. He couldn't figure out why it gave his mind cause to linger, but it stopped him dead in his tracks.

Sadie could hear voices and knew that it was her cue to come into the room. She glanced into the toaster, to give herself one last chance to appear to be somewhat decent. After a quick fluff at her hair and a tug at her clothes, she decided that she was suitable enough to meet her daughter's steady man. "Here we go", she chanted quietly to herself. It was meant to give her courage, for she knew that she would need all the strength that she could get.

Sadie walked into the room with her eyes cast downward, while wearing a courteous smile on her ageing, yet still very pretty face. "Hello, everyone", she said politely. She spoke

---

[8] Mi scusi, signore!" – "Excuse me, sir!"
[9] "Per favore, avanti!" - "Please, come in!"

The Elusive Mr. Velucci

in a gentle tone, and then braced herself for whatever would happen next.

Enrico placed his suitcase on the floor and then stood up again, giving everyone the impression that he was ready to be introduced.

Angelo placed his hand at Enrico's elbow, and faced him towards Sophie. "Papa, this is the girl that I'm going to marry."

Sophie was bubbling with enthusiasm at being introduced to her future father-in-law. "I'm very pleased to meet you, sir. My name is Sophie." As they shook hands she added, "I've heard a lot of good things about you."

Enrico's heart had suddenly swelled with an enormous amount of emotion; the girl was truly adorable. He turned to catch Angelo's eye, and then he smiled with approval before turning back to Sophie. "My son is a very lucky young man."

Enrico felt a strange sensation towards his future daughter-in-law, because she reminded him of someone else. He didn't know who, but the way his mind was reacting towards how she looked and their skin's initial contact, it seemed as if they had met before.

Sophie was caught up in the moment and reached out to hug the stranger. "Thank you so much. You're very kind." She was quite relieved that he liked her, and released a heavy sigh into the room.

Enrico's mind was racing, while he searched for answers as to how he knew this charming young girl. It was clear from her side that they hadn't met before, but there was something oddly familiar about Sophie that he couldn't quite put his finger on.

Sadie laid the large plate of small sandwiches onto

the dining room table, and took a second to check that everything looked perfect. As she spun herself around, she wiped her hands down the sides of her pants. Her eyes looked up, just in time to watch an older man take a step into the middle of her living room.

"Mom!" Sophie shouted. Her spirits were high because she was hoping that all would go well, and while she knew that her voice was a little loud, she didn't care. "This is Enrico Velucci, Angelo's father."

To Sadie, the world had exploded with a very loud bang. At least, that's how it felt. The very mention of Enrico's name, brought a huge amount of fear and intense anxiety to every pore in Sadie's body. The fact that he was standing there, in her home, had her checking her sanity over and over again.

She knew that she was staring, but she couldn't help it. He looked pretty much the same as he did at 19, but Sadie didn't recognize him at this age; his rough and tumble black hair had shiny hair gel in it. There was a flicker of grey amongst the darker strands, and all of it had been combed backwards and away from his face. His eyes were dark and the edges were wrinkled, and they shimmered like glassy volcanic rock. He was older and seemed a bit shorter, but upon closer inspection, Sadie gasped quite loudly when she determined that this was indeed, Enrico Velucci – her former student, and the father of her child.

And then, it was as if all the pictures of her past had flashed through her brain in a single swoop, so that she could remember him and their time together. Sadie could suddenly recall every single detail of Enrico's personality and

The Elusive Mr. Velucci

body; the feel of his skin against hers, how he smelled, how he laughed, and most of all, how his mouth felt against hers.

Enrico's eyes widened with great surprise, as he looked carefully across the room. When he realized that he somehow knew this woman, he choked on a mouthful of air.

Sadie was trying not to react, as her mind played back all the memories, but how could she deny knowing him? Vivid recollections were detailed in full color and sound, while goose bumps began to appear all over her body. She was wide-eyed and speechless as his name lingered around the edges of her mind, and it caused the hair on her skin to start standing straight up. 'Enrico?' her mind echoed.

Sophie's voice broke the trance she was in.

"And that is my mother, Sadie Adams", Sophie announced with pride.

Hearing her name made his heart flutter. Enrico suddenly felt off-balance and thought he was about to have a medical emergency. 'Was that really Sadie standing before him?' he wondered. His skin began to pale, as he tried to suck in another breath of air.

There was an immediate shift of energy in the room, if not on the entire planet, when these former lovers recognized each other. Maybe nobody felt it, but Enrico and Sadie did; it was dark and bright all at the same time, and made them both feel as if time had stood still.

Enrico thought he detected the twinkle of recognition in her gorgeous blue eyes, but was it from an attempt to be cordial over meeting the father of her future son-in-law? Or did Sophie's mother actually remember him as the young man who she taught English to, so very long ago.

Blood was rushing to every nerve and cell in his entire

body, and it left him feeling terribly disorientated. Flashes of seconds of them being together, tortured his senses and caused him to wonder if what was happening, was actually real. He had spent a lot of time trying to get hold of her, and now they were standing face-to-face. He couldn't believe it and didn't know how to respond.

Enrico didn't want anyone to know, but his chest was tightening and he was suddenly feeling ill, but he vowed not to die until he got some answers.

Did her heart stop? Sadie couldn't tell. Her muscles had gone rigid, giving her a stiffened posture, and her face had adopted a dazed look. 'Enrico?' she wanted to ask, but she had no breath in her body to push out the word. Her eyes were not blinking, but began to well up with tears of joy at seeing him again. Or were these tears of heartbreak for not having seen him for such a long time? She couldn't tell. But in case it was her former student and lover, she wished that she had taken extra time to look more presentable.

When Enrico saw her face light up, he immediately recognized her smile and the shape of her full mouth. His eyes slid down the silhouette of her body, making sure to capture every curve, and though she was older, he could see that she was still a remarkable woman.

Sadie was standing across the room, not being able to move or speak. She very much wanted to rush into his arms, but she couldn't; there was a secret which she had kept buried in her heart, and now was not the right time to tell it. Still, there were a thousand things which she wanted to say and ask. All of a sudden she remembered the introduction, and the words that clearly labelled who the older man in her home was - Angelo's father.

The Elusive Mr. Velucci

Sadie inhaled loud and sharp enough for everyone in the room to hear, but it was totally unintentional. '*His father?*' The words got stuck in her chest like a long knife, for she just realized that he must have gotten married. Sadie quickly cast her eyes downward, and began to fidget with an end of her clothing so that she wouldn't scream out or burst into tears.

Enrico had noticed what Sadie had done, and took a few steps towards her. When he was two feet away, he reached his hand out, and gently touched her forearm with his fingertips. "It's very nice to meet you", he announced formally. He tried to keep their introduction appropriate, but it was killing him that he couldn't gather her into his arms and hold her tight against his body for the rest of his life.

The touch of his hand was warm and tender, but Sadie felt that he seemed to want more. 'Did he recognize me?' she wondered. She desperately wanted him to, but knew that she couldn't do anything to make that happen. Sadie slid her hands down to her soft stomach and overlapped them. She wanted him to smother her with his lips, but appreciated that that wasn't about to happen.

He had now touched her skin, and it had been confirmed that this was indeed, Sadie. The reality of the introduction made Enrico's bones feel wobbly, but he didn't want to appear to be lame or unwell. In his head, he knew that he had apologies to make and explanations to deliver, but there were also a dozen questions for which he wanted answers to.

The eyes of the two oldest people in the room were locked, as if they were communicating by mental telepathy. In reality, neither of them knew what to say to the other.

"Mama?" Sophie called. Her mother had become very quiet in the last moment or two, and this worried the

Tina Griffith

bride-to-be. To break the silence and awkwardness in the room, Sophie tucked one hand under her fiancé's upper arm, as if to show complete ownership. She then squeezed him close to her own body as she spoke. "Mama, this is Angelo. My gorgeous fiancé." She looked into his face with the shine of euphoria and appreciation, that only a person in love can relate to. "Isn't he adorable?" she asked, as if he was a brand new puppy.

Sadie nodded in a mechanical way, almost as if she was a robot. She couldn't speak or move in a normal fashion, because the majority of her focus was on the other man in the room. Sadie had shared countless hours and experiences with Enrico, but she had not seen him since before their daughter was born. Therefore, she felt it only fitting that he be given the bulk of her attention.

"Angelo, this is my mother, Sadie." Sophie delighted in the fact that they were finally meeting each other; she had wanted to do this for a very long time, but outside elements had always gotten in the way.

"Nice to meet you", he stated in a heavy accent, but with perfect English pronunciation. As he leaned forward to shake her hand, Angelo was well aware that Sadie was more interested in his father.

Sadie reached her hand out, but her grip was weak and the shake action was quite limp. Sadie had grunted her greeting like a one syllable sound, but in her mind she had answered, "It's nice to meet you." She probably should have said more, but her mouth had gone dry and her eyes were prickling with unseen tears.

What nobody realized, was that her mind was confused and mentally replaying her wonderful months with Enrico.

The Elusive Mr. Velucci

'Did he also remember them?' Sadie wondered. 'Did he ever think about her or their time together?' She was a little anxious and wanted to know.

Angelo looked over his shoulder at his father's expression, and saw a glazed look of anguish which had spread over his entire face. He thought it was odd that Sadie was wearing that same exact look on her face, and couldn't understand why this was happening. These were the parents of the children who were about to get married. Shouldn't they be happy? His mind was exploding with these and other questions.

It was becoming clear to both Angelo and Sophie, that there was a tremble of uncanny awareness flying between their parents. And instead of faking happiness at meeting someone for the first time, the two older adults were speechless and standing as still as statues. The younger adults did not know why this was happening, but it was hard for them to ignore.

Sadie desperately wanted to race across the room with her arms outstretched while screaming his name, but she didn't. Dozens of thoughts were assaulting her mind, and all were asking loudly, 'Where have you been?' She could see that he was well, so why hadn't he tried to contact her?

Enrico took another step forward and reached out his hand to her. "Sadie", he whispered, in a tone that represented a million heartfelt apologies. He felt a knot in his stomach as he continued to lock eyes with her. Along with the apologies which he felt she was owed, he hoped that she would accept the quiet answers to all of her unspoken questions.

"Enrico", she sighed, her pulse was now racing. She

held out her hand to shake his, and the outside world had suddenly come to a crashing halt.

Angelo exchanged confused glances with Sophie, who in turn, shrugged her shoulders as if she didn't know what was going on. They both did what they could, to try to make sense of the uncomfortable situation which was happening between their parents.

A tingling sensation of familiarity, caressed the skin on both Enrico's and Sadie's hands. A powerful shudder shot between them the instant their bodies made contact, which made them both inhale with an uncontrollable force. Suddenly, the energy of forbidden intimacy was booming all around them, and yet neither of them could say a word about what they were feeling.

Sadie was trying to stay aware that her daughter and future son-in-law were in the room, and hoped that she wasn't being too obvious with her emotions. Even so, she wanted to smother the father of the groom with passionate kisses, hold him naked and close to her own body, and make love to him exactly how she had done, so long ago.

"Sadie", Enrico stated again, as if to tattoo the word into his memory bank. His dark eyes softened as he said her name, and he wished that she could know why; he had suffered a thousand painful deaths by her absence, and now she was standing before him, and he couldn't reach out to hold her.

As though her brain had read his thoughts, Sadie's entire body shivered as if she was standing naked and wet in a room full of strangers. Her heart pounded and screamed for him to calm her down, but she tried to keep her composure.

Enrico couldn't help but marvel that she was still as

The Elusive Mr. Velucci

beautiful as she had been at twenty-one. This made him both sad and happy at the same time, for she would never know how much he had missed her.

Their hands were still connected and a clear perception of what was happening, was exploding throughout her body. When his velvety voice said her name for a third time, it sent chills down her spine. She had forgotten what a lovely accent he had, and she could have listened to him speak all night long. Her lips suddenly parted as if she wanted to say something to him, but because her body had begun to throb with passion, she chose to stay quiet.

Enrico wanted to pull Sadie towards him, to hug her and kiss her, but he didn't. The muscles in his abdomen began to quiver, as he suddenly remembered all kinds of things about her. Like how she drank her coffee – two sugars, one cream. In his mind's eye, he could still hear the soft moan which had left her throat, when she sucked that first bit of steaming hot liquid into her mouth - it was one of his favorite memories of her. In fact, every time he came to New York, he had gone past that particular coffee franchise, and immediately thought of her... her lips cradling the edge of the paper cup, tasting the delicious dark flavored water, and her tongue coming out to lick all that had coated her upper and lower lips. It was quite sensuous to watch, and thus became one of his favorite memories of her.

Every inch of Sadie's body was craving him, for he was her first and only lover. After he left her life, Sadie had no desire to be with anyone else; she was pregnant, and then she was busy raising a child. She didn't resent him for that, instead she thought about him every single time she looked into her daughter's perfect face. He was there in Sophie's eyes and her smile, and in about a dozen quirky expressions that the little girl made on a daily basis.

Enrico glanced at Sadie's sensuous lips, and suddenly other memories came flooding back into his mind. 'The things that she had done to me that night, had me exhausted for days', he remembered happily. Desire was building inside of him for her, and he hoped that nobody else could sense it.

A tremor in Sadie's lower body brought heat to her thighs and groin. As she stood there aching for his touch, she hoped that nobody else could detect what she was thinking.

Enrico had never loved anyone as much as he loved Sadie, and now the anticipation of them rekindling what they once had, was almost unbearable. 'Would they get that chance?' he wondered. His body hoped they would, for he was now fighting an overwhelming need to be close to her.

The time had ticked away, and no-one in the room could fathom how long they had all been standing silent. Since the moment when the men had come into the home, the small space had taken on a new quality. Neither of the younger people could explain it, but to the parents, it was nothing short of recognition and lust.

Sadie and Enrico had become fixated on each other for far too long now, but neither wanted to break the spell. Their hands were still touching, and their eyes were locked but not blinking. Because they weren't talking or moving any part of their body, their children decided that enough was enough, and came over to break them out of the weird trance that they were in.

"Papa?" Angelo called softly. He had never seen his father act like this and was becoming terribly concerned.

"Mom?" Sophie wasn't sure what was happening, and

The Elusive Mr. Velucci

she was also a little frightened. "Are you ok?" Sophie's face showed serious concern as she shifted glances between Angelo and her mother, and then to Enrico.

Enrico's heart had emotionally exploded in his chest, with more love than he had felt in years. Yes, he had gotten married, but he had never forgotten about Sadie or their time together. It was pretty much all that he had thought about, since that day when the ship took him away.

Sadie couldn't believe that Enrico was standing in front of her. She was disappointed that she couldn't do anything to show him how much she had missed him, but she hoped that he could feel it in the impassable air which lay between them.

"Papa, come and sit down", Angelo ordered softly.

Enrico did as he was asked to do, and shuffled towards the three-seater couch. After making himself comfortable, he purposely patted the seat next to him, as a way of inviting Sadie to sit down, too.

It was a loving invitation, and Sadie did as he had requested.

Sophie and Angelo had watched the last few minutes in total disbelief, and it was as if time had somehow stretched out three times longer than it was actually happening.

Everything had become confusing and tense since Angelo and his father had walked through the door, and it seemed to be synchronized from a place that was beyond logic and reason. Ceaseless, inward questions tormented all of them, but nothing was said out loud. What was supposed to be a simple meet-and-greet to introduce their parents, had somehow turned into a silent battle of emotions between two seemingly stunned individuals.

Tina Griffith

Sophie couldn't stand it anymore, and broke the ice by asking if anyone wanted something to drink or eat. "We have plates over there and glasses over here." She pointed to the objects as she spoke, and was pleased that Angelo approved of her suggestion.

"Papa, Sadie?" Angelo said. "Would you like to come and get something to eat?"

The younger adults were relieved when their parents stood up and walked towards the table. They all ate in silence, but small words and phrases began to come out while the food was being wrapped up and put away.

The group talked about the wedding, how long Sophie and Angelo had known each other, what each of them were taking in school, and where they would live after they got married.

Two hours later, it was time for Angelo to take his father back to the hotel. The younger man turned and said good-bye to Sadie, and then he thanked her for a lovely evening. "It was very nice to meet you", he added politely. He then gave her a quick hug.

"Thank you, Angelo. It was very nice to meet you, too." Sadie smiled as she delivered her sincere good-bye, and then she turned her attention to Enrico. Her soul was begging him to stay with her, but her voice intervened. "Bye", she said softly, but she didn't want him to leave. More than anything, she wanted to cast morality and good judgment aside, but she knew that it was not possible.

Enrico took her hand and kissed the palm of it. "Ciao, Sadie", he whispered in a shaky voice. He also didn't want to leave, for fear that he would never get to see her again. He hoped that she could feel that he was fighting a huge

The Elusive Mr. Velucci

battle of personal restraint, because had they been alone, he would not have behaved himself in a very gentlemanly way; he craved her in every way possible.

A dejected stare burned from his eyes to hers, and they both knew that they would be crying from frustration before the night was over. They had so much to talk about and so much to make up for, and they both knew that nothing was going to happen tonight.

"Bye!" Angelo shouted to the girls in the room. That was Enrico's cue to leave.

"Bye!" Sadie called. Her heart was breaking and her mind was beginning to pout. 'I haven't seen Enrico in a very long time, and now I can't even talk with him!' Because Sadie could feel the tears eager to run down her cheeks, she rushed to her room before the men had gotten into Angelo's vehicle.

As she waved good-bye, Sophie realized that she was suddenly all alone. She was concerned about her mother, but decided to leave her unaccompanied until the morning.

They had adjoining rooms, and once Enrico got settled in his hotel room, he sat down on the edge of his bed. His eyes were scanning the carpet while his mind was swimming with all that had happened over the last few hours.

It was a rare occasion that the famous conductor had travelled without having it be for work, and now he was very glad that he had made the trip to America. Seeing Angelo in his New York environment was one thing, and meeting Sophie, his future daughter-in-law, was something which he had looked forward to for the last few months. But seeing Sadie again after all these years, was the finest privilege that anyone could have ever given him.

Angelo called Sophie the minute he was in his own room, and together they talked about everything that had transpired. They threw suggestions back and forth about what had happened, but they couldn't come up with a cohesive opinion. An hour later, they said good-night, and were no closer to the actual facts of what had taken place between their parents, than where they were before.

Enrico was still in shock that he had seen Sadie again, and now he was quite sad that they hadn't been able to talk. He ran over the details of their visit for a few long minutes, and then got himself ready for bed. The lights were off, the blankets were up to his chin, and he was all set to go to sleep. But as much as he tried, he couldn't calm his mind; all he could think about was Sadie and how awkward things had been between them. He wished that the events of the evening had been different, and that they had been there by themselves, but it didn't happen that way.

Sadie was emotionally suffering during that same hour, and had cried because Enrico had been in her home and she couldn't reach out and touch him. As she tried to go to sleep, her mind wouldn't shut down; it kept playing their visit over and over again.

Enrico had tossed and turned in the lumpy hotel bed, until almost 3am. He had so much to say to Sadie, but because he didn't get the chance, it left him genuinely wounded.

The only thing that they had been able to hold onto, was the knowledge that they would get to see each other again, at lunch the next day. They made sure to set their alarm clocks, and then began the merciful expectation of the loud ring.

The Elusive Mr. Velucci

They both bounded out of bed at 8am, as if they were late for an important meeting, and each took a lengthy shower.

While Enrico was getting himself ready for their luncheon, his thoughts were on Sadie and her beautiful daughter. He was consumed by the fact that nobody had said anything about the man of the house, and he decided that he would make a point to ask about that, when he saw them later.

Sadie made sure to look much more presentable than she had been the night before, and she hoped that Enrico would notice. She sprayed her favorite perfume on her neck and tummy, and she kept her hair down and loose – his favorite style. She felt as off-balance as a teenage girl who was about to go on her first date, and she hoped that Sophie wouldn't notice.

They all arrived at 12 noon, and sat down at a large table in the middle of the room.

Much to his disappointment, Enrico was seated on the opposite end of the large 4-seater, square table from Sadie.

Because of how Enrico and Sadie had acted the night before, Sophie and Angelo had decided to keep their parents apart. It wasn't meant to cause unhappiness, but done to relieve the tension.

Enrico was totally unsatisfied with this arrangement. He wished that he had the courage to ask if they could all switch seats, but he didn't want to cause trouble. Instead, he threw as many glances towards Sadie as was possible, without making it look too obvious.

Sadie was surprised by the seating arrangement; she would have liked to sit closer to Enrico, for that would have given them a chance to talk and get reacquainted. As it was, he was sitting crossways on her left, and she had to cough or drop a napkin on the floor, in order to conceal a momentary peek or two in his direction. Whenever Enrico caused a commotion in hopes of catching her eye, Sadie tilted her head to the side. She used the pretense that she was looking at Sophie, when all along she was stealing a quick look at Enrico.

By the time desert was served, Sadie and Enrico had become frustrated by the absurd situation. Their time together was almost done and they hadn't been able to have any kind of conversation at all.

"Here's your bill", the waitress announced happily. She laid it on the table in front of Enrico and walked away.

"Wait!" Sadie shouted, in Enrico's direction. It was a loud and bold announcement, and it had everyone around them looking at her in shock. "Let me help you pay!" It was a brilliant idea, and she was already searching for her wallet when her daughter spoke up.

"No, mom, what are you doing?" Sophie scolded under her breath. "The men are paying for us today. Leave it alone."

Her daughter's voice was firm and her eyes were cold, so Sadie sighed and had no choice but to back down. She lowered her head as if she had just been reprimanded, and somehow Enrico could feel what was going on in her heart.

"We'll be right back", he declared lovingly. He was smiling as he released an appreciative sigh, and had a strong desire to move closer. Angelo broke the awkward sentiments by tapping his dad on the shoulder. Enrico turned and walked away, but he hoped that he had left a warm impression on Sadie's heart.

The Elusive Mr. Velucci

When Sophie excused herself and went to the restroom, Sadie took that opportunity to observe Enrico and Angelo at the cash register. Her heart sank when she saw them talking and sharing a joke, and she wondered when it would be her turn to speak with Enrico … one-on-one.

The men came back to the table at the same time as Sophie, and they escorted the women out to their car.

Everyone was saying good-bye, but Sadie didn't want Enrico to leave. Her body was rocking from foot-to-foot and her hands were beginning to tremble. He was within her reach, but she couldn't touch him. She wanted to scream his name and tell him that she had missed him, but she couldn't. She wanted to hug him and kiss him until they were too tired to stand up, but that also couldn't happen.

Enrico had his eyes locked with hers and he could feel her pain. It was like a knife slicing through his skin, leaving an open wound that doesn't heal over time. A scar will eventually appear and it will carry on the memory of what had happened, but also of what might never happen again.

Sadie swallowed hard as her face went pale, while a salty tear trickled down her cheek. A flash of wild grief ripped through her body, from the notion that she'd never see him again. It was something which she knew she could never bear again.

Enrico needed to prolong their visit, so he asked if the ladies would like to spend the afternoon with them. He was shocked when Angelo opposed the idea.

"I have already made plans to do something with you, Papa", he said happily. "I'm sure you'll like what I have in mind." At least that was Angelo's hope.

Enrico wanted to spend some more time with Sadie, and

he had a strong feeling that she would have loved that, too. There was no measurement for the amount of affection that he had towards her, and he would have accepted as short as one or two minutes to show her how he felt.

Her lips were silent, but her heart was fluttering passionately under her breasts. She could feel her breathing accelerate, but she couldn't let anyone know what was happening; they've built a tapestry of lies, and the pull of one single thread could unravel the clues as to how they know each other. For now, this secret had to remain hidden. But how long can she last, when all she wanted to do was wrap her body around his? He was only a foot or two away from her. She could easily reach out, grab him by the lapels, and force her lips onto his.

While Sadie's eyes burned into his soul, Enrico suddenly felt the same urgings as he had had so long ago. His mind began to list all the things that he would say and do to her if they were alone, and soon his lower region was aching for the fulfillment of making love to her.

The strange silence and uneasiness from the night before, began to seep into this long and awkward moment. Sophie didn't want it to continue, so she made a harsh decision to end their time together. "Okay, well, good-bye everyone!" she called loudly, to both Enrico and his son. She then turned to face Angelo and mouthed, "Call me later."

"Bye, Sadie!" Angelo stated. He raised his hand in the air and waved in her direction. "See you soon."

While Sadie looked at him, she thought his ability to force a smile was truly remarkable.

Enrico had taken a step toward Sadie. He was staring into her face as they stood toe-to-toe, just less than one foot

The Elusive Mr. Velucci

apart from each other. He wished that he could stay and talk, but he uttered a quiet 'good-bye' instead. His heart broke into a thousand pieces as his son dragged him away.

"Come on, dad." Angelo had placed his hand into his father's elbow, and was leading him towards the car.

Sadie also wanted to linger in Enrico's company for a while longer, but with everyone else leaving, she had no choice but to get into her daughter's car.

Sadie's mind was juggling information way too fast for her to understand. In the space of five minutes, they were this close, and now they were driving away in opposite directions. She hadn't seen him in over twenty years, and then he was standing in her apartment, but they couldn't speak or touch. On another note, her daughter was about to marry his son – was that even legal? She needed to tell someone what was going on, but who?

As Sadie pulled the seat belt across her chest, she was clenching her jaw and trying not to cry. She wore a blank stare in her eyes, and her fingers were folded together while her thumbs took turns rubbing the soft flesh on the opposite hand.

"Mom?" Sophie called, after the motor had turned over.

Sadie stayed quiet as she watched Angelo's car drive away.

"You seemed distracted over lunch. Is everything ok?"

Sadie nodded, and then turned her head to look out the side window. She desperately wanted to cry, but held it in until they got home. Once the car was in her driveway, she ran into the house, went straight to her bedroom, and threw herself onto the bed.

Sophie was speechless as she wondered what was going on, but even though she was confused by the events that had happened over the past two days, she knew enough not to ask; she understood that they would talk eventually. She just needed to wait until her mother was ready.

Enrico was also very quiet on the drive away from the restaurant. "Are you ok, dad?" Angelo asked. He had hoped that this visit would be more jovial than it had been so far, and he was now becoming concerned by his father's odd states of mind; he was usually so bubbly, friendly, and a joy to be around. Angelo was quick to recall, that since they met Sadie, his father had seemed distant and disheartened.

Enrico turned to his son and nodded. "I'm ok. Just tired." He spoke in an abnormal but gentle tone, and hoped that there would be no more questions.

Angelo wanted to chalk his father's mysterious mood up to jet lag, but how did he want to explain this thing that kept happening between Enrico and Sadie? The staring into each other's eyes and not talking, was weird. The way that Enrico studied every detail of Sophie's mother was almost haunting, but in a curious manner. And on the other hand, there was a sparkle in his eyes that only appeared when Sadie was in the room. It was baffling on every level, but why? Angelo drove to the hotel while pondering these and many other thoughts, while his dad stayed quiet.

Hours later, Sadie emerged from her room, exactly how Sophie had predicted.

"Are you ok?" Sophie asked for the fourth time that day. She was sincerely concerned, because her mom's moods kept swinging from happy to distracted within seconds, and without warning.

Sadie nodded without looking in her daughter's direction. She was frowning, her head was bent forward,

The Elusive Mr. Velucci

and she appeared to stumble as if she had lost track of what she should be doing.

"Well, I hope you feel better soon, mom." Sophie walked across the room to embrace the person who she loved the most in the entire world. "If you want, we can cancel dinner tonight with Angelo and his dad, and we can do something all by ourselves."

Upon hearing that she would get another chance to be in Enrico's company, every pore in Sadie's body came to life. She spun around in a reckless fashion as she called out, "No, no! We can go! What time are we meeting them?" She was a little loud and appeared overly-excited, and it was quite clear that she could have been ready to leave in the next five minutes.

Sophie's eyes shot wide open from the tremendous change in her mother's mood, and it caused her to chuckle. "We don't have to meet them for another hour", she stated lightly. She was puzzled by her mother's fluctuating frame of mind, and now waited to hear her mother's response.

Sadie's insides were revved up with enthusiasm, but she couldn't tell her daughter why. "Maybe we can get there a little early, just in case", she urged. The words had flown out of her mouth with a great deal of intensity, and she suddenly felt very light.

A smirk fell across Sophie's confused face, but she agreed. They arrived ten minutes before the men did, and this time, they sat as couples – Enrico made sure of it. He purposely sat down in the chair directly across from Sadie's, while not paying any attention to where his son or future daughter-in-law sat.

Because Sophie and Angelo had noticed how unusual

their parents had acted in Sadie's home when they first met, and then again when they were having lunch that very afternoon, the young couple decided to keep a close eye on them during dinner. They worked like a tag-team and tried to dominate every conversation. They answered for their parent when Enrico or Sadie posed a question, and they even went to the bathroom in genders.

All Enrico and Sadie had left, was looking into each other's eyes and speaking by mental telepathy. While they were able to communicate just fine by this method, it was most often interrupted by one of their children.

"Dad, you should tell Sophie about the time we…."

"Mom, look at how Angelo drinks his tea; isn't it precious?"

"Oh, dad. I forgot to tell you about…"

"Enrico, can you please tell me what Angelo was like as a child?"

It didn't take long before Enrico and Sadie melted into a silent displeasure, for it was clear that they would not get a chance to talk to each other tonight, either.

Twenty minutes after they had arrived, Enrico tried to pass a note to Sadie, but it was intercepted by the waiter and accidently dropped onto the floor. The young man picked it up, and thinking that it was garbage, he threw it onto a plate which he had taken from another table, and brought into the kitchen for disposal.

Another time, Sadie dropped a utensil on the floor by her own foot, hoping that Enrico would pick it up for her. But faster than a speeding bullet, Angelo got up from his chair and rushed to her rescue. "Here you go", he said

The Elusive Mr. Velucci

sweetly. He was on bended knee and had lingered there while handing it up to her.

His goofy smile caused Sadie to believe that he assumed that he had just done a good deed. Sadly, a cheerful 'Thank you' was all he got in return. When he left, her eyes darted to Enrico's face, as she sucked her lower lip into her mouth from embarrassment.

There was an intense physical awareness of being so close and not being able to touch, and it was pulling Enrico towards a mild panic attack. He needed to touch her, to kiss her, and to feel her warm breath against his neck. Sadness clouded his features, as he realized that he might never get to tell her everything that she had the right to hear.

More time passed and Enrico was becoming desperate. Before they left the restaurant, he knew he needed to devise a way for him and Sadie to have some time alone … but what could he do?

Sadie watched him eat, paying particular attention to how his lips were curving around each forkful of food. She realized that it was silly, but she suddenly felt jealous of the items which he was eating; they got to be in his mouth, and spent a little time dancing with his skilled tongue. She cast her eyes downward and smiled.

Enrico saw her smile and an idea popped into his head. "You have a lovely city", he blurted out for no reason at all.

Sophie and Sadie nodded while exchanging glances.

"And I really like the place that we're staying in", Enrico announced nonchalantly. "The Carlton Hotel, right son?" He spoke clearly and added emphasis to what was important, and now waited to see if Sadie had picked up on what he was trying to do.

'Did he just give me a way to get hold of him?' she wondered. Passion was beginning to radiate from the soft core of Sadie's body, and it made her insides tremble with emotional fire. And while she would have loved to live in that feeling for a little while longer, Angelo's voice destroyed the vision in her mind.

"Oh, dad", the younger man interrupted. "I moved us to another hotel as a surprise to you."

The shocked look on Enrico's face let the world know exactly how he felt about that gesture. "Why would you do that?" he stated with a bit of resentment in his voice. He was too stunned to say more.

"Because the new one has a pool, and its closer to the Met and other places which I know you love to go to when you're in town." Angelo had only the best of intentions, and spoke with love and kindness.

Enrico didn't want to disappoint his son, so he calmed his anger and thanked him for always being so considerate. As he exhaled in sadness, his eyes locked with the woman who he was in love with. The older man only wanted to be with Sadie, but he had to keep that information to himself.

The dinner ended, and everyone went their own ways. All the days that followed, happened in pretty much in the same manner. In the entire week that Enrico was in New York, Sadie never got to spend one minute with him, that didn't include either Sophie or Angelo.

When it was time for him to go to the airport, Sadie shouted that she'd like to go, too. "I don't mind!" she begged loudly. She couldn't bear the thought of Enrico leaving without sharing a hug or a kiss with him. But as quickly as her hopes had risen, the idea had been rejected.

The Elusive Mr. Velucci

"No, Sadie", Angelo said politely. "That's too much of a bother for you. Let us take him and you stay here and rest." It was more of a command than a suggestion.

When Sadie heard the word, 'rest', her lower jaw dropped towards her chest. She suddenly felt like a ninety-nine year old woman who wasn't supposed to be outside or on her feet too much. Sadie stared hurtfully into each person's eyes, and while she knew that she wasn't blinking, she tried not to become unpleasant. She was furious though, with this young guy who she's only known for one week.

Enrico saw what had happened and he could see how it had made Sadie feel, so he tried to give his permission for her to come. "I would love to have your company, Sadie." He then held out his hand for her to take.

Sadie's heart soared from the considerate gesture. She reached out to lay her hand into his open palm, but before their skin had touched, Angelo insisted that Sadie might have other things to do.

"Oh?" Enrico's eyes widened with surprise as he looked back and forth between Sadie and Angelo.

"I actually don't", Sadie whispered sadly to herself. And before Sadie could further argue her point to Angelo, she remembered that she couldn't protest too loudly, without anyone knowing the reason why she wanted to stay close to Enrico. With sorrow filling every pore in her body, she pulled her hand away from Enrico's. She then lowered her eyes and her chin, and stood silent.

Enrico was dismayed by the fact that Sadie was not going to join them, and hoped that his son would tell him why, later. For now, he winked in Sadie's direction and wished her well. "Until we meet again", he said, in a suffocated whisper.

Tina Griffith

His heart had just been shattered into a million pieces, and even though he wanted to fight all the armies in the world in order to keep her in his sight, he knew that there was nothing he could do to change things.

They looked into each other's face, and it was as if they had made a silent pact to keep their past a secret. But at what expense? They had already lost a lifetime to be together, and what if they don't get to see each other again?

Sadie could see tears welling in his eyes, and Enrico could see that she was also fighting back the tears.

Sophie hugged her mom and spoke softly into her ear. "Angelo wants to take his father to the airport with just me, so that his dad gets to know the girl who's about to marry his son."

Sadie understood what her daughter was saying, but nobody was hearing what she was saying; she felt that this was her last chance to be in Enrico's company. She *needed* to be alone with him, even for two minutes.

Sadie caught Enrico's eyes and they spoke in mental thoughts without anyone hearing. A part of their souls were dying, but their children didn't know. She could sense the barely controlled passion that was spiraling in his body, and she hoped that he could detect that she felt the exact same way. Neither one wanted to walk away from the other, but they both knew that they had no other choice.

With a strong rush of anxiety now ruling all of her thinking, a brilliant notion popped into Sadie's head. She stood tall, clapped her hands together real loud, and in a strong voice she said, "Listen, everyone! I actually do have something that I have to do!" She turned and looked into Enrico face, and when she forced a wink with both eyes at

The Elusive Mr. Velucci

the same time, she hoped that he would understand the meaning.

Enrico smiled and winked back, but with only one eye. He remembered her younger self, her bubbly personality and free spirit, and he knew that she had something up her sleeve.

Sadie suddenly appeared to be much happier as she said good-bye to everyone. And as soon as they were out of sight, she hoped into her car and drove to the airport behind them. She made sure to maintain a great distance between their car and hers, and even parked several stalls away. Her eyes were fixed on them as they walked into the airport terminal, and she made sure to stay out of sight when she snuck in afterwards.

Sadie was pretty clever, and was able to go unseen by ducking behind anything she could find. She watched them like an eagle, and followed the trio until she caught Enrico's eyes.

When he saw her, Enrico's heart leaped into his throat. His first reaction was to shout her name, and then he realized that she was trying to meet with him in secret.

Sadie was wearing sunglasses and a large scarf to avoid being recognized, and she was waving for him to come over.

"I'll be right back", he announced, and then he was gone.

"We'll wait right here for you, papa!" Angelo called. He was confused and wondered where his father was going, but loved that he had a little extra time to say good-bye to Sophie.

Enrico walked straight over to where Sadie was hiding, behind the corner of the wall. Luckily, it was next to the men's bathroom and blocked by a large rubber tree plant, so Sophie and Angelo couldn't see what was happening. As Enrico got closer, his smile widened in approval, for he now had the highest regard for Sadie's intelligence; not only had she found a way for them to be together from the prying eyes and ears of their children, but they were able to talk and act freely from everyone within ear shot.

Sadie's face was beaming with joy when she saw him walking towards her. She smiled because his pace was hurried, and she couldn't wait to have him in her arms. Anticipation suddenly climbed up and into her throat; there was so much to say and so much time to make up for, but for now, she just wanted to hug him.

Enrico was smiling and almost out of breath, as he rushed avidly into her arms. He embraced her like he would never see her again, and now he never wanted to let her go. "God, I've missed you", he stated, as their lips met for the first time in over two decades.

He moved his mouth over hers, devouring its softness and moisture, and this time it was him who was forcing her lips open with his thrusting tongue.

She stood on tiptoe, with her arms wrapped tightly around his neck. Her lips were pressed firmly against his, with a hunger that came from not seeing him for such a long time.

As he roused her passion, his own grew stronger. Their senses twirled as if their passion had short-circuited their brains, and now they had to fight to not go beyond kissing.

"I'm so mad at you for leaving, but I'm so happy that you're here and in my arms", she cried happily. She couldn't

The Elusive Mr. Velucci

stop looking at his face or touching all the parts of his body; she wanted to memorize every single detail for later.

"I know, and I'm sorry for everything", he acknowledged. He slowly moved his hands downward, skimming either side of her body - from where her bra sat, to the middle of her thighs.

She inhaled sharply as his hands came back up and then pressed into the muscles on her back, pulling their bodies even closer together.

Realizing that their time was almost up, apologies flew out of their mouths with great speed, followed by how much the two of them still loved each other.

They were both trembling with the fear of him leaving, but the warmth of their groins against each other, gave them hope that this would not be the last time that they would be together.

"Dad?" Angelo called. He had watched his father head towards the bathroom, but now he had been gone for a little longer than was expected.

Sadie forced a smile and gave a tense nod of consent. "You should go", she stated sadly.

"I'm coming!" he called into the air. Enrico smothered Sadie's face with his lips, and hugged her body tightly against his own. He then professed how much he loved her, to make sure that she would never doubt it again. After he cupped her face with his hands, he memorized all that he saw.

Sadie didn't want to let him go, for he was the love of her life. She had waited for this moment for over twenty years, and hated that he would be leaving her again. Because she had been prepared, she handed him a piece of paper with her phone number on it. "Please come back, or at least call

Tina Griffith

me!" she begged. She raised her chin and presented him with all the dignity that she could gather, but inside, she was trembling; she wanted to hold onto him and never let him go.

"I promise", he swore, as he tucked her number into his coat's front pocket. "I have to go", he said tearfully, and then he walked away.

Enrico wished that he could have stayed in America a little longer, but surgery had been booked many months ago, and it was confirmed the day before he flew to New York - he couldn't put it off.

Sadie wanted to die when Enrico walked away. 'How could it be fair to see him, not see him, and then see him again, only to have him walk away from me?' she wondered sadly. Tears rained down her cheeks, while she stayed hidden until the three of them were out of sight. Once the coast was clear, Sadie ran outside and got into her car.

Because she had classes in the morning, Sophie arrived back at school two hours after the plane had lifted off the ground. Angelo flew to Italy with his father, while Sadie went home to wait for Enrico to call.

As Enrico was on his way back to Italy, he lifted his right hand to his mouth. He caressed his lips with his index and middle finger while looking out the window, and tried to retain every detail of their three or four minute rendezvous.

Many minutes later, Enrico fixated on other things that had happened over the past week, but one stuck out more than any other. When he left Italy to go to America, it was with the intention of being with his son, and meeting his future daughter-in-law and her parents. It totally blew his mind that Sadie was the mom of Angelo's girlfriend, and

The Elusive Mr. Velucci

because there was never any talk of a dad or husband, he wondered where Sophie's father was.

Sadie had settled into her pajamas and got cozy under the covers of her bed. She had her phone sitting right beside her, and had even turned up the volume on the ringer. As she looked at the time on her alarm clock, she calculated how many more hours it would take for Enrico to land in Italy. Knowing that she still had a little while, she turned on the TV and tried to relax.

The plane moved with great ease through the fluffy clouds, high above the ocean below, and it allowed Enrico's subconscious thoughts to come to the surface. One barely crossed his mind before another one followed closely behind it, but he soon settled on how much of his visit had been unexpected; seeing Sadie, being with his son in New York, and meeting Sophie were clearly the highlights of his short but wonderful vacation. And, he was quite grateful to his son for all the little tours which they had taken on their own. He was not happy that he had had so little time to spend with Sadie, though.

'Sadie' The word repeated itself in his mind. He was suddenly aware of the dull ache at the memory of the younger version of Sophie's mother, but he had to agree that the older version was just as lovely – if not more. Her beautiful grown-up face fascinated him, whether it was smiling, serious, or thoughtful. His attention suddenly filtered back to the day when they met, and it caused him to lower his face towards his lap. 'We were so very young, then', he reflected consciously. The tender memories of their last night together, travelled through his mind as vivid as could be. And being reminded of every detail of all that they had done, kept him aroused for the next few hours.

After the plane had landed in Italy, Angelo said that he had something that he needed to do, so they said goodbye. Enrico took a taxi and rushed to the solitude of his moderately-sized, brick and mortar home.

He raced inside, slamming the door behind him, and ripped his clothing off as he raced upstairs to his bedroom. He flopped on the bed and began to relieve himself, from the passion which had been built up during his flight. He was soon hurtled to the point of no return, and shuddered from an ecstasy that presented him with fireworks and bursting sensations. A moment later, he sighed with pleasant exhaustion, and slept for the next 5 hours.

The next day he got up, and after breakfast, he put on his Sunday best clothing. An hour later, he was driving towards the cemetery to visit with Maria. He didn't know if it was out of guilt or not, but it felt like he had somehow cheated on her.

The well-groomed, well-dressed man, stood at her gravesite with a beautiful bouquet of colorful flowers in his hands. He knew that the petals were shaking as he read her full name on the headstone, but he couldn't help being there. He took a deep breath, and that's when he noticed that his heart was beating faster than normal, and he could feel that the act of sobbing was not too far off in the distance.

Enrico had a lot to tell Maria since last month, and he began with the moment when he recognized Sophie's mother. "I haven't seen her in twenty years or more, and had no idea what I was walking into when Angelo drove me to meet his fiancé", he confessed. His voice was cracking from

The Elusive Mr. Velucci

the bewilderment of the past week. He could feel the tears forming but not one had escaped, and now his knees were starting to give out.

He felt weak – mentally and emotionally - and allowed his body to drop to the ground. Before he knew what was happening, he was sitting on the back of his heels.

"Maria", he continued softly. He bent his head in sorrow as he spoke. "I loved you very much, always know that. I thank you for making a large portion of my adult life, absolutely wonderful. You and Angelo gave me completion after my parents died, and I don't know what I would have done without you."

Enrico's chest was tightening and the tears were now flowing like a fountain. It almost felt like he was in a confessional booth - safe to say anything that was on his mind - and the words began to pour from a deep part of his soul. "And now with Angelo about to marry Sophie, Sadie will be a permanent fixture in all of our lives. I just hope you are ok with this."

And as if it was possible for the sun to get any brighter or warmer, it did. The heavens opened up and it felt like a blessing was being bestowed upon the grieving man; an understanding and a right to be happy came over him, all at the same time. That was quite powerful on its own, and then it felt like Maria was standing close by. Shivers shot up his spine, goose bumps popped up on his arms, and then an enormous amount of clarity simplified the entire matter.

'Everything happens for a reason', echoed inside of his brain.

Enrico stared down at the magnificently carved headstone, and a chill encased his entire body from head to toe. The whole thing suddenly made sense to him – like it was meant to be. Maria and Angelo had to be in his life, or he would never have been reunited with Sadie.

A groundskeeper was busy working not too far away, and watched with great interest, as a grieving man lowered his head, in slow motion towards the grass. And when his forehead was completely on the ground, his body went into spasms while crying a thousand tears.

The stranger had seen that kind of scenario many times before today, so he walked away and carried on with his work.

Enrico had many things to be thankful for, and after he said good-bye to Maria, he felt much stronger. He beamed from within as he walked to his car, for he suddenly realized how his future was going to play out. He now had no fear about the surgery, and he made himself a promise that after he had fully recovered, that he would count down the days until he could see Sadie again.

Enrico didn't know what their relationship would be, because there were too many factors involved, but at least he knew that he wouldn't lose touch with her again.

Enrico went to bed an hour after Angelo got home, and they talked for a few minutes before going to sleep. Very early the next morning, Enrico was in the operating room with a stronger determination to live.

It was not made public on purpose, but Enrico needed to have a tumor removed from the base of the hairline, on the back of his neck. The growth was in a tough spot, connected to some bone tissue in the spinal column, but the experienced doctors were hopeful that they would be able to clean the area up and leave him cancer-free.

The Elusive Mr. Velucci

Angelo was in the waiting room throughout the many hours while Enrico was having surgery. As he watched the time tick by, he had a feeling that something was wrong; this was taking much longer than they told him it would. When a doctor, who is also a family friend, finally came out to tell Angelo how the surgery went, there was something unnerving written all over his face.

Angelo jumped to a standing position and prepared for the worse, for he had a sneaky suspicion that things were about to move too quickly for him to process.

The conversation was held in Italian, and it had now been confirmed that there had been complications.

"He suffered a stroke, Angelo", Dr. Marco Lucia stated sadly. "Not a big one, but he lost his memory and his ability to speak, and that's enough to cause us to worry."

A large gasp escaped from the younger man's mouth, while a look of complete shock covered his face. "Oh my God!" he cried softly. Both hands flew up and landed flat against his chest, as if to protect him from the fear of the moment. In the next instant, Angelo's chin dropped as if he was imaging more bad news. His knees suddenly gave out, and he found himself sliding downward, only to land on the couch behind him.

The doctor sat beside the handsome younger man, and placed his hand firmly on Angelo's shoulder. "With proper care, your father is going to be ok. He will need lots of rest, and we'll put him on medication to help with the pain."

Angelo was relieved, and suddenly felt so alone. He was full-out crying and sniffled loudly, and he didn't care who saw or heard.

"I have to go and check on him", the doctor stated

kindly. He knew all too well how this kind of news could touch a person's soul, so he took the professional aspect out of his voice and behavior, and spoke to Angelo as someone who he has known for almost fifteen years, rather than as a doctor. "Give us an hour or so. We'll get him out of the recovery room and put him into his own private hospital room, and then I'll come back to get you."

Angelo nodded, and then stood up and gave the doctor a quick hug. "Grazie, Marco."

"You're welcome, but your father is far from being out of the woods."

The doctor's feet took him down the hall, at the same time as some friends of Enrico's came to see how Angelo and his father were doing.

After the hellos and the sincere offerings of condolences for his father's health were addressed, Angelo told them what the doctor had just said. They sympathized with him immediately, and led him to the chapel where they all prayed for a speedy recovery.

Before the small group left the hospital, the man who was responsible for booking all of Enrico's events, informed Angelo that he would take his father off of everything pertaining to work, until he was feeling better.

"Grazie, Santos." That was one thing that Angelo would no longer have to worry about.

Meanwhile, Sadie had been sitting in her bed in New York, wondering what was going on with Enrico. She had given him her phone number and thought he would call her once he had gotten home, but he never did. Because she didn't want to appear too anxious, she decided to give Enrico the benefit of the doubt, that his son was probably

The Elusive Mr. Velucci

beside him and it would be awkward to make a call without Angelo hearing. On the other hand, surely there would have been a minute or two that he could have snuck away to call her.

Sadie's moods were flying back and forth very quickly, and all she truly wanted, was to hear from Enrico. Her heart was breaking because she was missing him much more than she thought she would. Putting aside the fact that they have a history and a child together, they had just seen each other after a twenty year absence. Their reunion stirred up a lot of old feelings, and brought hope and new joys to her life.

Because he was not reaching out to her, Sadie was scared that seeing Enrico again, was all that she was going to get. That revelation made her anxiety go through the roof, and she suddenly had to fight her overwhelming need to be close to him. She closed her eyes and tried to relax, but all she could think of was him.

Without even trying, she could visualize all the features on his handsome face, as clear as day. It was only an image in her head, but it made her heart pound and her pulse race. She kept her eyes closed and imagined her body being crushed within his embrace. And even though this wasn't real, her senses were responding with smug enthusiasm. Her body suddenly leapt with a sting of excitement, while a delicious tingling heated her lower extremities. She reached a hand down and allowed her fingers to explore the warmth between her legs. A few moments later, she gasped in total delight, as intense pleasure flowed through her like warm honey.

Sadie was now completely satisfied, and so tired, that her nerves were throbbing. After returning from the bathroom,

Tina Griffith

she climbed back into bed. She grabbed the blankets and pulled them high enough to cover her shoulders, and then she slept for the rest of the night.

The doctor came to get Angelo about an hour after he had seen him, and brought him to his father's room.

It was mind boggling for Angelo to see his father laying in the twin-size hospital bed; besides the tubes which were going in and out of his frail and lifeless body, Enrico seemed a lot smaller than usual. Angelo had always looked upon the older man as tall, strong, and commanding. Seeing him like this, was kind of chilling.

Angelo held his breath and walked closer to the bed. He reached for Enrico's hand, and stood there without saying a word. There were many seconds where he would do nothing but study his father's face, and there were other flashes of time where he would try to decipher the readings on the loud machines in the room. He could feel himself growing angry and impatient because there was no logic for this situation, but he had no other recourse than to keep quiet.

As the hours ticked away, Angelo couldn't help but listen to the steady stream of each breath going in and out of his father's body. It was terrifying and he felt helpless, but he couldn't bear to leave.

Before midnight, a nurse came into the room to check Enrico's vitals. She was there for almost ten minutes, and before she left, she slid a chair over to Angelo, so he could sit down.

"Grazie", he muttered softly under his breath. As his body hit the hard plastic of the chair, he hadn't realized until that second, how weary his muscles had been.

The nurse could see how hard this was for the young

The Elusive Mr. Velucci

man, and asked if she could bring him a hot drink or something to eat.

At first, Angelo shook his head and said no. But when she assured him that it would be no problem, he relented and said yes. "Grazie."

The doctor came into the room first thing the next morning, and found Angelo sleeping with his head on the mattress, next to his father's hand. He shook him gently, and then told him that he needed to examine Enrico without anyone but a nurse in the room. "I won't be long, so give me about 20 minutes."

Angelo took that time to wash up, grab a coffee, and call Sophie. He felt much better after that little break, and couldn't wait to go back to sit with his father.

The doctor was still there when Angelo returned, and he had just finished writing down his findings. "Enrico is doing better, but we'd like to keep him in the hospital for another three weeks." Because Angelo's eyebrows had raised high on his forehead, the doctor smiled and added, "Two weeks is customary, I know, but we just want to make sure that he is well enough to go home."

Angelo was thankful for the good quality of care. The next day, he called his professor and explained the situation.

"I'm sorry for what you and your father are going through", the Dean stated sincerely. "And we can help you, but there are rules to which you would have to adhere to", he instructed.

Angelo raised his right hand as if it could be seen from across the ocean, and swore to abide by all the guidelines.

"Alright then, I'll see what I can do."

After thanking Dean Walters for understanding his

unusual circumstances, arrangements were made for Angelo to take some of his classes as a correspondence course. The large package of books arrived 5 days later, and Angelo did his best to keep up with his studies.

Sadie hadn't left the house in days, and kept checking to see if the phone was even working; it didn't ring except for when Sophie called, and even though Sadie had call waiting, she rushed her daughter off the phone with no remorse or explanation.

A week had gone by since the plane had taken Enrico and Angelo to Italy, and Sadie had fallen into a deep depression. Enrico still hadn't called, and this will be the second time that he had left her and didn't try to contact her. It was mentally and emotionally so hard on her, and she wasn't sure that she could go through all of that again.

By the beginning of the second week, she gathered up all of her courage and forced herself to go about her normal routine. Shopping for groceries was the first item on her list of things-to-do, and then she wanted to get her hair and nails done. As she walked out the door, she pushed away her uncertain thoughts and carried out her wishes.

Sadly, every minute of that outing had been quite daunting for her, because she feared that Enrico would call and not leave a message. It was a very heavy burden for her to carry, so she chose to never leave the house again, for anything more than an hour at a time.

The days flew by and turned into weeks, and when there still wasn't any word from Enrico, Sadie fell into an even deeper depression.

When Enrico was finally able to go home, an elderly

The Elusive Mr. Velucci

Italian nurse's aide, which the doctor had recommended, was there to fuss over him.

"There will be no interruptions to his convalescing", Dr. Lucia stated firmly in Italian. "Or his recovery could take a lot longer than we anticipate."

Rosalia, the nurse's aide, agreed by bowing her head while pledging to follow the doctor's rules.

Angelo solemnly agreed as well, and promised that nobody but him and the nurse would get near his father.

"Good. I'll stop by the house every two days, to see how he's doing."

"Thank you, Marco." Angelo turned and asked the nurse to walk the doctor out, while he stayed in the makeshift hospital room. He was grateful that his father was doing much better, and remained close to him while he recuperated.

Over the next fourteen days, Angelo and the nurse's aide, made sure not to disturb Enrico's rest with any outside nonsense. The phone and TV had been taken out of the room on day one, Angelo opened the mail and was taking care of what needed tending to right away, and all the rest was left for when Enrico was well enough to do it himself.

Sadie had no idea that Enrico needed to have surgery, so she was in absolute disbelief of why he had not called her. They had had a lovely few moments in the airport terminal, and he promised to keep in touch with her. Sadie lowered her head and groaned softly. She kicked an invisible stone with her foot and whispered, "Enrico may not be a poetic man, but he made me believe that he still loved me." She was suddenly overwhelmed by sadness, and collapsed in a crying heap on the floor.

Tina Griffith

Six weeks after Enrico had flown back to Italy, Sadie was still waiting for a call from him.

Sophie called her mom, as she did every single night, and they talked about school and wedding plans. She then asked her mom how things were going for her.

"Ok", Sadie replied quickly, and then she changed the subject. "Is Angelo back in the states again?"

The question was odd and straight out of left field, and Sophie was now confused. "No, mom", she answered. "He's still in Italy spending time with his father."

Complete surprise was etched all over Sadie's face, as she decided to probe a little further. "Doesn't Angelo have classes to go to?" she asked. She then pressed the receiver a little closer to her ear in order to hear the answer with absolute clarity. Sadie was a bit taken back that her daughter's voice and temperament were a little curt.

"He's not on the same schedule as I am, mom. I actually think he's on a break, or has just taken a few weeks off to be with his dad. I just know that he'll be back soon."

Angelo had been instructed not to say anything to anyone, for fear that the news of Enrico's surgery would leak out to the media. And because Enrico had suffered a stroke an hour after the surgery had started, this presented complications towards his recovery.

If the media found out about any of this, they would have been at the hospital, or now, at Enrico's home, waiting for any word on his condition.

As hard as this was, Angelo understood that he had to hide certain things from Sophie, and he hoped that his fiancé would forgive him, once she found out why.

"Ok", Sadie stated, but her voice had trailed off; she

The Elusive Mr. Velucci

suddenly felt like she was on the defense. "Do you speak with him often?" she asked, as misery twisted and turned inside of her.

"He calls me almost every night, but we don't talk for too long; he likes to keep the costs of our phone bills down to a minimum." A dreamy look came over her face and she cocked her head to the side as she added, "And then there are those times when he simply can't hang up from me, no matter what." She giggled as only a woman in love does.

Sadie adored hearing that her daughter was happy, but her real interest right now, was Enrico. "And how is Angelo's father?" she asked bravely.

"I'm sure he's ok. Why did you ask?"

Sadie hadn't counted on being questioned, so she tried to buy some time by swallowing and looking around. "He's going to be your father-in-law, right? We're all going to be one big, happy family. Isn't that reason enough to want to know how he's doing?"

Sophie thought her mother's behavior was very odd, but she brushed it off without batting an eyelash. "I'm sure he's fine, mom."

"Well, that's good." It was all too vague for Sadie to grasp, and because this left her angry, hurt, and confused, she decided to give up; she certainly didn't want to pry any more than she had already done. Sadie hated that she would have to wait another day or week for Enrico to call, but what else could she do?

"I'm going to bed, mom. Talk tomorrow."

"Okay, honey. Love you."

"Love you, too."

In the meantime, Enrico had been drugged up with

heavy meds to keep the pain at bay. It also allowed his body to have a peaceful sleep. In those short minutes when he was conscious, he was helped as he walked up and down the hall, and back and forth to the bathroom.

This moved the blood to his muscles so they wouldn't freeze up, and sent serotonin to his brain so that he could stay in a good frame of mind.

Nobody knew, but the whole time when Enrico was up and semi-alert, he was thinking about Sadie and wondering how she was doing. He tried to ask the people around him, but they claimed that they didn't know. These same people had no idea that the quiet, unanswered questions, left him emotionally weak and sad; he had loved being with Sadie after all those years of complete silence, and he couldn't wait until the day when they could be in each other's company again.

In Enrico's fourth week at home, as he was being walked back to his bed, he felt an overwhelming pang of anxiety. "What day is today?" he asked, but there was no reply. It seemed like such a long time ago since he saw Sadie's face, and he couldn't imagine what she must think of him, given that he had not called her as he had promised.

"It's Wednesday", she replied. Rosalia tucked him under the covers and gave him his pills. As the drowsy effect of the drugs began to work, she watched as a tear slipped out from the corner of his left eye.

Enrico was scolding himself, for he had done this to Sadie before. It took him all of twenty years to see her and to be in her arms again, and now that he had been given a second chance, he couldn't see himself walking away from her.

The Elusive Mr. Velucci

The drugs were kicking in and his mind was beginning to swirl. Before sleep could take over, he whispered her name as if he wanted her to take a step closer to the bed. "Sadie..." A moment later, all thoughts and emotions were gone, and his limp body was able to relax.

Angelo looked into his father's face with worry. He kissed the older man's forehead, stroked many of the strands of hair on his head, and after a few more minutes of just looking, he left the room. He did some homework and called Sophie when he was done, and then waited for the doctor's next visit.

"He's doing much better, Angelo", Dr. Lucia stated proudly. "I think he will be on his feet in another week. Why don't you return to America; be with your fiancé, get your life back on track, and plan your wedding. Your father will be just fine, and you can call me anytime." The doctor tried to sound confident so that the young man wouldn't worry.

Angelo stood next to the bed and held his father's left hand between both of his own. He looked into the doctor's face and replied, "Maybe you're right."

"I know I am." Dr. Lucia smiled knowingly in Angelo's direction.

After they shook hands, Angelo booked a flight back to New York.

When Enrico was finally able to get out of bed for more than just a brief walk, everyone was so happy for him. Not surprisingly, the first thing he did was ask if he could use the phone.

"Sorry, sir", the nurse's aide replied sternly. The 52-year old, newly-widowed woman knew the rules, and

Tina Griffith

had become as feisty as a mother hen about keeping them. "The phone lines have been down since yesterday morning, but we've been told that they will be back up in no time", she lied.

This confused him, but Enrico shrugged his shoulders and moved on. "Did we get any mail?"

"Yes sir, but Angelo took care of everything that was important. He did leave this for you to look at." She handed him all the nonsignificant items.

Enrico was very surprised that there was nothing but trivial bits and pieces for him to see or open, and again, he shrugged it off.

Enrico walked around the house as if he hadn't seen it for a while, and after drinking in all its glorious splendor, he turned to Rosalia. "I have a camel colored, double-breasted coat that I wear when I am travelling. Can you bring it to me?"

Rosalia's eyes widened and she stuttered on her one syllable word. "Uh-mmm…" Her salt & pepper hair, which had been neatly combed into a bun at the back of her head, now felt somehow tighter. The appearance of shock, which began in her eyes, eventually covered her entire face. And her aging arms were now folded and pressed securely against her chest area. "I don't know where it is", she said, but she didn't sound very convincing.

"I'd like to have my coat", he ordered, in a voice that was as cold and as sharp as a scalpel. His eyes were forbidding and wide open, as he waited for her to retrieve what he had asked for.

The 5'0", thin woman had been warned to keep Enrico calm, and she had a feeling that he would be quite upset by

The Elusive Mr. Velucci

the answer that she was about to give him. She took a deep breath, and with a great deal of remorse, she let the words fall out of her mouth. "It was sent off to get dry cleaned, along with a few other pieces of your clothing."

Something inside of Enrico's body exploded, and the blood drained from his face quite quickly. He suddenly had an overabundance of energy and wanted to shout really loud, but all of the muscles in his chest went tight, and then he couldn't breathe. The color of his skin had gone from tanned to pale, and before she could catch him, he had dropped to the floor.

Rosalia's old and wrinkled hands rushed up to her cheeks. She was borderline hysterical, and screamed wildly for someone to come right away.

A neighbor heard a woman's cries for help and called for a doctor.

Minutes later, Dr. Lucia and two men in an ambulance arrived at Enrico's home. The ailing man was examined, and the doctor proclaimed that his heart rate had gone through the roof. The men carried him up to the master bedroom and laid him down on the bed. The doctor, with the help of the paramedics, put an I.V. into Enrico's arm, and administered a strong substance to help Enrico sleep. After Dr. Lucia wrote down all of his findings, he presented the new instructions to the nurse's aide.

"This must not happen again", he ordered firmly. "Enrico Velucci is one of the dearest friends I have. Follow what I've told you to do, so that he can recover quickly."

Rosalia nodded, as sadness weighed heavily over her mind. She was tormented by the fact that it was her fault that Enrico was in this condition, and she mourned her actions.

"Grazie", the doctor added, once he witnessed her reaction.

There were five people standing in the room, and as everyone watched Enrico fall into a deep sleep, they all spotted tears sliding off the side of his face and landing onto the pillow. No-one knew why he seemed to be crying, but they hoped that it wasn't from him being in pain from the fall.

Enrico knew why; he was suffering emotionally. Without that phone number, he now had no way to get hold of Sadie. He was devastated to the max, as this had crushed his spirit more than anyone could ever guess. Of course he could ask Angelo to get Sadie's number, but that would draw suspicion – a consequence that came with penalties. So, it was with deep regret that he decided to wait until he felt better, and then he would try to get the number himself. Until then, he chose to suffer the agony of lost love in silence.

The doctor came to the house every single day, to monitor his vitals and to check his oxygen intake. A little more than a week after his fall, Enrico stated that he was feeling much better, and it showed; he was in good spirits and his stats had been brought down to a reasonable number. Even though there was a real fear that he could have a relapse, Dr. Lucia had no choice but to allow Enrico the freedom which he was requesting – but, it came with strict orders on what he could or couldn't do from now on.

"Agreed!" Enrico shouted. His statement was a little too loud, but he was full of self-confidence and couldn't wait to taste freedom again.

The Elusive Mr. Velucci

"Wonderful", the doctor replied. They shook hands, and after making promises to come back in a few days, he left the house.

The minute he was able to get up and walk around, Enrico asked for his mail, and to be informed of all that he had missed.

Since he was now aware of all the deceptions that had happened while he had been in his bed recuperating, his mindset wasn't as pleasant as it had been eight days ago. He now appeared stiff and reserved when speaking to people, and he acted like he expected them to jump to attention.

Rosalia felt a hot blush settle on her cheeks, whenever he called her name. She would always rush to his side, but she wavered when he asked for something which she knew would upset him.

Angelo had been told about Enrico falling unconscious, and has since received daily reports from the doctor. Today he was overjoyed to be able to speak with his father directly. "How are you doing?" he asked.

"They let me get out of bed, so that's good", he projected with pride. "I guess that means I'm getting better." Enrico chuckled softly at his trivial attempt at humor, and then remained quiet so he could hear all that Angelo had to say.

"I'm very happy for you, papa." And even as he said the words, his body wanted to curl tight enough, to stop the fear that he might not see his father again.

They talked for another ten minutes, and when Enrico got tired, they hung up.

Nine weeks after he had had the surgery, Enrico was given a clean bill of health. He was very grateful to be able to leave the house, and now his number one priority was to get hold of Sadie. He thought of nothing else since he had been told that his coat had been taken to the cleaners, and he insisted that he be the one to pick it up.

Enrico arrived at the store with a cocky, masculine grin on his face. He seemed to be smiling at nothing in particular, except for having a new appreciation for freedom, and for being in the outside world. He told the owner what he had come for, and a minute later, his excitement began to crash down around him ... again.

Very surprisingly, the owner still had the coat, but claimed that there was nothing in any of the pockets. "I check every pocket before an item gets cleaned", he professed.

Enrico's gaze was jumping from object to object, not knowing where to focus, while his mind was in a complete state of confusion. He did nothing but blink for twenty long seconds, so that he could try to understand the entire situation. He then became adamant and slammed his fists down on the counter. "I know there was a piece of paper in that pocket with a phone number on it; I put it there myself!" he shouted. His face was becoming red. "It was small and wrinkled, and I know it was there!" He was desperate and scared that this would be his only method to get hold of Sadie, and he felt like he needed to keep fighting in order to be heard.

"I'm sorry sir, but there was nothing in the coat." The owner raised his hands in the air as if he was surrendering, and took a few steps backwards, away from the counter. "Honest", he added for good measure. "I don't have it."

Enrico was in a level of misery that he'd never known before. Even after the death of his parents, he had not felt so lost or forlorn as he did in that moment. He was now

The Elusive Mr. Velucci

inconsolable, and apologized for his loud and rude behavior. Before he opened the door to leave, Enrico threw a few hundred dollars towards the owner, for causing such a scene.

The owner, still frightened by what had happened, waited until the customer got into his car and drove away. Then he swept the money off the counter and into his pocket, and closed the store for the rest of the day.

During the whole drive home, Enrico thought about other avenues which he could travel, that did not include asking Angelo or Sophie for Sadie's phone number. Enrico called New York Information the minute he stepped inside of his house. He asked for Sadie Adam's phone number, but it was unlisted. He tried calling Sophie's school, but because he wasn't on the contact list, the secretaries weren't allowed to give out any information. He even thought of hiring a private detective, and then decided that that was going too far.

Enrico's could see that he was running out of options, and struggled to figure out how he could get hold of his former tutor. His cousin, Paulo, popped into his head, and Enrico rushed to his phone list to find the number. He dialed what he had been given last year, but it was out of order, and his aunt and uncle were off on another holiday.

Paulo changed phones and numbers as often as other people changed socks, but Enrico knew he had to try. His aunt and uncle carried a pay-as-you-go cell phone, but didn't turn it on except for emergencies.

Just when Enrico thought he had lost all hope, Angelo called long distance. "How are you doing, papa?"

A smile ballooned across his cheeks and the features on his face brightened. "Fine, son. Just fine", he replied in

Tina Griffith

English, but with an Italian accent. He was dying inside, but he hoped that his son couldn't tell. "And how is everyone there – Sophie and her mother. How are they doing?"

"I had supper with Sophie tonight, and she's doing fine. I haven't seen or spoken with Sadie since you were here, but I'm sure Sophie would have told me if her mother was not well."

Enrico was quietly deciding what to do next. He couldn't just ask for Sadie's phone number, but he didn't know what else to do. "I'm sure she's ok", he replied. "Maybe say HI to her, the next time you speak to her."

To the outside world, that statement was delivered with courtesy from a future in-law. However, Enrico was hoping that he had sent a coded message to his son without him knowing.

"I will", he stated calmly. He thought it was very nice of his father to pass along his greetings to Sophie's mom, but it went no further than that.

Enrico sighed, and began to tap his foot against the ground. He was frustrated and hoped that Angelo might offer to give him Sadie's phone number, but he didn't. And instead of obsessing about it, he talked with Angelo for another little while before they hung up.

Once the receiver had been placed in the cradle, Enrico curled his fingers into fists, and pushed them high into the air. He then closed his eyes and screamed as loud and as long as he could. Afterwards, he felt so low that he wanted to cry; he was no closer to getting hold of Sadie than he was that very morning, and he didn't know what else to do.

Rosalia rushed to his side when she heard the loud, horrible sound. She saw his flushed face and the tears sliding slowly down his cheeks, and she ordered him to sit down.

The Elusive Mr. Velucci

"You must be careful!" she reminded him sternly. "You don't want to get sick again!" She walked him over to the couch, and once he was comfortable, she went to get him some tea.

Enrico had been convalescing so long, that he didn't even know what day it was. Before the nurse's aide came back into the room, he looked towards the calendar on the mantel. "Mmm…" The sound came from within his closed mouth, as his mind wandered. "I came back to Italy about 10 weeks ago", he said softly. After doing the math, he figured out that Angelo would be getting married in 3.5 more months. "Three and a half more months!" he cried, once the reality of the numbers hit him. Enrico hunched his body over and placed his eyes into the heels of his hands.

Rosalia arrived with the tea and asked if he was ok.

Enrico was startled and looked up right away. "What day is today?" he asked.

She was surprised by the question, and then she replied, "March 9." She waited for a big reaction, but was amazed that he had remained calm.

"Thank you", he stated kindly. "One more question. Did you take everything out of the pockets of my clothes, before sending them to the cleaners?"

Rosalia blushed and nodded. "There were two scrunched up gum wrappers and a piece of paper with numbers scribbled on it. I didn't think any of it was important, so I threw them all away."

Enrico lowered his head with utter disappointment, and sent her out of the room.

Rosalia bowed her head in shame, and even though she was reluctant to leave him alone, she went back to her duties.

Enrico got up and walked over to the calendar. He then

marked the date of the wedding with coal from the fireplace, to count down the days when he would get to see Sadie again. "Fourteen more weeks", he confirmed.

Sadie had waited all this time for Enrico to call, and since he didn't, she cried, pouted, and became very angry. Eventually she put him back into a deep crevice of her heart, and carried on with her life. She knew that she would see him at the wedding, and she was sure that he would have excuses for why he didn't call her. She also knew that she would accept each and every one of them.

In the meantime, every time she spoke with Angelo or Sophie, she asked them how Enrico was doing.

She wanted to ask for his phone number, but that would draw attention ... attention that would not work well in her favor. But maybe she could go to Italy and spend time with Enrico there? That thought was quickly knocked down; if he wanted her company, he would have gotten hold of her long before now.

As sad as it was, Sadie managed to get through each day with as much simplicity as she could. At night, when she was by herself, she cried many tears into her pillow. Sleep came and went, and the dreams were always the same - they started with her and Enrico standing face-to-face in her living room.

* * * * * *

As they looked into each other's eyes, her breath whispered over her lips, "Please don't go."

He gasped, in a sound that was half-pain and half-pleasure, as his eyes caressed her with hungry, invisible fingers.

The Elusive Mr. Velucci

She was disturbed by the raw power of her attraction to him, and yet she was powerless to resist his foreign charm.

He had a throbbing need to be inside of her, so he reached out and pulled her body towards his. "Marry me", he insisted, and then he ravaged her mouth with kiss after kiss.

Her eyes were blind with desire as she accepted his proposal. "Yes, I'd love to." Their lips met again, and she trembled in his strong arms.

Enrico broke the kiss and moved his mouth down her slender throat – one inch at a time.

She moaned as her body arched in response to his touch.

Upon seeing that she was ready, he picked her up and carried her to the bedroom.

He didn't get on the plane that night, and they were married the following Saturday.

* * * * * *

Sadie woke up most mornings on a wet pillow, from the tears which had escaped during the night. It was mostly from the realization that she was about to begin another day without Enrico in her life, but she often wondered if it was because she missed him and how he made her feel.

Time passed quickly, and neither Sadie nor Enrico had been able to get hold of the other. They filled their days with work and useless trivial things, and spent their nights dreaming about how great they were together.

It was now five weeks before the wedding, and Sadie had invited Sophie and Angelo for supper. She made a grand meal, made sure that her place looked extra nice, and hoped that she could steer the conversation to how Enrico was doing.

"Mom, this is amazing." Sophie hadn't been at her mother's home in a few weeks, and found that a lot of things had changed; it wasn't as cluttered as it had once been, it was strangely tidier, and it smelled different. She scrunched up her face and asked, "What's that scent?"

"Oh that?" Sadie replied in a nonchalant manner. "It's something that I picked up from the market about a week ago. I'm trying it out to see if I like it. What do you think?"

Sophie rolled her eyes and turned her back. "Whatever."

Unbeknownst to her daughter, Sadie knew what she was doing - Lilacs were Enrico's favorite flower. She hoped that Angelo would pick up on it, and that Sophie would get used to it.

"Well, I absolutely love it", Angelo commented happily. He had grown up with that familiar smell in his home, and he was very grateful to have had that flash of a memory from his past.

Sadie smiled quite proudly. "Thank you, Angelo. Aren't you a sweet boy?"

After they had dished the food onto their plates, they began to eat. Sadie waited for a few minutes, and then she asked Angelo about his father. "How's he doing, Angelo?" She stopped chewing and breathing so that she could hear every word of his reply.

"Oh, he's fine now", he began, and then almost choked on his food.

Angelo was well aware that his dad's health, financial, and social matters were of no concern to anyone, and now he had to backtrack.

The Elusive Mr. Velucci

"What I mean is, he was busy there for a while, but I think he's on some days off now."

Sophie whipped her head to the side to look in her boyfriend's direction. He was sweating and she wondered why he was being so evasive and nervous.

Angelo felt her cold stare against his face and continued, "I figure he's resting in his favorite place, or just plain taking it easy. That's what I meant." He lowered his eyes as a flush of dishonor covered his face. He gazed at whatever was left on his plate, and hoped that nobody could tell that he was dying inside.

"Well, that's good", Sadie stated. However, there was no truth behind her words.

While Sophie and Angelo exchanged information, Sadie slid into her quiet world. She was relieved that Enrico had been so busy, for perhaps that is why he hasn't called her yet. And now that he's on some days off, maybe he will find the time to reconnect with her. She hoped so anyway, as she missed him terribly.

An hour and a half later, they were standing at her front door and saying good-bye. The kids claimed that they had had an amazing supper and visit, and they each thanked Sadie for everything that she had done to make it so special. Promises were made, that they would be in touch soon, and warm, sincere hugs were given.

"Good-bye!" they all shouted at once, and continued to wave as the car drove out of sight.

Sadie was still confused about why Enrico wasn't calling, and wondered if she should try to get the number from Angelo. 'No', her inner voice replied firmly. 'If he wanted to talk, he would have dialed my number.'

Tina Griffith

Sadie felt she had no other recourse than to sit and wait for him to make the first move. She hoped that he would hurry; she ached for him, and the depth of her loneliness hit her broken heart like a sledge hammer. Her eyes began to glisten, and she covered her face with her hands. There was now a thickness in her throat, and then came another onset of tears. Before too long, she was crying herself to sleep.

The wedding date was approaching, and everyone was counting down the days. Sadie and Enrico were also marking it on their calendars, as they were eager to see each other again – each for their own reasons.

More days went by, and Enrico had still not called her. Sadie was becoming angry and wanted to know why Enrico had dismissed her. 'She had given him her phone number, so why had he not used it?' was a common phrase which she chanted regularly.

Enrico was truly upset about losing her number, and he desperately wanted to explain what had happened. He was willing to beg her to forgive him, and he hoped that they could then put this behind them.

A month before Angelo's wedding, Enrico booked the return ticket on a plane that was going to New York. Before the customer representative had tried to confirm the details, his mind had drifted to Sadie. It had been so long since he was in that airport, and he wondered if she would even want to see him again.

"Sir?" said the female voice on the phone.

"Oh, uh, yes?" Enrico listened to what the woman had repeated for his benefit, and then he agreed to everything. He cursed after they had ended their call; he had embarrassed himself by not staying focused.

The Elusive Mr. Velucci

Enrico picked up the phone again, and dialed a florist whose shop was near Angelo's apartment. He ordered two bouquets – one small and one medium – and paid for them by credit card. He also asked her to write down his phone number, should the clerk need to call him about anything pertaining to the order.

"I don't think that will be necessary, but I'll take it just in case", she said.

Enrico thanked her, and then called Angelo to tell him what he had done.

"Can you see to it that Sophie gets the bigger one, and please give the smaller one to Sadie." Enrico had goose bumps on his arms as he explained these very specific instructions.

The flowers were a ploy to grab his former tutor's attention, and to show her that he was still thinking about her. A lot of time had passed since they had seen each other, and he meant for these flowers to be the first step of smoothing the path to forgiveness. Enrico hoped that she would react positive and warm when she received them, and he was sorry that he hadn't done it sooner.

"Dad, what a great idea! Of course I will do that for you."

[10]"Grazie, figlio mio." Enrico continued to speak with Angelo for another few minutes, and then they hung up.

Sadie had lost faith that she and Enrico would ever be a couple, and now that the wedding was approaching, she was terrified; she knew that Enrico would be attending and she was scared to see him face-to-face. 'How would those first few minutes go?' she wondered. 'Would they pretend

---

[10] Grazie, figlio mio - Thank you, my son

that all the silence between them these past few months, didn't happen?'

'No', Sadie decided silently. 'It would be better if they stuck to being cordial to each other; a simple smile and a nod in the other person's direction was ok – nothing else.'

Sadie lowered her head and wanted to cry. She suddenly felt that it was obvious to everyone but her, that Enrico didn't want anything more than a distant friendship. With a deep intake of air into her lungs, and then slowly releasing it to all that was around her, Sadie hoped to feel a little better. She closed her eyes and asked God to give her strength. "Please let me get through this wedding with courage. I have to see Enrico again, I know that, but then I need to carry on with my life." She made the sign of the cross on her chest, and bowed her head. "Amen."

Sadie cleaned her house and then went shopping, while resigning herself to the fact that she would remain a single mother for the rest of her life. 'Maybe in time I will become a grandmother and that would give me someone to love.' It was a nice thought, but then Enrico creeped into the scenario - he would be the grandfather. Her face shriveled up and she made a loud sound. "Ugh!" She just realized that she would always be connected to him, but maybe not in the way she wanted.

As Sadie pulled into her driveway, she noticed that something had been left on her cement porch. Because her curiosity weighed heavier than putting the groceries into the house, she went to find out what the package was. After picking it up and carefully opening the cellophane layers, she saw the beautiful assortment of fresh flowers. Before she read the card, she brought her nose closer to the

The Elusive Mr. Velucci

lovely bouquet and inhaled a large whiff of its intoxicating fragrance. "Mmmm…."

A minute later, she searched for the card, but there wasn't one. It was a little confusing, so she looked towards her neighbor's homes, and up and down the street, but saw no-one. She was now wearing a quizzical expression across her face, while she unloaded her car and brought everything inside. After putting the groceries away and placing the flowers into a vase of water, she continued to wonder who the flowers were from.

As the days went by, Enrico had hoped that he would hear something from Sadie, but he never did. He called Angelo, but there was no answer. He left a message for his son to call him back, but because of all the last-minute wedding things that needed to be done, that call was never returned.

It was now a week before the wedding and all the plans had been finalized. The only thing that Sadie had to do, was get through the ceremony without drawing attention to what was in her heart.

Sophie called her mother three days before Enrico was scheduled to arrive in New York. In one part of their nightly conversation, she said that Angelo was going to pick his father up from the airport, and then she changed the subject to give her mom some in-depth specifics about the wedding and school - all of which Sadie was no longer listening to.

Upon hearing about Enrico, it brought a new state of mind to Sadie's already emotionally battered soul. Instead of pretending to be unpretentious towards him, she now wanted to run up and hug and kiss him. She lowered her eyes as a slight blush kissed her cheeks. Sadie suddenly felt

Tina Griffith

very silly, and wondered how any of it could be possible; all options to be alone had been played out, and every one of them had been unsuccessful. She even gave Enrico her phone number, and yet he has never called her.

Sophie's loud and very excited tone of voice broke her mother's daydream-like trance, and now Sadie was very alert.

"Oops! That's Angelo trying to beep through!" Sophie shouted. "I have to go, mom. Talk later!"

As Sadie laid the receiver in her lap, she realized that her heart was trying to convince her that a relationship with Enrico was not meant to be. On the other hand, if he even smiled in her direction, Sadie knew that she would melt and run into his arms. It was odd logic, but Sadie was still very much in love with that man, and she wanted to be with him more than anything.

Sadie placed the phone back into its cradle and got down on her knees. She positioned her hands into a begging pose, and prayed like she had never prayed before. After giving God a quick background as to why she was asking, she solicited his help in devising a plan where the two of them could have some time together - without the kids around. "Please", she begged, with all her might.

Tears were welling in her eyes as she stood up, and though she didn't have the least bit of interest to sleep, she crawled into bed. She watched TV until her body was so weary that it passed out from sheer exhaustion, and woke up the next morning feeling more sluggish than usual.

Two days later, only hours before Enrico's plane was scheduled to land, the phone rang.

"Hi mom!" Sophie began. She sounded stressed and full of energy. "I have a huge favor to ask you."

Sadie's eyes popped wide open from the enthusiasm which was bursting through the airwaves. Whatever was happening brought fear to her chest and a dryness to her mouth. She had a feeling that this was big, and now she had a hard time getting air to go in or out of her body. "Go ahead", she said softly. She then held her breath and listened to what her daughter had to say.

"I might have misspoke before", she began. "Both Angelo and I are busy doing some last minute errands, and Enrico needs a ride home from the airport. Do you think you could go and get him?" It was now Sophie's turn to be quiet and listen. Her eyebrows shot up towards her hairline, while she waited with baited breath.

Sadie couldn't believe it; her insides were pulsating, but she tried not to show much emotion. "Of course I can do that for you, sweetheart." Her muscles were quivering and she couldn't remember the last time when she had been that happy. Suddenly, a vision of the fantasy where they would run into each other's arms and stay there for the rest of their lives, appeared in her mind. It was in glorious color, with end-of-a-movie music playing loudly in the background.

"Oh mom, thank you", she stated sincerely. "You're a life saver."

Sadie blinked several times while coming back to reality. She then cleared her throat and asked in a calm manner, "What time does his plane land?"

Sophie provided her mother with all the details, and then they hung up.

Sadie checked her watch and muttered, "Two hours."

She knew that it took 40 minutes to get to the airport and a few minutes for him to grab his luggage, so that gave her about an hour before she had to leave.

During that time, she fluffed pillows, dusted lightly, wiped anything that needed attention, and dumped the almost-dead flowers into the garbage.

Sadie checked her appearance as she walked past the nearest mirror. "Nope, that won't do!" she gasped in horror. She changed her outfit, fixed her hair, sprayed some perfume on her body, grabbed her keys, and then left her home.

Sadie drove to the airport in total disbelief, and a little faster than the speed limit allowed. She was still in shock over her being the one to pick Enrico up, and trembled while wondering if what she looked like was good enough. She had a peculiar feeling in the pit of her stomach, and she hoped that nothing would change the current plans.

Enrico's plane was preparing to land, and all he could think about was seeing Sadie again. 'Would she be angry that I haven't called her?' he wondered. If he would've been by himself, he would have slapped a hand against his forehead for that stupid question. 'Of course she was going to be upset', he muttered in his head. 'This was not only the second time that I have done this, but she had made such an outstanding effort to make sure that I could contact her. And because that call didn't get dialed, it looked like I couldn't have been bothered.'

Enrico was very disappointed in himself, and it showed on his face and in his body language.

The plane had touched down and was now on the runway, which pumped Enrico's anxiety up to another level.

Sadie was standing inside the terminal, and terrified

The Elusive Mr. Velucci

and thrilled all at the same time. She had rehearsed what she was going to say to Enrico, over and over again, but now she couldn't remember any parts of her speech.

After a male voice announced that the plane from Italy had now arrived, a new worry entered her mind. 'What if Enrico became confused and upset because she was there and not Angelo?' Sadie didn't want to dwell on 'what ifs', but it did make her want to cry; he must have known that she would be waiting to hear from him, but he hadn't called her or tried to get hold of her in the past six months.

Enrico was collecting his items from the overhead compartment.

Sadie was pacing with nervous energy. She had now talked herself into a frenzy, and tried to apply the self-soothing trick. "It's going to be ok", she whispered quietly to herself. "It's going to be ok." She knew it might be awkward for Enrico to have her there instead of Angelo, but she would explain that she was doing the kids a favor. No matter what, Sadie was determined not to reveal her joy at seeing Enrico – at least not at first.

Enrico had come off the plane and was going down the escalator.

Sadie's mind was running a mile a minute. She was terribly confused, and her emotions were scattering in a zig zag pattern instead of a straight line. She looked up towards the ceiling and closed her eyes, and wished that this was all going to play out as well as she had anticipated.

Enrico picked up his bags and then checked the time. As he walked towards the entrance of the airport to wait for Angelo, he wondered if Sophie and Sadie would be there too, but he didn't want to count on it.

Sadie's probing eyes had been studying every male face within a twenty foot radius. She then spotted a man off to her left. He had two suitcases by his feet and he was wearing a camel-colored coat. His back was towards her, but there was something about him that seemed awfully familiar.

Minutes went by before a delicious shudder of warmth claimed her entire body. "Enrico?" she called, and she gave a little wave.

Enrico turned around when he heard someone calling his name. He was primed to see his son, but nothing could have prepared him for who was there. "Sadie?" He swung his head this way and that, in case Angelo was somewhere in the nearby area. After making sure that it was just the two of them, Enrico released a smile of relief.

Her beautiful face was beaming, and Enrico's heart was beginning to pound inside of his chest. He rushed towards her, wrapped his arms around her, and then he picked her up into the air. "Sadie!" He swung her around and around while they laughed about the amazing situation. And then, as she slid down the length of his body, they locked eyes. Seconds later, he pressed his lips very solidly against hers.

Sadie swooned, as did Enrico, and everything that they had shared on their last night of passion, came rushing to the forefront of their minds.

Enrico loved how she felt in his arms, and without using any words, his mouth was telling her how much he had missed her.

They had no knowledge of how long they had been saying hello, as sound disappeared and time had stood still. And there was no negative thoughts in their hearts or minds, just a huge ball of desire, which shone brightly between the two former lovers.

He pulled her body closer to his, encouraging her to feel his passion.

Her heart hammered against her ribs; he was teasing her and she was enjoying it, despite her silent protests from before.

The implication of how this visit might end, sent waves of excitement throughout Enrico's entire body.

Sadie noticed that his breathing had changed, and she was now aware that certain parts of him had hardened. This amused her, and she began to kiss him in a hot, demanding fashion. Not surprisingly, her own body was responding and now aching for them to be naked.

Enrico pulled away from her and stared into her beautiful face. "I'm so happy that you came to pick me up." His tone was apologetic and sincere, and full of immense love.

"I'm doing a favor for the kids, and I thought this would give us a little time to talk", she replied. Her stunning lips curved into an alluring smile, as her blue eyes stared into his dark brown ones.

"That it would", he agreed, with a sensuous quality to his voice. He matched her smile with his own, and reached for her hand. When he felt her fingers wrap around his, it sent his spirits soaring.

As they walked out of the building and towards her car, the enchanting reunion suddenly turned into an explosive moment. "Wait a minute!" she said, and she placed one hand firmly against his chest. "Why did you not try to contact me?"

Enrico lowered his eyes and chuckled. He agreed that it was a valid question, and one that totally deserved an answer - but not here, not in the middle of a dozen people. "Take me somewhere where we can talk, and I'll tell you", he begged with conviction in his voice.

Sadie hoped that he wouldn't try to snowball her with a ton of excuses, but deep in her heart, she knew that she wouldn't care; she was finally alone with him, and wanted to stay by his side for however long he was in New York.

Sadie was apprehensive, but obeyed, and drove him to one of her favorite coffee shops in the city. "Is this ok?"

He took a second to exam the outside of the quaint building, before he smiled his approval. "It'll be fine."

While having coffee and a piece of cherry crumb cake, Enrico unveiled the story. He told her about the surgery, the complications, and the bed rest. He then told her about the coat and the cleaners, and was almost in tears when he explained how hard he had worked to try to get her phone number. "Without getting the kids involved", he laughed.

Sadie could understand all of it, and was quite remorseful that he had gone through so much without her knowledge. "Angelo didn't tell Sophie about any of this, or she would have told me. Surely he must have known that you had surgery, right?"

Enrico nodded, and then described the terrible complications that could arise, if and when the press found out about his ill health. "Things like that have a habit of turning into ugly gossip, very quickly", he added. "I need to always present myself in tip top condition, and with exemplary manners and good taste." He was serious in what he had just said, but leaned in and added jokingly, "It's the curse of being recognized."

Enrico was famous for being a well-known conductor of various orchestras around the world. His work was admired by the Pope and the Queen, Rock Stars and Movie Stars, as well as the everyday, regular working class people. Any kind of gossip or scandal could ruin what he had built up over the course of his lifetime, and he hoped that Sadie recognized the importance of keeping some things quiet.

"I understand", she said quietly, and lowered her chin to her chest.

Enrico could see that her heart had been broken. Or perhaps she was upset about the lack of trust within the family circle. He reached out and covered her hand with his own. "Please know that I'm truly sorry for everything – the silence, and for not telling you about the surgery." His words were sincere, and he felt instantly relieved when he saw Sadie nod her head in agreement.

While she had been in her uncommunicative state, Sadie had been mulling over everything that Enrico had just told her – every moment that he had gone through after the surgery, and every pain that he had suffered all by himself. She felt awful and wished that she had tried harder to get hold of him.

"I am ok now, so please don't worry anymore", he pleaded. Enrico didn't want her to feel guilty or apologetic, so he changed the subject. "Can I inquire about Sophie's father, or is that too personal?" It was quite a bold question, and it was enough to snap Sadie out of her current mood.

Her first reaction was panic. Her second was fear. Sadie's face quickly turned a pretty shade of pink, and then she lowered her eyes before she spoke. "What do you want to know?" It was a topic which she knew would come up, but she hadn't counted on telling it today of all days.

"He's never around and you don't talk about him", Enrico began. "Because of how I feel towards you, I want to know if he's still in the picture." He leaned back until he was resting against the chair, and waited for her to reply.

Sadie wasn't sure where to start. After gathering her thoughts, she took a very deep breath and began. "For a very long time, I didn't know where he was. I did try to contact him, but failed in all of my efforts. And no, he has never been in Sophie's life."

Enrico looked down at his hands, and folded them very carefully on his lap.

Sadie took a second to breathe through her anxiety, and then continued to clarify their relationship. "It was a one-night stand, and it happened a very long time ago." Her eyes were also looking towards her lap, while her hands were playing with a napkin that she had torn up with her fingers.

Enrich looked up and could see how awkward Sadie was feeling, and he now regretted that he had asked about Sophie's father. "I'm sorry", he stated with kindness. "I hope I didn't offend you."

"You didn't", she replied quietly. She gazed lovingly into his eyes as she continued. "I adored that man, and I would have loved to have him in our lives, but he walked away and never came back."

Sadie was becoming a little upset, and it showed in her body language and in the tone of her voice. "And before you ask, he never knew about Sophie, because I never told him

The Elusive Mr. Velucci

about her." By how loud she had become, it was evident that she was angry.

Enrico wasn't about to back down now; he had become engrossed in the story and tried not to act jealous as he pushed for more details. "Why didn't you tell him?" He wasn't sure that he had the right to ask, but he felt that every man would want to know if he was a father.

The next paragraph of words came from deep within her heart. "He was only in town for a few months. We were friends the whole time, except for that last night."

Complete surprise was now etched on Enrico's face, as the provocative details began to emerge.

"And when he left, I thought he would come back, but he didn't." The way her declarations were gushing out, it was like Sadie was finally cleansing herself from all the waiting and wondering, and asking why he had let her go. "I can't tell you how much that hurt." The tears which have been teasing to come out, now jumped from her sockets and poured down her face.

Enrico's lower jaw had dropped towards his chest, and his eyes were as large as saucers of milk.

It was therapeutic and felt quite soothing for Sadie to have some freedom from the secret which she had been carrying for so long. "I loved him so much", she confessed. "I still do." Sadie's hands were covering her face, hiding the tears which were now drenching her cheeks and chin. "We actually haven't seen or spoken to each other since that night when we made love." She was now so completely lost in her own heartbreak, that she didn't realize what she had done, until the last few words had left her mouth.

Enrico was stunned beyond belief, and trying hard to

grasp as much of the information as he could. With sweaty palms, and eyes that were glistening from their own tears, he repeated some of her statements to make sure that he had heard everything correctly. "You said he was only in town for a few months?"

She nodded without looking into his face.

"That you made love on your last night together?"

She nodded again, while still keeping her eyes lowered.

"And he left you and never came back?"

Sadie slowly raised her eyes, until they were looking directly into his, and then she nodded. She had the exact same look on her face that a child does, when they know that they're in trouble.

All of a sudden, Enrico came to life. "Sadie, that's what I did", he stated loudly. He leaned back in his chair, tried to map out the timeline, and suddenly he couldn't breathe. He brought his body forward quickly, and searched her face for the answer. "Am I..." he asked, but his voice trailed off after the first two syllables.

She brought a shy smile to her lips, but it was full of uncertainty. "You are", she answered in a hushed tone.

As if he thought his ears hadn't heard correctly, he asked her again, full out. "Are you saying that I am Sophie's father?"

Sadie looked at him with more confidence than before and nodded.

His hands flew to his mouth and a short scream escaped. "I can't believe it!" he stated loudly. "I'm a father!"

Sadie was now crying from happiness instead of shame. She was relieved that her secret was out, and her face mirrored his same elated expression.

The Elusive Mr. Velucci

A small celebration erupted at their table, and it was joyous, but not too loud. Because the eight people around them were under the impression that she had just told him that he was about to become a father, nobody minded their disorderly behavior. Instead, some raised a glass and offered their congratulations.

Enrico was suddenly deaf, dumb and blind to everything that was going on around him. He was Sophie's dad, and that's all that mattered. It never occurred to him that this was even possible, because he and Maria had tried so hard to have a baby, and yet, were never able to conceive.

Sadie was thrilled that Enrico was delighted about the news. She had truly dreaded the moment when he came back into her life and found out that she had had a daughter – his daughter – without his knowledge. She was now thankful that he knew, and could feel nothing but love and happiness from his side of the table.

Enrico suddenly had a ton of energy. He wanted to get up and run somewhere, but he also wanted to stay there and hear more about Sophie and Sadie's life.

Sadie could see a few different expressions racing across Enrico's mind, and she decided to fill in the blanks. "I know you probably hate me for not telling you before now, but when I found out that I was pregnant, I went to the deli and it was closed", she explained.

"Closed?" Enrico was confused and threw his mind back to that time period. It took a short minute, and then a feeling of clarity enveloped his entire being, for he now knew what had happened. "My father had gotten ill, and then he passed away. All of our family members and friends came to Italy to be with us during that time period."

Sadie's heart softened like butter in a microwave. "So that's what happened", she sighed. "I'm so sorry for your loss." She had so much sorrow and regret in her heart all of a sudden, and it poured out in words and tears. She reached for his hand and looked deep into his eyes. "I really wanted you to know about the baby. I even went back to the deli several times after that, but it was either closed or had too many people inside, and eventually I stayed away because too much time had passed."

Before she could spit out any more words, Enrico stopped her. "Listen, I don't blame you; I take full responsibility. I said I would get hold of you and I didn't – twice!" He handed her another napkin and then reached out to hold her free hand. "Can you tell me more about our daughter?"

When he said the words 'our daughter', the strangest feeling came over her body. It was a strong mixture of doom and happiness that their child, a human being which they had created, was getting married.

Enrico had his own issues to deal with. He hadn't even gotten to know Sophie yet, and here she was leaving the nest. He was stunned by the very notion.

"Hey!" Sadie called across the table. Her tone was strong and she had a definite hunger for an answer. "I've got a question for you!"

The demand was loud and very unexpected, and since Sadie was now wearing a serious look on her face, Enrico knew that he should pay attention.

"If Sophie is your daughter and Angelo is your son, how can the two of them get married?"

Enrico suddenly broke out in a light laughter that she couldn't quite understand.

The Elusive Mr. Velucci

Sadie didn't find it funny at all, and glared at him in disbelief.

"Relax", he giggled.

Because of all the people sitting around them, he decided to speak in Italian from then on out.

"He's not my son by blood. I married his mother when he was already in school, and legally adopted him on that same day." Enrico made the statement with love and conviction, so that Sadie would know how he felt about the man who was about to marry her daughter. "He is my son on all levels, except biological."

"Oh, my gosh!" A huge sigh of relief unclouded her scary thoughts, and their children's future now looked a lot more promising. "Thank you for answering that very delicate question." Sadie took a second to breathe, and was able to relax a little, and then she wondered about Angelo's mother. "Does your wife not like to travel?" She spoke with the tone of a child's innocence, and searched his face while he took a second to reply.

Enrico was surprised that Sadie didn't know about his current situation, and he knew that he needed to discuss the fact that he was a widower and not a cheater, so that she didn't get the wrong impression.

"I'm sorry if I've steered you in the wrong direction", he began softly. His words were delivered in slightly more than a whisper. "Maria died on the day when Angelo was graduating from High School."

Sadie was dumbfounded and wanted to become invisible. "Gosh, now I'm the one who's sorry; I didn't know."

"Yah, I kind of figured that." He had reached out and now had his hand resting on top of hers. "It was a long time ago, but please know that I have only been with two women in my whole entire life – you and Maria."

As she looked into his eyes, she could see that what he had just said, was the truth. "And I have only been with you."

That surprised Enrico very much, but it also made him feel exceptional. "You have always had a special spot in my heart."

"And I have always had you in my heart."

They stood up slowly, eased into each other's arms, held on tightly, and kissed very passionately. It was tender and well worth waiting for, and it melted their souls.

Minutes later, after everyone around them had applauded and shared in their joyous occasion, they sat down and continued talking.

"So, I have a daughter", Enrico whispered across the table. He was beaming from ear-to-ear. "Does Sophie know who I am?"

Sadie blushed with alarm and automatically lowered her face. "No. I raised her to believe that her father had died in the war." She quickly lifted her eyes to meet his. "Since the moment you came back into our lives, I've wanted to say something, but I thought it best if I told you first."

Enrico smiled with compassion, while reaching out to touch her hand again. "We can tell her together, but not right now. After the kids come back from their honeymoon, that's when we will face this head-on."

Sadie never felt closer to another human being in her whole entire life, than she did in that one moment. He was not only the love of her life, but he was also the father of her child. "Thank you", she whispered. Her sentiment was said

The Elusive Mr. Velucci

softly, and it was filled with every ounce of emotion that she could deliver.

"No, it is I who should thank you", he stated sincerely. He was referring to the fact that Sadie had given him a daughter – a gift for which he didn't know how to reward.

Over the next hour, they had finished their lunch, talked about a hundred more things, and then decided to carry on with the rest of their day.

On the drive to Sadie's home, they held hands and stole a few dozen kisses, while they exchanged childhood details about their children. They were becoming closer, both emotionally and spiritually, and now they couldn't stop smiling. They made a pact to act accordingly in front of Sophie and Angelo, so as not to draw suspicion on what was really going on between them. For their own amusement, they created a few signals to let the other one know what they were thinking.

Blinking both eyes at the same time meant, 'I Love You'. Blinking one eye meant, 'I'm thinking about you.' Moving the eyes to the left or right meant, 'Go over there and I'll meet you in a minute.' And so on...

They were giggling and felt like teenagers who were trying to pull the wool over their parent's eyes, and they both thought it would be fun to see if this 'eye thing' worked.

When Sadie pulled into her driveway, she saw that Angelo and Sophie had already arrived.

Enrico couldn't help but study the outside of Sadie's home. The shape of the house, the neatly groomed grass, and the tiny array of flowers which were lined up across the front, were all perfectly thought out. The color of the siding, as well as the floral curtains which could be seen from the street, revealed her charismatic personality. But what attracted him the most, was her address; he now had somewhere to send little trinkets of love through the mail.

The first time he had been there, it was dark outside, he was tired, and he didn't think that anything about the house mattered. Now everything was important, because it belonged to Sadie.

By the time she parked the car, Enrico and Sadie were in great spirits, for they had made peace with their past. They were now looking forward to seeing what the future held.

As they entered Sadie's home, each child said hello to their parent first. Then they exchanged greetings with everyone else. Food had been laid out and everyone ate, but the visit ended after 40 minutes; Enrico had to get to the hotel and sleep, and Sophie and Angelo had one more thing to do before 9pm that night.

As they all said good-night, Enrico winked in Sadie's direction – with both eyes.

She in turn blushed, but tried not to show it. She then gave him a quick hug, making sure to put her phone number into his front pocket without anyone seeing. As she pulled away from him, she used her eyes to tell him what she had done.

Enrico placed his hand into his pocket and smiled when his fingers found the folded piece of paper. 'Thank you', he mouthed.

Sophie and Angelo were relieved to see how their parents were interacting; cordial, and not strange or statue-like as they had been at their first meeting. This pleased the future bride and groom, because they wanted everyone to act like a big and happy family.

The Elusive Mr. Velucci

Enrico called Sadie the moment he was alone. They talked for quite a while, and then hung up after expressing how they truly felt.

On the days leading up to the wedding, Enrico and Sadie spoke several times a day. If they met in person, they hid in the shadows so as to avoid suspicion from their children. When they were alone, it felt very liberating to kiss and hold hands away from prying eyes.

It was the night before the wedding, and they had already been on the phone for a few minutes.

"I can't wait until the day when we can recreate our last night together", Enrico stated fondly. Everything between the elegance and tone of his voice, was done deliberately to enthuse desire. And just the thought of all that they could do, made his skin glow and a part of his body rise to attention.

"It's been on my mind, too." Her cheeks were becoming warm at the very thought of being naked with him again.

Lovemaking had been talked about a few times in the past two days, and they both agreed that since they had waited this long, that they could certainly wait a little while longer. Their first true night alone would be on their children's wedding night, but neither Enrico nor Sadie felt that it would be appropriate to do anything then.

"We're in our forties and quite capable of remaining chaste until another, more opportune moment comes along", she stated, with less confidence than she had hoped to provide.

"I am anticipating that moment to come soon", he joked.

She blushed as she stated shyly, "Me too."

The morning of the wedding was busy; they all had

their hair and make-up done, the minister had to be picked up, the flowers were handed out to everyone in the wedding party, and everyone got into their outfits.

Enrico drove to the church with Angelo, while Sadie took Sophie. As soon as they arrived, Sophie was whisked away by her maid of honor, while Sadie was escorted to the front row of the church.

Meanwhile, Enrico was with his son, until the minister needed Angelo's attention. Enrico then went in search of Sophie.

'Knock, Knock, Knock'

"Who is it?"

"Enrico."

"Come in."

He opened the door to where she had gotten changed, and the first image of her in her wedding dress, made him weak in the knees.

"What do you think?" Sophie asked happily. She grabbed the dress with both hands and twirled herself around like a princess.

Enrico couldn't breathe; she looked like an angel. "You are so beautiful", he sighed. He was standing across the room from her and it felt like his feet were cemented to the floor. He had never been prouder in his whole life, but he couldn't tell her why. "My gosh", he cried. His hands were on his cheeks, while he continued to drink in all the beauty that he saw before him.

"And you are so kind", she giggled. "Where's my mom?"

"She's already sitting in the front row, waiting for you to walk down the aisle." He took two steps closer to his daughter. "How are you doing? Are you nervous?"

The Elusive Mr. Velucci

She had large oval eyes with thick black lashes, and she spoke to him like a little girl. "A little, but not much." She spun around to face the mirror, and marveled at how pretty she looked.

As Enrico studied the features on Sophie's perfect face, he recognized all the parts that reminded him of his parents; the cheekbones from his mother and the chin from his father. The hairline was exactly like his, and the rest of her was totally Italian heritage. Of course Sadie also added her DNA into this perfect human being, but Enrico giggled as he decided that Sophie had more Italian than German in her.

A woman knocked on the door and then poked her head into the room, and announced that they were about to start the music.

"Thank you. We'll be right there." Sophie turned to Enrico and asked if he was ready to walk her down the aisle.

Because Sophie grew up without a father, she asked Angelo if it would be okay for his father to walk her down the aisle. Her suggestion was met with a great deal of enthusiasm, and father and son agreed on the spot.

Sophie didn't know why, but she liked Enrico right away; he gave her the feeling that she had known him her whole entire life. He was Angelo's father, she felt safe with him, and he was very handsome, but he was also kind and attentive to both her and her mother.

Enrico swallowed hard, and then nodded. "I think I am."

Enrico had been more than thrilled by the offer, and now that he knew that he was her biological father, the task meant so much more to him.

"Okay, then let's get this show on the road." Sophie clapped her hands together, and acted as wild as a mother bear when she sent everyone out of the room. Once the small space had been cleared, she composed herself and reached for Enrico's elbow. Together they walked to their mark, and waited for their cue to enter.

While they waited, Enrico patted her gloved hand while he continued to smile.

The four piece band began to play 'Canon in D' by Pachelbel, and Sophie's heart jumped into her throat. "This is it", she announced nervously.

The double doors opened, and they walked in the beat of the lyrical music.

Enrico adored the classical song which the small orchestra was playing to perfection, for he has, on occasion, become lost in its rhythmic pattern and repeating intervals of harmonic progression. But today, he had been set adrift by another arrangement; his daughter's wedding.

With Sophie on his arm, Pachelbel's tender notes wafting through the air, and the sun streaming in from all windows, Enrico felt like he was in heaven; it was a moving experience that couldn't be explained in words, but it touched the deepest part of his soul.

Angelo's pulse quickened when he saw his bride for the first time; it was like everything he had ever wished for had come true in that one moment. His lips quivered, his heart exploded with joy, and tears burst wildly from both eyes. He couldn't stand still, and made little effort to hide his happiness from the crowd of people who were watching his every thought.

The orchestra was playing a familiar wedding march, and

its melody was consuming every molecule of air in the room. A bright light was streaming in from all the windows of the church, and sparkled against every bead on Sophie's gown. She had always been beautiful to Angelo - even in torn jeans and her hair pulled back in a pony-tail - but he had never witnessed anything so picturesque in his whole life.

Sophie was smiling and stepping in perfect time with the music, and the whole scenario epitomized poetry in motion.

Sadie stood up so that she could watch every second of Enrico walking Sophie down the aisle. The little flower girl was a step or two ahead of them, and was sprinkling red and white rose petals on the carpet for them to walk on.

Enrico was beaming. His shoulders were back, his chest was thrust forward, and he wore a wide grin that conveyed a happy secret. He had never expected to have this wonderful opportunity, and because he was actually living it, he felt like he had achieved one of life's most honored accomplishments.

"Are you ok?" the bride whispered out of the side of her mouth.

"I'm better than ok", Enrico answered.

Sophie's hand was gripping Enrico's left elbow - for moral as well as physical support. She had no thoughts in her head, other than making it up to the front of the church without falling.

Enrico placed his right hand lovingly on top of hers, and patted it a few times for encouragement.

Sophie was shaking but her eyes were dead set on Angelo. She was so in love with him, and couldn't believe

Tina Griffith

that she was about to marry the most wonderful man on the planet.

Enrico was staring directly at Sadie. He cast shades of love to her through mental telepathy, and thanked her for being in his life.

When father and daughter got closer to the front row where Sadie was standing, he blinked twice with both eyes, before tears began to blur his vision.

Sadie held Enrico's gaze, and mouthed, 'I Love You', back to him.

Many tears had already fallen down her shiny cheeks before that moment, and she was well aware that many more were sure to come.

When Enrico and Sophie arrived at the altar, they stopped walking at the same time when the music stopped playing. All was quiet in the church now, so the minister began the ceremony.

He cleared his throat and then looked out at the congregation. "Who gives this woman to wed this man?" he asked in a very loud and official tone of voice.

Enrico walked over to Sadie and reached for her hand. They faced the minister as a united force, and both replied, "We do", at the same time.

Angelo was nervous and in awe of the moment, so he wasn't aware of any silly indiscretion.

Sophie, however, caught onto to it right away. Her eyebrows pressed together by what had just happened, and because the minister had invited Sophie to come and stand beside Angelo, she had to push the situation to the back of her mind.

The Elusive Mr. Velucci

Enrico sat down beside Sadie, and they continued to hold hands throughout the rest of the ceremony.

After the 'I do's' had been recited and agreed to, the minister announced them as Mr. and Mrs. Angelo Velucci. The couple cheered, as did everyone else, and then they walked away from the altar while the orchestra played a happy tune.

Enrico and Sadie were brought to tears, as was everyone else in attendance.

Afterwards, they were delighted to take family pictures with the newly-wed couple – Angelo and Sophie were in the middle, Enrico stood on the outside beside his son, and Sadie was on the other side, beside her daughter.

The reception was majestic; the music, the flowers, the band, and the setting - it was all so perfect. During the dinner, Enrico sat on the far side of the wedding table, beside Angelo, while Sadie was on the other side, beside Sophie.

The first official song was, 'It Had To Be You', and it was meant for the bride and groom only. The lights dimmed, the music played softly, and hundreds of bright dots touched everything in the room. Sophie had her hands wrapped lightly around her husband's neck, while Angelo's hands were locked on the small of his wife's back. Minutes later, as the crowd heard the last few notes of the song, Angelo dipped his bride, just like they do in the movies. He then kissed her sensuously as the lights came back on, while everyone around them cooed and awed.

After the supper dishes had been taken away, someone announced that it was time for the father-daughter dance.

The foursome had also talked about this during Enrico's first week with Sophie, and it was planned that she would

Tina Griffith

dance with Enrico, while Angelo would dance with Sadie. That way, nobody would feel left out.

Enrico's heart began to pound when he realized that he would get to dance with his daughter. He took her hand in his and walked Sophie out to the middle of the floor, while Angelo walked with Sadie. 'The Way You Look Tonight' began to play, and the couples commenced the simple act of swaying in time with the music.

When the song was over, Angelo came over and hugged his father with all his might. "You did good, dad. Thank you for being here."

Enrico was quite overwhelmed by the entire wedding and couldn't speak, but he did display a feeling of love and gratitude towards his son. After smiling and nodding, he wiped the silly tears off his face with the back of his hand. He was walking back to the table, but before he got to sit down, there was another announcement.

"And now we'd like to ask the parents of the bride and groom to dance."

Enrico looked in Sadie's direction and he watched her light up. It was one of those looks that spoke a thousand words, without uttering a single sound. For unbeknownst to anyone else in attendance, they had danced together before tonight.

With her hand in his, Enrico led the stunning woman onto the dance floor, while everyone in the room watched.

Sadie's long gown glittered as she walked, and she wondered if she could even remember how to dance with him; it had been so long ago.

"Are you ready for this", he whispered, as he tried to control the dizzying current which was racing through his

The Elusive Mr. Velucci

body. Enrico placed one hand on her waist, while the other was holding hers out to the side.

"I hope so" she replied. Sadie was nervous. She stared into his eyes with all the love that she had in her soul, and trusted that he remembered what to do.

The intro to a slow ballad began to play, and Enrico held onto Sadie for emotional support; she was his safe place, and the true love of his life.

♪ I'll always remember the song they were playing

The lights dimmed and the music swelled. They were the only two people on the patterned floor, and they were dancing together for the second time in twenty years.

The first time we danced and I knew ♪

Sadie's memories were bringing her back to those moments of their first dance. He was governing their steps while gazing into her eyes, and she was yearning for him to kiss her – same as now. She recalled the ecstasy of being held tight against his strong body, while she hungered from the celebration of his mouth pushing against hers.

♪ As we swayed to the music and held to each other

Sadie hoped that nobody could tell how she was feeling, and clung strongly and silently to all the affirmations of their past, just as she would to a life preserver in a stormy sea.

Tina Griffith

I fell in love with you ♪

The feeling of Sadie in his arms again, was as powerful to him as when he was conducting a riveting piece of classical music. His eyes were glued to hers and they were burning with passion. Enrico was experiencing glorious flashbacks of their first time together – on the dance floor, and later in the motel. The images were vivid and making his blood pump violently throughout his entire body. A wry, twisted smile suddenly appeared on his face, as the memory of their first kiss came to the forefront of his mind. A kiss that was sweeter than wine, and will leave its imprint in his mind, forever.

Sadie stared at Enrico's pillowy-soft mouth, and her body tingled in remembrance of the first time their lips met. A sensual awakening began to spread over her entire body, as she recalled the many other things which they had done.

Enrico's mind was also summoning up every passionate act that they had tried, and it was leaving him somewhat breathless. Lust had now taken over the forecourt of his brain, and he could think of nothing else but their naughty hours of sex.

He felt guilty when Sadie had winced and gasped at the invading thickness of his hard member, and he wanted to believe her when she said that there was little pain after the initial shock.

It was a warm and velvety experience for Enrico, and he had to fight the rising climax in order to hold on a little longer. It took all of one minute, from full entry, when he felt his muscles tighten, to crying out in pure pleasure. They were still joined, but he had stopped thrusting. His moist body was now sprawled limply on top of hers, and he was taking a moment to enjoy the lingering effects of the shuddering waves of his first orgasm.

Sadie giggled as she wiped the tiny beads of perspiration off his brow. She then let her body relax under his, as a sigh of contentment escaped from her lips.

Once he found his breath, Enrico kissed her mouth and then pressed his forehead against hers. He then ran a hand playfully across her tummy, and found that her muscles were surprisingly taut with anticipation of another round. He gave her a smile that sent her pulse racing, and was ready to begin again.

As he grew inside of her, her body stretched to accommodate him. It took another few minutes before her toes curled, her back arched, and then her body became inundated with overlapping waves of extreme pleasure.

Enrico remembered how the bed groaned that night, but not nearly as loud as Sadie had. There were even moments when she treated him like male candy, and she was all too eager to lick and touch every part of his body.

When it was his turn, his mouth trailed the path along her collarbone to the hollow of her throat, and then went all the way down to her toes.

They were both virgins when they started their adventure, but Sadie had matched his heat and enthusiasm with her own.

As the steamy memories continued to pour into his mind, Enrico became so hard, he hurt. Very discreetly, he reached down and shifted his protruding member, and now he couldn't wait until he could recreate even an hour of what they had once experienced.

The audience clapped as the lights came back on, and

the parents of the bride and groom bowed. The song had come to an end, and they needed to walk back to their table. They were both reeling from excitement and being out of breath but happy, and each for their own reasons.

During the next hour, they communicated in long and loving glances, which spoke of memories and experiences that need to be relived.

Her stomach knotted and the muscles in her body stiffened, every time he looked in her direction.

An amused smile played across his lips, for she was like catnip to him – he craved her like butter to bread.

Sadie blushed while wearing a silly grin, for the last traces of her resistance to his advances, had now vanished.

Enrico was now convinced that he loved her to the very core of his soul, for other than being star-crossed lovers, she was his every hope and fantasy.

Sadie loved being the focus of his attention. And to be with him, on this day of all days, filled her with utter joy.

Enrico heard a rustling sound of people gathering as one, and pulled his drifting thoughts together. After he stood up, he saw what was happening, and laid all his focus on the reason that they were there.

Sadie searched the room for what had caught Enrico's attention, and her eyes soon met a pack of women crowding into a group. This intrigued her, so she stood up and watched, and saw that Sophie was getting ready to throw the bouquet.

A countdown led to screams of joy, and at '1', the bride tossed her bouquet into the mob of baying women.

The men were giggling and pointing towards this amusing exhibition, for the enthusiastic ladies were standing shoulder-to-shoulder with their hands in the air. Their

The Elusive Mr. Velucci

mouths were open and they were shrieking something high-pitched and incoherent, while being totally unrelenting about who was going to catch the bouquet.

A precocious twenty-five year old caught the beautiful spray of flowers, and immediately looked over at her beau of three months. He responded by smiling with embarrassment, and then he quickly swiveled his chair around. He was now chugging his drink as fast as he could, while pretending to listen to her tell him what this meant.

As Angelo and Sophie went around the room thanking their guests for coming, Enrico took Sadie out onto the dance floor again. Their eyes were closed as they held each other tight, and their bodies were molded as one. There wasn't a need for talking, because neither wanted to do anything but live in the moment.

They were dancing cheek-to-cheek, and looking more comfortable than some people might have wanted them to. Their fingers had been intertwined and lovingly secured by Enrico's left shoulder, and every so often, he would make a point to kiss the delicate hand of his beautiful partner. Their tummies were together, feet were taking baby steps, and they could have stayed in that position for another song, if not for the fact that someone needed their attention.

Angelo eventually caught up with his father, and he made sure to say thank you to him for coming to the wedding. "You made this day so much better by being here - not only for me, but for Sophie and Sadie as well. Have a good flight home, dad." They hugged with all their might, and then Angelo moved to Sadie.

"Thank you for making my dad so happy", he began. "And thank you for being so kind and loving to me."

Tina Griffith

She was moved by what he had said, and her tears were not so easy to hide. "Thank you for being a fabulous son-in-law. I know you're going to make my daughter happy, and I will try to keep your father out of trouble." She giggled at her own sense of humor, but pushed her face into Angelo's clothing so that he couldn't see how she really felt about Enrico.

Sophie hugged her mother next, and thanked her for absolutely everything. "Love you, mom", she said with tears in her eyes. "I'm going to miss you so much."

"I love you, too." Sadie was crying her own tears, but they were from a large bag of mixed emotions. "And you call me, anytime you feel the need."

Sophie turned to hug Enrico, and she whispered her own thank you into his ear. "I didn't have a dad when I was growing, so with you stepping in today, it made my wedding all that much more special for me. Thank you so much." She kissed his cheek before releasing her arms from around his neck.

Enrico developed a flushed appearance, and wore a grin that couldn't be contained. He was grateful to be surrounded by his family, and tried hard not to revisit the hurdles which could have prevented this moment from happening. "Thank you", he said, as warmth radiated throughout his body. "I loved being by your side today, and watching you marry my son. Believe me when I say it was my honor."

"You're very kind, thank you."

Soon it was time for the bride and groom to go off on their honeymoon.

"It's here!" someone announced loudly, when a fancy, white limousine had come to take the newly-weds away.

The Elusive Mr. Velucci

Minutes later, everyone chased after them, and they were shouting their good wishes, waving good-bye, taking last-minute pictures, and throwing hand-cut, paper hearts in their direction.

"Have a good time!"

"Have fun!"

"Don't drink the water!"

And then Mr. and Mrs. Angelo Velucci drove away.

Enrico and Sadie stood there long after everyone else had gone inside. They had their arms wrapped around one another as they watched the long vehicle drive out of sight, and they were dabbing at the tears which were dripping from their eyes.

Sadie reached up and wrapped her arms around Enrico's neck. She immediately thought back to when Sophie was born, and wondered what had happened to her little baby. "The time went by much too quickly", she mumbled, and then pressed her face into Enrico's shoulder.

Enrico draped his arms around her, and swaddled her with as much love and compassion as he had in his soul. A few minutes later, he looked into her eyes, and then he reached for her hand. "Let's go."

They went inside the building to grab what they had come with, and then walked to Sadie's car. She was distraught and asked Enrico if he could drive them to her home. After parking the car in her driveway, he asked, "Would you like me to go in with you?"

She nodded and got out of the car. She then walked up to her front door, with Enrico following closely behind her. "I'm going to get changed. Can you pour me a drink?"

Enrico went into the kitchen and did as he was asked.

Tina Griffith

He was walking back into living room at the same time as she came in. "Here you go."

Sadie reached for the glass which he was holding out for her. "Shall we make a toast?"

"To our children", he said quietly.

"To our new life", she added.

Neither knew what that meant, but they were sure that it included the four of them as a family, from then on.

While sipping her glass of rum and coke, they sat on her couch and talked. Enrico filled her glass when it was empty, but continued to sip his own.

Sadie was feeling a lot better by the end of the second glass of her alcoholic sweet beverage, and she invited him to stay overnight. "I just want to spend as much time with you as possible", she argued lightly.

He smiled his approval, and then wondered if they were about to break the rules which they had set for themselves.

"I'll go clean up the kitchen, if you want to use the bathroom first." She took the empty glass from his hand and began the short trek across the room. "It's the second door on your right." She pointed as she spoke.

Enrico gave her a cocky, masculine grin, and then hid himself away for a while.

Sadie washed the dishes in the sink, wiped down the counters, then locked the front door. After turning off the lights, she made her way to the bathroom.

It was midnight when Sadie came out, and Enrico was already tucked into her bed. She stood in her doorway as she looked towards him, and the double meaning of his gaze was obvious. "Behave yourself", she joked, as she walked across the room.

The Elusive Mr. Velucci

Not surprisingly, her outfit was cute, her hair had been combed out, she was displaying her bubbly personality, and she looked clean and refreshed.

"I'll try", he laughed. "But you aren't making this very easy." He was riveted by how she looked, and then his eyes moved slowly over the many splendid curves of her body.

Sadie knew the rules, but she found it hard to obey; he radiated a vitality that drew her to him like a magnet. "No, no", she laughed, as she wiggled her index finger in front of his face.

It was now Enrico's turn to laugh. With his hands up in a surrendering pose he said, "I give up." Truth be told, he would never give up on her again.

They decided to talk about his job and the weather in Italy, but as they locked eyes, each could tell that there was a deeper significance to the visual interaction which they were sharing.

While Enrico spoke, Sadie hung onto his every word, and trembled in the comfort of his nearness.

Enrico was telling Sadie about Sorrento and all its beauty, but mentally, he was caressing all of her finest qualities with his fingers.

As they lay there talking, her feelings for him were intensifying. As she watched his lips form each and every word, she wondered if maybe they could ignore the rules which they had so quickly made up. A second later, she remembered what Sophie and Angelo were probably doing, and her body quieted down. Her face became sober and pale, and she suddenly seemed to have no more interest in continuing their conversation.

Enrico couldn't help but notice the immediate change,

for it came without any warning, whatsoever. He bolted into an upright position and watched with great interest as Sadie prepared herself to go to sleep.

"What's happening?" he asked, while apprehension gnawed at his soul. At first, he thought it might have been something he had said or done. "Was it me?" His right hand flew to his chest, while shock covered his face.

"No", she chuckled lightly. Sadie didn't want to be blunt about it, so she added a lilt in her voice and stated, "I wonder what Sophie and Angelo are doing in this moment?" It was odd to think of their children having intercourse, but the statement needed to be said, in order for the parents not to have sex.

Enrico was suddenly very aware of what she was talking about, and he tried to calm his body down. "Yup, you're right", he said with total conviction. He immediately placed both hands behind his head, but a minute later, he rolled towards her and jokingly added, "Can you tell that to my lower body?"

Sadie rolled towards him while she broke out laughing, and pretended to slap him silly. They proceeded to kiss and cuddle for at least another hour, before they fell asleep in each other's arms.

The next morning, they had breakfast and reminisced about what had happened on the dance floor the night before.

"You felt it too?" he asked with surprise in his voice. Enrico thought she had, but it was nice that she had confirmed it.

"I did, and it was almost as wonderful as what had happened during our first dance together."

The Elusive Mr. Velucci

"Except this time we didn't make out", he laughed half-heartedly.

"You're right", she giggled. A minor blush appeared on her face, but she hoped that he wouldn't notice.

"We will have our moment, and it will be great", he promised, as he reached for her hand.

She held her eyes with his, and agreed. "I know it will, and I can't wait."

When her living room clock struck 11am, they realized that it was almost time for Enrico to fly back to Italy.

"I guess I should go to the hotel and pack my things." He didn't say the words with as much passion as he should have, but that's because he wanted to stay right where he was.

Sadie's heart rolled over more than a few times, with the suggestion that he would be going away. "I'll just have to go with you!" she protested – she was half kidding and half not. She felt like he was about to take her soul with him, and she didn't want that to happen.

Enrico looked into her face with every ounce of love that he had in his body. "I would like that, very much." He placed his index finger under her chin and leaned his face closer. He then took both of his hands and cupped her head, while gazing lovingly into her eyes. He kissed her mouth, and even though he wanted to do so much more, he controlled himself.

The kiss was slow and thoughtful, and not meant to bring them any excitement. Enrico gently moved his mouth over her lips while devouring her softness, and lingered as if it would be the last time they could enjoy a moment such as this one.

Sadie had her eyes closed, while a tear fell down her

cheek; she wanted to memorized the texture of his lips against her own, and recall the memory as often as possible.

It might have been intended to last but a few seconds, but their kiss lasted upwards of a full minute. No twists or turns were involved, just a head-on joining of two mouths together, but it was emotionally intense and left an impression on their souls.

When their kiss ended, they moved apart and stared tenderly into each other's eyes.

"I love you", he said with brutal honesty. The quiet mystery in his eyes beckoned her to say it back.

"I love you, too." Her voice was airy but audible, and her eyes were wide with devotion and joy. The nerves in her body felt scattered and unconnected, and her heart fell into her stomach as she tried to regain her composure; she really did love him with all her heart. She was fearful that he was going to leave and never come back, and she wanted nothing more than to kidnap him, tie him to the bed, and keep him with her for the rest of her life. Regret flowed through every vein, as she realized that she had to allow him to go back to Italy; she had no choice about the situation, and she knew it.

"Should we get ready to go?" Enrico asked calmly. He didn't want to leave Sadie again, but he had a concert to conduct in Riga in a few days, and he needed a day or two to prepare. "Come on, let's go", he insisted. He pulled her off the chair with both hands, and stretched one arm across her shoulders as he walked her towards the master bedroom.

Sadie's heart was already breaking, and he hadn't even left yet. They went into her room and got dressed unhurriedly, as if that would make the time magically slow down. When they were ready, they snapped a few

The Elusive Mr. Velucci

dozen pictures of themselves in different poses; some were completely silly, some were serious, and there were two pictures where they were kissing or had their cheeks pushed up against each other.

As they stood side-by-side comparing the photos, they made the other one promise to send 'this one' or 'that one' as soon as possible.

When they were finally ready to walk out the door, they took one last look around, and both felt like they were abandoning the life which they could have, and driving to a place where they would have to separate again. It was a depressing reality, but one which they both knew needed to happen.

They drove slowly to the hotel to collect Enrico's things, because neither wanted him to leave. They were in his room all of 10 minutes, and then walked back out again.

Because Enrico was used to travelling and living out of a suitcase, he had become quite organized in the past 10 or more years. The few clothing items which he always took with him, got washed or sent to the cleaners after each trip. The standard items remained in whatever bag it was carried around in; toothpaste, a tooth brush, cologne, a comb, a nail file, shampoo, conditioner, pictures of loved ones, etc… He travelled light, but made sure to carry all the amenities of home.

There was a nice restaurant on the main floor of the hotel, and because they still had a little time, they decided to share one last meal together.

Enrico reached his hand across the table and laid it on top of Sadie's. "You know that I don't really want to go, right?" He made eye contact with her, and stressed the sentiments with his voice and body language.

Sadie dropped her chin to her chest. "I don't want you to go, either."

"I know, but I promise that it won't be forever." His voice was unsteady and filled with apologies.

She caught his eyes, and her sudden coolness was evidence that she was not amused. "You've said that to me before, and we lost touch", Sadie snapped.

The lines of worry deepened along his brow and around his eyes. "I promise that that will never happen again … ever!" he added fiercely. "We won't let it."

Sadie didn't believe him and her face dropped. "I want to believe you."

Enrico was committed and felt the need to prove it. He stood up and went to her side of the small table. He got down on bended knee and spoke from his heart. "I will be spending the rest of my life with you, Sadie Lynn Adams, so you better get used to that. I have to leave you today, but when I retire next year, I will be around you so much that you will get tired of me."

His words woke her up and she was suddenly in good spirits again. "You want to spend the rest of your life with me?"

"I do, if you'll have me."

A very bright smile found its way through her recent mask of uncertainty. She reached over and wrapped her arms around his neck as she chanted, "Thank you, thank you, thank you." It was in a low voice, but it was filled with excitement, and she made sure that Enrico could definitely hear every word.

He returned the hug, and together they shed a few tears of happiness.

The Elusive Mr. Velucci

They spend the next twenty minutes in the restaurant, talking about their future and their kids, and then they made their way to the airport.

After parking her car, they walked into the terminal. She waited off to the side while he got himself checked in, and then they said their final good-byes.

"You call me!" she insisted harshly. Sadie had her index finger wagging in his face in order to make her point seem stronger.

Enrico couldn't help but laugh at how demanding she tried to sound, and he complemented her statement with a smile.

"Promise me!" she commanded. She had tears in her eyes which were about to fall down her face, and she wanted nothing more than to keep him there with her.

He crossed his heart and used the boy scout pledge with his hand, as he recited what she told him to say. "I promise to call you, no matter what."

"Even if you can't move or speak, get someone else to call me", she insisted.

"I promise", he chuckled, and held her by both of her shoulders.

She gazed into his eyes and hoped that he could feel what was in her heart. "I wish I could go with you", she stated truthfully. If she did not have to stay in New York because of work, Sadie would have loved to watch him perform.

"Me too", he sighed sadly. He reached out and pulled her tight against his body. As he had her bound in his arms he said, "You will never know how much you mean to me.

I know I screwed up in the past, but I will never do that again."

Sadie began to sob. "I hope you mean that, because I can't lose you again."

"You won't have to, trust me." He kissed her forehead, and then laid his cheek in that same spot in order to preserve the memory forever.

An announcement shot out from the overhead speakers, ordering all passengers to go to their gates.

"I guess it's time." Enrico was now beginning to tear up.

They hugged and kissed like he was being sent off to war, and then he walked away.

Sadie's heart was breaking as she watched him give his ticket to the attendant.

"Bye!" he called over his shoulder, and then he disappeared through the endless hallway which led to the plane.

"Bye", she called softly. She was waving, but he was no longer there.

As he walked down the long corridor, Enrico thought about what she had said about going with him.

Sadie's heart fluttered as she suddenly remembered him saying that he had booked a window seat. She made her way over to the large panes of glass which had a view of the runways, and she spied into each one of the round openings on the plane which was flying to Italy. She was being awfully impulsive, but she hoped that she could see Enrico's face, one last time.

Overhead, the music in the airport began to play a romantic slow song. The lyrics were sentimental, and her mind was instantly thrown to the end of the movie.

Suddenly, she had an ache in her chest, chills up her back, and tears in her eyes, and all because he would soon be gone.

♪ Scattered pictures,
of the smiles we leave behind

Sadie was trying to make out all of the faces which appeared in the tiny windows on the plane, but it was so difficult; the weather outside was not the best that it could be, and the people inside the plane were more blurred than she had anticipated. She now felt like she was losing something more valuable than her own life, but there was nothing she could do to change things.

Smiles we gave to one another
For the way we were ♪

Before the song had ended, Sadie was overcome with worry, and crying an endless amount of tears. She reached into her purse to see if there was anything to wipe the salty water off her face, and became instantly startled by a nearby stranger.

"Can you use this?" The male voice sounded as if it had come from directly behind her, and it made her jump. Sadie turned around and almost fainted; Enrico was waving a tissue and wearing a goofy smile.

"What's happening?" she asked, as she jumped into his arms. Her mind was sprinkled with a million more questions, but they all disappeared into thin air; nothing else in the world mattered, as long as her storybook prince was there with her.

"I just couldn't leave you again, so I booked a later flight." He was smiling from ear-to-ear, and after seeing her reaction, he knew that he had made the right decision by staying.

"And I didn't know how I was going to let you", she cried. She stared into his eyes as if she was looking at a mirage.

"So, how about if we spend the next five hours together?"

Sadie's eyes shot open as wide as they could go - with surprise as well as for joy. "Yes!" she shouted loudly, and she kissed him hard and long. "Did you already change your ticket?" The adrenaline in her body was racing faster than normal, and her mind had not caught up yet.

Enrico had to laugh at her unworldliness, for she was clearly not as experienced in things like travelling as he was. "Yes, I've already done what needs to be done, so we can go whenever you're ready."

"Yeeeah!" Sadie shouted loudly. She was childlike and beaming as bright as the noonday sun, and in complete awe of his brilliant idea. "I still can't believe you're really here."

"Well, let me prove to you that I am." He grabbed her by the waist and moved her body so that the front of hers was tightly molded to the front of his. He then lowered his head and kissed her with an intensity that was both dreamlike and erotic.

His entire scheme was spontaneous, and she knew that she would have to reward him. Sadie captured his lips with a tantalizing gratitude, and the outcome was more than satisfying.

Minutes later, when they were walking to her car, they both inhaled noisily while trying to catch their breath.

The Elusive Mr. Velucci

They spent the next few hours seeing the sights, holding hands, kissing as often as possible, and talking up a storm.

"I'd love to take you to Italy", Enrico stated. "You'll get to see my home and where I was born, and maybe I could persuade you to watch me conduct an orchestra?"

Sadie was overwhelmed and let out a breathy little moan. "Yes to all of it!" she professed with a great deal of enthusiasm. She wrapped her arms around his neck and squeezed him with all her might, and then she smothered him with a hundred kisses.

Enrico was laughing because he had never known enthusiasm like hers before. She was such a delight to be with and he vowed to never let her go again; being with her felt natural, as if they had always been a couple, in every sense of the word.

When it was time to drive Enrico back to the airport, it wasn't as bad as it was a few hours ago. There were still tears in their eyes, but because they had had a little more time to say good-bye, it was a little easier to let go.

Sadie parked the car and they walked into the airport, hand-in-hand.

Enrico pulled her body towards his and hugged her tightly. "Bye", he whispered, so only she could hear. He then stared into her eyes as if he was speaking to her by mental telepathy. "I honestly don't want to leave, but I have to."

"I know", she said sadly. She wrapped her hands around his back, and intertwined her fingers as if she was locking him into that position.

"I can't wait to show you Italy." He studied her hair, her eyes, her nose, and her mouth as he spoke, while the back of his index finger stroked her cheek.

Tina Griffith

"I can't wait to see it." A delicious shudder shot through her body at the thought of them in Italy together.

"I would like to spend a full week or two with you. Do you think that can that be arranged?"

"YES!" she shouted at low volume. "I will make it happen."

As Enrico gazed into Sadie's eyes, he could see that they belonged together. After Maria died, he didn't know how to go on, but Sadie brought him back to life in ways that he could never have imagined.

Sadie had never loved any man other than Enrico, and that's why it was so easy to give him her body and soul.

They hugged tight, one more time, and drew in all the sounds and aromas that they could. Then they heard the overhead announcement, which meant that he had to go.

"I love you", he said, and picked up his suitcase.

"I love you, too", she replied, and then she watched him walk away.

Sadie went over to the big windows, and examined each round opening on the plane. When she saw him waving, her spirits picked up, and she waved back with all her might. Minutes later, the airplane prepared to taxi to the runway.

Sadie was quite teary-eyed as she followed the movements of the plane, and began to cry when it raced down the runway. Once it was in the air, Sadie lowered her eyes and wondered when she would hear from Enrico again.

Enrico arrived in Italy many hours later, but during his flight, he couldn't help but smile as he thought about Sadie and their future.

Enrico took a taxi from the airport, and because he wanted to make sure that he never lost her phone number

The Elusive Mr. Velucci

again, he hand-wrote several copies, and placed them in different rooms in his home.

After taking a day to readjust to the climate and ambience in Italy, Enrico repacked his suitcase and flew to the Baltic States. He was greeted in the airport by several representatives of the hall, the orchestra, and the city, and delivered to his very grand hotel by limo. Over the next 24 hours, they treated him like a king, by offering him the best of all they had to offer. And after giving him two hours to get himself ready, they chauffeured him to the venue. Once he got there, he had three hours to practice and work out any kinks, and then he conducted the Latvian National Symphony Orchestra, in the Great Guild Concert Hall in Riga.

His performance was magnificent. And he experienced an overabundance of gratification, when he received a standing ovation from the more than 650 people in attendance. "Bravo!" they shouted, as they clapped and threw flowers onto the stage. Enrico stood proud and tall, and drank it all in.

He spent the next day walking around the beautiful city of Riga, and soaked in as much of the culture and natural features as he could see. Later that night, he flew back to Italy, and began making arrangements for Sadie to join him.

Enrico couldn't wait for her to see his home, where he grew up, and how he lived, and he also wanted her to see his favorite spot in the whole world – Sorrento.

He had told her all about the place of his birth, in the hours before his flight left New York. When he described the beautiful Amalfi Coastline, she became giddy and her eyes went wild with excitement.

"It's a series of small bays, beaches, villages and towns", he

Tina Griffith

began. "And they all share the same glorious backdrop of rugged high cliffs."

He made it sound so romantic, that Sadie couldn't help but sigh.

Enrico was reminiscing and loved the expression she wore when he was mentally illustrating where he lived. He was now home and missing her a great deal, and he needed to blink a few times to stop the tears from running down his face. As he continued to unpack, his only thought was of her. An hour later, he was in bed and dreaming of the moment when Sadie would be there with him.

Sadie was in New York, getting ready for her trip to Italy. She spoke to Enrico on the phone every second night, and in spite of her busy schedule, thoughts of him intruded into every hour of her day. She was thrilled to be going on her first trip abroad, and hoped that she didn't sound too childish when she asked what she should bring. "Does it rain there much? Is it cold? Should I bring a lot of sun screen?" she asked. She honestly didn't know, and hoped that he would not hold that against her.

Enrico chuckled, and answered every one of her questions with honesty. He was looking forward to Sadie coming to Italy, and he made sure that his home was in perfect shape for her visit.

Sophie and Angelo had just come back from their two-week honeymoon in Hawaii, and drove straight to Sadie's home.

During dinner Sophie asked, "How was everything here?" She left Enrico in her mother's care, and because of their strange relationship, Sophie was a little concerned.

The Elusive Mr. Velucci

"Oh, it went very well." Sadie decided not to tell the newly-weds that Enrico had delayed his flight, or how much time they had actually spent together. And in order to divert Sophie from posing another question, Sadie turned to Angelo and added, "Your father is a total delight; I loved visiting with him, and drove him to the airport in time for him to get checked in."

"I'm so happy that you and Enrico got along so well, mom", Sophie gushed. "He's an awfully nice man."

"Me too", Angelo agreed, and lowered his head in a moment of reflection; he suddenly remembered how much his father had grieved after his mom died.

Enrico had been in a horrible amount of emotional pain, and for a long time. Because it's been a few years since the family of three became a family of two, Angelo loved that his father was wearing a smile again.

Sadie had had enough of them talking about her, so she changed the topic. "Hey! Let me see some pictures of your honeymoon!" It was a strong request, but she knew that she didn't have to push too hard in order to grab Sophie's attention.

A small squeal came from Sophie's lips before she ran to get her purse. She pulled out a large envelope and said, "I just happen to have them all handy, but I have to warn you, there's a lot." The new bride had suddenly come to life, and her voice had gone from happy, to over the moon with giddiness.

Sadie spent the next two hours listening to all the details of their glorious honeymoon, and she loved every second of it. Sadly, she wished that Enrico could have been there to enjoy it too, but she knew that he would get his chance, soon enough.

Before they all said good-night, Sadie took a large lungful of air for encouragement, and then made an announcement. "Hang on a second. I wanted to tell you that Enrico has asked me to go to Italy for a week or so, and I said yes." It wasn't meant to have been blurted out, and now she waited with baited breath to see how the news would be taken.

Terri was a sucker for romance and sighed, "Aww...." She had been completely mesmerized by the entire story so far, as had everyone else in the room. She had switched to decaf coffee after her third pumpkin spice latte, and had devoured an entire plate of nachos - including sour cream and lots of melted cheese.

Halley was still sipping what she had left in her cup, and throughout the past hour, she had been watching her friend with a great deal of hilarity. She had never seen Terri so uninhibited before, and knew without pause, that the black dress would feel a bit tight if she tried to put it on again in the morning.

Because Halley had taken another break in the story, a few customers took a chance and rushed to the bathroom or outside for a quick smoke. Others ran to the counter and placed another order for food and/or drink, while the manager came over to Halley's table and offered them whatever they wanted. "It's on the house", she added happily.

"Nothing for me", Terri announced. She leaned herself backwards into the padded seat, and took a deep breath of air into her lungs. She was full, mentally exhausted but happy, and nothing was going to stop her from hearing the rest of the story.

"I'll have a decaffeinated coffee", Halley stated kindly. When it arrived, she thanked the manager and waited until everyone was seated. It was quite evident that they all wanted to know more, and she was now at the point where she didn't mind accommodating them.

As the manager walked back to the chair near Halley and Terri's table, she hushed the crowd to silence. "Sh-h-h-h-h!! Everyone, calm down."

Halley was loving the attention and teased, "Shall I continue? Or have you all had enough." She flashed a shrewd smile across her lips, for she already knew how they would answer.

Everyone gasped as if she was serious and shouted, "Continue!"

She turned her attention to Terri and asked the same question.

Terri scrunched up her face and released a theatrical groan, which came from somewhere deep inside of her soul. After a reflective inhale and exhale, some of the tension had been released. And then, after propping both of her elbows onto the table, she gazed at Halley with a dreamy look in her eyes. "Please continue", she pleaded softly. Terri so wanted Enrico and Sadie to end up together, and was nervously tapping one of her toes while urging Halley to tell the rest of the story.

Halley had never seen this side of her friend before, but here she was, her chin was resting in the palms of her hands, and her eyes were as round and bright as a full moon.

"I can't believe that Sophie will let her mother go!" someone in the crowd shouted.

Terri called back, "I can't wait to find out what happens when they're alone in Italy."

Halley was smiling and had her hands in the air as she stated, "Ok, let's start from there."

Angelo was extremely happy by the news, and shouted in joy and disbelief. "Congratulations, Sadie! You will love it there!" He was truly sincere and rushed over to hug her.

Sophie was mildly delighted and totally skeptical. "I'm happy for you mom, but does this mean that you guys are dating?" Her tone of voice and body language stated that she was a little put off by the announcement.

Sophie had already decided that Enrico was a nice guy, but he was Angelo's father, so she had to be nice to him. She wasn't sure why her mother was being so nice to him; with them living across the ocean, they'd hardly ever see each other. 'How could that possibly work if they decided to become a couple?' she wanted to know.

Angelo's eyes shot open as wide as they could go. He was terribly confused with the accusation that his wife had just made, but he wasn't sure if he should get in between a mother and daughter. His face spoke volumes about how he was feeling, and even though he was a brand new husband, he knew enough to keep quiet.

Sadie met her daughter's eyes with authority, and pleaded for her to understand. "We are friends, Sophie. We are also family."

Sophie crossed her arms and laid them against her chest before she spoke. "That doesn't mean you have to be *that* close."

Tina Griffith

Angelo reached his arm out and stretched it across his wife's shoulders. "I'm sure that my father meant well. He's a very generous man, who extended a very kind invitation to your mother." He pulled Sophie's shoulders closer until her body squeezed between his hand and shoulder.

Sophie lowered his eyes and relented. "I guess." She suddenly felt silly, and turned to hug her mother. "Sorry, mom. I'm going to trust that you will have an amazing time."

"Thank you." Sadie hugged her daughter, and showered her with a lot of love. Over Sophie's shoulder, Sadie winked in Angelo's direction.

'You're welcome', he mouthed. He was clearly happier than Sophie was about Sadie going to Italy, but he hoped in time that his wife would see that her mother and his father made a cute couple.

After the kids left Sadie's home, she rushed to her bedroom and called Enrico. She told him all about the visit - photos and all - and then explained the feelings which Sophie had about her going to Italy.

Enrico felt responsible for the rift between Sadie and her daughter. He wasn't prepared to hear that Sophie has that much bitterness towards him, and it made him feel awful. For a brief moment he tried to see Sophie's point, but he soon brushed it off; he was clearly not used to how a young woman's mind worked. "We will certainly talk about that situation, once you are here", he cooed into the phone.

"Thank you", she sighed. Sadie felt much better after speaking with Enrico; he had a way of saying just the right thing, at the right time. "Night, Enrico."

"Talk soon, my love." Enrico blew a few kisses into the phone before they hung up.

The Elusive Mr. Velucci

The next day, without letting Angelo know what she was up to, Sophie called her mom and invited her to go for lunch.

There was something about the request that didn't sit well, but Sadie agreed to the time and day.

They met at Moxie's, and sat in a table in the quietest corner of the room. After ordering their lunches, Sophie began her barrage of questions towards her mother. "I want to know what is going on between you and Enrico." It was direct and quite clear, and Sophie held her terrifying gaze until her mother answered.

Sadie was sitting in a pool of bitter shock, but she knew enough to keep her private life to herself. "Nothing but friendship", she replied firmly.

"How do I know that?" Sophie asked, in a tone that was on the edge of being rude.

Sophie's mind couldn't help going back to her wedding and the moment after she had arrived at the altar. The minister asked, "Who gives this woman to wed this man?", and Enrico ran over to her mother and stated that they both do. Sophie then flashed back to all the quick glances and awkward smiles that had passed between them since they met, and none of it made any sense.

"You don't, but why can't you trust me?" Sadie's eyes fell to her plate when the food arrived, and while she ate, she thought of many ways how she could run out of there and still keep her daughter's respect and friendship.

Sophie was not pleased with her mother's answers, but even though she could feel that there was something more going on, she could also see that she might have upset her mother with her silly questions. 'Did she have the right to interfere to this degree?' she wondered. 'Enrico was Angelo's father. What if it didn't work out? Wouldn't that make it awkward at family gatherings?'

Her mind continued to have doubt regarding the truth of their relationship, but Sophie decided to ease up on her interrogation for today. "Sorry, mom", she sighed. "I think I'm just looking out for your best interest."

"Thank you", she said, but her voice was borderline cold. Sadie was relieved that the question part of their visit was over, but she knew that her daughter wasn't about to give up that easily.

Four days later, Sadie found herself out with Sophie again, and now she was in the middle of a rapid fire game of 'riddle me this'.

"Did you sleep with Enrico? He's my father-in-law and your in-law. You know that wouldn't be appropriate, right? And with you living here and him living overseas, how would you work out a relationship?" Sophie ended her grilling session with, "Please tell me that you two aren't thinking of dating."

Sadie was left wide-eyed and bowled over by her daughter's humiliating outburst, and didn't know if she wanted to go through this again. "Hang on", she stated firmly. Her left hand was hanging flat in the air and ordering Sophie to wait a minute. She dropped her fork on the table, leaned forward, planted her feet flat on the ground in front of her chair, and spoke as a mother who's child needed to be scolded. "It's not your business, but no, we didn't sleep together. However, I do think we have found a basis for mutual agreement." Sadie held her stare until she felt that

The Elusive Mr. Velucci

her daughter had heard every word. Only then did she let go and glance towards her plate.

Sophie could definitely feel that her mother was upset, and it made her sit up and take notice.

Sadie popped a forkful of food into her mouth, and chewed it for a few seconds before she continued with her speech. "You and Angelo are our common place for happiness. Please understand that whatever affects our children, will concern Enrico and me."

It was obvious how Sophie felt in that moment, and she tried to calm herself down before any tears emerged.

Sadie changed her tone of voice and facial features in order to appear more apathetic. "I'm sorry, but we are a family now. And until something changes, we are all going to be friendly."

Sophie felt like a little girl who had just been caught with her hand in the cookie jar. "I'm sorry, mom. I probably shouldn't be interfering in anything that concerns you, but I just want you to be careful."

Sadie swallowed hard and then locked eyes with Sophie. "I thank you, but I'm a big girl and I know what I'm doing."

Sophie's mind snapped back to the protective mode, and her eyes went wide with wild curiosity. "What does that mean?"

"Sophie!" her mother snapped, as if to bring her to her senses. "Nothing has happened! After you left to go on your honeymoon, we talked, we laughed, and I drove him to the airport like you asked. During those hours, we got to know each other and he asked me if I've ever been to Italy. I said no, and he suggested that I go, and that he would show me the sights. That's it!" She paused for a moment to collect her thoughts. "We are friends, Sophie", she stated, in a voice that was softer and quieter. "He invited me to go to Italy, and I said yes." With her hand in the air like a boy scout, she promised not to sleep with him. "Can we leave it at that?"

Sophie's beautiful dark eyes teared up and she suddenly felt very foolish. "I'm sorry, mom. Of course you can be friends with Enrico. I'm not sure where all this emotion is coming from." She stood up and raced towards her mother to give her a hug. "I love you. Please forgive me."

Sadie accepted the gesture, and was relieved that this topic was now closed. "I love you, too. Now enough!"

When the embrace ended, they finished their lunch and went their separate ways, much happier than when their date started.

A few days later, Sadie was taken to the airport by Angelo and Sophie, and given an authentic send off. After Angelo offered her a sincere wish to have a great time, Sophie shot her mother a look that suggested she not do anything that they would all regret later. Sadie rolled her eyes, moaned out loud, and laughed as she walked away.

Because she had never flown before, Sadie was filled with a ton of apprehension. She hated the feeling when the plane left the ground, but luckily, it only lasted a minute or two, and then everything was ok. Aside from a few moments of turbulence here and there, she quite enjoyed the flight.

Sadie ended up sleeping for five hours during the night, and very intentionally, inspected every detail of the plane when she was awake.

When they were landing, she made sure to watch out the window so that she could see as much of Italy as possible.

Enrico was waiting for her when her plane touched

The Elusive Mr. Velucci

down, and as soon as she spotted him, she raced into his arms.

[11]"Amore mio!" he called when he saw her. His eyes teared up with absolute happiness, and when she leaned against his body, he felt more alive than ever.

"I've missed you", she cried. She was astonished at the sense of fulfillment which she felt, the instant she landed in his arms. Now that she was on Italian soil and they were together, she knew that this was exactly where she was supposed to be.

"I've missed you, too", he admitted in a low tone. His usually deep and rich voice was filled with emotion, and he was choking on his ability to speak. At the same time, many tears of gladness were blinding his eyesight. He hugged her as he pushed his face into the nook between her neck and shoulder, and sighed with pure contentment. "I'm so glad that you're here", he whispered sincerely. Enrico kissed her forehead and then they went off to search for her luggage.

Enrico drove her to his home, where, while she unpacked a few of her necessary items, he scooted into the kitchen to make her something wonderful to eat.

Sadie came downstairs thirty minutes later, and she couldn't believe what she was looking at. The first thing she noticed was how many lit candles were in the room; they were so beautiful and eerie, and had somehow cast a romantic spell in the small space. The second thing she noticed was the glorious music of a famous trumpeter - one who is noted for his starry-eyed melodies - playing softly in the background. This particular song was oozing a gentle

---

[11] Amore mio = My love

aura of nostalgia, as it dispersed its delicate essence around the room.

There were two place settings of expensive dishware and silverware on the marble table top, which were sitting directly across from one other. In between them was an antique set of candle holders, that appeared to be supervising a lunch of deep fried polenta crusted Brie. It was laying precariously on a large dollop of tomato apricot jam, and served with an endive salad on the side.

The first few notes of 'Cinema Paradiso', began to travel throughout the dimly-lit space, in the exact moment when Enrico came into the dining room from the kitchen. "Viola!" he announced when he saw her. He spread his arms out wide, and invited her to come closer. "Please. Enjoy."

Sadie's eyes were jumping here and there, inspecting each and every item before her. She was in awe of what he had done for her, and was mesmerized at how giving he was.

Enrico pulled her chair out and waited for her to sit down. As her bum touched the seat, he closed his eyes and sniffed the fragrance of her loose hair. He then unfolded the linen napkin and laid it gently across her lap.

Sadie lifted her smiling face towards his, and as if cupid's arrow had reached her heart, she was more in love than ever. As she watched him move to the opposite side of the table, a shiver went up her spine. Whether it was intended or not, the whole scenario encouraged intimacy.

Enrico used his fork to cut into the Brie, and he persuaded Sadie to do the same thing. He added a bit of jam to the fork and brought the utensil to his eager mouth. "Mmmm…." he sighed.

Sadie's turn. The glorious symphony of flavors had filled

The Elusive Mr. Velucci

her sense of smell long before she sat down, and now she was about to introduce the delicious foods to her tongue. She picked up her fork, scooped up the exact combination which Enrico had had, and placed the entire thing in her mouth. Her taste buds were immediately transported towards a most magnificent food orgasm; the sweet and savory combination was pure magic.

"Well? What do you think?" His eyes twinkled as a smile stretched its way across his lips.

"I honestly can't believe it", she sighed pleasantly. Sadie's eyelashes lifted and she locked eyes with Enrico.

Enrico watched her with love and curiosity, for he had much hope that she would enjoy his cooking. "And?" He hadn't been this interested in creating a meal for anyone in many years, and he really wanted to impress her.

"It is way more amazing than I can describe", Sadie declared. "I mean, WOW!"

That's all he needed to hear, for his heart was now bursting with happiness.

As more of the meal was being consumed, another dozen compliments were given. While coffee was being served, they sat back and talked for a long time, while they gazed into each other's eyes. When the table was cleared, Enrico showed Sadie all the highlights of his home.

Sadie was quite impressed with how beautiful everything was, and she envisioned herself visiting again and again.

After the tour was done, Enrico asked, "Do you feel up to going for a short drive? I'd like to show you a bit of what the city has to offer."

"I do", she announced happily. "Let me grab a jacket." She rushed upstairs and came down again, quickly.

Tina Griffith

Over the next few hours, Enrico drove Sadie around Sorrento in his Mini 1 convertible. "This is the most picturesque town on the Amalfi coast", he began, as he pushed his BMW into the next gear. "As you can see, it's perched high on the cliffs and has stunning views - from the Bay of Naples to the distant Mount Vesuvius."

"Oh, my", she gasped in sheer admiration of all that was around her. Enrico was driving a little faster than she would have liked, and she found it necessary to tie her silk scarf with an extra knot, so that it wouldn't blow off her head.

Enrico pointed off to the side and continued to recite the many interesting facts about his country. "This road hugs the cliffs of one of the most spectacular drives in all of Europe. Orange, lemon, and olive groves are everywhere, and over there are some of the world's most famous vineyards. But what makes this place even more special, is that all of this is close to the sparkling Tyrrhenian Sea."

Sadie's heart was beating for joy, while her eyes were wide open to all that Enrico was describing. The landscape was breathtaking, and almost too much for her to drink it all in at once. She turned her head to look at Enrico, who was sporting Hollywood sunglasses and looked like a Greek playboy, and she fell in love with him all over again. The sun was bright and warm, he was smiling and tanned, and with the wind blowing through his wavy black hair, this was the image which she could look at for the rest of her life.

Enrico could see how impressed she was by his countryside, and felt that it was so worth the time and trouble that he was putting forth, for her to know everything that she was seeing. "Tomorrow we will sample the local

The Elusive Mr. Velucci

specialties; extra-virgin olive oil, mozzarella cheese, and Limoncello - the local liqueur. I've even arranged for us to make our own Neapolitan pizza!"

Sadie was teary-eyed and speechless. She was beaming from one ear to the other, and sighing with a merriment that her heart had never felt before.

"Perhaps I will take you to Maiori, which has its own beach and tree-lined walkway? The hills and cliffs form a wonderful backdrop, but the town itself is not that hilly."

"It all sounds incredibly amazing." Her head was rocking from side to side while looking at this and that, and her eyes were having a grand tour of sheer splendor.

While keeping one hand on the steering wheel, he reached over and placed his free hand on her upper thigh. "We will do a bit of walking there, but don't worry; it's easy to stroll through the narrow streets and lanes. And because of their interesting shops, cafes and churches, I'm sure that you will not be bored." Enrico removed his hand from her leg, and placed it back onto the steering wheel.

Sadie was living in a moment where she had somehow forgotten everything and everyone else, in the entire world. She was giddy, disoriented, and her head was filling to the point of capacity. She couldn't believe how beautiful this place was, and she wondered how she had gone through her whole life without knowing that this paradise existed.

By 8pm, Enrico had brought Sadie back to his home. His delightful companion was exhausted, so they opted to have a glass of wine while sitting quietly. Before 9pm, Sadie had mellowed enough and wanted to go to bed.

Enrico had prepared the guest room for Sadie to sleep

in, but she had insisted that they sleep together in his big bed - the same as they had done in her home.

This pleased him very much, and Enrico was already on his side when Sadie came into the room.

The master bedroom was quite masculine and darker than her bedroom at home. The drapes were heavy with bold colors, and held open by decorative ropes. The large area rug looked quite expensive, and allowed people to see a small portion of the gorgeous buffed flooring beneath it. The bed was high and soft, and the bedding and pillows were fit for a king.

As she climbed into the bed, her heart pounded; she was very aware of him observing all that she had to offer.

They were inches away from each other, laying on their backs on separate pillows, and the round swell of her breasts suddenly tempted him.

Sadie noticed the change in Enrico's breathing, and when she turned to look at him, she saw the color of his cheeks go from tanned to red. The twinkle in his eyes told her what he wanted, but a few short weeks ago, they had talked about waiting for the perfect moment. Since this was not it, she tugged at the blanket until it covered her up to her neck.

Enrico recognized the meaning behind the silent gesture, but he didn't want to obey. Instead, his face was lit up as he reached his hand under the blanket, and lovingly caressed her nearest breast.

Sadie felt the nipple tighten to a sharp peak almost immediately. "Enrico, we shouldn't", she protested softly.

Because she didn't brush him away, his hand made its way across her chest to the other breast, and he kneaded it ever so gently. "Sadie", he breathed, in a way that warmed

The Elusive Mr. Velucci

her tensed muscles. His accent was slow and sexy, his breath was minty, and his body was warm and smelled of Old Spice. His muscular chest was touching the right side of her body, and it was all she could do not to give in.

Sadie's eyes fluttered shut, as she moaned and her toes went rigid. She now had a loose grip on the blanket, and all thoughts to ending what he had started, disappeared.

In a bold move, Enrico threw caution to the wind, and forced the blanket to fly off of her upper body.

When the cool air kissed her exposed skin, something in her head popped and she became instantly aware of what was happening. "Enrico, we can't", she said, as shame washed over her. She was looking directly into his eyes as she covered herself up again, and then spoke from her heart. With a request for forgiveness, she reached over and caressed his chest. "I'm sorry."

As much as he didn't want to admit it, Enrico understood and rolled onto his back.

Sadie's body was still warm with passion, and as her pulse quickened with a forbidden longing, she moved herself securely beside him. She nestled her head against his chest and arm, while her leg lay gently on top of his.

He in turn, wrapped his arm around her waist and held her very close. "It's ok", he whispered. There was knowledge behind his words, but not much truth.

It wasn't easy for either of them to be that close and not be able to extinguish the flame of desire; they both relished the opportunity to rekindle what had happened over twenty years ago. However, this was Sadie's first night in Italy, and because they had many days and nights ahead of them, they decided to be content to lay in each other's arms.

Tina Griffith

Over the next few days, Enrico took Sadie to the finest places to eat, and also to the smaller locations which tourists usually miss. The medieval architecture of both the churches and the cathedrals, were enlightening as well as awe-inspiring. Sadie was most fascinated by the millenary ruins of Pompeii, and its fascinating archaeological museum. She absorbed as much as she could see and smell, and found it all to be a truly humbling experience.

Enrico loved that her eyes sparkled with great interest, and that she had sincerely enjoyed everything which had caught her eyes and other senses. She was like a kid in a candy shop, and kept asking for more and more. And while he was interpreting it all for her, it was as if he was actually basking in it for the first time, himself.

Sadie loved observing all that Sorrento and Naples had to offer, but she also loved spending some time in Enrico's home. He was an amazing cook, and Sadie enjoyed watching him prepare their remarkable meals. When the food was ready, they usually brought everything out to the large balcony, where they dined while staring out at the glorious Bay of Naples.

On her forth night in Italy, minutes after they had finished eating, they danced under the full moon while it frolicked across the waves of the dark blue water. The background music was soft and the red wine was fruity and cool. The scenario had calmed their souls and eventually tore down their protective shields. This enabled them to work towards having a nice ending to a glorious day.

When Enrico saw the perfect opportunity, he lifted Sadie's glass from her hand. He set it down on the ledge behind her, and then brought her body closer to his own.

The Elusive Mr. Velucci

He guided her hands to reach around his back, and then cupped the back of her head while he brushed his mouth against hers.

Sadie tasted his sweetened lips as if for the first time, and she swooned. Without much coaxing, his tongue found its way inside the warm cave of her mouth, and fought a silent battle with everything that it touched. A minute later, as Enrico was playfully biting her earlobe and then nuzzling the nape of her neck, it was becoming clear that he had hopes of going lower.

Sadie was completely entranced in the moment, and had lost count of how many times his lips had made contact with her skin. He had already trailed kisses all over her face and neck, and was now moving along the length of her collarbone. She lifted her chin and moved her head to the side to give him better access, and a charming thought made her smile; if he kissed her every single day from now until forever, it would not be enough. She was head-over-heels in love with him and wanted to spend the rest of her life in his arms.

Enrico was reading her body language, and interpreted her movements as gentle encouragement. He was delighted that she was not trying to stop his advances, and employed his hands to move things to the next level.

As he pressed the tip of his nose into her cheek, his right hand slid slowly down the length of her spine. When he reached the bottom of her lower back, he pulled her groin towards his own.

She could feel the heat of his body against her chest and tummy, and then the growing hardness behind his zipper, against her leg. It was all so surreal; her long dress, the half-moon, the evening air, the music, the view, and being in Enrico's arms.

He touched his forehead against hers, and without saying a word, he pleaded for her to take him to bed.

Sadie would have loved nothing more, but because they had pledged a promise, they couldn't do much more than what they were already doing. She stroked his cheek as she kissed his mouth, and hoped that he could feel her emotional pain.

Sadie was very appreciative to be in Italy, and it was more than magnificent to be there with Enrico, but she couldn't break a trust. A tear fell down her cheek as she explored how unbelievable it would be, to be able to fulfill each and every one of their wishes; they were two grown adults in a romantic city in Italy. They were alone in a storybook fantasy setting and could essentially do anything they wanted, but there would be consequences to deal with afterwards.

Their relationship was sweet and quite complex, and while they wanted to rush into bed, they knew that that couldn't happen. Sadie swore to Sophie that her and Enrico were just friends. She even promised to keep things between them uncomplicated. But as she stood so close that a whisper couldn't wriggle through their tightly woven bodies, she realized that it was not an easy task; her longing for him was overpowering her common sense.

Enrico recognized what was happening, and it broke their impassioned mood. The certainty of lovemaking was suddenly shattered, and both of their hearts fell like heavy bricks. They realized that they could still lay in each other's arms, so they chose to go to bed.

The Elusive Mr. Velucci

As he brushed his teeth, he felt that it was so unfair that the woman he loved was close and willing, but that he couldn't have her. But he knew the score; he and Sadie had talked about this at great length, a few short weeks ago. He had agreed to wait back then, and now he had to hide his disappointment as best he could.

Enrico actually couldn't wait until they could be together - naked and in the same bed - so he could satisfy each and every lustful thought that he had. The fact that it might not happen this week, annoyed him, but not to the point where he would want to give up.

After Sadie crawled into bed, she looked deep into Enrico's eyes. She could see the hurt, but no matter how much she wanted things to be different, she couldn't get past the part where she had promised her daughter that they were just friends. Without speaking, they wrapped their arms around each other and held on for dear life.

In the dark of the night, the lights were twinkling in the sky, and the moon was serenading them with its clandestine magic. Their lower bodies throbbed with a yearning that could not be fulfilled, and their skin was glowing hot with a desire that could not be snuffed out. The window was open, and the slight breeze washed over them and was able to cool them down.

As Sadie cuddled up to him, she weighed all of her options. She loved her daughter and never wanted to be caught in a lie, for that could truly destroy their life-long bond. Sadie was extremely interested in being in a relationship with Enrico, and couldn't wait to make love to him. She adored this man with every cell in her body, and it was killing her that she was missing out on something quite wonderful. She pushed her face into his chest and whimpered from the obvious confusion of the situation.

Enrico could feel Sadie sobbing and understood what she was feeling. He equated it to a permanent sorrow which seemed to constantly push her down, or an old wound which throbbed heavily in the rain. He knew because he had his own emotions to deal with; he had just met his daughter, she had married his son, and he wanted to keep them both happy while rekindling a relationship with Sadie.

'Sadie' Just the mention of her name sent shivers down his back. He had hoped to consummate their relationship at some point during her trip to Italy, but something cautioned him to tread slowly.

He was getting old and time was not on his side. He loved Angelo and Sophie, but they needed to know how he felt about Sadie. He was in love with her, and had been for the past twenty-odd years. They could be grandparents in the next few years, and he felt that he had the right to be with Sadie throughout that experience.

Sadie hoped that Enrico could see how tormenting it was to be that close to him and not to be able to touch every part of him.

Enrico glanced sideways and saw Sadie suck her bottom lip into her eager mouth. When she traded the top lip for the bottom, it made parts of Enrico's body come to life. He suddenly felt ill-equipped to undertake the task of keeping their promise, for all he wanted to do was rip her clothes off and kiss her all over.

Enrico desired Sadie in every way possible, and it was all he thought about since she arrived. Because her vacation time was winding down and they had not been

The Elusive Mr. Velucci

able to explore the differences between their teen bodies to their adult ones, the unwelcomed tension stretched tightly between them.

Sadie was well-aware of the heat that was emanating from Enrico's body; it surfaced from every one of his pores. She pressed her body closer to his and let one of her hands fall lightly in the middle of his chest. She didn't move a muscle, but could feel that he was savoring the moment.

The last twenty-four hours of her visit were the most difficult; anxiety rushed to the outer shell of every movement he made and every thought she had. Everything took on a suggestive appearance; how they spoke, how they ate, and how they looked into each other's eyes. Without speaking a word, they had been able to work through the deafening silence which loomed between them like a heavy mist, but it was at times, quite difficult. This didn't make them stronger, but it did cause them to reach a point where things needed to be resolved – one way or another.

Enrico woke up early so that he could make her a fancy breakfast. He made very little noise so as not to wake her from her last slumber in Italy, and the result was perfection.

Sadie came down the stairs just in time to watch him place the dishes of food on the table. She sat down in her usual spot across from him, and waited for him to sit down. "It looks amazing", she said softly.

"It's Porcini flan with pecorino crust", he stated proudly.

"And these? What kind of eggs are these?" She pointed to what she was asking about.

"Quail eggs from the market which we went to yesterday."

She remembered him buying them, but it never occurred

to her that she'd be eating them. "Quail eggs", she repeated quietly. "They're very tiny."

"But very tasty", he added, and proved it by placing a half of one into his mouth.

"I'm sure they are." Sadie felt a knot in her chest, which came from them not doing something as natural as having sex. She was sorry about that, and hoped that he truly understood. Her eyes met his, and then clouded with visions of their past. She tried to send him a private message, and instead, drank in the sensuality of his perfect physique. She was putty in his powerful presence, and she knew it, but she had to leave him without having the satisfaction which she so longed for.

Sadie cut an egg in half just as he had done, and placed it on her fork. The silky smooth texture danced between her tongue and the roof of her mouth, and it was pure bliss. The sensation and flavor experience was immediate, and caused her eyes to close without being asked. After the remnants of the egg slid down her throat, she cut into her flan.

Sadie was elated by the food, the smells, and by all that Enrico had done to make this trip amazingly wonderful, and she hoped that he knew how much she appreciated his efforts.

Enrico studied the emotions which streamed across her face, and he could see that she was both happy and sad at the same time. He knew that she was happy about being there with him, and with all that they had experienced together. He also saw how sad she was about leaving, and how dejected she was that they couldn't do all that they had wanted to do. He could tell how difficult this was for Sadie to deal with, and he felt sorry for her.

The Elusive Mr. Velucci

Enrico closed his eyes and looked into his heart. As much as he wanted to keep her captive and naked in his home for the rest of their lives, he was aware that he had to calm his body down. He wanted her more than anything on this planet, but he needed to accept that nothing was going to happen on this trip.

Hours later, Enrico drove Sadie to the airport. They had hugged many times while she packed her belongings, even though silent wishes for her to stay, lingered in the air all around them. They held hands while he drove, and stole long glances on the trip downtown.

They walked inside of the terminal and made promises to talk again soon, and each of them glowed with an untamed inner fire. Sadie checked her baggage and ran back to give him one more hug.

"Bye, my love!" he called sadly. His words weighed heavy in the air.

"Bye!" Sadie waved as she choked back tears, and then her expression stilled and grew serious.

Enrico had tears in his eyes as he watched her walk down the hallway towards the plane, and his face was devoid of excitement. As she disappeared into the dark corridor, he took a step forward as if he wanted to call her back. He stopped himself before shouting her name, because he didn't want to make it even harder on her; letting her leave at all, was one of the most grueling things he'd ever done - besides burying Maria.

Sadie was already missing Enrico, and she hadn't even reached the entrance to the plane yet. After she found her seat and sat down, she looked for him in the large windows of the terminal. He wasn't there, but she hoped that they would get at least one more chance to be together.

Anger seeped into her body, and she continued her thought as if she was revealing a promise. 'And if that ever happened, I swear that nothing and no-one will ever stand in the way of us expressing our love.'

The plane fired up its engines and raced down the runway, as Sadie broke down in tears; she had officially left Italy without having sex with Enrico. It broke her heart, but it also gave her the confidence and determination that she needed, to tell the kids the truth.

Enrico waited until Sadie's plane had taken off, and then he went home. Even walking out to his car felt different, for there was suddenly a huge void in his life. He drove home in silence while looking all around him, and wished that she was there beside him.

Stepping into his home felt odd, because he had never heard an echo resonate with so little life before. The kitchen was no longer a joy to be in, and his bedroom was now the loneliest place on the planet. He slid into misery very quickly, and watched the time tick away, until her plane landed in New York.

Hours later, once it was safe to get off the plane, Sadie took extra care to make sure that she was the last passenger to disembark. While she was in her seat, there was a connection to Enrico. When the stewardess and pilot came over and insisted that she leave, she knew that her dream vacation was officially over.

Sophie and Angelo were waiting for Sadie at the entrance of the airport terminal. From their first glance of her, they could see that something was terribly wrong; her face was

The Elusive Mr. Velucci

pale and withdrawn, and her body appeared to be quite sluggish.

"Mom!" Sophie shouted when she saw her mother. She assumed that the symptoms were due to jet lag, but her instincts were telling her otherwise. "Are you ok?" she asked sadly.

Sadie groaned something that could have indicated that she was ok, but it came out too muffled to really understand.

Angelo placed his arm around his mother-in-law, and welcomed her back to America. He wanted to ask her how her trip went, but after getting her luggage, he walked her out to the car in silence.

Sadie got into the back seat, while the newly-weds took up the front.

During the long drive home, Angelo and Sophie shared glances with each other, in hopes that the other person could read their mind. Angelo took a few peeks at Sadie from the rear view mirror, but she never looked back.

Sadie stared out the window like a dog who knew he was going to the vet. She missed Enrico terribly, and she was consumed with what he was doing in that very moment.

When the newly-weds dropped Sadie off, they invited themselves in without asking.

"I made us all something to eat", Sophie said, and held up the foil wrapped meals.

Sadie looked, but because she felt obligated to entertain the very people who had brought her home, she didn't pose any objection.

Angelo carried the luggage into the house, while Sophie carried the food. There was nothing for Sadie to do, so she plumped herself down on the longer couch.

It felt odd for Sadie to be sitting there - her knees were pushed together and her shoulders were forward, like she was trying not to take up a lot of room. She felt like a stranger in her own home.

"I hope you're hungry, mom", Sophie stated happily from the kitchen. She had spent the better part of two hours making a few snacks and sandwiches for her mom to nibble on, until she got around to making a decent meal for herself.

Sadie wasn't hungry, and sighed in defeat. She knew that her daughter would force her to have even the tiniest of bites of whatever she had made, and now prepared herself to be bloated.

While Sophie was fussing about in the other room, Angelo sat down next to Sadie.

'Please don't feel compelled to talk to me', Sadie's mind screamed. She immediately lowered her eyes and gave the illusion that she didn't need or want to be bothered.

Angelo spoke in hushed tones so that Sophie couldn't hear, and he hoped that it would be exactly what Sadie needed. "My father loves you, Sadie", he began quietly. "He tells me all the time."

Her neck and upper body pulled upwards, and her eyes fluttered open as if she was in shock. "You know?"

He chuckled quietly as a pink color materialized on his cheeks. "I am a man, and of Italian descent, and yes, I can see how happy my father is when he's around you."

Sadie felt much lighter after hearing his words, and more relieved than she could express. Tears of joy began to flood her eyes while both of her hands flew to her chest. "Oh my gosh", she sighed quietly, as her face was suddenly beaming with happiness.

The Elusive Mr. Velucci

"My culture is a lot different from yours", he explained. "And I do not mind if you begin a relationship with my father." Angelo's sincerity and mannerisms were kind and very honest, and Sadie could feel that he was being genuine. "My mother died a very long time ago, and my father has been quite lonely ever since."

"I'm sorry about your mom Angelo, and thank you for your blessing." She stated the words slowly and with great meaning, as she looked straight into his gorgeous dark eyes. "Your father means the world to me."

"And you make him very happy." Angelo turned playful for a moment, and dug his elbow into her rib very gently. "I know that you like him."

Sadie blushed and lowered her eyes. "You can tell, eh?" She was embarrassed but very glad that he didn't mind.

"I can tell." He then added softly, "I can't speak for Sophie, but you definitely have my approval." He reached over and gave her a solid hug.

Sadie wrapped her arms around his neck and squeezed. And for the first time since they met, Sadie felt warm and motherly towards him. "Thank you", she whispered in a sincere tone, two inches away from his ear.

Their embrace broke apart, but they remained sitting side-by-side. They were both smiling, but a few tears had taken their time to slide down their cheeks.

Sophie came into the room with a tray full of hot drinks and finger food, and set it down on the coffee table. As she stood up, she could feel that something had changed. She wasn't sure why the ambience had flipped so drastically, but because both her mother and her husband were smiling, she was grateful, and decided to leave things the way there were.

Tina Griffith

The next hour of their visit was much more cheerful than anyone thought it would be. They talked about the flight, what Sadie had done in Italy, and Angelo asked how his dad was doing.

Sadie answered all of their questions, one at a time. She added that she would show them the pictures of her trip, the next time they came over. *This would give her the luxury of sorting through them first.*

Sophie left her mother's home with a feeling that there was nothing to worry about, for she honestly felt like Enrico was only going to be friends with them. "Bye, mom", Sophie purred. She was glad to have her back home.

Angelo held the door open to allow his wife to walk to the car ahead of him. He then turned and winked at Sadie. "I will call my father once I'm alone, to tell him that we spoke and to give him my blessing", he whispered kindly.

"Thank you", Sadie mouthed quietly. She truly appreciated Angelo's encouragement and support, but she wondered how he would react once he found out that Enrico was also Sophie's father. "Bye!" she called, as Angelo started the motor of the car. "Be safe!"

She watched them drive away, and then she closed and locked the door.

It was 9pm and Sadie was alone for the first time in over a week. She unpacked the necessary things from her suitcases, while getting herself familiarized with being at home again. When the clock struck 11pm, Sadie remembered to call Enrico.

[12]"Ciao, Bella", he said softly. It was 5am in Italy, so he was quite sleepy, but because Sadie was on the phone,

---

[12] Ciao, Bella = Hello, Beautiful

he suddenly felt happier. He switched on the light and put himself into a sitting position.

"Ciao, Enrico!" She was sad because they were apart, but very glad that they had connected by phone. She told him that she loved him and missed him very much, and then she asked him how he was doing.

"I'm much better now." He was smiling from ear-to-ear, while pressing the receiver even tighter against his head.

"I'm so glad, because I'm much better now, too."

"How are Sophie and Angelo?" he asked. Enrico already knew, but he wanted to hear Sadie's voice.

"They're both fine", she said. Sadie proceeded to tell Enrico all that had happened since they left the airport, and then she shared the conversation which she had had with Angelo. "It was quite unexpected and oh so beautiful", she added.

Enrico was pleased that she had arrived home safely, and then he told her that he and Angelo had just spoken. "He told me about the conversation, and I told him that I was very proud of him."

"I am also very proud of how Angelo interpreted our relationship. And that he gave us his blessing." Sadie went on to express concern over Sophie, but Enrico encouraged her not to worry. "Let's wait and see how that will play out", he added.

"You're right, of course", Sadie replied. She glanced at her pillows and wished that he was right there with her.

They spoke for another few minutes, and then said goodnight. They felt a thousand times better after hearing each other's voices, and they spent the next few hours dreaming that they were together.

Tina Griffith

The next morning, as Sadie was having coffee, she heard a noise outside and pulled back one half of the sheer white curtain. The birds were singing and flying everywhere, and the neighborhood kids were outside and having fun.

Sadie enjoyed seeing all of her familiar surroundings, and then her mind drifted back to Italy - to Enrico, the sights, the sounds, and the foods. She had had such a lovely time with him, and she wondered when they would be in each other's arms again.

By the time her porcelain cup was empty, she had already made plans for the rest of her day. Shopping, cleaning, and doing laundry were the top three things that needed to be done. Anything else would have to wait. Because Sadie wasn't scheduled to go back to work for two more days, she didn't want to push herself too hard. Instead, she found herself prancing around the house and singing along with the radio, while she dusted and fluffed the pillows.

With work keeping her busy during the day and talking with Sophie and Enrico at night, Sadie had no time to feel too lonely. Before she knew it, days had turned into weeks, and now it had been two months since she last saw Enrico.

He had just woken up, and was talking to Sadie before she went to bed. They were chatting about him conducting an orchestra near his home town, and when he was done with that, Enrico played coy, and casually informed her that he was coming to New York.

"What! When?" Sadie had screamed her inquiry into the phone at full volume, and bolted into a sitting position in that same second. Her eyes had popped open wide, her hearing suddenly became quite sharp, and she slowed her

The Elusive Mr. Velucci

breathing down so that she could listen to what he had to say.

"In two weeks", he replied, and then cautioned her about how to act in front of Sophie. "We don't want to give her any reason not to like the fact that we're, uh, friends." The term made him laugh, because he wanted to do so much more with Sadie, but Sophie expected them to act like acquaintances without benefits.

Sadie obviously couldn't wait to see him, and tried to think of where her calendar was. In that moment, her mind was scrambled with a lot of emotions and information, but she needed to make a mental note to mark Enrico's arrival date as garishly as she could.

Enrico went on to explain that him coming out was an impromptu trip, and it had been arranged by his son and daughter-in-law. "All they said was that they wanted us all to be together for a few days."

Sadie had a look of confusion on her face, but truly didn't care what the reason behind his visit was; she was beside herself with happiness and couldn't believe that he was coming to America. "I can't wait to see you", she cooed into the phone.

"I can't wait to see you, either." He blew a few dozen kisses into the phone, and then listened as she did the same. It was 6:45am in Naples and Enrico needed to start his day. He said good-night to Sadie and wished for her to have a good sleep. "See you soon", he added.

"See you soon." The call had ended, but Sadie kept the receiver tightly pinned against her chest. "He's coming here in two weeks", she chanted dreamily. Her eyes were cast across the room looking at nothing in particular, while her mind was fantasizing all that they would do once he arrived.

It was 12:45am in New York when they hung up, but Sadie was no longer tired. Because she had to go to work in the morning, she put the phone on her night stand and crawled under her covers. Her mind kept repeating the wonderful news over and over again, and she soon fell asleep and dreamed of him being in the bed with her.

The next time that Sophie called her mom, she told her that Enrico was coming for a visit, and that her and Angelo had made plans for them all to go out for a special dinner.

"Oh, that's wonderful!" Sadie acted surprised on purpose, because she didn't want Sophie to know that Enrico had already told her. "And how's school?" she asked, not wanting to stay on that topic for too long.

"Fine", she replied coolly. She went into a little detail about her new courses and the homework that's required, and then she told her mom about Angelo and his school.

Sadie listened to all that was being said, and was relieved that she had diverted the attention away from Enrico.

Mother and daughter spoke for another few minutes, and then they hung up.

The night before Enrico's plane was to arrive, Sadie was a nervous wreck. She had cleaned her home a few times already, but wanted to make sure that everything was perfect. She had her hair and nails done that morning, and changed her outfit four different times. She wanted to look exceptional, for it would be the first time in over two months that she had seen him.

Sophie and Angelo drove to the airport in their car, and Sadie drove in hers. They met inside the doors of the arrivals

The Elusive Mr. Velucci

area, and then walked to where Enrico would be coming down the escalator, together.

When Sadie and Enrico saw each other, it was like the heavens had opened up and lightening had hit them right smack in the chest. Their hearts began to beat even faster, smiles appeared and became brighter as Enrico got closer, and nervous sweat formed in every pore on their bodies. The energy and desire between them was electrifying, and could be felt from across the room. Adrenaline was racing while breathing was becoming limited, and they both wanted to rush into each other's arms.

"Dad!" Angelo called. He hugged his father first and Sophie hugged him second.

Sadie gave Enrico a polite side hug with one hand, but wanted to do so much more.

Enrico closed his eyes and breathed in her scent, while his free hand reached around to her back and squeezed her body closer to his own.

They didn't linger in their embrace, but when they bodies moved apart, their eyes stay locked together.

"Dad?" Angelo called.

Enrico's attention had now been diverted, and he knew it was for the best; he didn't want to do anything which would cause Sophie to continue to dislike him.

"Do you want to go in Sadie's car?"

The color from Sadie's face went from pink to white, and she felt like she was about to faint. After watching Enrico and Angelo nod and smile, she wondered what was going on. "Um, sure", she confessed, without showing too much emotion. Inside, she was exploding with the highest measure of enthusiasm. "That would be fine", she added while looking over her shoulder.

Sadie glanced in Sophie's direction, to see if she was ok with these arrangements, and because her face showed no objection, Sadie breathed a small sigh of relief.

Angelo took his father to get the suitcases, while the girls were left behind. Neither spoke, but it was clear that they were both thrilled that Enrico was there – each for their own reasons.

As they walked back, Angelo pulled a piece of paper out of his pocket. "Here's the name and the address of the restaurant", he said, as he handed it to Sadie. "We'll see you there in about twenty minutes?"

After Enrico and Sadie had gotten into her car, they immediately held hands without making it obvious to the outside world. They didn't kiss or show too much affection, but they did talk up a storm.

"You look so good", he said, as he focused on the road ahead of the car.

Sadie's cheeks were beginning to feel the heat from the blush on her cheeks, followed by a cramp from smiling too hard. "You look amazing, as always."

"I wish that I could kiss you." He also wished to do a lot more to her, but he knew that that would come in time.

"I can't wait to kiss your beautiful mouth", she gushed like a teenage girl. He smelled wonderful, and he looked more handsome than she remembered.

"It's so good to see you", he cooed, as he moved his thumb up and down the skin of her hand.

"I can't believe that you're really here", she added, and then silently thanked God that she drove an automatic.

The Elusive Mr. Velucci

They had talked by phone, three hours prior to him boarding the plane in Italy, but it somehow felt like they hadn't seen or heard from each other in months. They both felt impulsive, and their spirits had lifted the instant their eyes met in the terminal. And being able to talk freely, and hold hands for as long as they were in the car, was quite magical. Both had to admit that it was kind of romantic to have a relationship in secret, because it added another level to their already extensive desires.

Enrico told her all about his flight, while she remained perfectly content to listen to his romantic voice and delicious accent. They stole glances back and forth while they expressed how much they had missed seeing the other, and then they talked about how they could sneak away when no-one was looking.

"Perhaps after dinner, I could suggest that I drive you to your hotel", she stated boldly. "In reality, I would drive you to my house." She suddenly felt daring and instantly wicked.

Enrico certainly didn't disapprove of her idea, but he was hoping to think of ways to avoid Sophie from finding out.

Minutes later, they arrived at the fancy restaurant, and pretended like they were distant family members. As they walked, they couldn't help but admire the building – inside and out; the restaurant was clearly one of the finest eateries that New York has to offer.

The exquisite decorations, the 13-foot ceiling, the way the room was laid out, and the assorted clientele, made them both inhale with awe the minute they stepped over the threshold.

As they moved themselves towards the small table in the front entrance, a young and very attractive hostess greeted them. "Welcome to Manhattan's on 5th", she said sweetly.

"My son is expecting us. His name is Angelo Velucci."

Tina Griffith

She looked down at the open book to see where he was sitting. "Oh, yes. Follow me." And before they got shown to their table, Enrico announced that he would be the one paying the bill.

"Yes, sir." She smiled, and then continued to take them to their seats.

"Papa!" Angelo called when he saw his dad. He stood up to give him a hug, followed by Sophie.

Enrico pulled the chair out for Sadie, and then pushed it back in when she was comfortably sitting down. He then sat down right beside her.

"How is everyone doing?" Enrico asked to both his son and daughter-in-law. The conversation needed to pause unexpectedly, when the manager – a big fan of Enrico's – came over to say hello.

After introducing himself, and getting to know the names of everyone else at the table, Mr. Boylan instructed the waitress to give Enrico a huge discount.

"You're very kind", Sadie stated. "Thank you."

"It is my pleasure, for I love this man's work." The distinguished manager bowed as he replied.

"Thank you, Mr. Boylan." Enrico was very appreciative of the kind gesture and offered the man an autographed menu, to which he accepted whole-heartedly.

"Enjoy!" he added, and then walked away.

"I didn't know you were that famous", Sadie stated with pride. She was sitting on Enrico's right, and looked across the table while smiling at her daughter.

"You've gotta get out more, mom", Sophie said bluntly. It was not to hurt her mother's feelings, but said in hopes that Sadie would calm down a bit; Sophie was beginning to get a little embarrassed by the display of silliness which her mother was displaying.

Sadie had been the brunt of her daughter's harsh comments for a couple of years now, and while she didn't like it, she was almost used to it. But there was something that she was not used to, and that was how her newly-married daughter looked tonight; she was glowing and Angelo had a weird smirk on his face. "Are you ok?" she asked quietly.

Sophie blushed and lowered her eyes. "I'm fine, mom. Really."

Enrico looked at Sophie and then at Angelo, and he could see that something was going on between them. "Ok, what gives?"

Sophie and Angelo hadn't planned on making their announcement until desert came, but they looked at each other and decided that now was as good a time as any. "We're pregnant!" they shouted in the same voice.

"What?!" Sadie screamed. Her hands rushed up to her face and she didn't know who to hug first.

Enrico could not have been prouder. While his face broke out into the biggest smile of his life, he stood up and went over to hug Sophie. "Congratulations!" He then moved his attention to his son. "Angelo, congratulations! This is wonderful news!"

Before Enrico made it back to his chair, Sadie had reached out, and because they were still standing, she gave Sophie and Angelo a hug at the same time. Her mind was racing a mile a minute and not much was making sense. "Oh my gosh! I'm going to be a grama! Am I old enough? I'm certainly not ready for this. Oh my gosh!" She was exploding with happiness and forgot herself for a minute, and wrapped her arms around Enrico's neck to congratulate him on becoming a grampa.

Angelo and Sophie couldn't help but chuckle at how pleased the grandparents seemed to be.

The unmistakable excitement was contagious and loud, and spread around the room quite quickly. This caused the manager to come and see what the special occasion was all about. When he found out that his favorite conductor was about to become a grandfather, he ripped up the bill and advised his staff that the entire dinner was free of charge.

Handshakes and appreciation were delivered tenfold, and then the foursome concentrated on each other.

"When are you due?" As Sadie asked the question, her eyes automatically scooted down to her daughter's tummy.

Sophie turned to her mother and replied, "In just less than 7 months."

Enrico searched for that particular period of time in his mind, in order to see if he had any bookings planned for when the baby arrived. The delightful news had caused a heavy overload on his emotions and his head was already much too clouded to think straight, so he decided to put that off for another time.

Sadie beamed with pride and joy, and wore her delighted reaction all over her face. "Congratulations to both of you", she stated happily.

"Thanks, mom", Sophie said quietly. She flashed her mother a warm smile.

As Angelo looked into his father's face, he couldn't help but release a favorable sigh; it had been such a long time since he'd seen his father that happy. When Angelo turned to look at his glowing wife, he could tell that his eyes were

The Elusive Mr. Velucci

glistening while his skin had become warm to the touch. He then turned to Sadie, who was positively lit up about the prospect of becoming a grandmother.

A victory smile spread quickly across Angelo's mouth – a smile that was so strong that it could melt steel. He looked around the table and had somehow fallen in love with the interaction that was going on among his family members. The banter was productive and happy, and as he glanced from one person to another, he decided to stay quiet so that he could treasure the moment.

Enrico and Sadie were bubbling with joy, and quietly cheered and laughed at the prospect of expanding their family unit. It wasn't easy to be so happy and not be able to reach out, but they made a promise to keep a bit of distance between them, and knew that they needed to honor it.

Two hours after arriving at the beautiful restaurant, Sophie was getting tired and suggested that maybe Enrico would like to get to his hotel.

Angelo immediately turned his head towards Sadie and asked, "Could you drive my dad to the hotel so that I could take Sophie home?"

Sadie was in shock, but flashed a smile to hide it. "Sure", she stated nonchalantly. She didn't know how that had happened, and she wasn't about to ask any questions; she was just very grateful that she would get to spend more time with Enrico.

Angelo winked in Sadie's direction, and then smiled knowingly as if he had planned this all along.

Sadie had an overabundance of love for her son-in-law in that moment, and she knew that she would be forever indebted to him. 'Thank you', she mouthed slowly.

Angelo blinked at her with both eyes, and then escorted his wife out to the car.

Enrico was also ready to leave, but wanted to take another minute to speak with Mr. Boylan. After thanking him for the lovely dinner, he passed him a business card. "If you call the man who does my booking, he will give you as many tickets as you will need." He paused and then continued. "I think my next concert in New York is in three months. I look forward to seeing you there."

"My wife, Cathie, will be so thrilled." Mr. Boylan was very excited and quite appreciative, and used two hands to show his gratitude. "Thank you, and you come back soon."

There was a twinkle in his eye when he replied, "I certainly will." With a grandchild on the way, Enrico could envision making many trips to New York in the future.

Because their children were out of sight, Enrico reached for Sadie's hand as they walked to her car. The moment they were inside and the car was moving forward, he placed a kiss on her cheek.

"Congratulations on becoming a grama", he laughed. He had more love in his heart than he could imagine, and he couldn't see being a grampa with anyone other than Sadie.

"Thanks, grampa", she teased, but there was love behind her playfulness. Being grandparents would tie them together for the rest of their lives, but she wanted more, and she knew they would get that, but the question was when?

Enrico hunched his upper body forward and tried to talk like an old man who had no teeth. This made them both laugh, and it connected their souls even more.

"So, grandparents, eh?" Enrico sighed, when they had settled down. He marveled at the miracle of life, and how

The Elusive Mr. Velucci

things just fell into place. It also made him think about the other elements which they were battling - some of which haven't been made public yet.

Sadie nodded her head in agreement, without actually saying any words. She was keeping her eyes on the heavy traffic ahead of her, but wanted him to know that she subscribed to his way of thinking.

Enrico's mind went back to the topic of exposing their secret. "We should probably tell them soon, right?" He was fishing and he knew it, but he wanted to begin the rest of his life without coasting through any complications.

"But when?" she asked. She was nervous about how it would all go, and if they would all be speaking by the end of the conversation.

Enrico turned his head to look out of the side window, while trying to come up with an answer to Sadie's question.

He had not been there for Sadie when she was pregnant, and therefore he lost a lot of time to be with Sophie. He did not plan on doing that with his grandchild. And, he wanted to share that experience with Sadie by his side, as grandma and grandpa. The trick was how.

Sadie drove in total silence, because the reality behind the word 'pregnancy', suddenly flooded her mind with a ton of memories.

Saying good-bye to Enrico, watching the ship leave the dock, and then finding out that she was pregnant with his child, were all underlined moments in her life. Enrico coming back when Sophie was engaged to Angelo, was nothing short of a happy miracle. Telling the kids that they had fallen in love twice during the past twenty odd years, could destroy their family unit as it is right now – but there was no way around it; Sadie had been pushed away from Enrico a few times already, and she wanted to make sure that he would never leave her again.

As she parked her car in front of the hotel, Sadie squeezed his hand as she looked directly into his face. "We should invite the kids to come to my house for supper in the next day or so, and then put everything on the table", she said as clear as day. "We could tell them how happy we are about a baby coming, and then slide into our own relationship – how we know each other, and that you are Sophie's father." Saying the words out loud, made it all feel more real.

A few solitary tears were falling down Sadie's face, because everything was getting to be too much for her to bear. She turned to Enrico while her puppy dog eyes were begging him for comfort. "Tell me that everything will be ok."

He let go of her hand and leaned in for a hug. Enrico was now choking back his own tears, and needed a minute to let it all sink in. "Give me a day to figure out how to word it, so that nobody goes away angry."

Sadie forced a smile at her handsome suitor, and then asked him if he would like her to walk him up to his room.

Enrico took a long second to study her expression, as if to see if there was a hidden message in her offer.

Sadie saw the gleam of interest in his eyes and playfully slapped him in the chest. "To make sure that you get there safely, silly", she laughed. Her mood went from worry to happy in mere seconds, and her skin was now glowing from what he thought she was implying.

"Uh, ha", he replied, and then he mirrored her laugh.

The Elusive Mr. Velucci

"What am I going to do with you?" she teased. She got out of her car and lifted the tail gate.

"I happen to have a list, if you're interested." He pretended to reach into his pocket, which had her giggling like a shy teen. He then grabbed his suitcases and they went up to his room.

Sadie stayed and chatted with him for about an hour, before she realized that Enrico needed to catch up on some sleep. "We'll talk in the morning", she said, as she began to walk away from the bed.

He grabbed her lower arm before she got to the door. "You don't have to go, you know."

"You know that I don't want to." She leaned her torso into his body, looked him square in the eye, and laid a flat hand against the side of his handsome face. "I'll see you in the morning", she breathed softly. She kept her eyes engaged with his while she kissed his lips as light as a feather. She lingered in that pose for a full minute, and then she reached for the door knob.

"I love you", he called, as she was walking out of his room.

The door was not quite closed when she replied, "I love you, too." The overall feeling which was now running rampant through her veins, was enough to keep her smiling until she arrived at the entrance of her home.

They met privately for breakfast the following morning, and she was able to speak to him by phone as often as possible. During their talks, they had thrown ideas back and forth on how to tell Sophie that Enrico was her father. They realized that Angelo would also be shocked at first, but Enrico convinced Sadie that Angelo will not dwell in

Tina Griffith

the negative aspect, as much as Sophie would. Because of this, they decided to put all of their efforts into how to make Sophie feel better.

It was Thursday morning, and with Enrico leaving very early on Saturday, Sadie decided that Friday night seemed to be their only option for dinner. As they drank the last bit of coffee in their mugs, Sadie spoke from her heart.

"I'll ask our kids to come to my house for supper tomorrow night", she offered tenderly. She was blinded by love and nervous as hell, but she didn't want to wait too much longer for the truth to come out.

"That's a good idea; we really need to straighten this whole thing out." Enrico's nerves began to flutter in his belly, as he weighed the pros and cons of what they were about to do. Sophie could very well reject him and her mother, for hiding this secret for all these years. On the other hand, she could be so happy to finally have a dad in her life, that she might rush into his arms with unbelievable exhilaration. And then again, she could run out of the room in tears, and there would be no grandbabies for him or Sadie to love or hold.

Enrico's face lowered into his hands and he wept quietly. The ugly fear of what might happen, ate away at his sanity and reduced him to a gibbering wreck.

Sadie rushed over to comfort him, but while she rubbed his back and tried to soothe him, she felt her own tears falling down her cheeks.

They were in a corner booth, at a dimly-light breakfast restaurant, and because nobody heard or saw what was happening, they were able to work through their sorrow at their own pace.

The Elusive Mr. Velucci

By the time a waitress had come around to offer them more coffee, the couple had regrouped and appeared to be much calmer.

"I hope we're doing the right thing", Sadie murmured. She locked eyes with Enrico and felt she needed him to reassure her that everything would be ok.

Enrico wrapped his hands around both of hers, and kissed every single one of her finger tips. "I promise that I will do whatever I can to make this work", he began.

"I know you will."

"Please know that I will move mountains for you, I will block you from harm, and I will make sure that your daughter does not end up hating you. But first and foremost, I will do whatever it takes to keep you or our family, together."

Sadie rushed into his arms and they hugged each other very tight. Minutes later, the bill came, and Sadie and Enrico decided to go shopping for Friday night's supper. Shortly before noon, they allowed themselves 10 minutes to say good-bye, while making promises that they'd see each other again soon.

Angelo picked his father up at the hotel at 1:00, and was delighted to be able to spend the entire afternoon with him. He drove Enrico around the city, and when they parked near Central Park, Enrico was overjoyed; it was one of his favorite places to be.

As father and son walked along the winding pathways, they talked about insignificant things like the weather and school. They soon came to a rather unique bridge which overlooked a beautiful pond. It was surrounded by full trees, colorful flowers, two park benches, and a handful of people, who were also there to enjoy the good weather.

Father and son placed their elbows onto the cement ledge while peering into the dark water, and after a minute or so of complete silence, Enrico spoke up. "I have something to tell you, but I'm not sure how you will take it", he stated in a serious tone.

Angelo hadn't been prepared for a serious talk, so he became instantly worried. "Is it your health, papa?" His body tensed as he waited for the bad news.

"No, Angelo", he said quickly. "I'm fine", he promised. He laid a hand flat against his chest as confirmation.

Angelo's eyes closed and he sighed loudly with relief.

Enrico stared down at the water rippling beneath them and continued. "You know how I feel about Sadie, but there's so much more that I need to tell you."

Maintaining their pose, but turning their faces towards each other, Enrico talked while Angelo listened. As the words poured out, their hearts pounded as anxiety surged through their bodies. The paragraphs of information were difficult for Enrico to reveal, but it was also challenging for Angelo to absorb.

Angelo had known that there was something going on, since that first night when he saw his father with Sadie. The way they acted was weird, but now that he knew how they met and that they hadn't seen each other in twenty years, it all made sense.

When Enrico told Angelo that he was Sophie's father, that was a little more complicated for Angelo to digest.

"I didn't even know that Sophie existed, until I met your fiancé and her mother", he confessed. Enrico's voice was fragile and shaking, as a hot tear rolled down his cheek. His eyes were round and slightly patient, as he waited for his son to forgive him for not telling him these details sooner.

Angelo put his arms around his father, and hugged him as if he'd never see him again for the rest of his life. "We are ok, dad. I'm not upset with you about this, or anything else. What happened between you and Sadie was a long time ago – I totally understand that.

"I love her, Angelo." Enrico was referring to Sadie.

"I know, because you told me, but also because I can see it in your face and in your body language."

"I want you to know that I also loved your mother very much", he vowed firmly. He positioned himself so that they were facing each other. "Maria came into my life when I had no-one. She gave me a good life, and she gave me you. My marriage to her made me whole again, and when she died, a part of me died, too."

"I know, papa." He turned his head and stared into the water below them.

"I truly thought my life was over, but when I saw Sadie again, after all those years of being apart, I couldn't breathe."

Angelo felt sorry for his father in that moment; he could see that this confession was definitely hard on him. Enrico had always been a tower of strength, and now he looked like he could be knocked over with a feather.

"Angelo", Enrico continued. "I want us all to be a wonderfully, happy family. You and Sophie, and me and Sadie." Enrico's chest went tight, his face was turning red, he couldn't catch his breath, and he reached out to the railing for support.

Angelo helped his father to the nearest park bench,

where they sat and waited for someone to come and help them. Enrico was checked out within minutes, and told to go home and relax.

"He seems fine, but his blood pressure is really high", was the major consensus. "I'd like him to see his doctor as soon as possible."

"I'll make sure that happens", Angelo promised.

After thanking the officer on a horse, and the paramedics who had rushed to his father's aide, father and son were driven back to the car on a ground keeper's cart.

Enrico finally felt free from the secrets, and was now sighing with relief; the pressure of having to hide Sadie or Sophie from Angelo, had now been lifted.

Angelo watched his father's face, and hoped that he was going to be ok. "Will you be telling Sophie any of what you told me?"

"I'd like to, if you don't mind."

"I think she should know."

Enrico turned to look into his son's eyes. "Sadie and I want to tell her tomorrow night.

"Tomorrow?" It came out as a question and a statement, because Angelo was trying to process the speed of which this news was going to be delivered.

Please note that Sophie will not know that you already have this information, so I'm hoping that you can help me explain the finer points."

"Of course." Angelo was very happy to help his dad, especially if it meant that Enrico would calm down.

Angelo drove them to the house he shared with Sophie, and Enrico was able to lay down for an hour before he was called to the table. All throughout dinner, Angelo kept an

The Elusive Mr. Velucci

eye on his father, without letting Sophie know why. The conversation was kept light, and Enrico was driven back to the hotel minutes after desert was finished.

"You call me if you don't feel well, ok?" Angelo stressed. He had a firm lock on his father's eyes, while his hand was gripping Enrico's right shoulder.

"I promise."

They hugged, and Angelo could see that his father didn't look too bad, but the younger man felt horrible about leaving his dad alone. "Call me before you go to bed tonight, so I don't worry."

Enrico was facing the other way, but swung a single wave behind him as a way of letting his son know that he shouldn't worry.

Angelo did worry, all the way home, and hated that he couldn't tell Sophie what was going on.

Enrico dialed Sadie's number, the minute he closed and locked his hotel room door. He told her that they had had a really good time at the park, for which she was quite pleased. "And I told Angelo everything that's going on between you and me."

Sadie's eyebrows raced towards her hairline. "You did? How did he take it?" She was in a state of surprise, and now listened to all that Enrico had to say.

Enrico smiled while he replied, "Just fine, and he agreed to help us tell Sophie that I'm her father." He had been sitting on the bed, and now made his way to the large window on the far wall. He pulled one half of the sheer curtain to the side, and observed everything that was four floors below him.

Sadie tilted her head back and exhaled with relief. "Oh my gosh, that's amazing."

"I thought you'd be pleased."

Something in his voice caused her gut feeling to come alive. "Are you ok?" she asked. Her eyes flew open and her ear pressed harder against the receiver.

Enrico walked back to the bed and sat down before he answered. He didn't want to scare her, so he told her what had happened in the park, but he made sure to minimize the severity.

Sadie's knees buckled and she suddenly felt helpless and overly concerned. She knew that she couldn't do anything to help him through the phone line, but she spoke the next sentence with a great deal of love. "I'm going to hug you when I see you, no matter who sees or cares."

He thanked her in Italian, and made sure that each word was delivered slowly. The sentiments of his next few sentences were dripping with immense love, and were meant for her and her alone. "I want you to know that I love you very much – more than you could ever understand. I want to spend the rest of my life with you, because you're the one I belong to – body, soul, and mind."

Sadie had goose bumps on her skin, and her face was now glistening with freshly shed tears. She cradled the receiver with two hands as she answered him in perfect Italian. "I also love you very much, and I promise to stay beside you until the end of time; you are my heart, my life, and my reason for living."

They spent the next few minutes swooning, mixed with crying and laughing lightly, and then they discussed things that didn't pertain to their family. They each blew kisses into

The Elusive Mr. Velucci

the phone before saying good-night, and then they wished each other to have a good sleep.

Sadie picked Enrico up from his hotel on Friday at noon, and they rushed into each other's arms when he opened the door. While giving and receiving many kisses and hugs, he tried to convince her that he was ok. Sadie still needed to be sure, so after an endless search for any signs of injury, she walked Enrico to her car and drove him to her home. They had been able to spend almost three hours together before the kids showed up, and they not only looked much younger than their ages, they acted it.

When Sophie and Angelo arrived, they were surprised to find Enrico in Sadie's kitchen; he was helping to cook and serve, and it looked as if he had always been a permanent fixture in their lives.

"Have a seat and supper will be ready in a few minutes", Sadie announced. She had a lilt to her voice, and a trace of laughter that lingered in the air long after she spoke.

"And it'll be the best meal you've had in years", Enrico added. He was speaking to everyone, but only had eyes for Sadie.

Over the next half an hour, they ate a lovely light meal and talked about the new baby. They all listened to how Sophie was feeling these days, and how school was going for both Angelo and Sophie. When the meal had ended and the table had been cleared, Sadie determined that it was time to change the subject. "Shall we move to the living room?"

Enrico brought the large tray with the bite size deserts, while Sadie carried the hot and cold drinks to the coffee table. As they all sat down, Enrico glanced at Sadie while an intense expression of worry spread across his face. Their eyes were locked and it was clear that they were about to make some sort of announcement.

Because she was filled with worry, Sadie's heart began to pound and her eyes teared up; there was a huge possibility that she might lose her daughter's respect and love in the next few minutes. She looked into Enrico soul and realized that the fear of living as if he was merely a distant family member, was not how she wanted to conduct the rest of her life. This gave her the emotional strength that she needed to move forward.

Sadie turned her attention towards Sophie and Angelo, and hoped that Enrico was the one who would start this very difficult conversation.

"We have something to tell you", he began. "And it's not going to be easy for anyone, so please bear with us."

Fear flashed through Sophie's mind. "Mom? Are you ok?" she asked. She suddenly felt ill and terrified, and she wondered why Enrico was doing most of the talking.

Sadie reached her hand over to touch her daughter's knee. "Yes, honey. I'm ok."

Enrico shifted his hips in order to sit closer to Sadie's body, and then he reached for her hand.

Sadie took it and braided her fingers with his, and then she wrapped her other hand around is forearm. They both hoped that the next few minutes would go well.

Sophie had a blank expression on her face, and her eyes were searching for someone to tell her what was going on. As a feeling of fight-or-flight settled in her body, she suddenly felt like she wanted to cry. "Ok, what's going on?"

"You guys might want to take a deep breath", Sadie said bravely, and then she silently asked the heavens to give

The Elusive Mr. Velucci

her strength. She was sitting directly across from Sophie, but while she was talking to her daughter, Sadie's head was facing downward towards her lap.

Sophie's upper body rushed forward as she spoke. "Mom!" she called sharply. "What's going on?"

Sadie was terribly nervous and hanging onto Enrico's hand as if he would disappear in the next second. "Sophie", she said softly. She had butterflies in her tummy, her tone was apologetic, and she spoke with as reasonable a voice as she could manage. "Honey, there's something I need to tell you about your father."

Sophie turned her head to the side and shared a strong glance with Angelo. She watched him nod, and then she turned back to her mother and asked, "What exactly do you mean?" Her skin became prickly, her hands raced to the tiny bump on her tummy, and her heart began to pound in her chest. "Is he alive?" Her eyebrows had pulled together as she shot a grimacing look across the room. "Do you know where he is?"

Angelo sat quiet, and glanced first at his father, and then at Sadie. Even though he knew what was coming, his mind was racing as he reached out to hold Sophie's hand.

Sadie took a cleansing breath and continued. "Do you remember how I've always told you that your father was a soldier, and that he had been killed overseas while he was fighting a war?"

Sophie's eyes were glistening and wide open. She nodded stiffly because this part was common knowledge.

"Well, that wasn't exactly correct."

"What?!" Sophie's whole world had shattered in that one

Tina Griffith

single second, and she felt like she was sliding off the face of the earth and had nothing to hold on to.

Sadie released her grip of Enrico's hand, got down on her knees in front of Sophie, and then began to cry as the words poured out of her soul. "Your father came into my life for a little while, that's true. I loved him and he loved me, that's also true. He left the country before I found out that I was pregnant, but it wasn't to go to war." Sadie was sobbing so hard, that her body was shaking with each breath she took.

Sophie was beyond stunned and couldn't move for fear of how this story was going to end. She looked around the room at everything that seemed familiar, in order to hold onto her sanity. She looked back into her mother's tearful eyes while being terribly confused.

The strong clutch which Sophie had on Angelo's arm, suddenly got tighter. He patted her hand as her fingers dug into his skin.

It was not hard for Enrico to see how difficult this was for Sadie, so he boldly stepped in. "It was to go to Italy, where his family lived."

Because Enrico had taken over the story, Sophie wasn't sure who to look at or listen to. 'And how and why would Enrico know anything about her father?' she wondered.

The ambience had suddenly shifted significantly, question marks were flying everywhere, and the room had now become too small to hold the attractive group of four. Both parents had become strangers right before her eyes, and it was now dawning on Sophie that her dad was not only alive, but that he might be in the room with them.

There was a tornado of emotions spinning inside of

The Elusive Mr. Velucci

Sophie's body, sending a vast amount of energy and thoughts to her already disorientated brain. She was suddenly experiencing the strong sensations of excessive strength and speed, and now felt the need to stand up. She took many deep breaths as she paced around the room, while she tried to put the pieces of the puzzle in the correct order.

Angelo caught the eyes of both Sadie and Enrico, and was a bit perplexed as to how this was going to turn out. His wife was pregnant, and she was going through something rather devastating to understand. He wasn't sure if he should step in to help or not, and a moment later it all became clear; with a wealth of reluctance, he decided to wait until he was asked.

"So let me get this straight…" Sophie stopped moving her feet for a second, and pointed to her mother while she delivered her thoughts. "If I'm getting this right, are you telling me that Enrico is my father?" And before she could hear anyone answer, she turned back around and debated what she had just said. "But that can't be right, because Enrico is Angelo's father." With that shocking revelation rolling around in her head, Sophie turned around again and froze on the spot. "Does that mean that we are brother and sister?" The room began to spin, her knees gave out, and she could feel herself floating to the ground.

Everyone raced towards Sophie, and caught her before she hit the carpet. The men placed her limp body onto the couch, while Sadie ran to get a cold cloth for her daughter's head. Angelo raised his wife's head so that she could take a few sips from a glass of water, which had been pushed gently against Sophie's lips.

Everyone saw the pregnant woman lying there, pale and

not moving, and it was quickly agreed that all of this could have been too much for her to handle.

It took a few minutes before Sophie recovered, and when she did, she seemed angry and moved her body away from her husband.

"What?" Angelo called with a ton of curiosity. "Honey, what's the matter?" As he edged himself closer in order to soothe her, he saw Sophie recoil his advances, as if his fingers were laced with acid.

"Seriously, move!" she shouted. Her eyes were fierce, and open as wide as possible. Her eyebrows were pushed together, and she looked like a dog who was ready and very willing to pounce.

Angelo's ego had been bruised to the max. He was pouting and shrugged his shoulders dismissively, and then walked to another part of the room. He leaned himself against the nearest wall, and turned his head away from the rest of the people in the room. He suddenly felt hated, as if he was the enemy, but he didn't know why.

Sadie rushed to his side and tried to comfort him. "I'm sorry", she whispered apologetically, as if she had caused all of this to happen. She gently caressed his arm from shoulder to elbow while she stated, "Please know that none of this is your fault."

A very small part of him knew that he hadn't done anything to warrant that kind of behavior, but the rest of him wondered what he had done to make her hate him so much.

"First off, you are not brother and sister", he declared adamantly. Enrico, who had planted himself on the coffee table, inches away from Sophie's face, touched her arm with his hand and continued. "Sophie, I married Angelo's mother many years after your mother got pregnant. Maria and I had gone to elementary school together, but we lost touch after High School."

The muscles in Sophie's body were trying to relax, as she allowed herself to listen.

"We met by accident after my parents died, and we rekindled our childhood friendship. Angelo was already in elementary school when we began to date."

"So you aren't Angelo's father?" she asked in a tender manner. She so badly wanted him to say yes, for then her marriage would be legal and not awkward.

The warmth of Enrico's smile came from deep within his heart. He leaned forward and gave his answer. "No, my darling. Not by blood, anyway."

Sadie helped Sophie ease into a sitting up position, while Angelo spoke from across the room. "We are not blood relatives, Sophie", he began. "My mother and I met Enrico a few years after my father died. This man here, is basically the only father I've ever known or loved. He means the world to me, and I'm so lucky to have had him in my life."

As if he needed to stress the point further, Enrico added, "I am also quite proud to be Angelo's father; he is my son, for all intent and purposes, and he will always be my son."

Sophie reached out for Enrico and gave him the biggest hug possible; she had just seen his true personality shine all around the room, and now she knew what a good person he was.

When their embraced ended, Sophie met Angelo's eyes, and she begged him to forgive her. "Please", she pleaded.

A tiny smile ruffled the corners of his mouth, as his

defenses slowly melted away. With his hands in his pockets, Angelo wandered over to his pregnant wife and they hugged.

"I'm sorry", she said between kisses.

Sadie walked across the room to be with Enrico, who had moved himself to the love seat. They snuggled together as they watched the interaction between their children.

Sophie was now very alert, and her heart was pounding as she tried to get everything to sink into her brain.

Angelo stretched his arm across his wife's shoulders and kissed her temple.

"That's my son who's kissing you", Enrico called from mere feet away.

Angelo turned his head, and threw a smile at Enrico that filled the entire room with a sense of tranquility. "That's my dad who's talking." Angelo extended his hand out towards the man who had raised him. "And it turns out that he might be your dad, too."

As if they could read his thoughts, Sadie and Enrico nodded their heads in an unhurried manner. They both had tears of joy spilling down their faces, and they were both smiling.

Sophie turned to Angelo, and as if she needed to be sure, she asked, "So you have no blood line to my mom or to Enrico?" she asked in an accusing voice. It was said as a challenge, but meant as a joke.

Angelo smiled and closed his eyes, and then he shook his head no.

Sophie turned and focused on her mother. With anger beginning to ravage her soul, she fired off her next question. "Why did I grow up thinking that my father had died?" She then looked to Enrico and asked, "Why were you not a part of my life?"

They immediately went into a defensive mode, but while Sadie was ready and willing to answer, it was Enrico who stepped in and took over.

He stood up and cleared his throat while he adjusted the belt on his pants, but he didn't move his feet. Seconds later, he smoothed down his hair as he confessed, "I had school to go to, and then my father got sick and eventually died. My mother became ill soon after that, and then she died, too. I just felt lost and buried myself in homework and a part-time job." He paused to collect his thoughts, as he hadn't spoken or thought about that time period in years.

Everyone in the room kept quiet and watched as he struggled with his emotions. After he had composed himself, he continued. "I studied day and night, and thought of nothing else for months and months. After I wrote my final exam, I looked up, and I noticed that life had continued on without me." A tear dripped down his cheek, and he wiped it away with the length of his left index finger.

Sadie reached for his hand, as a tear fell from her own eye.

He focused on Sadie's face as he spoke the next few sentences, but he was talking to Angelo and Sophie. "My first and last thought every day, was of Sadie. I missed her very much, and wondered how angry she must be because I hadn't reached out to her." He turned and faced Angelo and Sophie. "Time raced faster than it normally did, and because it had already been so long, I assumed that she had found someone else to love." He threw his hands in the air while he delivered the next sentence. "I felt like I had no choice but to carry on with my life."

Angelo walked over and hugged his tormented father. "Oh, papa."

Enrico permitted his son to hug him, but then he gently persuaded him to back away. "I'm ok", he whispered into his son's ear. He faced Sadie and squeezed her hand to let her know that he was not getting too upset.

Sadie looked up at Enrico with more love than she ever thought was possible.

Sophie had tears of sadness rolling down her cheeks, but turned to her mother and asked, "Why didn't you try to get hold of him?" Her arms were crossed and placed firmly against her chest, and it seemed like she was impatiently waiting for an answer.

"Oh my gosh, I did, Sophie", she stressed loudly and with conviction. She fell onto her knees and continued. "As soon as I found out that I was pregnant, I tried several times to get hold of Enrico, but I failed miserably with each attempt. I had no idea where he was or what he was doing, and because we didn't have each other's contact information, I thought I was supposed to live without him." The sentiments were now becoming too much for Sadie to control. Her hands rushed up and were covering her eyes, while her sobs could be heard in every part of the house. She suddenly felt like she had committed a horrible crime, where she was going to be hauled away to jail and would never get to see anyone ever again.

Enrico bent down and wrapped his arms around her. "To be fair", he interrupted. "She was hired to be my tutor and I was her student. We didn't 'hook up', as the kids say,

The Elusive Mr. Velucci

until my very last night in America. When we woke up the next morning, I only had time to race to the terminal and get on the ship, before it left the dock." Enrico stopped talking and concentrated on helping Sadie get back up on the couch.

Angelo could see that Sadie was distraught, so he rushed over to help her. Together, he and his dad fussed over her until they were sure that she was ok.

As Sophie watched her husband and their parents interacting, her entire face showed contempt and disbelief. After Sadie had gotten settled, Sophie began another round of questions.

"So you had no way to get hold of each other? How come I don't believe you?" she stated firmly. She was trying to be courteous, but even she could hear the patronizing tone in her voice.

The next few words in Enrico's speech were delivered in a fragile and shaking voice, for his heart was breaking from all that was going on, and he was quite worried about how the evening would end. "Sophie, please", he pleaded strongly. "Things were so different back then. There were no cell phones, and we didn't think to exchange phone numbers or addresses. For months I was being taught English and I promise that we were just friends. We were young and we were only supposed to be together for a few months, but we fell in love. However, we didn't express how we felt until hours before I was scheduled to leave. And then we didn't see each other again, until the night I met you."

He spoke to Sophie but had turned his attention to Sadie. The instant they locked eyes, their hearts melted at the same exact time. "At your wedding, we danced as the

Tina Griffith

parents of the bride and groom. And maybe it was the music or the lighting, or even the moment, I don't know, but your mother looked somewhat different to me; not like the young girl she once was, but like an angel."

Enrico was sitting on the couch, but his soul seemed to reach across the 5-foot space to Sophie's heart. "When I was asked to walk you down the aisle and dance with you as the father of the bride, it was like one of my biggest wishes had come true." He lowered his head and softened his tone of voice. "I had always wanted to have a child, and now I find out that I have a daughter as well as a son." He paused to catch his breath. "I only wish that my parents could have been there; they would have loved you both." He looked into her eyes again, so she could feel how strong he had meant that last sentence.

Sadie stroked his back and his hair, and offered him as much comfort as she felt he needed. It was quite evident that this situation was too much for him – for all of them – but the words needed to come out.

As she was watching the loving interaction between Enrico and her mother, Sophie's whole stance was softening. They were holding hands and giving each other moral support, and honestly looked like they were a couple who were deeply in love.

Sadie shifted in her seat until she was facing Enrico. Her hands were holding his, her muscles were relaxed, and she was gazing at him with total love in her heart. She was well aware that three sets of eyes were watching her as she spoke the next few sentences, but these were words that needed to be said. "I felt something for you from day one, but because I was your tutor, I was forced to keep my

The Elusive Mr. Velucci

feelings to myself. As the months went by, it got harder to hide what was in my heart. Our last night together is one of the best memories I have; we danced and we kissed, and then we spent the rest of the night sharing our love in a very passionate way."

Sadie turned towards Sophie and persisted. "We didn't know what we were doing or that I would get pregnant, and after Enrico left, I was all alone." She lowered her head and continued. "I ended up scared, tired, and didn't know what else to do, so I raised you all by myself." She stopped to wipe a few tears off her cheeks and chin. "I sacrificed everything to keep you happy and safe, and I acted as both a mother and father to you."

Sadie turned back to Enrico but was talking to Sophie. "When you began asking questions about your father, I didn't want you to hate the man who helped make my beautiful daughter, so I lied to protect his honor." She laid a hand gently against Enrico's cheek. "I loved him then, and I love him now."

Sophie couldn't help but swoon, as large tears of pitiful sorrow fell down her cheeks.

Enrico spoke to Sophie, but he was still looking at Sadie. "I didn't know I had a daughter, until that day when Angelo introduced me to you and your mother. Since then, I have gotten to know your mother again, and I've grown to love you both, more than my own life." He moved away from Sadie, stood up, and walked towards Sophie. He reached out his hands to her and invited her to stand up. In a voice that was rich and full of love and dominance, he added, "Had I known about you, I promise that I would have been there for you and with you, to do whatever a father does with his little girl."

Angelo felt he needed to have his voice heard and acknowledged loudly, "I am your child, in every sense of the word, and I can firmly attest that you were and are an excellent father."

Enrico smiled and nodded towards his son, with approval, love, and thanks.

Sophie posed a question to Sadie and Enrico, "Why did you guys wait so long to tell us that you knew each other?"

Enrico looked towards Sadie and she looked into his eyes, but he spoke first.

"When we met after being apart for so long, I was completely dumbfounded to be seeing your mother again; she looked the same, but she was different."

Sadie spoke next. "I looked across the room, and I wasn't sure if Enrico was the person I knew from twenty years ago."

Enrico turned and spoke to Sadie. "You were older, but you were still so beautiful. I didn't know if you recognized me, and it took me a few long moments before I was convinced that it was you."

"Same here; you were older, but there was something very familiar about you that I couldn't quite put my finger on. And after I heard your name, I couldn't breathe."

"I had that same experience; just the mention of your name brought back all of the memories of our time together."

"I know!" she agreed wholeheartedly. "It was like, I wanted to believe that it was true, but it had been too long since I'd seen you, and I wasn't sure how you felt about me anymore. I didn't want to put myself out there, only to have you reject me." And then her voice became a little

The Elusive Mr. Velucci

angry. "You left and never bothered to contact me again, you rat."

Enrico chuckled, but because he knew it was all in fun. "I know. With everything that was going on with school and my parents, my whole way of life had changed so much, and the time went by much too quickly. But I did come to America, three different times, and I went to your apartment and knocked on your door."

Sadie was stunned. "What?" She, along with Angelo and Sophie, were very surprised.

"There was never an answer, so I left you letters, but I got no reply."

Sadie took a minute to think back to that time period. "But I didn't get any letters from you." She now had a concerned look on her face.

It was Enrico's turn to be concerned, and his voice was now stronger than before. "I put them into your mail box. The one at the front door of your building", he insisted.

Sadie suddenly knew what the problem was, and began laughing lightly. "There has always been a mix up where my mail should be; the numbers are marked wrong, so I got my neighbor's mail and he got mine. We waited for it to be changed, but after a few months, we just swapped keys."

"Why didn't you get my letters?" He was still in disbelief.

"That tenant moved out when Sophie was about five years old, and because of the condition of that apartment, it took a few months before they could rent it out again. We also got a new landlord around that same time period, and I know that he used that mailbox himself; for junk mail, for his credit card bills, and for anything he didn't want his wife to see or know about. And as far as I knew, I was receiving my mail."

Enrico had his head down and looked quite emotional. "I wrote you such loving letters. It's a shame you never got to read them."

"Awe..." Sadie stated. She rubbed his arm as a way of calming him down. "It's ok."

"No, it's not", he began. "I gave up hope that I'd ever see you again, because you never wrote me back."

Sadie felt awful. "But I didn't know about the letters."

"I know, but because you also didn't answer your door, I took it to mean that you had moved on with your life."

"But I didn't. I thought about you every single second of every single day." Sadie turned to Sophie, and while she held her hand out, she said, "And here's the reason; she looks just like you. She's been my constant reminder of the love that we shared."

Sophie blushed, and studied everything about Enrico without anyone noticing.

"Again, had I known... ", Enrico added softly. He looked into Sadie's eyes and he wanted to kiss her so badly.

"But you saw each other again and again", Sophie stated with anger in her voice. "We saw a connection between you, but you never let on that you knew each other." Sophie was being assertive and turned to get confirmation of her statements from Angelo. "Right, honey?"

Angelo nodded, because he was also curious.

"Honestly?" Sadie replied. "We weren't sure how to tell you, for one thing."

"The other reason, is that we weren't sure of what was

The Elusive Mr. Velucci

going on between us, or how it would affect the four of us in the long run", Enrico disclosed.

"Are you a couple?" Angelo asked point blank. He already had his answer, but he wanted it to be out in the air for everyone to see.

Enrico looked towards Sadie, and she turned towards him. They smiled as only lovers do, and displayed tons of affection without saying a word. Then they faced their children.

"I would like to marry her, and live with her for the rest of my life. I just didn't know how you guys would take it." He was speaking to both children, and reached for Sadie's hand while he waited for an answer.

Sophie whispered into Angelo's ear, and then announced that they needed a minute. "Can we use your bedroom, mom?"

Sadie was startled, but agreed. "Uh, yes." She wasn't sure why they had to leave the room, and watched in fear as they walked away.

Sophie took Angelo's hand and marched him down the hall. When the door shut, they talked quietly amongst themselves.

In the meantime, Enrico took his hands and cupped them around Sadie's face. He then placed a very long and loving kiss upon her lips. When the kiss ended, she wrapped her arms around his neck and hugged him hard. "I hope they come back with a good answer", she sighed. Her head was now resting on his shoulder.

Enrico could feel the tension in her body and tried to calm her nerves. "No matter what they say, I will stay by your side for the rest of my life." His voice faded into a hushed stillness, as he waited for a reply.

Sadie lifted her head and stared into his eyes. "I love you, Enrico Velucci. And while I respect my daughter, I want to be your wife."

Enrico smiled and his heart began to pound with delight. He hugged her hard and tight, as a tear or two escaped from his eyes. "I love you so much."

Behind the bedroom door, Sophie asked Angelo what he thought about the whole situation. "Am I being too harsh?" she asked kindly.

Angelo could see that the past half an hour had taken its toll on his wife, but he hoped that it would all turn out well in the end. "I can certainly understand how all of this could upset you and leave your head spinning, but there's a lot of advantages to them being a couple. You will have a father and not just a father-in-law, your mom now has a wonderful man in her life who totally adores her, and he wants to be part of our family on a different level."

Sophie lowered her head and tried to comprehend all that he was saying.

Angelo continued. "Yes, it's true that there were some lies told, but it was not to hurt you. I believe that your mother tried to protect you, and have you continue to love your father with all your heart." He brought her body up against his and continued. "She loves you, Sophie. Anyone can see that. She might not have known if or when Enrico would ever come back into her life, but she made sure that you had a father figure to be proud of. How can you blame her for that?"

Sophie flaunted her sad eyes into her husband's

The Elusive Mr. Velucci

handsome face and asked, "Why did they take them so long to tell us the truth?"

Angelo wrapped his arms around her back and pressed his forehead against hers. "I think that they just needed time to work out their differences before they could confide in us. There must have been a lot to talk about, because look at how long they had been apart. And have you watched them together? They really do love each other."

Sophie heard all the words and allowed them to sink in. She pressed her body very tightly against Angelo's, and held onto him for another few minutes. "I love you", she added. He was a good man, and she now suspected that he will be an excellent father.

"I love you, too."

The bedroom door opened, and the newly-weds walked hand-in-hand down the hallway towards the living room. After they sat down, they looked at both of their parents, but it was Sophie who spoke up.

To Enrico she said, "I don't know what to call you, but I'm really glad that you are in my life, and that you walked me down the aisle."

Enrico inhaled a very large breath of air into his lungs, while a shiver raced up his spine. "Thank you", he sighed, as a few tears fell down his face.

Sophie turned to her mother. "I'm still upset that you lied to me about who my father is, and I will forgive you, but it will take time. For now, I want to know you both as my parents."

Sophie turned to Angelo and added him into the

Tina Griffith

conversation. "These are our parents now, and will be the grandparents of our child", she stressed.

Sadie was now crying buckets of tears; she knew that she had hurt Sophie, and she hoped in time that her daughter would realize that she didn't mean to cause her any heartache. "Thank you", she whispered.

She wanted to hug her daughter, but wasn't sure if it was appropriate in that moment. As Sadie looked into her daughter's eyes, she could see that the whole scenario had been very confusing – to everyone.

Angelo rushed across the room to hug Sadie. He could tell how upset she was, and he could tell that she needed to have some comforting. As Angelo wrapped his arms around his weeping mother-in-law, Enrico stood up and threw his arms around the two of them.

Sophie was sitting on the long couch across from them, and watched them as they gathered into a group hug. She was newly-married and newly-pregnant, and her hormones were jumping all over the place. A lot had happened in the last little while, and she believed that she had the right to be emotional.

It took another minute for her to get a handle on the situation, and then she figured that if Enrico was going to be in her life anyway, she might as well let the past be the past and enjoy the present. Sophie let out a huge sigh, for she knew it wouldn't be easy, but she would try to be accepting of the awkward situation.

Sophie's eyes looked nonjudgmentally at the small group, while her body insisted that she join them. She stood up, while still being reluctant, and went over to join in on the cluster hug. She stood in between her mother

The Elusive Mr. Velucci

and Angelo, but her fingers had expanded enough to touch Enrico's back.

When Enrico realized what had happened, he looked into Sophie's eyes and tapped her lovingly with his hand.

Sophie smiled back, with a ton of appreciation and love.

A few minutes later, the hug ended and everyone went back to where they were sitting before. There was a new mood in the room now – one of surrender, forgiveness, and absolute love.

Enrico took Sadie's hand in his own, and looked into Sophie's eyes first, and then into Angelo's. He then repeated his question from a few minutes ago. "So, do we have your blessing?"

Sophie and Angelo exchanged knowing glances with each other. They giggled and shrugged their shoulders, and then they looked at their parents. "Yes", they said at the same time.

Enrico grabbed Sadie's hand and they both stood up shouting, "Yeeeah!!" They kissed each other in front of their children, hugged their bodies very close together, and felt like they had just scored a victory in the name of love. "Thank you, so very much!" they shouted into the air.

That night, Sophie and Angelo said good-bye to their parents at Sadie's front door. They both had their suspicions of what might happen while they drove home, but Sadie promised that they were saving themselves for the wedding night, and that she would drive Enrico to the airport on time.

Sophie was relieved while her husband wished them well. "Night! See you both tomorrow!"

Tina Griffith

That night, they slept together in her bed, but again, there was no sex. They cuddled and kissed a lot, and reached out to touch and caress a lot, but Enrico didn't get past second base. Not because they didn't want to, but because they now had something special to look forward to.

They talked at great length, about their children, their wedding, and their honeymoon, and every word and thought had been delivered in soft tones, and with immense love.

The morning came much too quickly, and neither of them wanted to get out of bed. But because Enrico's things were still at the hotel, they knew they had to. Sadie made breakfast while Enrico got himself cleaned up, and then they ate while enjoying the coffee and buttered toast with jam. They got dressed slowly, as if to lengthen their time together, but then time got the better of them and they knew they had to hurry up.

Angelo and Sophie met their parents at the airport. They were delighted by how happy and serene Enrico and Sadie looked – as a couple, and as loving individuals.

"I'm very glad that you came", Enrico said proudly. He had tears in his eyes when he saw them in the terminal. "Thank you for being here."

"We couldn't let you leave without giving you one more hug", Sophie said softly. She wrapped her arms around his waist and embraced him like a little girl does to her daddy. "You have a safe trip, grampa."

Enrico giggled, but the tears were already getting ready to rain down his cheeks. He kissed the top of her head and thanked her for the very kind sentiments.

Angelo also gave his dad one more hug, and wished him to have a safe flight. "Talk to you soon, ok?"

The Elusive Mr. Velucci

"As soon as I get home", he promised.

Angelo and Sophie left, and now he was alone to say good-bye to Sadie.

Enrico steered her over towards the large windows - the exact same one where he had handed her a tissue. He pointed to the plane which would take him to Italy, and made her guess which window was beside his seat.

Sadie thought this was a silly game, but she did just as he had asked.

While her mind was busy, Enrico pulled a ring out of his pocket and got down on one knee.

Enrico bought the 1.00 carat, pink sapphire, round cut, platinum gold engagement ring, a month after visiting the dry cleaners. He was on the verge of dropping into a deeper depression after he had learned that her phone number had been lost, and was spending a lot of time walking around and window shopping in the malls. He bought the precious ring five minutes after seeing it, and promised himself that if Sadie would forgive him, he would ask her to marry him, so that they would never have to be apart again. He has carried it with him, ever since.

When Sadie turned around, she was undeniably shocked and confused by what Enrico was doing.

Enrico's eyes were locked on hers, as he executed a very thoughtful, thirty-second, well-rehearsed speech. It began with, "I want to do this officially", and was followed by, "Sadie Lynn Adams, will you marry me?"

"YES!" she shouted, while exhilaration flooded her body. Her mind had exploded and she couldn't even spell her own name in that moment, but she knew that she wanted to marry him. It was what she had waited for and dreamed about for most of her life.

"Good. Now let's see if this ring fits." He took it out of its protective case and placed it on her ring finger.

She was shaking as he slipped it on, and gasped when it fit. "It's so beautiful", she sighed. Tears were flowing down her cheeks and dropping onto her blouse, but she didn't care. She had her left hand out and was admiring how lovely the ring looked. "I love it, so much", she gushed.

"Good." Seeing Sadie's face light up, made Enrico very happy. "I'm glad you like it", he said quietly. Enrico knew that he needed to get checked in, so he glanced at his watch to check the time. "I'm afraid that we have to say good-bye for now, but I will see you again real soon."

They touched their foreheads together, and whispered some tender words that only the two of them could hear.

"Thank you for the ring", she said quietly. "I love you, and I will talk with you as soon as you get home."

He smiled while looking directly into her eyes. "You're welcome, and I really do promise to call."

They shared another few dozen kisses, and then he walked away.

"And this is where we come in; we're doing their wedding", Halley announced loudly to the eager crowd. "Sadie wanted outside help, because her and Enrico want it to be the most special wedding that anyone has ever seen or been to.

"That is so sweet." Terri dabbed a tissue against her eyes to wipe away her tears, and then used the same napkin against the bottom of her nose. *sniff* "This is such a beautiful story, and they love each other so much", she said in a quiet tone.

Halley moved her body towards her friend and patted her hand while trying to comfort her. "Are you ok?" she giggled.

In a nonchalant manner, Terri suggested that she was fine. "I just adore how they got to the point where they're finally able to be together", she added. There was an intensity to her lowered voice, which was meant to show that she was rooting for them to be a couple.

Halley looked over her friend's shoulder and noticed that there was an enormous change in the ambience in the entire room, and it was not just at their table; everyone in the coffee shop was crying softly in the background, even though some were trying to cover it up. As her eyes scanned each of the tables, she watched as life began to seep back into the crowded space. And it became even more clear, when the feet of those people going to the bathroom or to the counter,

Tina Griffith

moved sluggishly across the floor; nobody was worried about making noise now.

Chairs had been turned to their original positions and conversations began to break out in muted tones, as they all took turns guessing how the story would end. The majority hoped that it would be 'happily ever after', but there were a few skeptics who insisted that Sophie would somehow try to break up the marriage between her mother and Enrico.

Meanwhile, the manager flipped the sign on the front door to read 'open', and then walked across the room to thank Halley for telling the beautiful love story of Enrico and Sadie.

Halley smiled while wearing a placid look on her face. "It wasn't my intention to grab everyone's interest, but I'm glad that they were all entertained."

"As was I", she replied with conviction. After she walked away, other people came up and quickly gave Halley their thanks. They didn't linger at the table too long, but wanted Halley to know how much they appreciated her giving them one of the best afternoons in a long time.

"You're welcome." She wore a shy but proud smile across her face, as she spoke to the twenty or more people who were there that day. "It was my pleasure."

As if she had been suddenly shocked back to reality, Terri checked her watch and jumped when she saw that she was running behind. "I have to go, but I'll call you later, ok?"

Halley had been taken by surprise by the sudden declaration, but nodded and added, "That'll be good, because we still have some last minute things to do before the wedding day."

The Elusive Mr. Velucci

"Ok, bye."

They hugged, and then Halley watched as Terri sauntered her fabulous body towards the front door.

Her perfect hips swayed side-to-side, the slight bounce in her step was precise and quite elegant, and the high social energy which emanated from the wannabe actress/model, kept everyone who was watching, from breathing in a normal rhythm.

Terri knew that people were looking, so she walked as if she was on a Paris runway, and being judged by the ten top fashion designers in the world. She arrived at the front door, and before she could reach out to turn the brass handle, a man had jumped up and turned it for her.

"Allow me", he whispered softly, as he pushed the door wide open. His lips were approximately an inch away from her ear, and his breath smelled of strong coffee.

Terri knew she had inhaled a little too sharply, but his sensual voice had given her soul a shudder of excitement, which had oddly confused her otherwise, cold exterior. From the corner of Terri's eye, she could tell that he stood her same height, that his shoulders were wide and straight across, and that his cologne reminded her of freshly ironed, white linen shirts, that had been hung to dry in a quiet, woodsy area. He hadn't shaved that morning, but he had combed his hair, which was a wonderful combination in her book.

It took a mere second for her to catch her bearings, and then she remembered that she was in love with a brilliant man named, Tim. This gave her inner strength, and encouraged her to not give the stranger any ideas.

Terri puffed out her chest and raised her physique a little

Tina Griffith

higher. She didn't change her facial expression or even look in his direction, but merely walked around him and stepped outside. Before she reached her car though, Terri felt a cold shiver race through her entire body. It caused all of her muscles to go limp, while a smile tickled the corners of her mouth. She recovered quickly from the stranger's kindness, and was able to continue on with the rest of her day.

Once the door to the coffee shop had closed, it was evident that the aura inside the café had changed. Something huge had happened there today, and it had unmistakably altered everyone's perception and mood.

The assembly of strangers who had been there by coincidence, had somehow come together as a united group with one cause. They very much enjoyed the impromptu story, and they all realized that the many facets of it, would fill their hearts with love and questions as to how it would all turn out, for many days to come.

Halley was still stunned by Terri's rather abrupt departure, but she gathered up her things, left a handsome amount of money on the table, and then she made an unhurried exit.

While she gave the crowd something quite interesting to listen to and talk about, she wasn't given the awe factor that Terri had been given, when she was the one leaving. But, Halley took a great deal of happiness with her just the same, and she now wore a proud smile across her pretty face. She waved good-bye to the manager as she stepped into the outside world, and hoped that when someone was in need of a wedding coordinator, that they would keep her in mind.

After getting into her car, Halley allowed herself to relax. A good minute had passed before she steered her light blue, Nissan Versa through the semi-busy traffic. All the while, she reveled in the fact that she was on her way home.

Soon after leaving the coffee shop, Halley found herself humming to, 'Our Day Will Come' - one of her favorite wedding songs. Before she got to the chorus, a new level of happiness filled her soul.

A week later, Halley and Terri were meeting with Sadie at her home, to talk about the final details of the wedding. It was exactly one month to the day before the ceremony would take place, and everyone was getting nervous.

In that same moment, Enrico was in Hong Kong acting as a guest conductor of the Hong Kong Symphony Orchestra. He had just stepped inside of the Concert Hall of the Hong Kong Multipurpose Cultural Centre, and he was completely blown away by the enormity of how grand the building was. As his eyes made a slow sweep of all that was before him, he guessed that there were over 2,000 seats in the oval, two-tiered auditorium. It was beautifully finished with high quality oak and decked out with gorgeous heavy curtains, and he couldn't wait to hear how the music resonated throughout the room.

Halley opened her detail binder while Terri explained all that had been done, as opposed to what was left to be approved and checked off the list.

Sadie's thoughts were on what was happening with the wedding, but also with her daughter; the baby was due in two weeks, and anytime the phone rang, she automatically assumed that it was Sophie.

"We're confident of where the wedding is going to take place and who's going to perform the ceremony, and now

The Elusive Mr. Velucci

we just have to make sure that all the rental clothing will be properly fitted and ready for the big day", Halley stated.

Terri turned to her friend and added, "And also that the reception area will be decorated with the precision with which we expect, and that the caterers will arrive on time, if not minutes before."

"You're right", Halley agreed, and made notes in her binder.

Sadie was thrilled that it was all coming together, and that almost everything had been discussed and checked off the 'things to do' list.

"You've made your hair and nail appointments?" Terri asked.

"Yes", Sadie replied.

"And your dress? Have you had the final fitting yet?" Halley asked.

"That happens next week."

Halley added notes beside both of these entries. "Check and check!"

Sadie wished that Enrico was there to do some of these things with her, and that Sophie would not go into labor during the twenty-four hours before the wedding.

"So? Are we done for now?" Terri asked to both Sadie and Halley. She wanted to go and make a few phone calls, to ensure that every single thing would be executed with perfection.

Halley and Sadie looked at each other and nodded. "I think so", they responded at the same time.

"Ok", Terri began. "I'm going to do a quick follow-up with the musicians and the minister, as well as a few other people on this list. We'll stay in touch and meet again, two weeks before the actual ceremony." Terri leaned in and gave Sadie a quick hug, and then turned to Halley. "We'll talk later." They hugged and then Terri left.

Halley stayed a few minutes longer, to see if Sadie was ok. They had not known each other for too long, but they had developed a wonderful bond over the past few months - much like that of a mother and daughter.

"You were a bit distracted today. Are you ok?" Halley asked. Her voice was soft and filled with concern.

Sadie lowered her eyes as she clung to hope that everything would go as planned. "My daughter is about to have a baby, as you know, and I hope that the delivery, as well as my wedding, goes well."

Halley could understand that, however she couldn't guarantee it. "No matter how it works out, you will have a husband and a grandchild before the next full moon." It wasn't meant as a joke, but it made Sadie smile.

"Thank you", Sadie said, as her eyes and heart lit up. The words made a whole lot of sense; it wasn't that the wedding had to be perfect or that the timing of the baby was that important, it was the fact that Sadie was going to be a grama and a wife in the next thirty days. She looked into Halley's eyes and added, "You are wise beyond your years, my friend."

Halley leaned in and gave her a big hug. "Thank you. I just don't want you to worry about anything; we're working towards creating your big day. This is the wedding that you've dreamed of your whole life. I just want everything to be perfect for you."

Sadie was overwhelmed by the thoughtfulness and caring that Halley had shown her. "Thank you."

The Elusive Mr. Velucci

"You're most welcome." She touched Sadie's forearm as she spoke. Halley gathered up her things and said good-bye, and then walked to her car and drove away.

As Sadie closed the door, the phone rang.

"Hello?"

"I'm taking Sophie to the hospital!" Angelo shouted in a voice that was filled with high-level anxiety. "Her contractions are running five minutes apart, and she's in a lot of pain!"

Something inside of Sadie's head exploded and she couldn't comprehend anything else, but what was happening with her daughter.

"Can you hear me?" Angelo asked loudly. He was frantic and not sure how do to this on his own.

"Y-yes, I'm here", she answered. "I'll meet you there."

Sadie dialed Enrico's number, but the call went straight to voice mail. She left him a message, but she didn't tell him what it was about.

Enrico was in the midst of his one and only rehearsal, and couldn't hear the phone, even if he wanted to. The run through was remarkable - no problems, no sour notes, and nothing needed changing. It was as if they had done this a million times before today. And the quality of sound that he heard in that venue, was equal to sitting in a warm bath, while someone massages your shoulders and neck with the finest baby oil on the planet. It was all Enrico could do not to swoon or sigh during the last song.

Sadie tried to drive within the speed limits and between the lines, but she was filled with torment. Her thoughts were running amuck, worrying about the silliest things possible, and because she was panicking, nothing was making sense.

'Enrico's not here, the baby is early, and if the pains are five minutes apart, why didn't anyone call her sooner?' her mind screamed.

All that could keep Sadie sane, was the fact that Sophie was going to be in good hands. She was sure that Sophie's doctor was already there and waiting, and he was pretty fussy about who worked with him. Sadie took a deep breath, held it in, and then released it into the air. After doing this a few times, it seemed to clear her head.

She arrived and parked, and raced into the hospital like a rabbit who was being chased by a pack of wild dogs. Her heart was pounding, her eyes were wide, and her only thought was, 'where is my daughter?'

The lady at the front desk directed her to Sophie's floor and room, with words and arm gestures.

"Thanks", she called over her shoulder. She raced to the elevator and arrived at Sophie's labor and delivery room, a few minutes after that.

The first thing she saw, was Angelo pacing around the room with a terrified, wide-eyed look upon his face. Tears flew out of his eyes the minute he saw her face, and he rushed over to give her a hug. "Thank you for coming so quickly."

Sadie was appreciative of the hug, but her focus was more on her daughter. "How are you doing?" she asked, as she stroked the hair off Sophie's forehead and cheeks.

Sophie was in the middle of another contraction and couldn't talk, but she grunted how she was doing. "I'm at 5cm and wish this was over."

Sadie knew very well what that meant; it felt like

only last year that she had given birth to Sophie, and she remembered every single detail.

The pain was unbelievable and almost tolerable, the hot water in the shower was very helpful, and just when she thought she couldn't do it anymore, the baby came out.

As Sadie looked at her daughter, she wished that her labor would go just as easy.

Angelo was having a small panic attack, and one of the nurses noticed. She walked him out of the room, sat him down on one of the two chairs in the hallway, and asked him to bend his upper body forward.

He did as she suggested, but he worried that he should be in the room with Sophie.

"She's going to be ok; her mother and a nurse are in there with her."

Angelo wanted to fight the woman who was arguing with him, but he didn't because she was emotionally stronger. She kept a firm hand on the back of his neck, while she tried to get him to calm down. It didn't take long before Angelo's thoughts and racing adrenaline, slowed down enough for him to think clear again.

Once the nurse recognized that his body had changed, she let him sit up. She gave him a cup of cold water with ice chips in it, and a cool towel for his head. "I'll go and check on your wife, but you sit here for another minute." It was an order, and not something he could protest.

Angelo understood and did as he was told.

The nurse came back a few minutes later. "Your wife is now dilated to 6cm, but it's still going to be a long time before you get to meet your child. I'd like you to sit here for another ten minutes or so, and then you can go back inside." Again, this was not a suggestion.

Angelo agreed, as he didn't know that he had another choice. Plus, he wanted to be in good shape for when Sophie needed him.

Hours later, on the other side of the world, the lights dimmed, the curtains opened up, and 'La Traviata' by Verdi was about to begin. The audience rose to their feet, and clapped loudly when they were introduced to the guest conductor, Enrico Velucci. He bowed as they cheered, and then turned around to face the well-dressed group of talented musicians.

Little did Enrico know, that as he raised his baton to strike the orchestra in their first song of the night, the baby's head had crowned.

"Push!" yelled the doctor. His hands were right where they needed to be, and the nurse beside him, had a warm blanket to wrap the baby in. Another nurse was monitoring the machines which were hooked up to Sophie's chest and arm, while Angelo stood close and kept quiet.

He had never felt so helpless before, and swore that he would never touch his wife again, for fear that she would end up in this situation a second time. His face winced and his body cringed every time Sophie screamed out in pain, but all he could do was encourage her to keep going.

As Sadie watched her daughter go through labor, she wished for it to be over soon. She also wished that Enrico had been there – as a first-time grampa, but also to help Angelo get through this. Every time she glanced in her son-in-law's direction, he looked like he was about to pass out. He stayed upright though, and she made a point to congratulate him on that, later.

As the opening notes of the first song began to play, Sadie's face popped into Enrico's head. It was not such a coincidence that he thought about Sadie in that very moment, since the song was about a woman falling in love with one of her suitors.

"One more strong push!" the doctor ordered loudly.

As the first song reached its pivotal end, the baby had been successfully released from Sophie's body.

Enrico bowed as the audience clapped, in the same moment as when the baby had discovered its first cry.

Hours later, after Sophie and her baby had been cleaned up, Sadie was able to hold her grandchild. She cooed and awed at the beautiful little face, and thought of nothing else but how much love she had, for this tiny bundle in her arms.

Enrico's concert was now over, and he couldn't wait to hop on the plane and get back to New York. As the taxi drove him to the airport, he checked his phone and saw that he had missed quite a few messages. His body went through a dozen or so different emotions as he listened to all that Angelo and Sadie had to say, and then he couldn't contain himself any longer. "Yeeeeeeah!!" he screamed with utter delight. He suddenly had a newfound energy surging through his body, and a brand new reason to get on the plane.

Angelo and Sadie stayed in the hospital with Sophie until morning, and were still there when Enrico came into the room.

Enrico knocked on the door with the knuckle of his

right index finger, and peeked his head into the room. "Is it ok to come in?" he asked softly.

"Papa!" Angelo called, and rushed over to greet his father. "You missed the most wonderful event."

Enrico was choking up from the many emotions which he was experiencing in that very second.

Sadie stood up and walked over to Enrico. They wrapped their arms around each other, and stood crying for what seemed like forever. Afterwards, they kissed on the mouth and stared into each other's eyes, without feeling the need to speak.

"Hi, grampa", Sophie called. She looked exhausted, but spread her arms wide open to welcome him home. "I'm glad you got here so quickly."

Enrico bent down to give her a hug, but was careful not to crush her. "I wouldn't want to be anywhere else", he stated with an amazing amount of love.

A nurse knocked once and then walked into the room, carrying a newborn baby. "I hear that grampa hasn't seen the newest member of the family, yet. Is that right?"

Enrico looked into everyone's face to make sure that this was not a dream; up until this point, it all felt so surreal. And the fact that this baby was his grandchild, was completely overwhelming to him.

The nurse wasn't anticipating an answer, but she did wait until he held his arms out before she handed over the precious child. Once she was sure that the head was held properly, she walked out of the room.

Enrico had never felt like this in his whole entire life. A wonderful piece of music gave him chills, and being with Sadie made the world a much better place to live in, but holding this child – his true grandchild – was the strangest and most delightful experience he'd ever had.

Sadie walked over to him and gently moved her body next to his. She brought one hand up and laid it across his shoulders, while they both looked down and admired the new baby.

Angelo loved what he was seeing, and did the same as Sadie.

Enrico was now blessed on all sides, by the people he loved the most in the whole world. He could also feel Maria nearby, and wished that she was there in person; she would have loved being a grama. He made a mental note to introduce this child to her, when Sophie and Angelo came to Italy in the future.

"Don't you want to know what it is?" Sophie called. She suddenly felt all alone, and wanted a little bit of attention to be on her.

Her question caused Enrico's whole demeanor to shift. "Y-yes", he replied. He was happy enough that they had a baby to fuss over, but it would be nice to know if it was a boy or a girl.

"I'll give you a hint. The baby's name is, Skyler Angelina Velucci."

Enrico looked into Angelo's eyes and sobbed uncontrollably. "That's beautiful", he said.

Sophie explained how they arrived at the name. "She's going to have Velucci from you guys, and I wanted her first name to begin with an 'S', to keep that tradition going on in our family. We used 'Angelina' for three reasons; it's the female version of Angelo, it was his mother's middle name, and it means 'Angel' – a messenger of God.

Tina Griffith

Angelo had tears in his eyes, but he continued from where Sophie left off. "This little girl is a gift, and is going to be connected to all of us for the rest of her life."

Sadie sighed from the beautiful sentiments, and could feel her tears begging to come out, yet again.

Enrico couldn't stop looking at how exquisite the delicate creature in his arms was. She was gorgeous in every way possible, and when she moved or yawned, it brought another quality to the already perfect human being.

A nurse came in and stated that she needed to take the baby away for a few short minutes. Before anyone had a chance to object, she gently removed the newest Velucci from her grampa's loving arms. When the door closed, the foursome were alone, and took a minute to let the situation sink in.

Sophie's doctor came in with a clipboard, and asked how she was doing. After examining her, he recommended that she stay in the hospital for another day or two, and then she could go home.

Angelo stayed at the hospital for the rest of the day, while Sadie and Enrico went to her place to get changed and reacquainted.

Enrico showered and ate, and then they both climbed into bed to rest. When they woke up, they made their way back to the hospital in order to give Angelo a chance to go home and get cleaned up.

Sophie and the baby went home at the end of the following day, and began their new lives as mother and daughter. It was an amazing experience, one which required a lot of hands-on training, but it was also something that

The Elusive Mr. Velucci

she was truly enjoying; every moment was completely new, and there was a lot to learn.

Angelo had asked for some time off from school and was graciously given six weeks, but that wasn't supposed to start yet. Because the baby had come a little early, Angelo had to call the dean and explain the current situation.

"Congratulations, Angelo!" he shouted. "I would have no problem if you wanted to begin your time off now, but you would have to make up the school work by the end of the current semester."

Angelo agreed, and thanked Dean Walters with an enormous amount of gratitude. A little while later, Angelo called his boss at his part-time job, and asked him for some time off. He was most grateful when the answer was an astounding, yes.

Over the next two weeks, Enrico and Sadie went to Sophie and Angelo's house as often as possible. They always brought presents, diapers, food, and toys with them, and whatever else that was needed or wanted. They also got to hold their darling little granddaughter, as much as they wanted.

During those two or three hours when the parents came by, Sophie and Angelo spent ten minutes saying hello, and then went to bed for some much-needed rest. Grama and Grampa didn't mind, as they were in their glory with their newest little family member.

They took turns feeding, cuddling, singing, and telling the baby a story. Sadie was in charge of changing the diapers, but Enrico handed her all the items which she asked for. Enrico was in charge of giving Skyler her bottle, while Sadie sat beside them and cooed.

Tina Griffith

Before Sophie and Angelo had gotten up from their naps, supper had been prepared by the skilled and loving hands of Grampa Enrico. The dishes were always washed and put away by Sadie, and sometimes Angelo helped out. That left Sophie and Enrico to bond.

Now that her hormones were not rushing around and making her crazy, Sophie had a much softer attitude. While she watched Enrico with his granddaughter, she became better acquainted with him. She was sorry that they had not known each other while she was growing up, but after spending some time with him this past year, she felt sure that he was going to be a fabulous grandfather.

Sadie had also had been able to bond with Angelo. While doing dishes, she asked him how he liked staying home, and how great it was to have a baby in the house.

"It's weird not being at school or work, but being at home with a baby and a wife is work in itself. There's always something to do, and I never get a minute by myself", he confessed.

Sadie heard a little sadness in his voice, but understood that everything was still pretty new to him. For that reason, she was very sympathetic, because she had gone through the same thing when she was his age. "And I had to do it all alone", she reminded him.

"I can't imagine that." Angelo looked at her with a higher level of respect. He and Sophie were having a hard time, and there were two people taking care of the house and the baby. Angelo shook his head in total disbelief; he had no idea how Sadie had done this all by herself.

"You do what you have to", she sighed.

When they weren't fussing over their beautiful

granddaughter, Enrico spent the rest of his time at Sadie's home. And while they slept in the same bed, they refrained from having sex. It wasn't easy, but the anticipation of the wedding night, made it all worth it.

Two weeks before the day of the wedding, Halley called Sadie, just as promised.

Enrico walked into the room while Sadie was on the phone, and he asked who she was talking to.

Sadie held a stiff index finger in the air until she finished the conversation. "She weighed 7 pounds and 2 ounces, and she was 20 inches long. Oh, she's a beauty. Lots of black hair, really dark eyes, and she's as cute as a kitten."

Sadie paused, and then she laughed and continued speaking. "Ok, I'll see you then."

Sadie turned to Enrico and told him that the wedding planners were coming by the house tomorrow.

Enrico was delighted, and couldn't wait to see how the wedding plans were shaping up.

Because Halley's home was also used as their make-shift office, Terri and Halley met there the night before going to Sadie's home. They got together once a week just to talk, but tonight they wanted to make sure that every detail of the wedding had been checked off.

Halley had already poured the chilled wine into glasses, and was carrying them into the tiny living room area, when she heard Terri knock on the door. "It's open!" she called.

"I'm here!" the dark haired woman announced, as she walked into the room.

"Here's your wine." Halley's voice had dripped with excitement, while a recognizable joy gushed from every pore in her body.

Terri reached for her glass, as a supreme look of confidence shone across her face. "To a successful wedding", she cheered.

They pushed their glasses together and giggled at the hollow clinking sound that it made, and then they sipped their delicious red wine as they celebrated another job well done.

A half an hour later, everything had been checked and confirmed, and now it was time to breathe.

"Question!" Terri stated, with a hand in the air. "Can we talk about Enrico?" Terri's eyes had suddenly glazed over with extreme interest. "What does he look like. I know you've

The Elusive Mr. Velucci

told me a few details here and there, but you've actually met him, so I want to know your perception of him."

Halley had to compose herself before she gave Terri a description of Sadie's fiancé. "He's gorgeous, but I guess I shouldn't say it like that. He has dark features, long lashes, he's taller than me, clean shaven, and he likes to dress well. He also looks very fit, has shoulders a yard wide, a perfectly symmetrical mouth, full lips, and a swath of wavy black hair that falls casually onto his forehead."

Terri swooned, and then felt the need to take another sip of wine.

"Because he's famous for conducting orchestras around the world, his hobbies, his interests, and where he went to school are all common knowledge – anyone can find that information on the internet", she stated with confidence. "He keeps his financial status quite private, but you can bet that it is almost as absorbing as how he looks. Should I go on?"

Terri's body language showed that she was more eager to meet him than ever. "He sounds delicious." It was strange, but she found herself sighing over a man who she had never met or seen before. "Go on."

Halley found it difficult to think about Mr. Velucci without swooning, because she had agonized over him since they met a few months ago. The fact that she couldn't have him herself, caused her head to swim through a haze of silly teenage emotions and desires. For this reason, Halley was glad that her meetings were with Enrico's fiancé rather than him, for his nearness was both disturbing and exciting to her.

"It was easy for Terri to see how awkward this

conversation was to Halley, and now she wanted to know as much as possible. She knew full-well that she was prying, but her curiosity was getting the better of her. And despite that it was not good business ethics, she wanted to know as much as Halley would tell.

Halley could feel that she had been defeated. She swallowed hard, lifted her chin, and met Terri's gaze with a little fear. She gulped the rest of her wine down really quickly, and then went to refill her glass.

"Come on!" Terri urged. She was sitting on the edge of her seat, both physically and mentally, and wanted her request to be received as a demand, rather than a polite invitation.

As she walked from the kitchen back into the living room, Halley had lowered her voice. It was now in a slightly darker tone than before, and it gave the story a sense of mystery.

Terri could definitely feel goose bumps trying to push their way out of her smooth-as-satin skin, and it made her feel somewhat cautious of what Halley was about to say. Her almond-shaped eyes were now as wide as a full moon, and it felt like her heart had begun to beat a little harder.

"Ok, are you ready?"

Terri felt like she was sitting in a dark, haunted house, and that someone was going to jump out at her, sometime in the next few minutes. "Yes, but speak slowly so that I can hear every single word you say."

Halley spoke volumes, and for as long as she could, and when Terri didn't comment, Halley paused and looked around. She was stunned to find that two large bottles of red wine had been finished, a mickey of vodka had been emptied, and several empty containers of Chinese food were laying haphazardly on the kitchen table and counters. What made her laugh, was the fact that Terri was passed out in a fetal position, and mumbling something about a beautiful love story.

Terri had hung onto every single word that left Halley's gorgeous mouth, but she was nervous about parts of the story and ended up drinking too much. And when she rested her head against a cushion from the couch, she accidentally fell asleep.

Halley's eyes drifted to her lap, and she noticed that her hands were cradling her almost empty wine glass. She tipped it up and finished the last few drops of the now-warm purple liquid, and then she stood up. She was woozy – her head was spinning with alcohol and passion – but she wanted to straighten up before going to bed.

Halley looked towards her friend, and decided to take care of her before doing anything else. She took the handmade, quilted blanket which her Auntie Effie had lovingly made for her, and placed it on top of Terri's body. Halley then gathered all of the empty containers and bottles from the living room, and brought them into the kitchen.

As she moved around the room, the sentimental effects from telling the powerful love story hit her hard, and she suddenly felt overly emotional. The quiet numbness and mock happiness from the alcohol in her blood stream, plus the relief that Terri had not heard the ending of the story, put a smile on Halley's relaxed face.

Halley closed her eyes in silent thanks, that Terri hadn't heard the inflection in her voice when she talked about the moment when she shook hands with Enrico, or when he spoke directly into her eager blue eyes while they were being introduced. Terri didn't know how loud Halley's heart had been pounding in her ears whenever he looked in her direction, or that her smooth skin had turned pinker by the minute, whenever he spoke to her.

Halley suddenly remembered how her body had raced from being fine one minute, to being very warm and sweaty the next. It was bizarre, and she hoped that nothing like that will happen tomorrow.

As Halley took a last look at her best friend asleep on the couch, she was grateful that some things were going to be kept a secret.

To Halley, Enrico was princely in every way possible, even though he was old enough to be her father. Still, that didn't seem to deter her from falling in love with him.

Halley flipped the light in the living room off, and walked to her bedroom. As she climbed into bed, she sighed, "Sadie's a very lucky woman."

The next morning, Terri opened her eyes first. She could tell that she was at Halley's home, and then everything else began to make sense. She stumbled down the hall and into her friend's bedroom, and then climbed into bed with her. Both girls said good-morning to the other, and then rolled over and went back to sleep.

Hours later, Terri woke up to the smell of a fresh cup of hot coffee, which was being held mere inches from her face.

"Morning!" Halley called, but not too loudly. She waited until Terri got into a sitting position before she handed her the cup. "How did you sleep?"

Terri was not a morning person, but she was more than grateful to be there with her best friend in the whole world, and to have some coffee in her body. After two sips, she

The Elusive Mr. Velucci

moaned and then answered. "I loved that story you told, but I don't think I heard the ending."

Halley blushed and tried to confuse the issue. "I'm sure you did, because I remember how you sighed and said how beautiful it was."

Terri made a face, took a sip of her coffee, and kept her eyes down while she searched her brain for the ending.

Halley tried to hide a giggle, because Terri was easy to fool.

"Oh, yeah, right. I remember now." Terri obviously didn't, but she chalked that up to still having alcohol in her system.

Halley was more than relieved. She had been caught up in the story while telling it, and had gotten quite lost in many of the wonderful moments before the end. Halley felt safe that Terri had not heard how she truly felt about Enrico, and now she knew that she would have to make sure that she never talked so freely about someone again.

As Halley walked out of the room, she noticed the time. "Okay, let's finish our coffees and get ready to go; you're meeting Enrico in three hours."

Terri was suddenly very wide awake.

Sadie jumped to attention when the doorbell rang, and insisted that Enrico come into the room to greet their guests.

Enrico had met Halley before, and greeted her with familiarity. As he was looking into her eyes and holding her hand between both of his, he stated, "Halley, it is very nice to see you again."

Halley swooned and sighed, and felt her knees going weak. "H-hi!" she whispered.

When he turned to Terri, he could actually see the color of her cheeks turning rosy pink. "Well", he began. "I've heard so much about you." As he wrapped both of his hands around her left one, he continued, "It's very nice to meet you."

Terri, who couldn't stop staring into his eyes, was on cloud nine and never wanted to get off. "Thank you", was all that came out of her mouth.

"Come in!" Sadie insisted. "Please, have a seat." She had her left arm extended and pointed towards the dining room table. "As you can see, we have tea and treats waiting for you."

"Thank you", Halley said, in a very proper voice. She stepped past Enrico and inhaled the scent of his aromatic cologne, and hoped that he couldn't tell how she felt about him.

The Elusive Mr. Velucci

It had been a few months since they last saw each other, but her inner stirrings were still as strong as ever.

Terri couldn't help staring, because she now knew firsthand, exactly what Halley was talking about; the man was gorgeous. He exuded confidence and vitality, he was more handsome than words could describe, and he smelled absolutely heavenly. He reeked of old school charm and manners, and he gave you the impression that he cared very deeply about how other people were feeling.

Terri was reluctant to leave the small confines of the front entrance, and would have rather lingered near him, for as long as time would allow. But when Sadie invited them to come even further into her home, Terri blinked and tried to pull herself together. "Thank you", she stated quietly, and hoped that nobody had noticed how preoccupied her mind had just been.

Enrico sat on the same side of the table as Sadie, and held hands with her while they discussed the plans for the wedding. He kept good eye contact with both of his guests, but it was quite clear that he was only interested in whatever made Sadie happy.

"Oh!" Sadie stated energetically. She left the table quite abruptly, as everyone watched in surprise, and came back with a list of people who had confirmed their attendance at the wedding. "It's mostly our families who are coming, but we've also invited a few friends that have made a difference in our lives."

Enrico glanced at the list and nodded his approval.

Halley was sitting directly across from Enrico, which caused Terri to be a little jealous. While they directed the conversation to both the bride and the groom, Enrico was

Tina Griffith

definitely made to feel more important. Papers and pictures of what to expect on the day of the wedding, were flipped so that he could see them without causing strain to his neck or vision.

When Halley was speaking, Terri took that moment to study all of Enrico's best attributes. She tried her best to control her deep, savoring breaths, but she couldn't hide the look of yearning which had now spread across her face, while she gazed into his dark Italian features. He had an intellectual look about him and a captivating personality, and trusting eyes that weighed down his thick, black lashes. And when he spoke, his accent made every word feel and sound more alive and romantic, than anything she had ever experienced before in her life.

When it was Terri's turn to talk, Halley used that moment to romanticize over whatever Enrico was doing or saying. She wore a silly grin, but didn't know it, and wondered if he could see into her soul.

"I'm so impressed by all that you girls have done", he said kindly.

Terri had been caught off guard by the sudden enthusiasm in his voice, and laughed lightly to catch his eye. "Thank you." She then stared at him with a beaming expression, but he was busy doing all he could to make Sadie feel absolutely adored.

When he turned and looked in Halley's direction, she was in shock. Halley immediately lost all sense of time and awareness of her surroundings. A mental fuzziness invaded her mind, her heart began to race, and she could feel the blush on her skin develop rapidly. It embarrassed her, so she

The Elusive Mr. Velucci

lowered her eyes and pretended to glance at the many treats on the table.

Enrico was very perceptive, and he could see that he was causing both of these ladies to feel uneasy. Because he felt that Halley needed to have more of his attention, he reached for the plate and placed it in front of her. "Please", he insisted. "I made these Italian Ricotta cookies especially for you."

Terri's head swiveled to the side with a whooshing sound, as her mind screamed, 'What?'

Halley locked eyes with the handsome conductor, and without looking at the plate, she reached for one of the delicious morsels which he was offering. "Thank you", she sighed softly, and brought it to her lips.

Enrico moved the plate so that Terri could also try what he had made. "Please", he insisted. "Have one. I know you want to."

Terri had her eyes fixed on his while she reached for a tasty treat, and thanked him by smiling and nodding. She placed the freshly baked goodie in her mouth, and just as Halley had done, she moaned with great appreciation.

"These are really good!" Halley announced with enthusiasm.

Terri agreed, "Most definitely."

"I told you that you should open a bakery", Sadie giggled. She placed her arm around his elbow and squeezed.

Enrico patted her hand lightly, while he stared lovingly into her eyes. His whole face lit up when he replied, "I just might have to do that, then."

A half an hour later, after all the details had been confirmed, it was time for the girls to leave. Both of them would have liked to stay longer, but Enrico and Sadie had plans to see their granddaughter.

"Thanks for everything", Halley added sincerely. It was great to see Enrico again, and the cookies had not only tasted amazing, but it was interesting to note that he had made them with his very own hands. She swooned from the image of him in a white apron and nothing else.

Enrico reached behind the door and presented her with a small, pretty bag. "These are for you."

Halley's eyes shot open. "For me?"

"For you and Terri", he chuckled. "That is, if you can share."

Halley couldn't speak, but her mind was screaming that she'd totally share anything he asked her to.

Terri didn't care; she was using her last few seconds to drink in everything she could, about Enrico Velucci. She stared into his eyes while she reached her hand out. "Bye", she whispered. She almost melted when he turned her hand over and kissed the back of it.

"It was my pleasure to finally meet you", he professed kindly.

"Thank you", she said. Terri's voice had trembled, as she continued to stare at all that made him so attractive. She was in awe and thought she might faint, but instead, she held the kissed hand firmly against her chest and covered it with her other hand, as if she was trying to preserve the moment for eternity.

"You are welcome, but it is I who is thanking you, for all that you have done to make our wedding so special", he insisted, in his romantic accent.

The Elusive Mr. Velucci

"Wow!" floated out of Terri's lips. She was completely idolizing the man in front of her, and knew that she would never forget this moment for as long as she lived.

Enrico reached for Halley's hand and kissed the back of it, just as he had done to Terri. He then held it tight between his own, while he professed his glowing gratitude. "And you. Thank you for all you've done for us."

Halley was completely lost in his accent, his words, his mannerisms, and his attractiveness. "Th-thank you", she stuttered. She then realized what she had said and tried to back pedal. "I-I mean, you're welcome. It was our pleasure."

"Totally our pleasure", Terri added. She was wide-eyed and pale, and looked like she had just met her fairytale prince in real life.

"Bye, girls!" Sadie was having fun watching them swoon, but she still wanted to go and see her darling granddaughter. "We'll talk soon."

As they drove away, both Halley and Terri were amazed at how that meeting had gone.

"Do you think he noticed that we acted like dorks?" Terri asked.

Halley made a face, and then tried to make light of their behavior. "Naw. I think we covered our tracks really well." Secretly, it weighed on her mind that they might have come across as silly women who acted a little star-struck.

"It was like meeting my favorite movie star", Terri began. "And he was within our reach." She turned and continued. "I don't mean that I wanted to grab him or anything, but this famous, really good looking man was right there." She stared out the front window as her fantasies took over.

Tina Griffith

"Yah", Halley replied, with a dreamy quality in her voice. "I know what you mean." She spoke while staring out the front window, but as her mind drifted in and out with romantic notions, she kept her eyes focused on the road.

Two weeks later, they were all standing on the shore in Sorrento – Enrico's favorite place on the planet. There were many lit candles, big and small, cleverly dispersed all around the immediate area. There were white flowers and petals everywhere; in Sadie's hair, on the ground, on the backs of chairs, and attached to the whimsical wedding arch. Along with many twinkling lights, there was a white, sheer fabric which had been laced through different sections of the arch. The last two feet of this flimsy material, had been allowed to hang close to the ground like a delicate curtain, so that when the gentle breeze kissed it, there was added movement to the already glorious moment. Through the arch, everyone could see the beauty of Naples – the curly blue waters, the lovely scenery of Italy, and the orange-yellow sun, which was slowly dropping behind the glorious mountains. The whole scenario made an amazing backdrop, to where Enrico and Sadie were about to be wed.

Angelo was the best man and Sophie acted as the maid of honor. Baby Skyler was also there, and being held in the protective arms of Halley James.

Terri wore the headset today, and was responsible for making sure that everything ran smoothly. It was only her second time to direct an entire wedding, and because she had so much riding on this, she vowed to do an amazing job.

Once everyone was seated, Terri instructed the 10-piece orchestra to play the wedding march.

The couple had chosen 'Over The Rainbow' as the song to which Sadie would walk down the aisle, and had asked that it be played in a slower tempo than usual.

Everyone stood up when she came into view, and as Enrico took his first glimpse of his new bride, he turned into mush. He was blown away by her beauty and endless energy, and couldn't believe that he was finally going to fulfill his life-long wish, of being by her side for the rest of his life.

With each step that she took forward, Sadie's heart pounded more and more. She kept her eyes locked on Enrico's, and because he was crying, it made her cry as well.

Not surprisingly, the beautiful music stopped, the instant she stood beside her groom. As she handed the large floral arrangement to Sophie, a hush fell over everyone in attendance. A few birds could be heard chirping or singing off in the distance, and the constant splash of water against the beige sandy beach, only enhanced the already romantic mood.

Enrico's eyes suddenly fell to the locket which she wore around her neck. He reached out to lift it off of her skin, and his eyes grew wide with amazement. "You still have it", he sighed tenderly.

"Of course", she replied softly. Sadie nodded while smiling, and they both teared up.

The minister stood tall and proud as he began the ceremony. He delivered his speech with great admiration, of all that this couple had gone through in order to be together. "Dearly beloved", his voice boomed. "We are gathered here on this miraculous day, to witness the blessed

The Elusive Mr. Velucci

union between Enrico Velucci and Sadie Adams. This is a great celebration on which we come together before God, to recognize the scared love and dedication that is shared between these two people."

The minister's speech went on for another eight minutes, and then he asked the bride and groom to face each other. "Please hold hands as you repeat what I'm about to say", he stated strongly.

Sadie and Enrico stared at each other with an overpowering love. As they held hands and listened to the minister's words, they could feel that the other person was shaking. As they gazed into each other's eyes, they could detect the elation of the moment, emanating from the person who would soon be connected to them in marriage.

"To commemorate this union, we ask that you exchange rings." The minister held one up and showed it to the entire congregation as he spoke. "This circle symbolizes your eternal love and commitment to one another."

As he lowered his arm, and placed one flawless band of gold in Enrico's hand and the other in Sadie's, the orchestra began to play 'Hallelujah', softly in the background.

As the 'I do's' were being recited and the rings were placed on their fingers, the crowd wept. After this part of the ceremony was done, the minister spoke again. With his hands and face raised towards the sky he stated, "Let the memory of this day, always remind you of the promises which you have made in the past half an hour."

He then looked at the bride and groom and declared that they were now man and wife.

The crowd rose to their feet, and clapped and cheered loudly while Enrico and Sadie squealed in delight.

The beautiful music, the surroundings of Italy's best scenery, and the endearing moment, brought tears and goose bumps to every person in attendance.

The minister spoke specifically to Enrico, when he leaned forward and said, "You may now kiss your bride."

Their eyes sparkled while their hearts soared, with more love than any two people ever had in their souls. As they moved their bodies together to embrace their first kiss as a married couple, neither one could contain their emotions.

Enrico took control of the moment, cradling her head with one hand while pulling her lower back towards him with the other. He provided her with plenty of kisses, and each one was given with the heat of anticipation for what would happen later.

Sadie was completely overwhelmed by every single moment of the beautiful service, and kissed her husband again and again.

The minister cleared his throat, and when he finally had their attention, he announced loudly, "It is with great pleasure that I introduce you to, Mr. and Mrs. Enrico Velucci."

Enrico and Sadie smiled and held hands, while turning to face their friends and family. The newly-weds then took their first steps down the aisle, towards their bright future together. White flower petals were strewn towards the 3' wide walkway, as the crowd of forty shouted their congratulations.

After the pictures were taken, everyone moved into the large tent, which had been erected thirty feet away from the wedding arch. The magnificently large shelter had been

The Elusive Mr. Velucci

decorated to perfection, and looked like something out of an elite wedding magazine.

The talented musicians, who had moved from the outdoors to the indoors, had taken their place on the elevated stage, and were now playing softly in the background while everyone ate.

Enrico and a few others had taken their time to prepare the glorious amounts of food, which everyone at the reception was able to enjoy. Three different kinds of pasta, meatballs in sauce, Italian wedding soup, caprese salad, crispy prosciutto wrapped asparagus, and cheesy arancini rice balls, were just a few of the delectable items which were offered on the buffet style menu.

After the multi-layered, butter cream wedding cake had been cut and served, a DJ took his turn to play music for people to dance to. It was then when the duties of the wedding planners had been completed, and now they too, could join in on the wonderful festivities.

Tim, who had flown to Italy with Terri and Halley, was excited about spending the rest of the evening with his girlfriend. Up until that point, he had spent the majority of the wedding by himself.

As Terri removed her bulky headset, she released a strong sigh of relief.

Halley rushed over to congratulate her friend with a huge hug. "You did amazing!" she shouted, above the music and people's voices. She grabbed Terri by the shoulders, and it was easy to see how impressed she was with how her protégé had conducted a perfect wedding. "I'm so proud of you!" she stated sincerely, as she looked directly into Terri's eyes. "In fact, I think we should form a partnership."

Tina Griffith

"What!?" Terri gasped. Her eyes opened up while her mind questioned what had been said.

"I know I started this Wedding Planner business, but I want it to be a fifty/fifty venture from now on."

Terri couldn't speak, she was so happy. She rushed into her friend's eager arms and shouted, "Yes!" They jumped up and down while expressing their joy, and minutes later, they tipped a glass of Dom Perignon to toast their new relationship.

Tim joined in on the clinking of the glasses, and it was then when he saw Terri in a new light.

He had unknowingly studied her all evening, as she interacted with the guests and the bride and groom, and he noticed something within her that he hadn't detected before. This was the real Terri, and not a fake version which she so often portrayed. Today she had been creative, professional, tender, and able to laugh freely. In this environment he could see her for who she really was; a charming, responsible, and down-to-earth woman.

The moon was full and bright in the clear night sky, the music was perfect, and the food and drinks were endless. The water was rippling as it sauntered to the rounded shoreline, and licked each rock that it touched. And the twinkling lights, all over the reception area, gave everything a magical dreamlike quality. But when a ship's horn tooted its congratulations for the couple who was getting married, that's what shocked Tim's mind into doing something significant.

He gulped the last bit of courage from his second glass of champagne, and then set the empty vessel on a nearby table. His eyes then scanned the tent, until he found the

The Elusive Mr. Velucci

dark-haired beauty who he was looking for. Without having to think twice, he walked over to her and invited her to go outside.

Terri was surprised, but did as he requested.

Tim took her drink and handed it off, and then he led her into the fresh air. He walked hand-in-hand with her, until he was sure that nobody could hear what he was about to say. He then positioned them both, so that they were standing face-to-face. As he gazed into her eyes, he prepared himself to speak.

Terri felt nervous, because she didn't know what he was doing. He had an unusual look on his face, which caused her to shiver while holding her breath. 'Is he about to break up with me?' she wondered fearfully.

After Enrico and Sadie walked around the large tent, giving their thanks to everyone for coming to the wedding, they slipped away without anyone noticing.

They had waited until after they had had their first dance as man and wife, and then hopped into the stretch limo and made their way to the Bellevue Syrene Hotel in Sorrento.

Tim was nervous, but felt that if he didn't say these words under the brilliance of the Sorrento sky, he never would. He reached for Terri's hands, and held them in his while he spoke. "We haven't known each other for very long, but I find myself falling more and more in love with you, with every day that goes by." His knees were weak and he had tears in his eyes, but there was something pushing him to keep going.

Terri's breath got caught in her throat and she looked like a deer facing headlights. Her heart was pounding and

Tina Griffith

she was filled with relief, and now wanted to listen to all that Tim was saying.

Tim's body was shaking, as was his voice, but he managed to muddle through his tender speech. "I think about you every morning when I wake up, and I dream about you every night when I go to bed. Terri, I've known a lot of girls in my life, but I've never wanted to marry any of them."

While wearing white silk pajamas and holding full glasses of pink champagne in their hands, Sadie and Enrico toasted their new relationship. "Here's to your last day as an innocent woman", he mocked. He raised an eyebrow and nodded shrewdly, while presenting her with a playfully evil smirk.

Sadie blushed and dramatically threw one hand to her chest. "Why, Mr. Velucci", she stated, in a fake southern accent. "What did you have in mind?"

Enrico took one step towards his new bride and replied jokingly, "I happen to have a list."

Her eyes shot wide open while she drew in a large breath of air.

Tim got down on one knee, and reached out to hold Terri's left hand.

Terri gasped loudly while her free hand flew to her mouth. This was definitely an unexpected surprise to her, however, it was something that she had hoped would happen at some point down the road.

Enrico took a sip of the sweet and bubbly liquid, switched the radio onto a commercial-free, romantic music station, and then placed his glass on the nearest flat surface. He was looking into Sadie's eyes as he took a few steps

The Elusive Mr. Velucci

towards her, and after letting out a gratified sigh, he rested his folded hands on her lower back. As he pushed into her body, he leaned his face towards hers.

Sadie felt like she was living in one of her dreams, and touched his chest with a playful finger to see if he was real. The glow of his smile warmed her skin, and she tilted her chin towards him.

Tears were beginning to crawl down Tim's face. "I love you, Terri. Would you do me the honor of becoming my wife?"

Terri burst into tears, and shouted 'YES' four times in a row. She then flew into his arms and kissed him until his lips were swollen.

Enrico kissed his bride with a hunger that belied his outward composure. He was ready for her, and with every sound and whisper that came from his mouth, he was pledging to love her forever.

Sadie's kisses were daring and she held nothing back. And as her hands roamed eagerly over his muscled male flesh, she could feel him coming to life.

Enrico didn't want to rush things, so he tried to calm his body and mind while he fought against the pleasurable rush that was building within him. A moment later, when he knew that he was losing the battle, he exhaled loudly through gritted teeth, while riding the storm of oncoming sensations.

Sadie couldn't help but give in to the same scandalous pleasure, and she moaned as her body vibrated with overall satisfaction.

"I don't have a ring on me", Tim stated apologetically.

"But when we get back home, maybe we can shop for one together?"

Terri had been overwhelmed by the last few moments, and all she could do was nod while continuing to cry tears of happiness.

Tim rushed into her arms and buried his face into hair; he suddenly felt happier than he ever had in his entire life.

While Enrico's lips stayed connected with Sadie's, he ripped open her pajama top and completely exposed her ample breasts. He then watched as her back arched and her eyes closed, as if to soak in the erotic flavor in the room.

Sadie hadn't been properly prepared for what he had done, and it caused her to inhale quite loudly. Her head was now spinning from the sudden onset of adrenaline which was hurrying through her body. Or was it from the exhilaration of what was about to happen next?

Enrico had spotted the bright flare of desire that had sprung into her eyes as she moaned, and it tickled his interest to do more. Without wavering, he puffed out his chest while wordlessly begging her to do the same to him.

'Was he daring me?' she wondered. Sadie could see the sparkle of excitement shining on his handsome face, and in one swift movement, she tore his top open and pressed her naked chest against his.

Their breathing was now strong and deep, but not in sync, and the bodies of the newly-weds were glistening with beads of perspiration. It was then when they realized that the perfect moment – the one which they had both longed for - had finally arrived.

Meanwhile, Terri and Tim stepped back into the tent. He flagged the DJ so that they could make an announcement, and when the music stopped, Terri screamed to all who could hear, "I'm getting married!"

And while everyone was shouting their happiness over the news of the surprise engagement, Enrico and Sadie removed their pajama bottoms and climbed into bed.

With the moon shining in through the hotel window and the fire crackling away in the small fireplace, Enrico covered his bride with his hard and eager body. And as the bed trembled, their hearts soared, for they had finally ended their long pursuit to be together.

The End

Tina Griffith is also the author of the following books;

Under The Nail Polish
Behind The Wishes
A Bewitching Sequel
Some Habits, Are Hard to Break
A Second Later...
The Handsome Farmhouse Ghost
Charlotte's Decision
Spencer Brown
Synchronicity – A Love Story
Dating.com

Printed in the United States
By Bookmasters